PROMISE OF DESIRE

"Dora," Rogan murmured, "you'll soon want me as much as I want you."

Dora's only answer was to moan from somewhere deep inside herself. As they touched, she felt the heat rise in her body, and suddenly she felt weightless as a consuming sweetness washed over her.

He pressed against her and she shivered as he searched the swell of her breast. "You'll desire me soon, Dora; I have already promised you that." Her feet left the floor and she was being swept to the bed in his sturdy arms.

This powerful, handsome man who, only hours before, had been a stranger to her, was now, she thought for one insane moment, having his way with her. . . .

ZEBRA ROMANCES FOR ALL SEASONS
From Bobbi Smith

ARIZONA TEMPTRESS   (1785, $3.95)

Rick Peralta found the freedom he craved only in his disguise as El Cazador. Then he saw the exquisitely alluring Jennie among his compadres and the hotblooded male swore she'd belong just to him.

CAPTIVE PRIDE   (2160, $3.95)

Committed to the Colonial cause, the gorgeous and independent Cecelia Demorest swore she'd divert Captain Noah Kincade's weapons to help out the American rebels. But the moment that the womanizing British privateer first touched her, her scheming thoughts gave way to burning need.

DESERT HEART   (2010, $3.95)

Rancher Rand McAllister was furious when he became the guardian of a scrawny girl from Arizona's mining country. But when he finds that the pig-tailed brat is really a voluptuous beauty, his resentment turns to intense interest; Laura Lee knew it would be the biggest mistake in her life to succumb to the cowboy—but she can't fight against giving him her wild DESERT HEART.

Available wherever paperbacks are sold, or order direct from the Publisher. Send cover price plus 50¢ per copy for mailing and handling to Zebra Books, Dept. 3060, 475 Park Avenue South, New York, N.Y. 10016. Residents of New York, New Jersey and Pennsylvania must include sales tax. DO NOT SEND CASH.

WILD ISLAND SANDS

BY
SONYA T.
PELTON

ZEBRA BOOKS
KENSINGTON PUBLISHING CORP.

ZEBRA BOOKS

are published by

KENSINGTON PUBLISHING CORP.
475 Park Avenue South
New York, N.Y. 10016

Sixth printing: May, 1992

Printed in the United States of America

Ancient Myth

Long, long ago there reigned a supreme deity who was called by the name Zeus. One evening Zeus called to him the cunning craftsman of the Olympians and commissioned him to fashion a thing most fair. So Hephaestus mingled together the bloom of the rose, the voice of laughing water, the beauty and power of seduction, the art of flattery; he also added the sea's beauty, and its treachery too; and the doe's heart of love. All these, the gods' choicest gifts, Hephaestus blended cunningly into a shape that Zeus described to him.

Zeus himself then breathed upon the image to give it substance, and it lived. She, this thing created, looked upon them with the glorious wonder of one suddenly awakened to life. She was likened to a goddess. But . . .

"Behold," Zeus announced. "We have made the first Woman. She is of my shaping thought. She shall be named Pandora, all-gifted, all-giving."

Zeus then sent Pandora to the Titan Epimetheus. When the Titan saw this beauteous creature he was beside himself with joy and desire and made her that very same day his wife. Now Epimetheus had been warned by the gods not to take any present from Zeus but the woman. However, Pandora had with her an amber box, which unbeknownst to her contained all kinds of misery and an evil secret. Epimetheus had no heart to cast away the box, of which she seemed so fond, and Pandora was glad that she might keep the wondrous amber box that shone like translucent gold in the sunlight. She viewed it with pleasure day after day.

At last, as it came to pass, Pandora could resist her desire no longer. She must see what was inside the glorious box. Half-fearful of what she might find, she laid her hand upon the lid and raised it very gently, very slowly. Suddenly out flew a swarm of tiny hummingbird-winged sprites that soared upward and away—away through the open door before she could close the lid. She wept then when she saw that her box was empty, but she had loosed all manner of evil that flew out over the earth and that even now remains in our midst.

Epimetheus, having found her weeping, asked, "Are you sure all the sprites have escaped?"

"Yes."

Later she looked again and to her startled amazement found that one still remained inside, the lid having been shut down before the smallest sprite could escape. With its rainbow wings drooping, this tiniest of sprites clung weakly to the golden rim. Pandora did smile then. For something told her that this one precious thing left was Hope.

Part One

Blossoms

Chapter One

Paradise!

Pandora St. Ives had always cherished the same fantasy—that of being pursued by a tall, compelling stranger, *malahini,* as they said in Hawaii. In her daydreams, in her night visions, he pounded barefoot after her. After capturing her, he would bring her to the sand, with gentle force, and strip off her *holoku;* then, bursting into flames, they would make wild, sweet love to the luau drums; the paradise flowers, having fallen from her hair, would be crushed into the sand. In the moonlight, Pandora would give her virginity to him—only him. In the sand, the flowers, always . . .

The green chain of islands seemed to have been pulled from the Pacific by a huge, magical hand. Complete with glistening beaches, lush valleys, majestic mountains with rainbow-misted peaks; blossoms and junglelike feathery plants of every imaginable color; and palm trees, juxtaposed against one another and the blue sky that waved to the exotic birds soaring over the wildly beautiful landscape.

Here on Oahu, which is roughly diamond-shaped,

9

were once two immense volcanoes; from them erosion has fashioned two rugged, parallel mountain ranges. One range, Koolau is twice as long as and older than the other, Waianae, and the two are connected by a high saddle.

Long ago people of many other stocks than Hawaiian came to the islands voluntarily or were brought to work on the sugar or taro plantations. The Hawaiians seemed destined to disappear more through intermarriage with other races than through an excessive death rate of pure Hawaiians. Even now, in any schoolroom in the islands, the children may be of fifty different combinations of racial ancestries.

Recently these islands became a state of the United States. Hawaii had become a full partner in the American system.

Below the jagged heavenward mountains, a soft breeze was blowing in off the rainbow-tinted sea. A slender young woman, barefoot and beautiful and perpetually sun-tanned a golden hue—a sort of fairy princess—sat with legs crossed, down the beach from the bungalow here on Oahu where she had lived for two years with her guardians, her aunt and uncle.

Such long lonely years, to Pandora St. Ives.

She now busied herself weaving a floppy hat out of the leaves of the *hala*. A half-eaten coconut lay in the beige sand; the milk had been drunk. Her sharp knife for cutting the leaves into strips also lay beside her.

Long hair, streaked with glorious strands of a pale copper shade, curtained her unsmiling features on one side, while on the other her hair was tucked behind one ear and held there by a white tiare flower.

Always Pandora wore flowers, sometimes red, the color of passion here, but she as yet was untouched by the transports of love.

When Pandora was at home, on the beach, she dressed scantily, the aqua-flowered sarong, which was her favorite, clinging to her almost boyishly sleek hips and revealing her willowy graceful legs—long slender legs set off by shapely feet warmly tanned like the rest of her. She did not possess the bronze skin or dark brown or black hair of her relatives, but was as fair underneath as her mother, Linda, had been.

From the sun-splashed beach, Pandora gazed wistfully out to sea and up at the crystal-blue sky. Day and night she had become accustomed to the sound of the surf pounding the shore, and when she was away from this for any length of time, inside a building like the school in Kailua, she imagined she could still hear it.

The island paradise had become a part of Pandora. Both the sea and the sky seemed to be melded together, into a swirling glacial blue that was reflected in her eyes which were framed by long, flaxen lashes.

The rare beauty of the valleys and the misted green mountains rose and fell behind her; Honolulu, Waikiki, and Diamond Head were not far away. But all this undying beauty did not alter the new apprehension that had settled in her breast this day. She had good enough reason for her sadness.

Born and raised on this Pacific island, the farthest Pandora had ever been away from home was Hawaii—the largest in the cluster of islands. She had gone to school in Honolulu, and she had also been taught by her schoolteacher mother, Linda, prior to her death. In Honolulu she had excelled in her academic studies, especially reading and mathematics.

Some say that travel in Hawaii is to the islands what Paris is to travel in France. Those who come here from the mainland never get to the "outer islands"—Mamma had said—a term somewhat distasteful to those who live on those islands, but surely most tourist attention *is* devoted to Oahu. This subtropical island has increased steadily in popularity and a great many people who come every year are fashionable folk, even exclusive. The waters are colored in a dozen blue hues that challenge artist and dabbler. Nearly naked bathers and surfers, of many nationalities, swarm the whole area, while artists stroll with their brushes and palettes, even on Kalakaua Avenue.

To Pandora the Hawaiian language had become easy to pronounce, Linda having taught her that each vowel has only one sound, as in Spanish. "Just let the accent fall the easiest way, Pandora darling; that is pure Hawaiian, anyhow," Linda St. Ives, always the teacher, had instructed. But Pandora, who had always been possessed of a quick, keen mind, had already known that. Of course having grown up on the islands . . .

She closed her eyes now in remembered pain as she thought of her mother's and father's bodies in their watery graves . . . their gravestones that stood above the mossy earth.

In the past the word "worried" hadn't meant much

to Pandora. But she could not cleanse worry from her thoughts now. And even if she could, she knew the outcome would still be the same. To be free instead of a prisoner was all she wanted, to be relieved of the fearful thought of becoming the bride of a man whom she so detested. Oh, damn; she felt as if her heart was aching sometimes! She would love to tear herself free . . . but where would she go . . . ?

A ripple of excitement surfaced from her despondency. She would love to visit San Francisco someday, where her older cousin, Cara Kalee, had gone to live. Cara, disowned by her father for her notorious acts of lust, was her guardians' only offspring.

According to Pandora's geography book in school, Cara's home lay twenty-one hundred miles west-southwest of San Francisco. Would she ever see San Francisco? Probably not, she told herself now.

But, beneath her bed in the bungalow, she had enough money hoarded, *just* enough, to board a ship and join Cara in California. And unbeknownst to her aunt and uncle, Cara's address was also beneath her bed.

Her temptation to go to San Francisco grew with each passing day. Especially now. Marriage to Akoni Nahele? No. Never! But that was exactly what her Uncle Mauli had in mind for her, now that she had just turned twenty.

"Heah, Pandora, *haole wahini,* with the blood of your ancestors flowing in your veins," Mauli would admonish, "you should long ago become bride to one like Akoni Nahele. I wait no longer. Heah me!"

The very thought of marriage to Akoni made her

shudder, even under the hot sun. He was ugly, fat, lecherous beyond reason, and she would rather be dead than to marry him. In fact, she would seriously think of drowning herself in the Pacific first, or Nahele himself if he touched her again!

"There she be!"

Her Aunty Iola, Uncle Mauli, and Akoni Nahele were ambling down the beach toward her, a line of waddling fat. Her uncle's dark lips of a purplish hue were set in a thin line, attesting to his determination.

Pandora stood agilely, brushing sand from her bright sarong and seemingly endless legs. The virgin-white flower now seemed to wilt in her hair, even as Akoni's eyes, black and bold, set above a broad flat face, devoured her slim form greedily, resting on her gently swaying breasts as she stood.

Akoni's wealthy Hawaiian parents had died when he was just in his teens and after that he had lived with his grandmother in their sprawling house, a plantation on the north shore. Now that Akela was gone too, Akoni lived alone in the huge wind-blown house situated on an old taro plantation. He owned a smaller structure on the land and rumor had it that he planned to sell the plantation, or already had, but would keep the one parcel on which the wood-frame house stood. To think that Akoni would have the heart to sell that lovely, but run-down, plantation, a grant from King Kalakua to Nahele, saddened her greatly. Sold to a stranger, no less. Actually this was now none of Pandora's affair, and she hoped it would not be in the future.

She did not care one whit if Akoni was wealthy or not, she felt no love for Akoni and that was that!

But what was she to do? She loved Aunty and cherished her and wanted only to please her.

Aunty Iola's hair, thick and sable brown and shiny, like her father's had been, was combed back from her wide forehead and parted down the middle and drawn into the usual tight bun at the nape of her neck. Her round face wore a look of defeat, and today Iola's floral muumuu sagged worse than ever. Iola had pleaded her niece's case and had lost again, said her fixed countenance.

Akoni Nahele's bold desire was bluntly plain to see, even in his billowy white trousers. This always happened to Akoni when he was near Pandora St. Ives. She knew the private parts of the male anatomy well; Aunty had long ago, along with Pandora's mother, told her what went where—and why. But Pandora just knew there must be something more to life than merely making fat little babies. A good feeling, that made one warm and thrilled inside, like when she had been kissed by a handsome sailor on the beach not long ago. She should have stayed with him on the moonlit strip to learn more of that pleasurable sensation, instead of running away home like a silly little coward. But he had not been the man of her dreams; this she had known.

"You are sure she still virgin?" Akoni Nahele had pressed her uncle for the truth.

"I be sure," Mauli had answered. "We know, both Iola and me, we keep eye on her. She is pure as Sacred Falls of Kaliuwaa. I know she is big girl, long ready for *honi-ipu*, but she is good girl. Heah, no man has had her!"

Pandora had overheard this conversation and it

15

made her shudder again to bring it to mind. She had saved herself for only one man—yet to come into her life.

Pandora now gathered up her things. "Coming, Aunty!" she called up the beach, lifting one hand to flip a long wave behind her shoulder.

Unhappily she gazed around at the lush, dazzling beauty of the island paradise. Oh, how she felt like running. *Now*. Then again she had always loved this place where she had been born. And life, oh yes, it had been lonely the past two years since her parents had passed away. The St. Iveses had been on the new vessel that had been wrecked at Diamond Head reef, as a result of a navigational error on the captain's part. She had almost cried herself into hysterics. Iola had tried calming her, and had finally succeeded after several attempts by praying on her knees with Pandora to her Christian God. Yes, she had lived through loneliness. But now this. Life had suddenly become another rough road for her to walk.

"You must find your own road, Pandora, and travel it," her mother, Linda, had often instructed her. "You are as adventurous as the sea winds, like a flower opening up, a sun rising, a passionate spirit with a vagabond yearning. There will always be hope, no matter what, for one so strong and beautiful. This is why I have named you after the Greek goddess, Pandora."

The haunting sensation these words always instilled in her did so now again. "But *Hope?*" What good did it do her now, she asked out loud, but low enough for her ears only.

They stood there now, the two men in their bright

16

floral shirts, completely threatening.

"Come to house now, Pandora *wahini*," Iola called gently.

Pandora loved her aunt, but what could *she* do? Like most women of the islands, her husband's wishes came first.

Mauli wanted Pandora to marry Hawaiian, and strengthen her heritage, however weak the strain. He had kept, as best he could, sailors ashore on leave away from her, and the garrison troops that were stationed on the island, too. She must be pure in body as well as heart when she went to her new husband.

They, the three, turned back to the bungalow that was set up on masonry piers above a blanket of scrub grass, walking slowly so that Pandora could catch up. To meet her doom, Pandora concluded.

While she walked, Pandora's life, as one dying, swam before her glacial-blue eyes. Memories came crowding to fill those empty places of loneliness in her mind. Her mother, lovely, not so dainty but fair of coloring, had been born and bred in America, the daughter of a French family of schoolteachers in New Orleans. Mr. St. Ives had been American also, but had been born on Oahu, and both he and Pandora's mother had been longtime *kamaainas* of Hawaii. Iola, too, professed Hawaiian ancestors, as Colter St. Ives had, but now he was gone, his lips sealed forever.

In the early nineteenth century a royal decree had ordered the Hawaiians to give up their paganism; Pandora's great-grandfather was a congregationalist missionary who had arrived from New England at that time. Ministers, teachers, physicians, printers, farmers, and businessmen; they introduced the

17

church, the school, and the press. After 1854 public instruction was no longer made in the Hawaiian language but in English. American teachers, textbooks, and methods became popular. Linda Sweet, Pandora's mother, had been one of those American teachers who came to the Hawaiian islands.

However distantly, Pandora's blood still mingled with that of a beautiful Hawaiian princess—the "rebel princess" she had been called—her great-grandmother who had married the handsome minister from New England. Their son, Colter, when old enough, had gone off to America to stay until he became a U.S. citizen. Upon his return, he had met the fair and intellectual Linda Sweet.

Colter St. Ives had owned a taro plantation on Oahu, but had accrued huge shipping debts that had to be paid on a lost, or perhaps stolen, cargo. So Mauli had informed Pandora after all the payments had been settled. Her uncle had taken care of everything, even the small funeral monument of her parents in Honolulu. But it was as if Pandora's future mattered not at all, at least not in terms of her own will. Sometimes she felt as if she was very much alone in the world. A very small world, all things considered.

The tropical sun was drifting high overhead as Pandora tossed her lion's mane of hair and took one more glum look over her shoulder at the blue ocean. She then turned toward the bungalow flanked by swaying palms. On the veranda she knew fresh fruit, watercress, and chilled lime juice awaited them for luncheon.

As she walked closer to the house, with every step

her resolve strengthened. It was all settled in Pandora's mind. She must harden her heart and depart Hawaii in the deepest hours of night—one night soon—before a marriage between her and Nahele could ever take place.

Pandora hurt so much. There was no way out of the trap. She stared out across the inky-black sky; the moon hung like some huge magical fruit, so close to earth, and dropped silver pieces of itself into the waters of the Pacific. The heavens wore its famous necklace of stars spreading across the night sky . . . and here she stood alone wishing to God that tomorrow would never come.

"Tomorrow," she murmured on a choking sob, "I will become Akoni's bride. . . ." That was the source of the ever-present horror in her glacial-blue eyes. He had leered at her and chuckled and talked lewdly, his dark eyes saying he would demand his rights as husband . . . finally. Each day he appeared uglier, more obese, more evil.

As in a fairytale she had sought the arms of her "prince," holding him against her breast in her dreams, as if he would keep her from that evil lecher, from his vulgar clutches. To torture her was Akoni's delight. . . . So great was her hatred that she could *kill* him with her own black-hilted blade before tomorrow ever came. Yet, how could she? She was no murderess.

Pandora still hoped that she could escape the cruel fate that awaited her. Didn't Aunty Iola realize what a vile glutton of a man Akoni was? Unaware of Pandora's distress, or pretending to be, Iola had cheerfully planned the luau that would follow the ceremony tomorrow.

"Not to look so sad. You have no worry, Pandora. Akoni will be good for you. You need a man, a husband, all womens do. Mauli and I do not want to see you alone. . . . Your uncle say it is time for you to marry, have babies. *They* make you happy, you will see, always babies make women happy . . . and much busy!"

She had so very much wanted to throw herself into her aunt's plump arms, cry to her once and for all that she felt not love for Akoni Nahele but sheer hatred! What mattered most to Pandora was that she had always dreamed the perfect love would come, like the prince in Linda's fairytales who would ride into *her* life to save *her*, fall in love with *her*, sweep her away to his castle beside the sea. . . . But why had she always dreamed *he* would come to her on a night like this? Was it because this was the night she had been dreaming and waiting for? To be saved? Why should the man, the "prince," of her dreams ever come? None of it was real, after all.

"Damn *you!*" She borrowed one of the curses she had heard a sailor use to another. She shook a slim fist toward the sea—from where "he" should come, her gold-threaded hair lifting from her shoulders and blowing back, giving her the look of a mythical being, like Halcyone, the fairy maiden, daughter of the beach and of the wind. She uncurled her fist, letting it fall back to her side.

"I wish . . . that I could be transported to another place and time, to become something that could not be hurt. Like the winged horse Pegasus . . ."

Or why couldn't she just be a bird that sailed up and down happily forever, upon the pleasant seas of Greece where her name was born? Her face would be like that of a nymph, her plumage like the rainbow; she would fly away and out to sea . . . to *him*.

"Will 'he' come . . . with the sunrise?" Then again, would her dream vanish with the dawn, never to be hoped for again? "Iola, Aunty, I cannot marry Akoni Nahele!" But the sea breeze snatched that up and tore the words like wolves at a sheep.

Back in her little curtained room in the bungalow, Pandora stared at the shadowy wall of the room in front of her. She sat there, just like that, staring, until the small area grew gray and misty with dawn. The awful day had arrived. She prayed she wouldn't be sick. . . . Ah, that was always a thought!

"No," she said. Iola would be brokenhearted. She could not do that to the aunty she had always loved.

Her dream of her "prince" had vanished and she sat still and motionless with terror as the horrible apparitions, the wolves, came slowly forward to claim her . . . the bride. Akoni Nahele and her Uncle Mauli.

Love, sweet and pure . . . dream where did you go? This was never to be. After all, her name *was* Pandora . . . but this Pandora had given up *all* hope. There wasn't a thread left. . . .

The dazed young woman, in the long flowered dress, lace gloves, and kid shoes, stood outside the new hotel in Honolulu. Morning had finally come. She waited for the carriage to take her to the waiting ship *Baghdad* that was making its return trip to San

Francisco. She pulled open the strings of her reticule, peered inside the bag, and repeated to herself once more:

"My name is Pan . . . Dora. . . . I am sailing to . . . San Francisco."

A random surge of wind rippled the hem of her dress and she struggled against tears that welled rebelliously again. Oh, why could she not remember more than just that?

What had happened to cause her to lose a corner of her memory?

Pandora . . . or Dora *what!* Did she not have a last name?

All she knew was that she must sail from here as soon as possible. If she did not, something . . . or someone would catch up with her.

Chapter Two

Between a dusty gray sky and a cool dove-gray sea, mists entwined around the tops of buildings until a fleeting wind frayed them out and chased them among the cluster of hills. Both city and hills tipped steeply down, to where the bay region and city snuggled close to the sea, an area veiled with mystery. The bay city long ago learned to deal with the world by water; during the gold rush, thousands had come by ship, having sailed clear around the Horn. The Pacific was San Francisco's empire and from here to Honolulu the sea was well-traveled; the port itself experienced the thrill of many sailings and dockings. Through the Golden Gate arching over the channel to the sea, lay mild San Francisco, with her rolling fogs and her delicate gray colors; the sun stayed for only short visits.

The Embarcadero curved at the bottom of the cobbled hills where streets ended and wooden wharves began. Ships sailed into home port all week long, their bowsprits rimmed with salt, their plain or carved figureheads dulled by the spray of open seas.

A kaleidoscopic crowding of memories hover there where the past mingles with the present, the pull of imagined tides with real ones, coming from the never-still sea. The swirling sea mists drift in from beyond the gate, bringing people of all nations; some land with secrets as dark as a storm blowing in from the horizon.

One such incipient storm blew tentatively toward the office structure and connecting warehouse of Thorn Navigation, located in the jigsaw blocks of buildings fronting the Embarcadero in the very heart of the shipping empire.

Within that office on a map, tiny ships with even smaller flags rose where affixed on the vivid blue of the ocean and near their ports of call.

A compelling figure at the head of the table in the conference room let his gaze slide from the huge walnut-framed map dominating the space on the wall opposite the long table where the men sat.

With gossamer-green eyes, he studied some beautifully carved models, proud of his cargo ships, especially the passenger liner, *Baghdad*. So far they had only one liner, but very soon there would be more added to his line. He also owned the schooner *Phantom*, but she was solely a pleasure craft, one he did not get to sail very often as his business took up most of his time.

His gaze drifted out the window and to the left, where the wooden wharves of the Embarcadero jutted out. An undefinable thrill shot through him; he could feel the tingling at his nerve ends, an anticipation to which he could not put a name.

In home port again, the *Baghdad* had sailed into the harbor just this morning from the Hawaiian islands. With strangely brooding visage, he had watched her proud entrance into the Bay of San Francisco, watched her sails folding as their canvas was being taken in and furled. The gilded carving of her siren figurehead had led her safely home again.

He, Rogan Thorn, owned her.

Rogan returned to the business at hand, leaning far back in his swivel chair as he glanced around slowly at each man in the conference room. He rested his gaze on the general manager of Thorn Navigation.

"Might we hear your opinion now, Mr. Bixby?" Rogan continued.

Bixby cleared his throat. "Yes, Mr. Thorn. I agree with Joe Pickett. They are planning to build all those fancy new hotels on Waikiki Beach, and I for one am for expanding our passenger service to Hawaii and the Orient. *That's* where the biggest money is—and we only have one *Baghdad*."

Rogan's mouth quirked at that. Now, Mickey Papet, in charge of contracts for commercial cargo, intervened in a low voice.

"In my opinion, we're going to be handling more *cargo* in the near future."

President Rogan Thorn drained the dregs of his coffee cup and grimaced. He half-stood then as he swiveled his chair to swipe a paper off the wooden file cabinet.

"Perhaps we can just reconcile both ideas, gentlemen?" he said.

Rogan Thorn was the only man in the room who indulged in the casualness of shirt sleeves rolled to the elbow. He sat down again in his swivel chair and passed a picture from a newspaper around the table.

Rogan went on. "Why couldn't we turn some of those new cargo ships like the *North Wind* into passenger liners that take a quota of travelers?"

Heads nodded, as these men studied the picture of a ship out of Boston that had been altered into a passenger liner. One head came up.

"Mr. Thorn, you say Todd Ashe is thinking of selling her? She's a rakish beauty, that *North Wind*," Joe Pickett said, twirling his pencil.

"Yes, she is," Rogan agreed. "Also, I have the first bid on her." A smile lifted his firm lips.

Contagious smiles then went around the table, as one and all instantly brought their powerful competitor to mind. Walter Riddock, president of the Wolfington & Riddock line, would turn an angry red if Rogan Thorn got to the *North Wind* before him. And Rogan, that crafty man, seemed to be doing just that, they told themselves. Rogan always got exactly what he set his sights on.

In ruthless San Francisco where weak men disappeared like ice under the sun, Rogan Thorn commanded both respect and liking—and from some a little awe. He quickly made friends with important and influential city folk and islanders. He was an important figure, both in San Francisco and Hawaii. Unlike Walter Riddock who had invested in plantations or ranches merely to provide cargoes for his ships, Rogan planned to restore his own plantation, which he planned to rename Briar Rose, and to live there four to six months out of the year. He had been reluctant to leave Oahu, the island he had just recently visited, but business had called him back to California.

26

Rogan Thorn continued now. "You know, many desire to go abroad, but haven't the money for luxury liners. Of course, we'd have to spend *some* money outfitting those ships—" His amused glance skimmed around the table. "They don't exactly provide top comfort for cruises."

Mr. Little, passenger-ticket sales manager, smiled enthusiastically at that. Alexander Moor, vice president of Thorn Navigation took control again, as he had done earlier in the board meeting. He had glanced just now at his pocket watch, surprised at how much time they had spent at this particular meeting. But it had been important to the company; competition was running high.

"Well, gentlemen, as far as I'm concerned that just about completes our business for today. Unless you've something else in mind, Rogan?"

The room was silent a moment more, and then Rogan Thorn waved a hand in dismissal. At once chairs scraped, and scratch pads flipped shut as the men stretched, took their empty coffee mugs, and filed out of the conference room. Mutterings and footsteps echoed up through the stairwell as they descended.

Now alone with his best friend, his confidant, and his partner, Rogan relaxed somewhat. He always retained some aloofness, though, no matter whom he was with at the time.

Rising to his feet and adjusting the front of his trousers, Rogan stretched his strong, lean body to get the kinks out. Running the narrow fingers of one hand through his wavy, chestnut hair, Rogan poured himself another cup of strong, black coffee with the other and then, taking long easy strides and looking out of the window now and then, he slowly walked about the room. His footfalls, like those of a hunting wolf, barely made a sound as he moved across the polished dark boards of the floor.

"Did you spend the night poorly?" Sandy asked, looking up from a stack of papers he had just arranged neatly into a pile.

"No." Rogan continued to gaze out to the *Baghdad,* his head tilted thoughtfully, his eyes taking on a lazy, sensual quality.

"Say, Rogan, how about joining me at that little French restaurant, you know, the one with the reputation for—ah—naughtiness?" Sandy lifted one blond eyebrow that was shot with white curling hairs.

"What? And risk a possible mugging—or worse?"

Rogan snorted into his cup of rolling black liquid, finally tearing his stare from the ship out there.

"Hey, I don't mean a honky-tonk dive of the Coast, man! I'm talking about a posh eating place where the traffic to the upstairs goes on hush-hush every night."

"Oh," Rogan murmured with much boredom. "I've been there, to those *places,* and was lucky to get back without a social disease."

"Not the *unmarried* whores. See, I'm talking about the married ones; they're clean, and the best in the sack!"

Rogan sighed deeply. "And I've had my fill of naughty women who play at being little ladies of the night. God . . . how repugnant!"

"Yeah, sure." Sandy's eyes lighted to a twinkling

brown. "But, old boy, when was the last time you had some fun—real sport?" He studied the features that were creased with experience of all sorts, and something close to sadness at times.

Thin nostrils wrinkled. "Fun? About as exciting as eating doughnut holes, your *married* women," he muttered.

"Hell, man!" Sandy pulled a man-sized pout. "You're all business and little play lately. Frankly, I'm very surprised at your actions. Rather, your lack of them." He smiled broadly to cool the other man's temper that could surface readily. "If you know what I mean? Hey, relax, and forget the business world for a while, huh?"

"Ah, not tonight, Sandy." Rogan slipped into his tweed business jacket. He left it unbuttoned, but still the material stretched tautly across wide shoulders.

"Hey, have you taken a giant leap from your senses? Rogan Thorn, lover boy, where'd you go?" Sandy continued to press the issue.

"I might be expecting company tonight." Rogan verbally shrugged off the question put to him. After leafing through some papers, he glanced up. "Not that the prospect excites me all that much anymore, but Cara and I, well, we get along, if you know what I mean."

"Only too well," Sandy returned with a sigh.

Rogan Thorn had become the eligible target for every scheming woman, every artificially attractive female who had knowledge of his vast growing wealth. Rogan kept it to himself, though, that he was utterly lonesome at times. No matter how many women, mistresses or otherwise, entertained him, there was still that something that mattered, something great and wonderful missing from his life. If he hadn't found it by now, he usually told himself with a casual shrug, he never would.

Alexander Moor knew that Rogan shunned clinging vines like the plague—also, phony society people, money-seekers who tried attaching themselves like leeches to Rogan's private life. Part of him always remained aloof and wary, even with his employees. Mostly, he avoided those who sought his friendship with unusual determination.

Not devoured by jealousy, Sandy, nonetheless, looked upon Rogan with a slightly envious eye. Rogan Thorn was a descendant of the Argonauts; he was from one of the city's oldest families. Rogan poured all his heart and soul into the company, just as his grandfather had. Whitelaw Thorn had founded the navigation company the very year Rogan had been born, in eighteen sixty-eight.

Before entering college, Rogan had worked initially as a dock hand, unloading freight from the many cargo ships that were part of the Thorn commercial fleet. While still in college, he had studied at the office, burning the midnight oil, learning the intricacies of the business in which he had always been highly interested.

Rogan had largely established himself in the Hawaiian merchant trade and his successful firm planned to exchange sail for steam—which was not far off—and eventually to encompass a large fleet of passenger liners. His focus was on Hawaii as the center of Pacific trade. Still, windjammers, his first love, would ply the Pacific for many years to come.

There was nothing on God's blue sea—or green earth for that matter—as beautiful and as graceful as a ship under full sail. No, not even a woman, to Rogan Thorn.

"Why don't you marry her, then?" Sandy interrupted the other man's thoughts.

"Who?" Rogan had ships on his mind.

Sandy smiled. "Miss Kalee. The woman."

"Are you kidding?" Rogan chuckled low. "Me, a confirmed bachelor?"

Sandy shook his blond head. "And here I thought you had suddenly gone and turned respectable at thirty! Really, you had me scared for a while. Marriage is nice, but so is cutting your throat or hanging yourself, they say," he joked.

From the second story Rogan studied the street below. Checking his pocket watch with the wall clock, he snapped the gold lid shut and slipped the timepiece into his trouser slit.

"Wizan is picking me up. Damn, the Chinaman should have been here with the carriage fifteen minutes ago. He's late. Wonder what could be keeping him, he's usually prompt."

"Geez, when you get down to stating the obvious, then I know it's time for me to fetch coat and go." Sandy realized that Wizan picked Rogan up every day promptly at four, so this was a break in the usual routine. Rogan must be fuming, he thought to himself. The man stuck to a strict schedule.

"Ah, finally!" Rogan exclaimed tersely, sighting his black carriage with the top down just rounding the corner.

Sandy Moor waved. "I'm off. See you Monday."

Rogan suddenly felt that he'd been unkind somehow to his longtime friend. "Say, Sandy, stop by this weekend. That is, if you can tear yourself away from your little French restaurants." He smiled, displaying even white teeth.

"Try I shall, to make it to the Thorn Mansion!" Sandy hailed.

Downstairs, Sandy had stopped to chat with Carolyn, the company secretary. Rogan preferred females to handle the paperwork, having decided long ago they could do a better job at that than men. Besides, a good woman was hard to find. Carolyn was the best when it came to figures—on paper.

Carolyn paused in her flirtation with Alexander Moor to wave to her boss as he descended the stairs. Sandy looked at Carolyn and smiled warmly. She was smart *and* lucky to still be with the company. She was not one of the long line of women who had obliged Rogan Thorn with her charms as well as her office skills. But Rogan had fired, many said cruelly, some of the others who, after sleeping with him, had become a pain in the buttocks; clinging vines he'd had to cut down and dismiss. But that was all in the past. Sandy had seen the change, indeed a great one, that had come over Rogan. Most of the employees were gossiping that he was working himself to an early grave. All work and no play. They decided that someone in his life, perhaps a woman, had to save him. But Rogan always set his sights high, and one day he was bound to become a shipping tycoon. This was inevitable.

"Say," Sandy began to Carolyn, "how about us,

you and I, painting the town tonight?" Sandy smiled to himself, sure that she would accept.

"I may be a flirt, Mr. Moor, but I am not unfaithful!"

Sandy smiled at that, thinking of those other married women.

Rogan brusquely shut the door, and then stepped onto the walkway. He stopped dead at the sight that greeted him. He could see the Chinaman busily fluttering his hands. He was bent over a figure lying on the leather seat of his carriage. Rogan could see the flowered skirt and knew it was a woman. But . . . what was she doing in *his* carriage. A muscle twitched along his jaw. If this was another woman professing to be his relation . . . come begging money from him . . . Rogan clenched his hands against his hips.

He moved forward. Just who was *she*?

Chapter Three

Wizan jerked up at his boss's arrival and his eyes nearly slanted up into his skull. Rogan could not tell if Wizan was smiling or crying. Shocked maybe. But then, Rogan was experiencing just a little bit of this himself.

"What's this, Wizan Sing? Who've you got there?" Rogan snapped as he walked like a brisk wind to his carriage.

Wizan could only wring his hands.

"Well?"

"Is all my fault, Mistel Thol'n. Oh! Oh! Was in hurry, getting veggies at market when I notice time. Oh, golly, knock her down when I turn corner too fast. She does not wake up, see?"

Wizan's finely boned fingers flew about in the air, frightening the mare, Bessie, into prancing in place.

"Stop that fool blubbering, and tell me just who she is!"

The soft rise and fall of breasts demanded Rogan's gaze when he bent over the young woman, his ever-widening eyes sweeping her from head to foot. Suddenly his whole being seemed to come alive; it was an incredible moment he would not soon forget.

"Velly solly, boss. But how *I* know her!" His dainty shoulders shrugged almost to his chin. "I just see her in front of carriage for first time ever. She come—poof!—and step in front of carriage. Never see her before—"

"Stop repeating yourself, Wizan Sing!"

"Solly, boss."

Rogan could not tell if anything was broken; that would take a doctor's intimate touch. He wished for a moment he'd taken up the practice. The scent of her hair drifted to his nostrils on the warm wind from the hills.

How beautiful she is, like warm honey, he thought, a light leaping into his eyes.

"Well, let's see what we can do to revive her—if that's possible. There's a small bruise rising on her temple." He studied her quickly again, with a little breathlessness. "Have you thought to feel for a heartbeat?" He glanced up over his shoulder to the worried Chinaman who was still wringing his hands.

Wizan's yellow skin blushed to livid olive. "You go ahead, Mistel Thol'n!" He nodded quickly, setting his silk cap askew, while Rogan placed his fingers directly beneath a rounded breast. Wizan grinned under his blush.

Rogan cleared his throat hoarsely, appearing a little flushed himself. "Uhmm, we should not move her, she might be injured elsewhere, Wizan."

"Forget it. I awready move her. How in world you think she get into carriage—walk by herself?" Wizan squeaked and his pigtail flew as he shook his tiny head.

"Don't get smart, Chinaman. Just get up on that seat and let's go!" Rogan ordered harshly.

Lifting her head and shoulders gently onto his lap, Rogan thought for just a moment that the spiky amber lashes had fluttered. But now she lay completely still again. His flesh, where he had touched the young woman, burned with an awareness of her.

After having placed her rattan suitcase near Rogan's legs in the carriage, Wizan scrambled onto the bouncing box. Rogan stared at the suitcase; then he frowned, wondering why he recalled the odd sensation he had had just that morning while gazing out at the *Baghdad*. Could his ship, or another, have brought this lovely creature from some foreign port? Or was she merely from the Bay area?

"Horsy, make tracks!"

Wizan flicked the buggy whip over the horse's nervously twitching ears and shouted at Bessie while he worked the reins to complete a circle and head up the cobbled hill to Thorn Mansion.

A crowd gathered on the corner, trying to peer into the Thorn carriage. And a large-nosed woman with an ugly daughter craned her neck to see what Mr. Thorn had there on the seat with him. Rogan suppressed the urge to stop immediately and to have Wizan put up the top of the carriage; but this would only draw more attention.

"How do you do today, Mr. Thorn?" Mrs. Peabody called from her daughter's side.

"Good day to you, Mrs. Peabody," Rogan returned; then under his breath as the carriage swept by, "Nosy bitch."

Now the young woman stirred and Rogan felt her

head roll agonizingly on his thigh. She faced his groin now, making his flesh burn with an awareness of her helpless position. Little shocks ran through him every time she stirred causing fire to ripple through his blood. His whole being seemed concentrated between his thighs. Not surprisingly, he began to be aroused. His hand moved to shield himself, just in case there should be any more nosy onlookers peering into his open carriage.

Aware of a hard body beneath hers, a blush moved up from Pandora's throat to her cheeks, but she kept her eyes shut tight. The flames on her cheeks were not from fever or shock. Oh, Lord, did he know what was happening to her lying here on his rocklike lap? Could he feel the quick hard throb of her pulse?

Back a few blocks, where the carriage had recently passed, a hard-featured man, with eyes that should belong to a frog, stepped back into the gray shadow of a warehouse. He wore flannel knickers, the jacket of a sailor, and the shoes of a miner. But Sly Binks was neither.

He glanced down, studying the reticule he had swiped from off the ground before the flustered Chinaman could notice. He stuffed the reticule under his jacket and headed back toward Walter Riddock's office. His boss would be fit to be tied when he heard the news that the young woman, Pandora, had come to an accident—especially when he heard in whose carriage she had been whisked away. Sly cursed himself for being so stupid. He had been tracking the young woman all afternoon, for he had to report to his boss where she would be staying. She had stepped out from an employment agency earlier, and the look on her pretty face told him she hadn't found a job. He cursed again; he must have frightened her into quickening her steps.

Well damn, Sly thought, at least he could inform Riddock where she might be staying. It wouldn't be for long, though, because his boss would go fetch her out of there. Just how Riddock would accomplish this move remained to be seen. Sneaking into Thorn Mansion would not be an easy thing to do.

Up the hilly cobbled street the Thorn carriage continued to slowly *clip-clop-whir* along. In her flowered, cotton dress, the young woman shivered and murmured incoherently. Rogan immediately shrugged out of his tweed jacket to cover her, damning his lustful feelings as he did so.

"Lord, she is a beauty," he kept thinking to himself.

"We stop at Dr. Hoyle house first, Mistel Thol'n?" Wizan shouted the question over his shoulder.

"Good idea, Wiz." Rogan looked down at the unconscious female whose head had again eased onto the most intimate part of his thigh. "Why didn't I think of that first?" he said, as if asking her, knowing she couldn't possibly answer him.

But this beauty appeared so vital and alive, whoever she was, that even though she could not acknowledge him, she seemed at ease and content to snuggle up to him. Lord, but was she safe from him? Rogan began to wonder, for he too, had never felt so warm and alive. He smiled for a moment mischievously to himself, hoping that she was uninjured.

They had reached the Nob Hill district, where the wealthiest citizens had built their enormous mansions. Wizan brought Bessie to a halt near a tall, turreted house, leaped out from his box and scurried up to swing the wrought-iron gate open.

The parlormaid answered the knocker. "The doctor is not in right now. He's out on a call." She held one arm akimbo with a feather duster still in it.

"Tell him please to come to Thol'n Mansion."

"I'll do that, when Dr. Hoyle returns." She shut the door busily on the Chinaman.

"Woman has velly bad attitude," Wizan clucked to himself on his way to the carriage.

The carriage was set in motion again. They hadn't far to go now. Rogan automatically brushed strands of straying hair out of the young woman's eyes. They fluttered half-open for an instant, and Rogan caught his breath before the diamond-blue eyes shut again. Starry eyes, contrasting with the gentle fires in her hair, he thought ardently. The ride maddened him; it seemed to be taking longer than usual. He damned his impatience to be home with this strange but lovely creature. What he would do about this delicate matter he was not quite sure just yet.

Rogan's heart beat stronger, though, as he considered what lay ahead. And even stranger, he felt his self-control slipping away.

The streets here were narrow and the sidewalks even narrower. With its archaic elegance, Thorn Mansion towered above its neighbors through addition of a severely peaked gable. It was as if Wizan had read his boss's mind, for he drove directly to the carriage house. He knew that rather than carry her from the street to the house and have the neighbors see, Rogan would choose to take her in the back way. His boss hated scandals and would go far out of his way to avoid one. But Mrs. Peabody was sure to talk.

Before Wizan could manage to reach the back door to the house, Rogan had carefully swept the woman from the seat and was already kicking open the heavy door.

"Freyda!" Rogan shouted in a deep rumble for the parlormaid who scrubbed floors, dusted the fine furniture, and laid the evening fires in the grates to extract the San Francisco damp from the bedrooms.

"Huh. Vhat is going on?" Freyda came rushing out into the hall from the drawing room, rustling her black, aproned skirt.

Like a brisk wind, Rogan passed right by the drawing room. The rattan suitcase still in his clutches, Wizan stood ready to aid in any way he could. But he wore a puzzled frown now, until he noticed that Rogan intended to carry his feminine bundle up the curving, black oak staircase.

Freyda stood gawking at Mr. Thorn mounting the stairs with care—and with a strange woman in his arms. She clapped a hand over her mouth in scandalized shock.

"Is not teatime, woman; go fetch washbowl and cloths to bathe young lady's face!" Wizan ordered the maid sharply.

Wizan Sing ran the house nearly single-handedly, with the efficiency of a new pocket watch. He had packed off many a servant with nary a good-by when one had taken it upon himself or herself to fly above this Chinese ruler of the roost. Wizan was too valuable to Rogan Thorn and so he allowed the Chinaman to hire and fire at his will. Besides that, Wizan had been with the Thorn family ever since Rogan was a wee babe.

"I go, I go," Freyda said crisply, compressing her lips as, with a swish of starched apron and cap streamers flying behind her, she hurried off to the water closet.

"Velly good," Wizan said after her and then whipped himself, too, into action.

Wizan reached the guest bedroom at the top of the stairs just in time to put the rattan suitcase down next to the bed and to busy himself with pulling down the quilted counterpane.

Rogan stood back to rub his chin with a finger, pondering his next move. He sighed. All he could do now was to wait for Dr. Hoyle.

Wizan took in the perplexed look on his boss's handsome face. But there was something different about him, something that had altered his appearance in the last hour. Wizan was at a loss as to what it could be that had caused the change.

"You know *her*, Mistel Thol'n? Is she daughter maybe to one of 'wealthies' in city?"

"How would I know, Wizan; it's almost impossible to become acquainted with each and every family that resides in the San Francisco and Oakland Bay area." His lowering gaze fell on the rattan suitcase. "Have you checked that to see if there's revealing information inside?"

"Oh, no! Much too personal to peep inside

woman's things."

Rogan turned to pace, missing the movement as her eyelids opened to mere slits. Blue orbs glittered around the room momentarily, then closed. Rogan whirled back to face Wizan who was cocking his head in the direction of the bed. He shook his head then as Rogan went on.

"In this case, Wizan, it's a necessity. Wasn't she carrying anything else, another smaller bag besides the suitcase? Women, most women, do, you know."

"Too busy with her to look around. No one else was on street either." He shrugged here. "Do not think so, anyway. I just pick lady up and went back to snatch up suitcase, all the time shaking like willow leaf. I worry that another buggy come by and run her over to squash her like bug; that is why I put her into carriage, boss."

Freyda entered hurriedly just then, with the items needed for ministering to whatever surface injuries the girl might have. Nan, the upstairs maid, stood by with a bowl and Freyda dipped her washcloth into it at once, wrung it out, and washed the lovely young face. Freyda thought for a moment she saw the lovely patient flinch as the cloth touched her, but the movement, if any, had been so fleeting she couldn't be certain.

"I don't know what is going on," she said, shaking her head, "but I do as I am told, yah." She tossed a look of mild bitterness over her shoulder to the sapient Chinaman, then went on. "It's only dat I am so vell paid here that I stay, othervise—I am sorry, Mr. Thorn." She wasn't about to add she didn't like the condition that went with the pay—meaning the

Chinaman's dictatorship.

"Boss, I think Freyda should look into young lady's bag now, find out maybe who she is, before she wipes pretty face clean off!" Wizan stood with arms crossed, imperiously over his black silk chest.

Freyda finished with a low "Humph!", wiped her arms and hands on her apron, and then went through the suitcase. Rogan and Wizan looked aside, just in case feminine unmentionables were revealed. Not that Rogan had never looked upon such items, quite the contrary, but he did it for the sake of the two pairs of female eyes watching him. Freyda closed the suitcase and slowly rose from her bent position.

"I don't see anything vhat has a residence on it, Mr. Thorn. Only a couple of changes of clothes, and vomen's unmentionables."

At the last word, Rogan hid a smile from the older woman. He continued to stroke his chin in deep thought as harsh lines of weariness began to darken the area beneath his eyes.

Pandora moaned low. Four pairs of eyes turned collectively in her direction, then froze. They waited in suspense for another response or movement. Unblinking, they waited. But nothing else happened to indicate that she was with them in the conscious world.

"Freyda, keep talking," Rogan ordered. "I believe the sound of another woman's voice will awaken her from her deep sleep."

"Vell, vhat should I say?" Freyda walked over to the fourposter again and picked up the girl's softly tanned hand, while Wizan and Rogan peered and hovered behind her.

"Helloo!"

"Vhat vas dat?" Freyda cried, spinning about in alarm.

"Hoyle," Rogan supplied, meaning the doctor. "Wizan—"

"I know; I go call him up here."

While Dr. Hoyle examined the young woman, the clock below struck six. Rogan and Wizan paced in the hall like expectant fathers. Freyda was stationed at the door, her hands clasped in the folds of her chambray uniform, as she waited in case the doctor summoned her for assistance.

Hoyle poked his head out the door. "She seems to be unharmed, Rogan." Then he pushed the door open wider. "But for that nasty little bump she received, there's nothing broken, no more bruises, and she's coming to, I think. How did she get the bump on her forehead?"

"I'll speak to you after we've seen her together," Rogan answered.

The handsome doctor led the way, and then halted, smiling in puzzlement that his patient had turned onto her side after he had left the bedside.

"Miss?" Hoyle said softly while touching her shoulder with a gentle hand.

Pandora murmured and gave the handsome doctor a long, lost look. She fluttered her lashes, and gripped the doctor's polished fingers. He smiled, and she forced a smile to her own mouth.

"How did . . . I get here?"

Her soft, breathy voice sent chills running up and down Rogan Thorn's spine, and he had an idea that she guarded every word she spoke. But why? he

44

wondered. This intrigued him even more. He waited for her lovely lips to move again, remembering the soft femininity of her form when her weight had rested disturbingly against him in the carriage and as he carried her up the stairs.

"You have had a little accident," Rogan put in, watching closely as her eyes flicked over him and then returned to Hoyle.

"Who are you, miss?" Hoyle now asked.

"What of your parents, where are they?" Rogan asked at the same time.

She shook her head while her thoughts scattered in every direction. Truly they did. "I do not remember anything about myself," she said this time in half-truth. Indeed, at that moment there was not much of her past she could recall for the strange men's faces, turned toward her in open admiration, unnerved her more than anything else.

"You haven't a fever," Hoyle supplied, "so you should be remembering very soon—at least let's hope so. I can recognize that you are in a state of sheer exhaustion, and are very hungry." He said this smilingly. "I heard your stomach rumbling a short while ago. When did you eat last?"

Pandora gazed directly into his dark brown eyes with the innocence of a child. "I do not know, really—I don't," she said truthfully, squirming inwardly when a growl rose from her belly to witness the doctor's words.

"Do you remember your name, at least?" Rogan put in.

Pandora did not glance again at the man with the deep baritone voice, but fingered the cool cloth she had been clutching in frustration.

"Do haunting pictures move fleetingly through your mind, young lady?" Dr. Hoyle put his new hunch into the question, but carefully, smiling as he did so.

"Yes. My name is Dora."

Two pairs of male eyebrows rose in surprise. Rogan leaned forward, hands stuffed low in his pockets. He was trying to stay in good humor, but aggravation was beginning to set in.

Rogan looked sharply at her. "That's *all?*" he rapped out louder than he had intended.

"Yes."

Pandora appeared startled by the question and kept her eyes averted from this masterful-sounding man flanking the doctor. She knew beyond a doubt, and without looking fully into the tall man's face— the man who had brought her here—that he was a strikingly handsome figure, much handsomer in fact than the good-looking doctor who had touched her intimately in his examination. She had been hard-pressed to lie still beneath his soothing hands.

"Hmmm," Rogan murmured, twisting his mustache upward. "Could I have a word with you, Hoyle?" He moved back one step; then added when the doctor hadn't moved, "Outside."

Dr. Hoyle bent to the young woman to pick up her long-fingered hand. "I'll check back tomorrow. Maybe you'll be remembering by then who you are; at least *all* of who you are," he ended with a brief chuckle.

"Thank you, kind sir," she said sweetly.

Rogan lifted an eyebrow at that. Rogan was

growing impatient when Hoyle paused again to give her a final order.

"Oh. Don't try to walk for a few more hours. Rest. Good day, young lady."

Pandora tried not to squirm when, at the door, both men glanced back to see her staring after them with feverishly bright eyes. Hoyle seemed a bit flustered and confused when they went outside the bedroom. But with the quick sympathy of a doctor for a patient, Hoyle felt sorry for the young woman who had suffered a lapse of memory.

"Now," he began, "what's this all about, Rogan? Can you fill me in on the details."

Although the door had been closed to a mere crack, Pandora was able to hear snatches of conversation. The maid had gone back to her tasks, as had the Chinaman, she guessed. She drew in quick, intermittent breaths at what she could hear the men outside saying.

"She may very well be . . . of the mind . . . amnesia, where people get sick . . . yes, as well as in the body."

Pandora could almost see the man she supposed was the owner of this house lift an eyebrow now while the doctor spoke.

"Yes, it would seem that way . . . but . . ." the deeper voice went on, lost to her ears as it dipped low.

". . . the authorities . . . find out where she came from . . . get her full name . . . keep her here . . . until then."

The other voice again. "What else . . . I do?"

The crisp voice of the doctor: "See no harm in it, Rogan . . . lost or runaway . . . young enough . . . strange . . . traveling light . . . that may be so . . . but do keep her from leaving. . . ."

"Thanks . . . Hoyle . . . tomorrow."

Long, tapered fingers worried the silken cream sheets while Pandora waited until their footsteps receded from the door. She was alone. Finally.

Alone. A terror from the past crouched at the edge of her mind.

Cautiously she sat up in bed to search about the room for her rattan suitcase. Indistinct mumblings and the rattle of tea things drifted in to her and at once she fell back to the pillow.

Oh, why had she waited so long to flee!

Still, she could hardly have jumped up from *his* lap when she had regained consciousness in the carriage, could she?

A picture formed in her mind. Windswept and seaswept. *She* had been swept away, too, compelled to flee.

More pictures. Of white sand, huge bright flowers, verdant green background, and trees alive with birdsong.

They might discover she was on the run . . . from what she herself did not truly know yet. She shook herself as one rousing from a nightmare.

"Later," she told herself frantically, "I have to get away from here!"

A strange new life was beginning for her; she could feel this in her bones, blood, muscles, and sinews. Only one thing must remain consistent in her mind: She must not let that tall man touch her again. *Rogan*, the doctor had said.

Chapter Four

Paris drank champagne from fine, dainty slippers, and so did San Francisco—"The Paris of America." So, this evening would Walter Riddock, to his never-ending delight and astonishment. The watchful eye of the city was on him—oh, yes, and Rogan Thorn—and Walter knew this; he, too, was highly respected and deeply loved; his adventures and misadventures alike were juicy material for constant gossip. There had been a great deal said about his actions in the dark at the theater; he shrugged. But Rogan Thorn had become a thorough bore, as far as Walter was concerned—and he wasn't much.

Walter's dark blue eyes glittered from the carriage that climbed the hill. He knew he was considered handsome and a bit of an intellectual; he had an eye for art and objets d'art, all lovely things for that matter. And he was very popular, especially with young couples. The theater held a strong appeal for him, especially the comedies rated risqué. He liked to sit in the fashionable audience surrounded by the rustle of silk and stiffly starched shirts, but he didn't much care for the current fashion for ladies to wear tailor-made clothes in public. Ugh!

He had gone to the Sutro Baths—the largest indoor tank in the world—and to study the bathers on the beach. But his enjoyment of that scene had been marred by those "daring young things" who wore nothing but the latest bathing suits that revealed *only* their faces and hands. The suits were mostly black, but on their limbs were those horrible new stockings with the shocking diagonal stripes. Why, even their hair had been hidden beneath rubber mob caps!

"God, how repugnant!" Walter muttered now. He looked around at his surroundings. "Driver, stop! I'll get out here." He pointed his walking stick. "Wait if you can, I shan't be long." He stepped out to the sidewalk.

So three hours after he had received the message—and Pandora's reticule—from Sly Binks, Walter Riddock was knocking on the door of the rooming house.

After having climbed three flights of stairs, Walter looked annoyed, impatient. He studied a crack in the ceiling with disinterest, poised to knock again when, with a yank, the door opened.

She caught him studying the meandering crack, just as Rogan Thorn had done several times before. Her long thick hair had been sleekly brushed and drawn back into a loose coil at her neck. Almond-eyed, she measured Walter Riddock, president of the Wolfington & Riddock line of cargo ships. She snapped out a greeting peevishly.

"Yes? What do you want now? I told you—" Then Cara found herself facing a stranger and not her busybody landlady, Mrs. Cirillo. "Well, well, who have we got here?" she asked in her best surmising tone.

"Miss Kalee, you don't remember me, I see. We have met before, though—" He stared at her softly rounded face, lips he knew could be deliciously warm—if one was so inclined—and large inquiring eyes.

Oh-oh, Cara thought to herself. She had heard this line before a million times.

"I have a feeling," Cara said sarcastically, "it will come to me soon. But—why don't you tell me first, so we can get over it without playing games, hmm?"

Cara tilted her brunette head to one side, waiting.

Walter gave a short laugh. "Walter Riddock, Sarah Wolfington's nephew. You worked for her, remember?" He jerked his face up a bit proudly.

"Ohhh, now I see. But I won't do it!" Cara began closing the door in his face.

But Walter stuck his foot in. "Wait a minute, Miss Kalee. Let me explain," Walter tried. "Could I come in for a minute or two?"

Cara tossed her dark head. "Only if your aunt owes me some money she forgot to pay me. Otherwise forget it, Jack!"

"Walter," he corrected. Now he lowered the boom. "Miss Kalee, Pandora—ah—St. Ives has come to California." He watched for her reaction.

Cara heaved a great sigh. "So, what about it? My cousin is in San Francisco; Pandora has finally run away from Paradise." She said this with bitter emphasis directed at her island home. "What has all this got to do with you, anyway?" she added with a brisk snap.

"Wouldn't you care to see your younger cousin? It's been a long time, I believe," Walter guessed.

"Mr. Riddock," Cara began impatiently, her fingers gripping the white-painted door with its blister of peeling paint, "I don't care to see Pandora St. Ives, or you, or anyone for that matter. I am going out tonight, to visit a friend. So, I do have to get dressed in a hurry, good-b—"

"You're *very* rude, Miss Kalee," Walter said quietly, "but still I ask that we might talk for a few minutes."

"We have been doing just that. No, I'm sorry, you can't come in. If you've met Pandora and you want her for your mistress or something like that, to hide her out here, you'll have to hunt up another place. I like living alone, you see," Cara said; then paused to ask, "Have you got a wife, Mr. Riddock? With all that money you must—"

"No, I don't have a wife!" Walter felt himself getting angrier by the minute.

"Well, if you don't want Pandora, and—"

"I *do* want her. I've been crazy imagining her lovely face ever since I—well, you see, while on business in the islands, your cousin was walking on the beach. I happened to see her—"

"And now you're in love," Cara mocked with puppy eyes. "I *do* have to get going! I've wasted enough time with—" She pushed against the door with her palms.

"Damn you, bitch!" Walter ground out between clenched teeth.

"Mrs. Cirillo!" Cara shrilled when he shoved the door and her into the room.

"Pandora is now at Rogan Thorn's house," Riddock hissed.

"*Mama mia*, what'sa going on up there? Eh? What're you shouting about, woman!" Mrs. Cirillo called up the stairwell. "You gonna crazy or something?" The landlady waited, but no answer came down. "Hey! You gonna paya the rent or amma I gonna have to kicka you outa here. *Hey?*"

"Yes, Mrs. Cirillo, I'll be down to pay it in just a little while!"

Dazedly Cara turned back to go inside her apartment. Having made himself at home, Walter Riddock waited for her, seated on a crimson couch around which plants rose as in a tropical garden. This plush living room was entirely out of keeping with the shabbiness Walter had seen on his way upstairs. He knew she hadn't earned enough working for his aunt to purchase all these fine appointments. Someone else must have, someone like Rogan Thorn.

Cara shut the door and faced Mr. Riddock squarely. She sauntered over to the sofa, her lush curves undulating sensually. Now, charmingly, she leaned close to Walter Riddock. The potent smell of her patchouli perfume rose up between them like a mystery cloud of the Orient.

"Tell me that *again*, Riddock, so I can hear it this time without Mrs. Cirillo shouting in the background," she said softly, with an ominous undertone. "Yes, I would like to hear how little Pandora has latched onto Rogan Thorn." She paused with a hand crossed over his wrist.

Walter tried not to flinch, for her long nails were

53

digging into his flesh. But he waited, ignoring the painful claws, for her to finish what she was saying.

"He is *my* lover, did you know that?"

"First off," Walter began, raking a nervous gaze over the mounds of flesh peeping out of her dressing gown. "Pandora St. Ives is not so little anymore. Quite tall, in fact, and the most beautiful young woman I have ever—admired—and wanted to possess."

"Possess? *Really*, Mr. Riddock," she muttered. Then, showing more interest, she went on. "Tell me . . . Walter, how Pandora has wormed her way into Rogan Thorn's house and maybe his heart?"

First Walter pried his wrist from her grip; then, from out of his silk vest he handed over to her the China silk reticule that contained a letter dated two years ago, written in Cara's own hand, with the address of this very same rooming house in it.

She flicked her eyes up at Walter as he said:

"We'll start here, with this letter. Then you tell me a little more about your cousin. A deal?"

"What do you mean 'we'll start here'?"

Walter cleared his throat. "You want to know how to get her out of his house, don't you?"

"A deal."

Chapter Five

The night fog had crept in through the Golden Gate and now sent its tentative fingers up the cobbled streets to Nob Hill. Lighted by the dim, diffused glow of fog-bleared street lamps, the row of houses was slick and glistening with the dampness. Pandora woke suddenly to find herself in a strange room bathed in tones of mauve and pale blue and soft gold. There were chairs covered in satin and velvet and mirrors reflected the soft glow of gaslight turned low.

The nightgown Pandora wore was strange, too. Then she remembered. She had been having a hard time remembering lately. A matronly woman had helped her into it before she slept. Tea things rattling . . . a maid named Freyda . . . warm liquid coursing down her parched throat again . . . But what else? What came before that?

Pandora stirred on the luxurious fourposter, but did not sit up just yet. She wanted to test her strength by moving her sore muscles one by one, starting with her toes. Her hand went fluttering to her brow. There was a bruise on her temple the size of a half dollar and she winced when she discovered it.

Of course, the accident. She remembered that much now. Running, yes, she had been fleeing from a shadowy man who had been following her most of the day. The only thing she could not recall was how she came to be in . . . San Francisco?

As she stared into her past, a kaleidoscope of memories shifted and then settled into nothingness —nothing but bits of black glass. Horror on a shadowed beach, far from here.

Pandora truly had been unconscious, at first, and then after awakening in the carriage on the way to this house, high on a hill, she had pretended to be. Up, up they had climbed and she now recalled her fear. But of what? Surely not of the man with the deep masculine voice; his green eyes had glittered over her as she had glimpsed the man, only momentarily.

They, whoever they were, must not learn where she was from, what had happened before. . . . Before she came to be here? And just where was she from, and what had happened to cause her to be so cautious and secretive?

The blood, so much blood washing up . . . on the black glass. The dark secret of a tide-washed shore. Yes! But whose blood had it been? A woman's? A man's?

"No!" Pandora sobbed aloud, coming upright in the massive fourposter. She covered her wretched face with trembling hands. "I can't remember, I must not!" she cried aloud.

"Why not?"

Pandora startled, peered over the tips of her fingers. Her heart stood still, but only for a moment as the tall man with the sparkling, unfathomable green eyes rose fluidly from a dark corner and came to stand beside the bed. He looked down on her with a heavy-lidded gaze.

It washed over Pandora slowly, then with more force, like breakers rolling up on the shore. She knew she was in a bedroom belonging to this green-eyed man, this stranger with the deep voice that rose to a higher pitch when he was perplexed. He had been angry, too. But why? Perhaps it was because she had imposed on his privacy. With his looks and wealth, he must have a wife. What was she thinking at this minute while her husband was with a strange woman in her guest bedroom?

She had to get out of this house and away from this man—and his family. A stirring of alarm was running through her body. He would be married to the kind of woman who would not stand for any trouble, of any nature, in her house.

"Dora?"

The sound of his deep voice sliced through her thoughts and stirred something in her. Something wild and thrilling she had never experienced before swept her from head to foot. She quickly suppressed the feeling and realized with shock that she had been staring at him openly, incredulously. He looked like a seafarer, one whose countenance had been tanned by the sun and blown by the salt winds. She tried to lower her eyes, but was mesmerized by the startling green of his, like sheer silk over jade stone, yet paler; strange eyes, more like the color of . . . waves underneath, before they break; with a fringe of the blackest lashes ever. Grooves slashed downward on either side of his wide lips, and there were shadows in evidence beneath his high cheekbones. He had rich chestnut hair, lots of it, and wavy, the kind a woman would like to . . . run . . . her hands through. Discounting his sinister mustache, he was by far the most roughly handsome male her young eyes had ever beheld.

"Why?" he repeated, more forcefully, still staring with those pale eyes that seemed to demand something of her she couldn't give. Not words . . . but something else.

Pandora blinked out of her trance, blushing profusely.

"I—I am just a little confused, that's all," she said, biting her lower lip unconsciously.

"And afraid," he put in.

She lowered her head. "Yes," she confessed.

Of course, she was afraid and why shouldn't she be? There was a certain dangerous magnetism about this man. She broke contact with his gaze by brushing back a wave of copper hair, and winced when the back of her hand came into contact with the bruise again.

"It's purple now, but has gone down a bit."

"What? Oh, the bump. Yes."

"You've had an accident. Do you remember that much?" Rogan asked, a frown growing on the bridge of his thin nose.

He had flaring nostrils, too, she noticed throwing a hasty glance at his face and then turning away to stare at the pattern on the carpet.

"Yes . . . that much," she finally answered.

"No more?" he pressed.

His knee bumped the edge of the bed accidentally as he shifted his weight. The indirect contact sent a little shock through her flesh. If he could do this to her now . . . several feet from her . . . then what if . . . She could not finish wondering.

"No more."

"Dora. Correct?"

"Yes . . ." Her pulse quickened. Why was he looking at her in this manner?

He heaved a deep, impatient sigh when Pandora kept shifting her gaze from his face to the quilted counterpane. "Dora *what?*" With a palm resting on the bedside table, he stepped a few inches closer to the bed. "Look at me, Dora," he commanded.

Her gaze ran across his lowered face and then glanced off to the marble fireplace. She could not remember her last name!

"I repeat, miss, I must have your last name. We really should contact . . . *someone.*"

Back to the fireplace shot her gaze, her lashes fluttering. The fireplace, with its dark-gray marble, was so shiny that the bedroom was reflected in it. The perfection of this room surpassed in elegance anything she had ever seen.

Hurry, think of something fast, she shouted at herself inwardly. A lie is a most terrible thing, her mother had always said. She had said that? She did have parents of course, but whether they were alive or not she could not recall.

"Do you have a headache, now, Dora?" he asked. "The doctor told me to call him back at once if—"

Her head jerked up, breaking his sentence. "Dora. Just Dora, I remember no more!" she cried heatedly.

Rogan was slightly taken aback by the sudden thrust of her words, and rubbed and blinked an eye, as if there were something irritating it. He stared hard at her now, and cleared his throat noisily.

"Miss—ah—Dora. Just Dora. I am Rogan Thorn. Welcome to my home." He paused to shake his head confusedly; then went on after another impatient sigh. "A relative, or if not that, perhaps a friend we can get in touch with?" He stopped himself. "I am sorry, you *are* 'Miss'?"

His eyes were sparkling oddly, Pandora thought. Or was it only because the gaslight seemed to brighten suddenly. Or was it merely the fuzz in her brain that made her think this?

"Mr. Thorn, why are you so very suspicious?" As soon as the question was out, she wished she could snatch it back.

Irately he ignored her question, thus causing Pandora to redden from intense embarrassment. Her question had been so out of place, she realized to her horror. He was so businesslike and so overwhelming that she felt mouselike by comparison, even though she was by no means a small woman. Pandora crushed her childish urge to stick out her tongue at him. Instead she pulled a long face. After all, this was his home, and she should take that into consideration; at least that much.

Oh, yes, and she should be thankful for his kindness, she added to herself. He could have contacted the police. Heavens! he might still do that very thing! She had to think of a way to go from this house as quickly as possible. Would he let her go? Or would he keep her? He was a powerful figure, she sensed that, and she . . . was helpless and did not know what had happened in the past that was too frightening for her to even dwell upon.

Pandora felt so out of place in this bed, *his* bed in *his* house, his *wife's* house. Strangers, for she did not know them from Adam.

Eyes narrowed and head set at a brooding angle, he seemed lost in distant thought, though his eyes rested upon her. Finally he spoke again.

"Are you sure you are this . . . Dora . . ."—he shrugged—"whatever? You aren't just fooling me about that, are you? You *are* afraid of the police, I can tell," he declared.

"Yes. I mean no! I am Dora . . . that is all I recall of myself. And I am so very sorry to have inconvenienced you." She twisted her long fingers together. "I am so sorry to put you through all this trouble, Mr. Thorn." She realized she was repeating herself, merely for something to say. "I will be leaving here now, if you will get my bags?"

"Bags?" A heavy brow lifted. "You have only the one suitcase—Dora."

When her legs had completed the swing from bed to carpeted floor, it hit Pandora. Her head reeled dizzily and she caught herself just as she was keeling sideways. But warm, vibrant hands were at her shoulders swiftly; he was pushing her back gently onto the soft pillows. She closed her eyes, rolling her head on the pillow to avert his stare.

It was then that Rogan noticed the strange cut of her clothes. He felt them where they lay on the table. No woman in San Francisco, or any other city in America for that matter, wore clothes like these. The flowered dress of simple but colorful cotton was very unfashionable. She could have stepped from a different time—or just a different place. Somewhere . . . but where had he seen dresses like this one before?

Rogan shook himself from his trance, and stopped fingering the cloth. Maybe he was just dreaming all this, and he would wake up soon. He would have yielded sooner to his impulse to kiss her if it had not been for her fear and the strangeness of the situation.

"Well," he said with a sigh, "where are you from, Dora? You haven't answered me, either, as to who your relatives could be. You are a complete mystery, woman, and I need some answers before you leave my house!" His voice was rising angrily.

How could this young woman, this lovely stranger, do this to him? He hardly ever lost his composure. When he did, though, with anger goading him on, his acquaintances ran the other way. For some strange reason unknown to him, he did not want this Dora to fear him or to leave his house, even though she was getting under his skin.

Wizan chose this moment to enter, quietly bringing hot coffee, pink slices of juicy ham between thin triangles of white bread, and a dish of Chinese rice cookies ringed with orange slices. Wizan's kimono-style jacket of black and gold shone in the gaslight as he set out the coffee cups of white Limoges china on the side table.

Pandora hardly noticed the food. She must have eaten some of the frosted cakes and drunk some tea that the maid had brought in earlier, for she didn't feel much like eating. She noticed that Rogan Thorn did not look very hungry, either.

"Mr. Thol'n, should I light lamp on the taboret now?" he asked, indicating the mahogany table with the Italian-marble top.

Rogan was so engrossed in staring at the gorgeous young woman whose hair cascaded down her back like copper fire, that he hardly noticed the Chinaman's presence. Wizan had never seen Thorn in such a state of total absorption. From the hall Wizan had heard his boss harshly question the young woman. Why was he being so mean? Could he not see she had lost her memory?

Engrossed wholly herself, Pandora stared openly at Mr. Thorn now. His eyes fascinated her. This was too much to bear. She had to escape from this house, especially from this man!

Rogan finally acknowledged Wizan's presence. "Yes, light the lamp if you want, Wizan. Then you may go," he said, just above a whisper.

When the servant had gone out on softly padding slippers, Pandora chose to answer at once. "I am on my own, Mr. Thorn. I have no relatives to speak of." Not that she knew of, really.

He had no business, this Rogan Thorn, putting her in such an embarrassing and possibly dangerous position. With thoughts of escape running through her mind, she decided firmly to get away from this man, to find . . . someone. She had to . . . find a woman? This man, of undoubted affluence and power posed a threat to her . . . freedom? Was that the word?

She just could not stand the thought of being caged again, by any man! Yes, that was it, she had been a man's prisoner before. Almost? Questions kept going through her mind without answers. Again the blood flashed before her vision.

Rogan attempted to try a new tactic, and this brought Pandora out of her trance.

"Maybe I could get in touch with your employer?" He knew he was picking her languid brain, but he couldn't stop himself. "You didn't just pop out of nowhere, Miss—Dora. Although your dress and manner begin to puzzle me. So, why can't you tell me why you mustn't remember? You said this earlier. What is so horrible that it must be put so far back in your mind?" he fired at her steadily.

Pandora gasped, her long fingers flying to her breast.

"Please, not so fast! You are mixing me up more than ever!"

He brooked no refusal to his harsh questioning, but plunged ruthlessly on.

"*Be* mixed up then! Let's have some outright answers, now, or else I'll have to get in touch with the police."

"The . . . police?" she stammered breathlessly.

"Yes. They should always come anyway when there has been an accident. Perhaps you are a runaway? You look young enough." He waited for a reply. "Well, how old are you?"

Before she could answer, Rogan thought about what he had just said. If he summoned the police, there would be gossip, talk, and newspaper coverage. His name involved with that of a strange woman. Scandal. God forbid!

The spellbinding gold of little lamp flickers played across Pandora's face, causing her in her helplessness to appear very young indeed.

"Twenty," she rapped out, guessing exactly.

"Liar," he said softly, then louder. "You don't look a day past seventeen! Why, your dress"—he indicated the flowered cloth on the table—"was made for a child of fifteen."

"How dare you!" she yelled.

"I dare anything I damned well please!" he shot back.

"Oh, no, sir, not with me!"

Pandora propelled her body from the bed, though her effort cost her dearly. She fought off the renewed feeling of weakness and nausea. She felt as if her body were weighted down—and her head throbbed awfully—as she wove her way to a chair and snatched up her suitcase which she had spied minutes before. She had no idea just how ridiculous she appeared in the nightgown with suitcase in hand. But neither did she much care.

Rogan did nothing more for now than to watch her, stuffing his hands into his trousers; but a predatory look leaped onto his face as he felt his desire for this gorgeous woman rise.

"Oh," Pandora breathed trying to support her weakened legs by clutching the chair back a moment before trying to make it to the door. It seemed such a long way off. Finally she straightened and moved normally, but slowly.

Rogan found himself catching his breath. He hadn't realized she was so tall, and as regal as a princess in her carriage, even in the nightgown that was too short at the hem for her long legs. The nightgown belonged to his mistress, Cara. She had left it the last time she had stayed at his house, several months ago.

Pandora continued to move slowly, placing one foot in front of the other, giving Rogan a glimpse of her lovely long legs when the nightgown rode high with each stride and molded the thin material to her thighs. His heart quickened as he found himself wondering about the rest of her body hidden beneath the gown. He could already see that her breasts were full and ripe; his gaze followed the softly rocking motion of them.

"Fool!" Rogan finally allowed himself to get upset. "You look utterly ridiculous in that simple rag, clutching that battered suitcase as if your life depended upon it."

"It does!" she retorted.

"You know what?" He didn't wait for her to answer. "I am beginning to believe that this accident made you a little touched in the head!"

She slowed her steps to yell back at him. "It is all your fault, Rogan Thorn! Your Chinaman's fault, excuse me!" Anger was feeding her strength.

"Oh, I take that back," he volleyed. "I believe you were dimwitted even before that! Now get back here, into the bed. No woman, sane or insane, is going to scandalize the Thorn name. I've not worked long and hard to uphold the name my grandfather set for this family in order to have a silly damned urchin ruin it all in one fell swoop with her long, tangled legs tumbling down *my* stairs!" His voice went lower then, became a threat. "I will keep you here, Dora, tied to that bed if necessary!" He advanced one step.

She spun about to snap at him, "How do you know my legs are long?" Anger goaded her to go farther. "I *am* going and do *not* try to stop me!" Pandora gasped

66

then as her head swam wildly and her eyes blurred. But she could see him coming, and she held up her hand. "Don't come near me, or I shall scream for your wife!"

Suddenly he was beside her, reaching out. "I am not married, Dora. What made you think that?" His hand moved swiftly as a sound bubbled from her throat.

Rogan had anticipated her scream and had clamped a hand over her mouth, unconsciously hurting her. Pandora closed her eyes to shut out the wild look in those pale green eyes.

"I hate you," she hissed low, "even if you are not married."

She could barely make out his breathless words.

"I want you."

Chapter Six

"No, don't pull away," he said in a commanding tone.

Though her first reaction was one of panic, Pandora felt his touch go through her arm like a flaming sword. When he caught her at the door, she fell in a swoon in the arms that gathered her close. Melting to him against her will, her body weak and trembling, she heard his intake of breath, and his words that seemed to come from afar. Her mind and body became a contradiction of feelings and emotions, mostly betraying ones.

Though Pandora feared his strength and what could happen should he call the law, she forgot all this and began to experience a new kind of warmth against his silk-clad chest. She dared to look up at him to see that his pale eyes had changed almost to a blazing emerald, but he gazed down at her with something close to wonderment, a soft yet strange expression growing on his face.

"Dora," he murmured, "you'll soon want me as much as I want you."

His hand slid down her back and her heartbeat increased. He felt so strong; he could crush her in his embrace easily. But would he really hurt her? Like rape? If he decided to take her by force, she wouldn't have the strength to stop him. She felt his muscular tension as he trust his fingers into her hair that cascaded like silk from a bolt. Rogan bent to breathe in the soft scent of her hair and Pandora felt the heat rise in her body, to her thighs, higher, between her hips, and to her breasts. She could feel the hardness between his legs pressing at her and she felt suddenly weightless as a consuming sweetness washed over her. She heard the whisper of clothing, but paid it no mind.

Rogan Thorn shivered with the soft, young thing against him. She seemed to be drawing sorely needed strength from him; and he was beginning to know a sense of giving. Something new for him, an emotion he had never known before, rippled through him. The pressure in his groin was becoming unbearable and he grew tumid. His body ached and throbbed and craved her softness. He wanted to thrust and enter her.

"Dora." He said the name caressingly. "*Lonesome. I have never been that, but if you go from me, I surely will be.*" He heard himself mutter this and he was bewildered by this unbidden flow of words.

Their eyes met and held.

"No." Pandora began to struggle weakly, uttering low cries, for she feared this physical arousal that she was experiencing for the first time.

She tried to turn her head aside, but he cupped her chin between long fingers.

"Dora, don't fight me," his husky voice commanded. "Don't be afraid. . . ."

She saw his head bend and his lips come to claim hers, possessively, mercilessly. Before they made contact, though, she instinctively placed her hands between their bodies.

"No, don't do that." He pulled her hands down to her sides and their lips merely touched in the movement.

Now those lips came down on hers to silence any further protest. First, like the brush of a butterfly flitting from flower to flower; then like a bee sting, shocking, as he sought to go deeper into her mouth; parting her lips, touching her tongue with the hot tip of his. She stiffened.

"Dora, open your mouth to me," he demanded with gentle force.

The only answer she gave was to moan from somewhere deep inside herself as darting sensations began to gather in her lower region. For Rogan's kiss was the first taste of desire she had ever known. This kiss lengthened, causing an unintelligible murmur of protest to rise from her throat and to bring a moan from her lips.

"Oh . . . oh . . . what are you doing to me—?" She didn't want him to stop, but she was suddenly very afraid.

Then, from somewhere came a small sense of past experience. Not of desire, no, for she had never been kissed or caressed as he was doing, though someone . . . had stolen kisses many times. She could not count as pleasurable those other wet kisses that someone had slobbered all over her face, her neck, and her breasts. Compared to that animal theft of her body and soul, this was like being transported to heaven, on silver wings. It was shocking, but she needed more of this man and what he was doing to her.

"Woman," he moaned near her cheek, his breath like a flame. "For you are woman, lovely . . . do you know what it is that you do to me? This moment could be so beautiful, if only I knew something of your past." He groaned near her ear. "Oh, God, what am I saying. It *is* beautiful, and I want you . . . want you . . . Dora . . . Dora." His voice echoed his desire.

In their moments of ensuing passion, the body heat between Rogan and Dora increased threefold. He pushed her back a little in order to see her face while he caressed her hips and buttocks through the nightgown. A question entered his eyes. Her own eyes, like a sea-blue mist flickered up at his in her gentle innocence.

"No?" he inquired, but hope sprang in his eyes suddenly grown huge.

"Yes," she said shyly, not knowing to what she had just committed herself. "I want you, too, Rogan."

Then as her girlish nervousness slipped away from her, Pandora wondered briefly if she had lost her will during the accident. Though her body said yes, her mind screamed, It's too soon. This was not right; she must stop this before it went too far.

"Forgive me, Dora, but you are driving me insane with desire. Please tell me quickly who you are, where you come from? Don't you remember anything?" He groaned huskily. "I must know that you do not belong to another before—"

"Please, R-Rogan, do not ask." She fell to hugging him close, afraid to let him go, not knowing what she

71

really wanted.

Wantonly and naturally but ironically with inexperience, Pandora pressed herself closer as she wrapped her long slim arms about his neck. Running her fingers through the thick chestnut curls at the nape of his neck, while he deluged her with a rain of kisses that created goose flesh at her throat, Pandora arched to him, her leg becoming trapped between his. A hardness stabbed into her belly and she shivered as he searched the swell of her breast, and her nipples swiftly hardened beneath his hand.

"Ah, Dora, your breasts are full and perfect in shape. Full, ripe, your skin like satin. Your lovely body was made for love. You will desire me soon, Dora; I have already promised you that."

"Oh, Rogan, Rogan, I—I already do," she cried, going limp in his arms.

Her feet left the floor and she was being swept to the bed in his quivering arms. This powerful man, who had only hours ago been a stranger to her, was now—had been—setting the scene for love-making and she, little fool, she thought for one insane moment, was letting him have his way with her.

He came down to the bed beside her, taking her hand in his. "Touch me, Dora. When we make love I want to be completely ready, know that you want me." He guided her hand downward, but worry flitted over his rugged visage.

When his hands slid down to come to rest between her own thighs, his fingers made a gentle exploration, moving back and forth across the soft flesh until she moaned. He was still guiding her with his other hand, but she drew back.

"I—cannot touch you—" She bit her lower lip. "What are you . . . doing? I have never—"

With that, Rogan was brought back down to earth as if a bolt of lightning had suddenly struck him.

"I thought so—you are a virgin!" He looked down at himself and noticed that sometime in the heat of passion he had unfastened his trousers. "Whoa," he said, silently cursing his haste.

He left her brusquely and stood, damning the throbbing in his swollen member. This was all happening much too fast. Situations such as this had gotten lesser men into trouble. He had much to lose hopping into bed with someone who was possibly suffering an attack of amnesia, or worse. She could even have a husband. And God, he despised scandal. What was even worse, he had never lost his heart to a woman; he had always guarded it carefully.

Pandora grew cold, so very cold now. She was suspended in a state of half-consciousness, but she could see the man buttoning the top of his trousers. She sat up with a shock that registered on her countenance.

"Damn me if you aren't!" Rogan said again, taking in the pale face of a timid virgin.

Pandora blushed deeply. "I must have"—she passed a shaking had over her moist brow—"passed out for a while. Did I?" she inquired innocently, truly wondering what had transpired between them. On top of everything else that had happened to her this day, she felt all hot and bewitched. Cold one minute; hot the next.

He muttered an oath. This puzzled her, for she had never heard such before.

"Forgive me," he said. "That's no language for a woman's ears." Then he went on to answer her question. "No, you didn't pass out, and neither did I." He concealed a worried frown from her as he went on. "Rest, Dora. Eat something if you can. But tomorrow, bright and early, I demand you come down and join me for breakfast. We have a lot to talk about, you and I."

He wouldn't be able to wait very long to have her, he knew; but later, there would be time enough for answers. First things first, just as in business.

Rogan slipped away from Pandora. Her arm dropped listlessly over the side of the bed. She was so, so tired . . . and cold. But her hands went over her lips, feeling, savoring the touch of a kiss as hard as a bruise. She couldn't understand why his kisses had left her empty, desiring something more; but it was a thing of which she was ignorant.

Pandora at once dreamed of palm fronds dancing in sea breezes . . . the sand . . . flowers . . . the "man" who would someday make her a woman beneath the stars. . . . Had her search for him ended . . . ?

Chapter Seven

The fog was thicker now as it crept in from the bay, cloaking the entire city with its eerie, clinging mist. Though she felt as if she were afloat, Pandora was no longer aboard the softly rocking ship that had brought her to San Francisco. She was in a haven against the damp fog, a bedroom hung with mauve and gold, outside of which a pale street lamp fought vainly to illuminate the house front.

Pandora had stirred at sounds from outside; a carriage bowling along the street; a heavy catch grating noisily, as if announcing the arrival of a visitor.

She had slept fitfully, but now she fell back into a wearied slumber, walking the tormented, dark, forbidding streets she ventured along in her dreams. The cherished dream was with her now no more; the image of the "man" became mixed with her nightmares.

Downstairs the outside gate had indeed opened and closed; then the heavy oak front door did the same. Wizan, wearing a mask of irritation, let Cara Kalee in finally, even though he still tried to send her away. But Cara was already peeling off her black kid gloves and preparing to search for Rogan herself if the Chinaman proved troublesome. He had, on some occasions, but never as much as now.

"Mistel Thol'n does not want to see anyone. He had velly busy day at office, and be mighty mad if I let you in!" Wizan maintained with guarded stance.

"Oh?" Cara brushed by him, ignoring his dainty body that had been set up as a barricade.

"You be velly solly." He shook his head for emphasis.

"Oh, he'll see *me*, Chinaman; he's been expecting me tonight. Didn't you know?"

Cara gathered her skirt and peered along the main floor where large sliding doors opened into all the rooms. She did not await his answer, but swept by the living-room door, pausing to glance up the winding staircase with its elegant finials and balusters; the polished handrails gleamed beneath a burning side bracket.

How many times Cara had gone up those stairs with Rogan, eager to make love—until they were both satiated. But that had seemed so long ago now. Before the problem had ever arisen; his problem.

A swath of light showed beneath the study door and Cara smiled to herself. Tipping her gleaming head, she waited for the glowering Chinaman to go back to wherever he had been busying himself before her arrival. She knocked when Wizan melted into the dark shadows at the end of the hall.

"Rogan? May I come in?" She adjusted the prim lace trimming the sleeves of her emerald-green dress.

The door opened shortly and Rogan stood there as if he had been on his way out of the room. But his chestnut hair waved over his forehead as if he'd raked a heavy hand through it in meditation—or perhaps irritation at being interrupted.

"Cara," was all he said. His green eyes appeared brighter than ever, Cara noticed, almost feverish and somewhat troubled. She decided she knew the reason very well.

"Naughty man, aren't you going to invite me in?" she purred, her brown eyes dancing with a playfulness she didn't feel.

"Not in here, Cara."

Rogan stepped out, closing the door behind him. "Let's go into the parlor." Wizan had lighted a fire there against the damp. "It's cozier."

Cara paused to frown as he swept past her, impeccably groomed even in his wine-colored smoking jacket and dove-gray trousers.

"You left the lamp on in the study, Rogan. Do you have someone in there you don't—" She cut herself off just in time, so she thought.

Rogan swung about. "Just the usual books and papers, Cara." His narrowed eyes were piercing. "Did you think I had company?"

"Just curious," she said, her voluptuous figure following his tall one back into the parlor.

"Why?" Rogan wondered out loud, closing the door brusquely when she was inside with him.

But Cara hadn't caught his low-muttered "Why?" Rogan continued on the tempting but tormented path he had been mind-walking that evening in his study. Dora. Dora. With her gold-threaded coppery hair, she was a beautiful and feminine young woman; one he guessed who was simple and natural, who had never used her feminine wiles to get a man or gain his favor. She had been sitting on his bed as still as a statue, a half-naked goddess; the brilliance of unshed tears caused her slightly uptilted eyes to appear even more blue. And now, he sensed, only too late, that his thoughtless attack on her shy womanhood had somehow hurt her. He would give anything to take back those hot kisses and bruising caresses if he could, if only to assuage his own feelings of guilt. But was that completely the truth . . . ? For the first time in his life a pang went through him for someone else's sake besides his own.

He turned from Cara so she could not see the pain in his face. At the same moment that he was turning away from her to go to the fireplace, her arms had been in the process of reaching out for his wide shoulders. She shrugged when he kept walking, as if he had not noticed her familiar gesture.

Cara set the Victorian rocking chair into motion with a careless hand, running her fingers over the floral carving in the wood and the shaped back of beige tapestry upholstery. She tossed her kid gloves onto the seat. She patted her hair, though not a strand was out of place. The straight mass had been carefully waved this afternoon; she had crimped it on her curling tongs.

Would Pandora have to use such things to curl her hair, Cara wondered, or did she still possess the same golden hair with fiery lights falling in countless waves below her shoulders, as she had when a young girl?

Pandora still dominated Rogan's thoughts. What would it be like to make love to her? Would she turn to jelly and quiver in his arms . . . ? Or would she turn wild, stretching out like a cat, purring and becoming passionate, to make love like a pagan goddess would have long ago? Would she giggle like Diane Ash or Sheila Meade, and bat her flaxen lashes when he was done? He would love to lay her down and cover her with himself and stretch her arms high over her head as far as he could put them and then . . . He turned quickly now to hide the telltale sign of his desire from Cara who had come to stand across from him. He cooled his ardent thoughts of what he would like to do to the young woman upstairs in his bedroom . . . his guest bedroom. . . . Lord, he couldn't even think straight. He knew Cara was studying him intently, but he couldn't bring himself to face her just yet. He knew, though, that she had an idea something wasn't quite right with him. How could he tell her?

When Rogan turned from her the second time, something within Cara seemed to snap. A jealous rage consumed her. She thought of Pandora lying in his bed, her cousin whose coming had torn her life asunder.

"So, Cara," Rogan said again, "tell me why were you curious?"

Cara thought fast. "Well, darling, you looked so dark and mysterious when you saw me standing outside your study door, that it was as if you'd been expecting someone else—and not Cara?"

"What the devil is that supposed to mean?" he snapped irritably.

Rogan had swung about, his back now to the small fire in the grate. With his features and eyes shadowed, his look was unreadable. Uncomfortable, Cara trained her gaze on the claret velvet seat of a Chippendale chair. Automatically she unbuttoned the top of her high-collared cape and let it fall to the floor. Her liquid-brown eyes danced provocatively as she stepped closer to him, delighting again in the manly scent of spice after-shave lotion.

"Enough of that, Rogan. We're supposed to be lovers, not sworn enemies tearing at each other's throats. Why are you so irritated tonight? Has something gone wrong at the office? That passenger-liner business again?" She stood before him now, shivering in remembrance of the nights they had once shared. "Rogan," Cara purred low, "what's wrong, darling?" She had asked this so often lately that it had become redundant.

"I wonder if she merely has a split personality," Rogan muttered to himself.

"What was that you said?" she asked him.

"I—nothing, Cara. I was just thinking out loud," was all he offered of his musings.

He stepped away, his arm brushing her shoulder and accidentally her breast. He remained indifferent to the contact, but Cara's fingers reached out again, missing him by an inch. He drew away and she wanted to cuss, but she had never done so in front of Rogan. Now her sultry brown eyes narrowed into catlike slits; the hazel lights in them glittered.

"This smacks of 'we're finished.'" Cara clenched her small hands into frustrated fists. "Are we, Rogan?"

"God, Cara." He sighed. "We have been friends for a long time. What more do you want from me?"

"Friends!" Cara gasped in outrage. "Is that all we've been to each other for *two whole years? Friends?*" Cara looked about the room in stupefaction, but his words had manifested her worst fears.

"Of course! We enjoyed each other's company now and then, went out to the theater, out to"—he smiled, not being able to help it, and finished with—"those little French restaurants you like." Cara should really go out for a night on the town with Sandy Moor, he thought to himself humorously. They both liked the night lights.

"What," she croaked, insulted, "what about your room—upstairs?"

"It's still there," he said instantaneously.

"*Funny.* You didn't let me finish. What'd we do there, in your bed, darling, twiddle our fingers half the night? Have you lost your mind—or your manhood, Rogan Thorn?" Cara was instantly sorry for throwing that in. Therein lay his problem.

Really, Rogan had been long wondering about that himself. Cara was not deliberately trying to be cruel, no. Something was wrong. Terribly. It had all started . . . what, several months back? He had felt jaded back then, come to think of it. Lord, he wasn't *that* old. In fact, tonight had proven his virility—up to a point. Was it only Dora's virginity that had stopped him? Or was it something more, afraid he couldn't make it again?

Frowning to herself, Cara set about to confirm his very own thoughts. "Now that I think of it, Rogan, you've been a cold fish and wallflower for quite some time now. Damn," she finally broke down and swore, unable to stop herself, "but this night puts the topper on it!"

"Yes, I suppose so, Cara," he muttered absently.

She allowed her gaze to roam over his back, remembering his nakedness in bed, so muscular and powerful. His chestnut hair curled softly; his front forelock was disheveled from his having run his fingers through it, no doubt. He was so handsome it made her heart wrench.

For a long time, Rogan had been having trouble making love. He had really and truly tried, she knew. He had consummated prematurely, but lately he had not maintained erection long enough to even begin the act. And now this! Cara wondered dully if crafty Walter Riddock had been right, after all. Her little Cousin Pandora—not so little anymore, Walter had corrected—must be something of a looker to catch Rogan Thorn's jaded eye. She rolled her eyes toward the ceiling. At once Cara snatched up her cape and gloves. This is not going to be easy, she told herself, clenching her hands tighter than before.

Tossing Rogan a parting glance, she saw that he appeared to be caught up in his own thoughts. Desire for him mixed with her anger. She squinted at him closely, but he never noticed this in his despondency.

"Good night, lover. I'll see myself out."

Rogan finally turned. "Cara, I'm—"

"Never mind, Rogan. It doesn't matter," she lied. She opened the door, but paused before going out.

Rogan stared into the marble, corner fireplace, and automatically reached for a slim cigar. He hadn't smoked for a long time, but now lit it, inhaled savoringly, and then blew out a wreath of smoke, watching the blue spirals ascend toward the ceiling and seeing in them a vision of beauty. A shiver of awareness coursed through him; there was almost an abandoned sensuality about her. He saw golden tresses with fiery lights rippling nearly to a slim waist and creamy tan flesh—where had she obtained such a glorious color? Natural? Her breasts were ivory-fleshed.

He moved mechanically to a chair. "We'll talk later, Cara," he said, but she had already gone out.

Chapter Eight

The gaslights hissed and burned low at the top of the stairs.

Treading warily, Cara paused on the first landing to peer down over the balustrade before going up several more steps to the second floor.

Looking all ways, Cara crept along noiselessly, almost on tiptoe. She turned the conversation of the last half-hour over in her mind, coming to the conclusion that she still wanted Rogan, even though their romance had been less than perfect for a long time now. Their *arrangement*, hers and Rogan's, had been nearly heavenly—for a time. There had been no ties. But Cara had always been able to flaunt her lover, a very handsome and wealthy one at that; there had been nights at the theater, days on his schooner, strolls through Chinatown, along the beach—Rogan loved to walk there—and nights, oh so many nights of wild, fulfilling love-making. She had been saddened when those times abruptly came to a halt. The most important part of their being together had suffered; they had been compatible lovers.

Yes, she still wanted him; she could not forget what they had shared intimately. It was never too late; she could still help him with his "problem."

Cara herself had not been a faithful lover. In fact, Rogan had not demanded this of her. But Rogan had been faithful to her to the end, as far as she knew. At least she had never seen *him* with another woman. But he had seen her with another man, without seeming to mind all that much. Or had he? she began to wonder.

But now, suddenly, there was a human being with whom she must contend—her cousin. She felt her heart sinking as she envisioned Pandora taking him away from her. To revive Rogan's virility—Cara knew it was still there, somewhere, lying dormant, waiting to be kindled anew—to do this, Cara wanted to be the flame herself.

Excited by this prospect, she saw new hope; maybe Rogan did love her just a little and this infatuation with her cousin would pass.

Cara started when the door up ahead opened and a maid backed out with a tray balanced on her hip. The servant closed the door silently. Hastily Cara sunk into the shadows of an ell, eluding Nan as she passed right by her.

Now Cara knew which room housed her cousin— the one on the right—for Nan had been carrying a supper tray.

Cara smoothed her skirt nervously, wiping off a sweating palm as she hurried over to the door to pause there a moment before slowly entering. She closed the door carefully behind her and leaned against it for a second to glimpse the room before she approached the fourposter. She moved forward with careful slowness. Her heart thudded in anticipation.

Would Pandora truly be as lovely as Riddock had described her?

Her eyes moved over the young woman in the bed as the low gaslight twinkled down; Cara took in every detail of Pandora's gorgeous countenance. There was the bruise, indicating that Walter's tale of the accident had been correct.

Yes, this was Pandora St. Ives, but not at all the willowy girl she had last seen several years ago! How long and graceful she appeared, even beneath the sheets!

"Pandora?" Cara questioned softly as she bent over the bed.

The young woman stirred. "Mmmm?"

Pandora slowly opened her eyes and only dimly saw the woman above her. She lay unmoving for a moment and then turned her head on the pillow and saw that the tray was gone. For a split second Pandora thought this shadowy woman was Nan, the maid, before the low voice spoke again.

"Pandora, don't you remember me?" Cara hoped not, but she smoothed the copper strands from her cousin's face. She drew her hand back as if burned. How silky is her skin!

"My name is Dora."

"Oh—yes, Dora," Cara readily agreed, blinking away a frown.

Suddenly Pandora's eyes widened and she snatched at the sheet to cover herself. "Who are *you?*" Without recognition she searched the pretty face above her. Had Rogan Thorn been lying, and was this his wife?"

"Mrs. Thorn?"

"No." Cara laughed at that softly, a gentle sound. "But who I am doesn't matter right now. I'm a friend, I'll say that much." Her voice went serious. "I have heard of your coming here—and you are in danger. You must come away with me, D-Dora."

Pandora raised herself slightly, frowning at the woman in puzzlement. "Really, you are not Mrs. Thorn?"

"Really; I promise I am only a friend," she went on to reassure her.

"I must come with you? But why am I in danger?" Her blue eyes were very big and inquisitive.

"Don't worry, and don't look so puzzled, Dora. You'll remember me soon," Cara said with promise in her tone.

Cara stood in indecision, not knowing whether to try to take Pandora with her or leave the house and forget this foolishness. It was only that Pandora seemed so lost and bewildered that Cara hesitated. But it was not until later that she would realize that Pandora St. Ives suffered from mild amnesia.

"You are going to help me . . . get away from *him?*" But a worried frown flitted across Pandora's brow. "Is it the police; are they coming to arrest me?" She rose swiftly to sit on her buttocks.

Eyes lighting, Cara nodded. "Yes, yes, the police! We have to get you out of here before they arrive!"

Cara paused here for a moment. Police? What had her cousin done to be afraid of the law? Perhaps she had only been having a nightmare . . . ?

"C'mon; we haven't a moment to lose. There's a dress there in the wardrobe. It's mine," Cara added without thinking.

"Yours?" Pandora was puzzled again about this strange woman's intent to help her be away.

"I—yes, I used to occupy this room—that is, when I worked here," she lied, seeing no other way out of her dilemma. "Now, can you get up and dress?" Cara asked hurriedly.

"Yes!"

Pandora rose urgently and went to the wardrobe immediately to flip through the dresses. "I cannot see; it is too dark. Which one is it? There are a few here."

"Take the deep-blue one, there on the far left, with the high collar," Cara said, "and dress quickly!"

Cara watched Pandora remove the dress from the wardrobe. Ugh! Cara thought to herself with distaste. One of the first dresses she had purchased when she had arrived in San Francisco and met Rogan Thorn. They had made mad, passionate love the very night they had met at a restaurant. That was before she had gone to the employment agency to which Rogan had referred her and obtained the job at Sarah Wolfington's as the old woman's companion. Cara had never once taken charity from Rogan Thorn; nor had he ever offered any, even upon learning that she had found employment at his rival's home.

With the dress finally donned, its bodice laced with nervous fingers, Pandora felt a wave of dizziness wash over her and she steadied herself against the fourposter. Alarmed, Cara moved toward her cousin, feeling as pale as Pandora herself looked.

"Are you all right?" Cara's voice quivered with concern.

Pandora brushed her aside with a wave of her hand. "Yes, let's be away!" She could see a pair of gossamer-green eyes already looking for her. "Hurry!"

Cara giggled softly at that. The situation could almost be laughable if not for the consequences should Rogan decide to come to bed early. By the look of him, though, he would spend hours wandering from parlor to study, as he usually did when he was perplexed over something. And so he had been!

When Pandora and Cara finally stepped from the bedroom, looking around with each cautious step, Cara told Pandora to wait a moment inside the shadowy ell while she went directly into Rogan's bedroom for something. She came out a minute later with some glittering items that she tucked inside her cape.

"What do you have there?" Pandora breathed, beginning to have second thoughts about this escape.

"Something I am borrowing from Rogan Thorn for a time. He won't miss them." She pointed to the items she had tucked into her cape. "Don't worry, Dora, I am not a thief."

Pandora stared and blinked at this strange woman for a moment, before she felt her hand being taken gently in a small but firm grip. Something passed through her then, a curious sense of familiarity.

"You said hurry, so let's go," this woman was saying to Pandora, still squeezing her hand.

The clock on the landing told the time, each bong louder than the one before.

In complete relief, Pandora felt herself being

pulled along to the back stairs by this dainty woman. Without a backward glance, they went down and out the door into the fog-shrouded night just as the twelfth bong sounded.

Dark mists cloaked their swift passage as they sped across the lawn to the gate at the very back of the fragrant, dewy garden. The door gave a low creak of hinges and a dog barked and howled across the way. Pandora's lungs burned from her effort to make haste and she was feeling light-headed again. Cara laughed inwardly at her cleverness. But Pandora pulled the borrowed cape closer about her, suddenly apprehensive and wondering if she was doing the right thing.

It was too late to turn back now. A carriage waited down the street, on the dark side of the corner.

Chapter Nine

Such a night it was. The atmosphere inside Thorn Mansion was charged with such excitement that the maids and manservants couldn't even go to sleep, but stayed up to see what was going on.

Often one had spied Rogan Thorn coming and going from his study to linger at the bottom of the stairs, looking upward, his hands stuffed into his trouser pockets, his implacable male countenance now brooding and then thoughtful, before he turned and went back to his study to remain awhile behind closed doors.

But Wizan was worried as never before about Rogan and as was his habit when worried or perplexed, he went to the living room and sat in the dark near the bay window through which he stared out into the mist-shrouded night. His thoughts carried him back to when Rogan Andrew Thorn had come into the world. Wizan had helped with the delivery. He had taken the squalling newborn into his arms, washed him, wrapped him in a small square of linen, and gently placed him in the basinet.

He had painted Chinese dragons in humorous caricatures on the supporting ends himself. The baby's mother had inspected him briefly, without interest. She would have nothing to do with the small "it" which was what she called Rogan; name him anything you want, she had said, she didn't care. She told Wizan to find someone else to nurse him, even though she could hear him crying piteously for his dinner.

Eileen Thorn packed all the clothes she owned and left before dawn of the next day. Elijah Thorn with Rogan's grandfather returned two days later to discover that the hugely pregnant Eileen had finally given birth, an easy birth, and had vanished just as easily. The father and grandfather were much too busy with their own interests to care; Whitelaw had his ships, Elijah his magic and the "cocktail route" of the city. And then came the women, so many mistresses for Elijah that Wizan couldn't keep count.

Wizan never told the lad, in all the time he was growing into a man, his mother's name, or just how cold and heartless a woman Eileen had been. But he guessed Rogan knew that much. Always he had lived inside his own empty shell, and if he ever sought to bring up a shadow or two with which to round out a portrait of her, his mother, he never had discussed his efforts out loud.

Wizan could still see Rogan at age thirteen staring, with stormy, defiant eyes the green of Wizan's mint tea, around at the sparse furnishings in the house. His hands had been thrust deep in the pockets of knee trousers that had been worn to a shabby state. His shirt sleeves, even rolled down, had not quite covered his bony wrists, and his long stockings had fallen in wrinkles on his skinny legs. But he held his head higher than all the other boys in the neighborhood. He was always quiet when things did not go his way, but Wizan knew how the lad's face could darken. It did so that day.

"I'm going to make us rich . . . richer than grandpa has made us, Wiz! I'll fill this house with all the best furniture and things . . . pretty things. Bold colors of velvet. Gold and silver. Fine curtains and draperies. I'll have shiny dishes and cut-crystal glasses in the pantry, ornaments in the drawing room, just like at Sarah Wolfington's. I'll buy you tunics and robes and trousers of nankeen silk, just like the ones in the windows in Chinatown . . . only better!" He paused to take a breath, then went on to vow grandly, his thin chest puffed out as far as he could make it go, "We won't always eat cheese sandwiches and cold chicken and jelly rolls." His brows were a scowling black band. "I'm going to have better and bigger ships than grandpa or Sarah Wolfington, I promise. Just you wait and see, Wiz!"

And all his grand promises came true. He indulged himself in his only love—he had to have ships, more and more ships. More money. A bigger name for himself. He had ridden fast on horses called "Grandeur" and "Success" and he raced with everybody who competed with him, always determined to win. Win he did; he wanted only to ride fast and hard with the reins of both intangible horses in hand.

Silence stretched out the minutes in the Chinaman's imagination. Only the tick-tocks of the clocks could be heard in the background as he thought now about the young woman upstairs, and an old Chinese proverb slipped into his mind: One who comes like misty rain soon floods the river. Another sound intruded on his reflections and Wizan shot up to go to answer the knocker, wondering who could be there at this late hour of night.

Rogan had been prowling the room sipping coffee laced with rum when Alexander Moor had knocked, and Rogan, knowing by the strength of the rap who was there, called to him to enter.

They had been discussing the accident and the mysterious Dora for half an hour now. Earlier that day, Sandy had grown curious when he had seen Rogan pull away in his carriage with a strange woman lying across his lap! He had called to Wizan, but the Chinaman had only driven on. And Rogan, well, he had been occupied otherwise evidently.

"A little smitten, at last?" Sandy wondered, adding, "Love at first sight?"

"It does seem extraordinary, but Lord, I just don't know. Love at first sight has always seemed a silly phrase to me; I preferred to call that instant insanity."

Sandy chuckled at that, nodding his blond head. "I agree."

Rogan sighed. "Maybe she has only bewitched me. It's too early to tell if—" He cleared his throat. "If I have fallen."

A blond eyebrow rose at that. But there was a look

94

of adoration in Rogan's luminous eyes that was unmistakable. Also vibrations emanated from Rogan; Sandy could feel them strongly in the room. Like a soundless wave of passion, he thought with some bewilderment.

At first when Sandy had arrived he thought Rogan must have been drinking, or he had been bewitched. Now he chose the latter, as Rogan himself had just half-admitted. It had to be that; men like themselves didn't just *fall* in love. That was utterly ridiculous!

"You don't even know her, Rogan." Sandy realized that his friend had been acting rather strangely of late, but this really was the weirdest he had ever seen him. "So, pal, what are you going to do with her—this—ah—Dora?"

"Dora, yes." Rogan smiled slowly. "I haven't exactly decided just yet. Either she's lost her memory, or she's running scared, from something—or someone."

Again Sandy's eyebrow rose. "The latter, I think. She has probably run away from home, maybe even a jealous husband. I mean she sounds nice from your description, but roses are lovely, too, despite their tiny but sharp thorns. She could be the daughter to some very influential family. Would you risk your sterling reputation by taking this lovely flower in? I mean, sure, you took Bo Gary in to be your ward, but this is a woman you've got here, and man, that could spell scandal."

"I suppose it could," Rogan said matter-of-factly.

Rogan had always had iron control over himself. This Dora had only captured his imagination,

Rogan rationalized, not his heart. No one woman could do that. He doubted if there was even such a thing as love. There had never been any love to speak of in his family. In fact, he didn't even know what that word was all about!

"But," Rogan began, as if arguing with himself, "this young thing makes me feel ten feet tall. No woman has ever done that before!" Rogan ended with a wry chuckle.

Sandy's mouth went slack. "You've already had her? Man, that was the quickest you've ever moved. I take everything back I said about lost lover boy today!"

"Heeeyyy, you've got it all wrong, Sandy, it hasn't gotten that far—"

"Yet," Sandy put in.

"Damn, how could I . . . I mean—" Rogan raked his chestnut hair back, damning his impotency. But Sandy couldn't know about that; no one but Cara knew he had a serious problem carrying through to fulfillment.

Now Rogan's mouth throbbed again and a thrill passed through him. He remembered a kiss he'd had not so long ago, soft as a rose petal; a rounded breast trembling beneath his soft caress. Then as now, he had no feelings of impotency!

Sandy unstoppered a brandy decanter and helped himself. "Well," he began, scratching behind his ear with a finger, "I think you'd better run the other way, and turn this Dora What's-her-name out—cruel as it seems, old boy—so she can go back to whatever she had been doing before Rogan Thorn met up with her—uhmm—accidentally. She may even have worked a dubious profession, for all you know!"

"Oh, I doubt that very much—" Rogan swung slowly about to face his friend squarely. "For you see, she's a virgin."

"That easy to read, huh?" He watched Rogan nod, then went on. "Do you also doubt that she has gotten under your skin?"

The door opened just then and both men swung their attention toward it.

Munching a sandwich with pink slices of ham spilling out, and holding a glass of milk in the other hand, Bo Gary entered just then. Rogan had stiffened at the intrusion, but now he relaxed to smile automatically at his ward.

"Don't you ever knock?" Rogan asked Bo, but there was fondness in his eyes.

"Nope," he said, waving his thick sandwich. "But my apologies to you two ... I mean if I have interrupted something?" He was about to go out again, having caught an underlying mask of seriousness on Rogan's face.

"You have my permission to stay, Bo. You might as well hear what we're discussing anyway. You'll find out soon enough," Rogan said, looking down at Bo's callused palms.

Bo Gary followed the green gaze down to see what Rogan had noticed and smiled sheepishly. "I've been working on the *Phantom*, sanding the paneled doors, and I've got one lacquered already."

The rhythmic creak of deck planks, the squeak of taut lines made fast to mooring bits, canvas sails

97

billowing: everything that had to do with ships lay in Bo Gary's dreamy Irish blue eyes. He even carried, as usual, a mingling of wood and sea damp on his sailor's jacket.

Bo Gary's clothes were a little better now. But the once-ragged urchin whom Rogan had taken to be his ward, and the skipper of the *Phantom*, had been penniless, homeless, a waif who had worked his way as cabin boy from port to port, searching for someone to take him seriously—and for someone who cared. Someone had done both, and Bo now made his home on the *Phantom*. Bo preferred it that way, when he was not roaming around his beloved Chinatown with his pretty little girl, his love, Susie. But Bo Gary always had a room upstairs at Thorn Mansion, at the back, because he liked looking out over the garden.

Rogan always seemed to be taking urchins in, Sandy was thinking privately now, as no doubt this Dora must surely be. Bo had also appeared like a sudden storm to wrack the serenity of Rogan's life on the cobbled hill. Then, of course, there had been Cara Kalee, but she had made her own way in the world. Sandy had bedded the dark-haired woman, after *her* seduction, only once, for he had found it laborious to keep up with her wild abandonment. But Rogan had kept her for close to two years. Now, it seemed, that was all over.

Rogan still prowled the room. He was chewing his lower lip thoughtfully when Wizan burst in, his felt-soled slippers skidding to a halt. He spun about, searching for Rogan, who at first frowned at this second intrusion, but soon realized that Wizan had good reason for barging in.

"She gone! Freyda check her room and she take bag and dress and—*poof!* She gone just like she appear. She go so fast she not even leave streak behind her!"

"Who! *Who* are you blubbering about, Wizan Sing?" But Rogan had a pretty good idea already.

"Freyda say she, Dora girl, not go out front door and I not see her go out back door." Wizan then waved his dainty hands in the air theatrically. "Maybe she fly out like bird from window upstairs?"

Rogan brushed by Sandy so briskly and with such force that the man had to step aside or have his feet trod upon. After making a thorough search of the house, up and down, cellar and attic, Rogan swiftly shrugged into his short coat and swept like lightning out the front door, trembling in his eagerness to find the young woman.

"Dora!" he shouted into the misted midnight, along the street where he trotted blindly. He saw a carriage pulling away from the curb up ahead, but as there were a few other conveyances out, he paid it little notice.

Alexander Moor, Wizan, and Bo Gary exchanged glances of utter bewilderment. Especially Bo, whose sandwich stuck in his throat at all the unusual excitement at Thorn Mansion. He had never seen such a commotion in this household. He saw Freyda and the parlormaid and Nan huddled close together in the hall, fearing that Mr. Thorn would come down on them hard for not having caught the mystery girl's flight. He listened to some of what was going on.

"I did not see young voman go when I take ashes

out of fireplace in da living room," Freyda was saying, trembling from head to foot. "No vone come down"—she scratched beneath her pert cap—"I don't tink, from upstairs. Not vhat I see."

"I saw no one myself," Nan offered. "Only that Miss Kalee as she—she—" Nan was so frightened that she could hardly speak now with Wizan glowering across to her.

"What she do?" Wizan questioned fiercely to the woman standing on the threshold.

"Well, she—she must have gone—upstairs to get a dress, b-because I saw her slip into the guest bedroom. She—she does have some of her—ah—clothes in that room!" Nan finally got out, embarrassed at having to say that.

"One where girl Dora was sleepy?" Wizan interrogated.

"Yes. M-Miss K-Kalee thought I didn't see her. But I had dropped something from the—the tray on the stairs. Whe-en I looked up—she thought I didn't see her—I did see her, Miss Kalee, go into the guest bed-bedroom!"

"Where she go after that?" Wizan asked suspiciously.

Nan shrugged bony shoulders, finally calming down enough to speak straight. "I couldn't say, Mr. Sang—ah—Sing. She just took her dress—the one was missing, Freyda said—and left, I guess."

"I must tell boss," Wizan announced to no one in particular, staring across the floor.

"Ah, why don't you let it go, Mr. Sing," Sandy put in. "You wouldn't want Rogan getting any more upset over this—this female baggage than he already has, would you?"

"Oh, golly!" Wizan clamped a hand over his mouth. "Scoundlel!"

Sandy corrected. "It's scandal, Wizan Sing." He paused, then went on. "I hate to think of Rogan involved in something—yes—like a scandal. There would be publicity for him then, the wrong kind, you know that."

Wizan saw the wisdom in the words. He was careful not to let any person or persons upset the calm efficiency of Thorn Mansion. He decided to take Mr. Moor's sound advice. Anyway, why, he asked himself, would Miss Kalee want to whisk the young woman away?

"Well, she's gone, and I think it's for the better," Sandy said stiffly, pouring himself another two fingers of brandy.

Bo shuffled out the door and leaned against the jamb, remarking, "Boy, she must have been *something* for Rogan to go out looking for her, and in this gosh-awful Frisco fog, too!"

"No cussy, Bo Galy," Wizan chided. "Mistel Mool right, boss soon forget she even come here. *Poof,* she come; *poof,* she go!"

But soon Wizan found himself frowning over his own words. As did the others gathered in and about the parlor door. That is, all but Sandy, who sighed inwardly. Rogan and himself were just not the marrying kind, not cut out for anything but the bachelor life. It was too good to lose.

He muttered to himself, "Rogan should have

bedded the wench in order to free her from his mind."
That always worked for him, anyway, when he was
hot for one particular woman and wanted to get her
out of his blood fast.

Bah! Women were impossible! Sandy tossed his
hands up as he went to fetch his coat.

Chapter Ten

As soon as Cara snatched off her high-collared cape and flung it onto a chair, a knock rattled the paint-chipped door. She cast a hasty glance at herself in the oval mirror over the graystone mantelpiece, patting her sable-brown hair above her flushed face. She sucked in her waist to accentuate the full curves of her bosom and hips. In anticipation of her caller, her firm breasts rose beneath the fabric of her dress and she felt a thrill pass through to her loins.

"Come," she called, not surprised in the least to find Rogan standing inside the door.

"Do you know of someone who goes by the name *Dora?*"

God, Cara thought to herself, he comes right to the point of his visit—but Dora? Could this be Pandora he was searching for? Of course, it must be, she decided; the name was close enough. What was her cousin up to? she wondered.

Cara did not answer at first, but a mischievous gleam appeared in her eyes that had not been there before. She ran her hand over a table, pretending to be searching for dust, instead of stalling.

"Well?" he asked sharply when she didn't speak.

Cara was smiling, her eyes filled with a glittering heat as she brought him a glass of brandy, his favorite, but as she reached his side a dark scowl appeared on his face while he studied her motions closely. She was suddenly a little afraid of him; she knew his temper and his lashing tongue that could mock and ridicule.

"What are you hiding, Cara?" he said while frisking her visibly.

"Hiding?" She gave a short little nervous laugh. "Nothing. Why would I want to hide anything from you, lover?" She ran her small fingers lightly along his, clutching the glass. "So, who is this woman you are hot on the trail after?" she asked, knowing he indeed sought her cousin.

Cara wondered now, as she returned his scrutiny, why she had never realized Rogan Thorn was the most handsome, compelling male that any woman could imagine in her wildest dreams. There was only one other who came close to matching him in good looks—but he, Joe, was far away, and she was here, desiring the only man in her heart at this moment.

"How do you know I'm searching for her?" he wondered, automatically sipping from the glass of brandy he didn't really want.

Cara's lips trembled, because at this moment she desired to be kissed by him, and she had a feverish desire to undress before his cynical stare. He was not the least concerned with her body, though; she could understand Pandora was the one he wanted. For all the other women in his past, herself included, Rogan had never once displayed this much concern—and he was feeling something else, too.

"If you think I'm hiding something, or someone, Rogan, why don't you take a good look around? You know where everything is in my apartment, lover; you've been here often enough." She gave his male person a meaningful scrutiny.

Unsmilingly Rogan set his glass down onto a small mahogany stand. For a moment his glance brushed hers. The cold indifference in his luminous green eyes shook Cara to the core of her being. To think she might be losing this man and all they had shared as lovers, and yes, friends, made her feel curiously close to tears. There was also at the back of her mind the problem of what to do with Pandora. How long before Rogan discovered Pandora was housed at the Widow Wolfington's?

What was more shattering, Cara thought despairingly, was that her first impression of this night had been correct. Rogan was much enamored of her cousin. The silly little bitch; Cara could scratch her eyes out. Perhaps this infatuation of Rogan's would pass given time. But he could not do anything about the situation now.

"Will you stay awhile, Rogan?" Cara half-begged as she gestured toward the overstuffed horsehair sofa. No response. "Well then, maybe you can explain why you are looking for this—uhmm—Dora. Let's be, as you say, friends—I can maybe help you over this thing?"

"What do you mean by 'thing'?" he said snidely.

"Well, I can hardly believe"—she paused for a breath, then continued—"that you of all people would be deceived into letting that sneaking tart into your house!"

He took a step toward her. "You know her?"

"Oh, yes, I mean I've *heard* she has really been making the rounds today, Rogan!"

He went very pale. Then, collecting himself, he asked almost savagely, "What the devil are you talking about?" He dug his fingers into her shoulders and shook her roughly. Cara winced with pain, as he went on. "The young lady, Dora, met with an accident this afternoon, by my own carriage, driven by Wizan! He brought her to my home, sent for Hoyle, and now she's vanished—no doubt in a dazed condition. And you stand there telling me she's some whore or something close to it!"

Cara gasped out her next words. "And you think you are responsible—for her welfare?"

"Yes, damn it! She may be hurt!" he hollered back at her.

Cara dug her nails into his wrists. "Rogan, let go of me! You have no right to hurt *me* on *her* account!" But her words were drowned in his rage.

"Tell me what in hell you're blubbering about!" he had been shouting.

"I said what I meant, Rogan. She fooled you, damn you. You just go ahead and ask Walter Riddock!" She bit her lip then, chiding herself for bringing him into this.

Rogan curled his upper lip and his words emerged in a snarl. "What has that bastard got to do with Dora?"

Cara tossed her dark head. "He met up with her, too." Her jealous anger goaded her on. "I would look around my house were I you, Rogan. She might have robbed you of some precious jewelry, just as she did—at Riddock's Summit House." She was in deep now, but she plunged on. "Go ahead, ask him, damn you!"

Just looking at Cara, and hearing her curse like a man, Rogan came to the conclusion that she was much like the other females he had bedded in the past. This city was full of women who hid beneath a rough, coarse exterior. He almost had allowed himself into a situation—a most *comfortable* one— from which he could not have extricated himself easily. There was nothing, he realized, nothing at all unique about Cara Kalee.

In his mouth Rogan gritted his teeth, but outside, his eyes danced with fury. "How do you know this female is the same Dora—Walter's thief? And mine now you say?" he questioned, staring at Cara hard and incredulously.

Cara went sashaying to the table beside the sofa to snatch up a small handbag made of network from the lower shelf. Intentionally swaying her hips, she brought it to Rogan, smiling triumphantly as he took the bag brusquely.

"Look here," Cara said, reaching out to fold back the opening.

Rogan looked over the bag's contents which merely consisted of a tortoise-shell comb and matching hairpins, ribbons of bright colors in pinks and lavenders. "So? This tells me nothing!" he snorted.

"Oh-ho, yes it does, Rogan. Walter discovered this bag in his carriage this morning—first she nearly fainted dead away in the street and he brought her to Summit House. She rested in a room upstairs, then robbed him and disappeared!"

Rogan stared at her hard. "Still, this does not prove that it was Dora." He said the name with much familiarity.

Cara sucked in a breath before going on. "Look again, at the long strands of hair. What shade of hair was this Dora's, Rogan, tell me?" She made a wry grin.

Rogan lifted the comb out now. Long strands of sparkling copper hair shot with gold were caught between the teeth. "Well, well," Rogan exclaimed. "A beautiful damned thief." First she fooled Walter Riddock, and then him—no one fooled Rogan Thorn and got away with it!

He stuffed the bag into his tweed jacket. "I'll take this, if you don't mind," he said, not caring if she did mind.

Rogan strode swiftly to the door and wrenched it wide. He paused as Cara put a sly question to him. "Are you going home to check your jewelry box, lover?"

"Of course . . . what else!" he snapped tersely.

Then, after shutting the door firmly, he was on his way downstairs. Cara hastened to the window, putting a knee onto the window seat to watch Rogan run to catch a hack just rounding the corner.

Cara rushed to drag her own reticule out from beneath the sofa. She took Rogan's signet ring with the steed's head carved in a cameo fashion, one layer over the other; and a pair of diamond links. She promised herself when Pandora had been sent back to Hawaii—after Walter tired of her, and he would, for women did not interest that devious man all that much—she must devise a strategy to return the

108

jewelry to Rogan's bedroom. That would take some doing, to be sure!

Now to pay Walter a late-night visit at Summit House, before Rogan had the same idea . . . but first he would return home and discover the missing jewelry. Good.

Damn, Cara, she complimented herself, you are the sly and crafty one!

But Cara never did visit with Walter. He had gone out with his pasty-faced cronies to do whatever it was that men of their kind did.

Thorn Mansion was kept apart from its neighbors by an iron fence. At the heavy gate, also fashioned of iron, Thorn's symbol of a sharp-hooved horse rose forbiddingly from the center post. And from the very top of the house's gable rose a weather vane, also a brass steed.

Pandora's sweet scent haunted Rogan as he crossed the hall to his own bedroom. His countenance bore an edge of steel, and his steps were brusque and dangerously paced. He was frustrated in mind and body, knowing what he most desired, his loins throbbing with the need for the one who had betrayed him, time after time.

His black look flitted around the room until it settled on his heavy jewelry box. It had been carelessly left open as if whoever had rifled it had been in a hurry.

He quickly went to it, at once recognizing that Cara had been correct. His family-crest ring was gone, as were a pair of diamond links. Anger pricked him anew and he whirled about, a curse snarling his lips.

For the next quarter of an hour, pacing and cursing, he argued with himself, mostly against visiting Riddock. Why should he? As for Dora, why should he want another man's leavings when Walter was done with her.

Yet . . . something didn't ring right about Cara's story. She had roused suspicions in his mind. The woman seemed to be concealing something, but what? *What?*

As for Dora Whatever, he would handle the thieving slut in his own way: she would pop up again somewhere, in his path, and when she did . well, he would teach her a lesson she would not soon forget.

Chapter Eleven

The late afternoon drew to an end as the last of a brilliant April sun dulled. Streamers of gray vapors, bearing the smell of the bay and the wharves, had drifted in from seaward and a thick gray fog would inevitably muffle the bay.

Drivers had ceased to thread their way along the Embarcadero and onto the docks. But in the late-day jostling, the noisy bustle of longshoremen loading and unloading cargoes mingled with the movements of drays, express wagons, and hand carts.

Rogan turned from gazing darkly, broodingly, out the window and went to perch on the edge of his mammoth desk. Letting one leg swing freely from the knee, he took a sip of strong black coffee and then pushed the mug aside.

"Cold already, huh?" Sandy said, stuffing some papers into a leather case as he prepared to leave for the day.

"Very," Rogan replied, still quiet.

Gray shadows showed beneath Rogan's wave-green eyes; there were new crinkles at the corners, too. Sandy could tell that Rogan had not gotten much sleep in the last few days. He could almost pity his handsome friend. . . . What had gotten into Rogan? The mysterious Dora? Nah! Rot! It had come on long before *she* had arrived on the scene.

Maybe Rogan just needed to get away for a while.

"I think you need a change of scenery, Rogan, friend. Why don't you take a little trip with the schooner, like to one of the Pacific islands? I'll take care of things while you're gone, you know that," Sandy suggested carefully.

"Not now. It hasn't been all that long since I sailed to Oahu."

"But that was business; now it should be pleasure," Sandy reminded him, drawing a picture of a hula girl with his waving hands.

"Maybe in a month or so." Rogan bent to cup his knee, his action halting its swinging.

Catching the familiar movement, one that often preceded a pronouncement by Rogan, Sandy stopped what he was doing, a waiting expression on his face.

"I'd appreciate it, Sandy, if you'd check on any current ventures in which the Riddock line is involved," Rogan said, shortening the name of his competitor as usual.

"Play detective again, hmm? Nasty business, snooping and prying around and rubbing legs with the Riddock employees." Sandy chuckled the words out.

"I'd like to know if Riddock plans expansion of cargo or passenger routes. Maybe you can overhear some information that will help Thorn Navigation." A dark brown eyebrow lifted drowsily.

"Tsk, tsk, nasty," Sandy repeated, but his huge muscles flexed just the same, giving him the look of a Viking.

"I know, but the Riddock line is our most powerful competitor, remember, and we'd like to stay ahead of the game," Rogan reminded him.

Sandy nodded with another clucking of the tongue. "You're edging closer to becoming the shipping tycoon of the Pacific trade, and you still want to play games?"

Sandy picked up his empty mug with the charming, topless mermaid painted on its side—a souvenir from Chinatown. He took in Rogan's definite nod. "Well, then, ay, ay, private investigator Alexander Moor at your service, Captain Blackheart."

Rogan chuckled low, but his smile did not linger. He was staring across to the window again, out to where the *Phantom* was moored. A faraway look seemed to drag his spirit out to her.

Thinking there was more afoot than Rogan was letting on, Sandy said, "So, anything more about the mystery girl?"

Rogan swung his gaze sharply about. "No. But you can keep your ears peeled for any information that would be helpful pertaining to—Dora. Just Dora, with the red-gold hair. As long as you're at the game," Rogan finished, raising an eyebrow in a sinister fashion.

"Ah-hah! Now I get it; you're more interested in the lost Dora than Riddock's current ventures. I know, I *know*, you told me over breakfast just yesterday: if she's a thief, as Cara and Riddock seem to think, then you want the poor thing punished— but your *own* way. Right?"

"Correct. But I didn't say a thing that excluded me

113

from thinking Dora a thief—I just don't know yet. As I said, I'll handle it my own way. Hell, I might even decide to let her off easy, if she was that hard-up for money. Otherwise—'' He merely shrugged, letting it hang.

"How about letting me in on how you plan to punish her, if she's found?"

Rogan cracked his knuckles one by one, smiling wolfishly. "I don't think you'd care to hear the gruesome details, Alexander, my friend." He dropped his heel to the floor, sliding his buttocks off the desk in the same action.

"I know what you'd really like to do to her," Sandy said with a lascivious grin.

"Yeah? What's that?" Rogan curled his lips.

"You'd like to throw her down on the floor and ravish the hell out of her—just like a nasty old pirate. True? Hey, see, you're smiling deviously! I just knew it!"

After a warning tap, the door opened up. "Just knew what?" Carolyn said. "That I am the most ravishing secretary in the city?" She lowered some papers down onto the massive desk, giving Rogan a cautious smile of greeting. Her boss looked even worse than he had earlier that morning. "Have you been keeping late nights or something? You look just terrible—I mean, compared to your usual gorgeous self, you do." She smiled a toothy grin.

"Really," Sandy said, smiling. "Falling in love and being robbed all in one weekend is pretty much stress for one man to handle. But Rogan can weather it, once the 'hots' for his pretty thief have vanished.

114

Boy! Some men do crazy things to get a woman they want."

Carolyn looked from one to the other with an astonished eye. "What's this I hear? Rogan in love—" She was cut off as Sandy rushed over to snatch her by the arm and to usher her out of Rogan's office. "But—I want to hear—"

"Let's go, sweetheart, I'll let you in on *some* of the details. But not in here." Sandy went out chuckling as Carolyn buzzed questions in his ear. "I'm afraid objects are going to begin flying at our heads," he finished.

Alone now, Rogan murmured the name, "Dora." No, he would turn his thoughts from her. He glanced at the huge face of the clock on the wall; he imagined its hands spinning back in time, back, back . . .

Whitelaw Thorn, his grandfather, and a friend had seen the possibility of hauling commercial cargo, and so had built three small schooners and soon had a thriving business going. His grandfather had built the mansion on the cobbled hill, too, for his son and grandson. But ten years later, Rogan's father, Elijah, had died in a fire while "visiting" a lady friend, an actress in a Palace Hotel room.

Elijah Thorn had been forever walking his "cocktail route" with his bag of magic. He had been a magician, and many had marveled over his fantastic card tricks and his *Thorn illusions* that had seemed supernatural. At the time there had been a popular song about this Thorn legend. But Rogan, as a lad, had not been much interested in the magic Elijah had taught him.

115

Rogan had never known a mother's love; only the caring hands of the Chinaman. He never even knew his mother's name; no one had ever told him. He had never asked, either. All he knew of her was that she had been a San Francisco belle. She had left his father the day after she had given birth to Rogan, their only child.

Whitelaw had made the company grow and expand; he had sent sailing ships to the Orient and to the Pacific islands ahead of any other commercial shipping firm. He had worked so hard that there wasn't any time left for his grandson. Wizan had taken up the duties of both mother and father, caring for the many needs of a lonesome child.

Whitelaw had added merchant and passenger ships to his line and had extended their ports of call to the Orient and the islands of the Pacific, as well as to Australia. Then he had died of a brain fever, the doctor had said, and Rogan, a young man almost twenty, had taken over.

Rogan gazed out to the Embarcadero now. He remembered having lost two of his ships to Sarah Wolfington, Riddock's shrewd aunt—the famous Black Widow. After Whitelaw's death, she had claimed the biggest share in them and had come up with the papers to prove it. But for Rogan Thorn and ambitious men like him, San Francisco was still young and lay at their feet. Rogan had sought to soar above his competitors in the shipping business, out to prove, if only to himself, Wizan, and God, that his grandfather's dream of a certain kind of shipping dynasty would finally be realized.

His thoughts turned back to the mother he'd never known. A woman calling herself Mrs. Derby had visited him at his office several years ago, professing to be his mother. She needed money badly, she said sobbing, and could she come and live with her son? Her husband was frightfully ill. Coldly, not knowing whether or not she had been his mother, Rogan had turned her out, but not empty-handed. An article had appeared in the paper several weeks later—though Wizan had tried as best he could to hide it—Rogan had discovered this bit of news for himself. He had been shocked when, having turned to the article in his office, it read that a Mrs. Derby, widowed two years, had shot herself in the head. A neighbor had reported that Mrs. Derby could not see prolonging what she deemed to be a painfully useless life. No one wanted her anymore, so the story went. Her small apartment on O'Farrell Street had been littered with a mountain of whiskey and gin bottles, the neighbor had added. For several months after the incident, Wizan had found Rogan hell to live with.

Rogan's jaw was set now as he scowled darkly out the window. He sat there for an interminable time, then stood, then sat again, lost in the depths of thought, until the last glint of sun yielded to the coming dark.

Over the next two weeks, new lines appeared in Rogan Thorn's lean face and a harshness became evident in his manner. It was as if by dating as many women as possible, he could tear something painful from his memory. The night usually ended the same way: *Good night. It's been nice. Maybe sometime soon.*

He did not care anymore about the stolen jewelry, for that could be replaced—if indeed stolen it had been by . . . Dora. Of all the women he wined and dined and tried to sleep with, he could think of only one and his emotions raged passionate, tender, violent, or gentle by turns. One woman's memory, one woman who had seemingly vanished into thin air, like Wizan had said, *"Poof!"*—was disturbing, enchanting—this excitement churning in his vitals would never leave him.

But just when he needed warmth from a woman, his manhood betrayed him and made a fool of him— that is, when he got as far as a bed. Which was not very often.

But today Rogan had tried harder than usual. Sunset bathed the cobbled hill with orange, scarlet, and vermillion; and Rogan was ending another very short visit with an old flame of his. Again he was left unsatisfied by the ritual of love-making, a short session that ended without pleasure for him. Before penetration he maintained an erection, but could no longer find it possible to carry through to culmination. Matters were indeed becoming worse.

The Tiffany lamp was burning romantically low; a bottle of champagne lay on its label on the plush rug. His clothes and Sheila's were scattered around the tousled bed.

"It is getting late, Sheila," Rogan announced as casually as he could under the circumstances. He rose from the bed. "Anyway, Bo Gary will be here shortly to pick me up. He's taking a break from his two

118

loves," ending as if everything had gone smoothly.

"The ship and the little Chinese girl," Sheila guessed correctly, hiding a frown.

Sheila rolled over, her blond hair shimmering about her enticingly nude breasts and down to her pinched waist. She began to pout as Rogan quickly pulled on his trousers. Then she protested.

"We have only started—anyway I want you again, Rogan!" Suddenly she grinned. "Even though you had a hard time of it. Say, love, how long have you been having the *trouble* . . . Rogan?" she blurted.

"I'd rather not discuss it, Sheila," he said tersely.

"Well, I enjoyed *you* pleasuring me, Rogan. Aw, why don't you c'mere, I'll try harder—this time for you."

Rogan shrugged into a dark gray jacket and adjusted the front of his trousers. He looked down at her in the mussed bed, and damned if he did not feel his desire for her rise again. He sighed deeply then, too weary to have a go at it again, even if she was a tempting morsel of a woman.

"You need your beauty sleep, for partying, Sheila, and I have to be at the offices by eight tomorrow morning, as usual."

Sheila stretched again, invitingly, catlike, remembering the fast in-out motions that had ended all too soon. "Ooh, I shall miss you— But! I'll be at Millers' country house this weekend for the very big, important party of this summer. So, love, will you be joining us this time?" She caught his perusal and ran her eyes down the elegant length of her golden-tanned body. "Why are you staring? Don't you like what you see? You are frowning—as if I've suddenly changed into a frog or something equally horrible!"

In an odd, indefinable moment in time, Rogan had found himself seeing not the fun-loving Sheila Meade, a member of the "smart set," the ultra group of San Francisco society, but another woman— slightly younger and slimmer—who looked lost in his big bed. An enigma of womanhood. God, how the copper-haired vixen tormented his days and long, lonely nights.

"Oh, I see! Don't worry, Rogan darling! I always take precautions, never take a senseless risk. Oh! What *am* I saying—we needn't have worried today anyway!" She laughed that off lightly while picking up a small hand mirror to check her face for smudges of lip rouge. She peered up over the mirror, smiling. "Coming?"

"What . . . ?"

Seated on the edge of a plush-upholstered gilt chair, Rogan lifted an eyebrow at the question. Sheila snapped her painted fingers and laughed loud.

"Rogan! To Millers', silly!" she snorted shortly and Rogan went on to frown. Looking in the mirror again, she missed his brooding expression, and continued. "The men will don scarlet coats and very fluffy cravats; the ladies white satin and powdered wigs! Three hundred guests will not be unusual, darling! If you come"—her laughter trilled—"we shall make it three hundred and one! Oh, it will be the finest party . . ." She glanced around the hotel room, somewhat wistfully. "Oh, but I do hate giving up this darling room to someone else, and I *hate* even more going back to stay at Ma Sissy's country house!" she said contrarily.

Ugh! The gathering of the clans, Rogan thought dispiritedly. He said out loud, "Yes, I have been invited again, Sheila, but"—he sighed—"I'm afraid I won't be attending."

"Oh? Not again! I so hoped to see you there this time—and attired in such fine regalia. You would be *sooo* handsome! Like a really true Englishman!"

After slipping on his high-necked shoes, Rogan stood, saying, "I have to keep an appointment that day with a man about a ship. I'm thinking about purchasing Todd Ashe's *North Wind.* She's a beauty." His eyes glittered as if dreaming about a woman he loved, instead of a ship.

"Ohhh," Sheila murmured with a pretty pout. "Our good-looking millionaire won't be coming. Ma Sissy will be so *damned* disappointed! You are a man with ships and women on his mind—in that order!" Sheila exclaimed as a chuckle rose from deep within her throat to burst out like a thousand champagne bubbles.

If only Sheila had known what or who was on his mind she would have turned green with envy. Rogan headed for the door.

"Before you go, there's more, darling! Wait till you hear!" she said, bouncing on the puffy bed. She forced him to pause.

"I've something that just *might* entice you into accepting Millers' invite."

Strangely a little thrill of anticipation ran through Rogan's blood and shot up his spine. What could entice him into partying with the cleverest and wittiest people of the city and peninsula, the set that said and wore the smartest things, and indulged in more wild merriment than any other group of San Francisco society? It had better be good, more exciting than elaborate suppers at midnight, wearing silly costumes, and dancing until three in the morning.

Sheila made ready to drop her bomb.

"Widow Wolfington is going!" she announced, but could not suppress another round of laughter that bubbled up from within. With a toss of her yellowy blond hair, Sheila waited for his reaction.

"Wonderful," Rogan muttered, bored. "That is about as enticing as warmed lettuce salad." This last, having been inaudibly spoken, he moved toward the door, but halted his hand on the knob when she went on.

"Sarah *darling* is bringing along her *new* companion!"

"So?"

"Everyone is talking about her. She's a sweet young thing with a *look* of demureness about her, and she's . . . *get this* . . . extremely fond of the old bag!" She bounced onto her knees. "Haven't you heard, Rogan? Where have you been hiding yourself these past few weeks!" Then she grinned, displaying perfect pearly teeth. "You old fox, you! No, don't go yet." Again she prevented him from turning the knob. "More astonishing, darling, is that no one knows where this dewy-cheeked doll popped up from. She could be from a dozen, a hundred places, but, oh, the gossip about her that's circulating! She has to step on the toes of brutes that ogle her constantly. Cara"—she snickered over the name—

"Cara is spreading wild gossip that *she* is a thief—oh, and a whore! That's a corker if I've ever heard one!"

"Is *that* so," Rogan snapped sarcastically, feeling muscles go taut in his loins and back.

"That jealous bitch, Cara. She's going to spoil all the fun we could have gossiping about the Black Widow's companion. Sheesh, the gorgeous idiot might not even come to Millers' party and that would indeed be a sad state of affairs. A disaster!"

"Well," Rogan began softly, with an ominous undertone. "You can at least let me in on the mystery girl's name, can't you?"

Sheila shrugged across to Rogan. "Dora. That's all she knows of herself, the stupid ninny—" She giggled. "Just Dora!"

Sheila had leaned over to turn up the Tiffany lamp in the darkening room, and now she burst into a fit of giggles, pointing her finger at Rogan's paler face.

Frowning darkly, Rogan bent to catch a glimpse of himself in the bureau mirror. "My God, and I almost went down to the lobby like this!" He pulled his handkerchief out of his trouser pocket and rubbed his lips and cheek hard to remove the red lip rouge. In an even darker mood, he turned back to Sheila and her wide grin.

"Well, I've taken the damnable stuff off, so what's so hilarious now?" he snapped with irritation of a twofold nature, his mind flitting away from this empty-headed, painted *broad* with whom he had been wasting his precious time.

"Oh, Rogan, I can't help it; you looked just like a clown! You know, like one of those at the circus who perform magic tricks? Yeah, like your pa, Elijah, used to do!"

Thoughtfully Rogan stared at her for a full minute, not really seeing anything, just looking clear through her. Then, without another word or "good-by," he slipped out the door. Sheila shrugged powdered shoulders, hummed a tune, and went back to studying herself in the mirror.

Chapter Twelve

The husky-sweet voice continued to read from the book of poems:

"Floral apostles that in dewy splendor weep without woe, and blush without a crime."

"By Horace Smith," Pandora finished.

"That's enough, dear." Sarah Wolfington patted the girl's slim hand indicating that she should close the book. She went on, as if she hadn't been listening to a word of the poem. "You shall wear pink satin, Dora, my dear, and fashion your own hair in flowing love locks."

Pandora smiled graciously, though she would rather be like the other women attending the party and wear white satin.

Ever since Pandora had come into the employ of the woman known as the Black Widow Wolfington, her countenance had undergone a striking change. She owned a new wardrobe now and had learned how to do her hair in the most popular of fashions. In two weeks' time, Pandora had also learned much about the old woman of whom she was already extremely fond.

Eccentric Sarah Wolfington, eighty-one years of age, had been widowed for twenty years. She was still sprightly, and could always be seen dressed in black since her husband's death. Pandora deduced that Sarah had never quit mourning—but certainly not in sackcloth and ashes as Trudy, the maid with uppity airs, often announced. Though it was entirely black and somewhat severe, Sarah Wolfington's wardrobe was in the height of fashion.

Pandora's nose wrinkled again. The lush Victorian elegance that was Sarah's home wore an ever-present peppermint smell.

Earlier this afternoon, Sarah had taken her young companion to a little restaurant which served the most delicious seafood. Looking about herself, somewhat nervously since it was her first time there, Pandora had skewered a giant shrimp onto her fork, then dipped it into the heavenly yakitori sauce. After her first taste, Pandora had forgotten her surroundings and dug in.

Now at four o'clock they were sharing fruit and tea. Pandora loved juicy orange slices; she never seemed to get her fill of them. But she tried to nibble daintily at the tidbits of fruit arranged like a tiny sunburst on the small tray. The tea was in tiny Chinese cups, and accompanying it were tiny napkins and even tinier sandwiches. When because of rain they did not have tea at a restaurant, Pandora had a great desire to wolf down the whole tiny tray of bread-and-meat hors d'oeuvres.

"For a young woman, my dear," Sarah was saying now, "you certainly have a ravenous appetite. You must *really* practice a little more control, Dora. I realize you have a lot of places to put the calories, being so tall and willowy, but my goodness! You wouldn't like a thick waistline, either. I know many women who are tall—and obese, too!" she hissed the word "obese" in distaste. "Also it is very unfashionable to be so hungry all the time."

Pandora eyed the fresh chocolates in the open valentine heart—the box a memento of days gone by for Sarah—and shut her eyes to the delicacies that unceasingly tempted her sweet tooth. She was starving!

Sarah eyed the pinched waist and the prominent cheekbones of the young woman. She drew back a little to study her further.

"Perhaps . . . you are right, for now, Dora. You may have some chocolates to fatten—I mean *fill* out your figure a tiny bit. We do not want you to appear like a scarecrow in the stunning creation Alice is stitching up for you, now do we?"

Pandora immediately reached for a few of the chocolates; they bulged in her cheeks now as she chewed the sweet morsels slowly, savoring each bit that slid down her throat. When Pandora reached for a few more, Sarah tapped her hand.

"That's enough for now, Dora. Wait awhile; then you may have some more." She smiled as the younger woman sat back with a sigh, licking her lips.

I do feel like a bag of bones, Pandora thought to herself. Though she was by no means underweight by present standards, she felt a bit on the light side lately; and it was as if her *head* were in the clouds, too. But, wearing only chemise and petticoat, she had studied her curves as she stood before the cheval glass in her bedroom. She had nice breasts, but her waist and hips . . . had they been this thin before . . . ?

No, stay out of the past, she chided herself.

"Dora, let's go out to the back porch now." Sarah stood and Pandora along with her. "Uh-uh, bring along your book. Don't leave it, dear; you may read to me if I choose again. Or, perhaps we shall just chat."

On the porch, Pandora began to perspire, even though they sat in the shade of the long porch. Her burgundy velvet jacket and black satin skirt with matching velvet bands running down the front had been comfortable that morning in the coolness of the moist clinging fog, but now the sun had burned it away. She removed the jacket and folded it neatly on the porch-swing seat. Sarah at once snatched it up and shook it out.

"Dear no! You mustn't fold the velvet. It may crush. You still have so much to learn"—she sighed—"Dora dear. I love being your tutor, though." She laughed in a delightful tinkle. "It takes up the tedium of the day. I taught Miss Kalee everything of charm, fashion, and grace. Oh yes, and poise. But oh! how she crucifies the English language! She was very much like you, dear, and I'm sorry if I am frank—but she was a simple creature till she came to me. Oh! What is it, dear, have you a sudden headache?"

Pandora continued to press her temples with her fingertips. "It is just the name . . . Mrs. Wolfington—"

"Heavens! *My* name? Why should that—"

She was cut off gently.

"No. Not your name. You said *Miss Kalee*."

Pandora frowned, blinking while staring at the sun moving brightly in the garden, dancing across the orderly rows of azaleas and camellias.

"Oh!" Sarah clapped a hand to her cheek. "Does the name ring a bell?" she asked.

Indeed Sarah could have kicked herself in the shins. She ran her eyes cautiously over the young woman beside her on the swing. Ironically it was Cara who had brought Dora to her, to be taken under her wing, so to speak. She had been ill, Cara said, so take good care of Dora. And Walter had paid his Aunt Sarah a visit the very next day and said almost the same thing. Sarah had prided herself now for having lifted Dora from her despondency.

"Kalee!" Pandora exclaimed jumping up from the swing. "Now I know. I came . . . to San Francisco . . . looking for someone by that name."

She stared down into Sarah's face beseechingly. "Oh, Sarah, I am beginning to remember!" She frowned then, her shoulders falling. "A little, anyway."

"You have been staring at the sunshine too long, Dora. We will go inside now."

"No. I mean, please, tell me who is . . . Miss Kalee?"

Sarah heaved a bosomy sigh. "Sit back down, child."

Pandora sat, blinking into the older woman's face expectantly.

"Cara Kalee, she is only a friend," she said, as if that explained everything.

Pandora rushed her next words. "The woman who brought me here, she used to work for you—your

129

former companion.''

"Yes.''

"Sarah, maybe *she* can—help me remember where I'm from!''

"*I* will, dear, someday, you'll see. But, yes, Cara used to work for me; the ungrateful tart came to me several years ago from the employment agency. Not once did Miss Kalee thank me for all I lavished upon her—clothes, good food, the rules of etiquette. She . . . she was so lost in a strange land. I believe I did more for Cara than she did for me. Yet, not even when I introduced her to the man who is her lover did she thank me. At least I introduced them *formally;* she had only been *acquainted* with him before that.

"But now, I've heard, he has different women, all of them beautiful but vacuous, like some of the smart set that cling to his arm each night. So wealthy, so handsome, and so pestered by women! The poor man used to be so reserved, but maybe one doesn't know a wolf for its sheep's clothing. Tsk, tsk. Not only have the gambling establishments become his haunts, but even the honky-tonk dives of the Barbary Coast . . . !''

Slipping the ribbon between her long slim fingers in studied motions, Pandora fiddled with the marker in the book. Little sighs escaped her lips. Sarah rambled on.

". . . The last few weeks he seems bent on taking in every facet of local color, and bent on his own path to destruction, too, with his new recklessness and all. Always with several thousand dollars spending money in his pockets, it's gossiped!''

Sarah smiled shrewdly here. "He won't be our

most powerful competitor at the rate he's going!" she sniffed.

Pandora finally realized that the conversation had taken a turn away from herself. "Who is *he?*" she wondered out loud now.

"He?" Sarah blinked her confusion of the moment. "Oh, you would not know him, dear," Sarah covered up at once. For some odd reason all his own, Walter had given her strict orders to keep poor dear Dora out of Rogan Thorn's path. She just had to wait and see what her nephew was up to. One thing she did know: Walter planned to have Sarah introduce Dora to him at Millers' party.

"Oh," was all Pandora muttered.

After a long silence, Pandora expressed her curiosity over something she had heard. "You have a business, Mrs. Wolfington?" she asked softly.

"Why, yes, of course. Did I not tell you?" Sarah frowned over this and went on. "Walter Riddock, my nephew, is president of the Riddock line—*our* company. I prefer to call it Riddock, I guess because Wolfington added to it is such a mouthful," she rambled on, "anyway, Riddock has a more business-like ring to it."

"What will I call myself—when we attend the party?" Pandora asked suddenly.

"What's that, dear?" Sarah opened gray eyes that had closed for a moment.

"People will wonder, at the Millers' party. Will I call myself Dora . . . just Dora?"

Sarah shook herself again. "Your last name has not come back to you yet?"

The young woman beside her shook her head a

131

little sadly.

Sarah began to nod in the swing again, then jerked her head up. "Don't look so sad, child. It will come to you soon—everything. You know"—Sarah perked up—"this is all very exciting. It's almost scandalous, the manner in which you are being gossiped about." Sarah shifted as if tickled. "Even—oh! They are beginning to call you the Mystery Girl. Is that not interesting now?"

"Mrs. Wolfington—"

"No—no, you must call me Sarah, child!"

"Sarah, could . . . I mean I couldn't possibly wear the pink gown. It is lovely, but with all the others wearing white—" She shrugged helplessly, unable to go on.

"You mean you will be too conspicuous?"

"Yes. Exactly."

Pandora already realized she would be on display, like a scarlet rose in a bunch of white camellias. Sarah very much wanted her to attend, and Pandora *was* fond of her employer. But she felt so out of place, so lost in this society she was being gently urged into by Sarah. So far away from home . . . how far? Something else struck her as strange now, too. Cara Kalee and this sweet old woman; they knew more than they were letting on.

"Well then . . . you are accompanying me, correct?" Sarah said.

"Yes, but I don't see—"

"Dora, my plans for pink for you have changed!" Sarah rose from the swing and went inside the door to pull the bell cord for the maids' quarters. She turned about, framed in the doorway, her silver hair like a delicate halo about her head.

"You shall wear *black*, Dora, as I shall. You see? I am ever in mourning and so are you . . . for what you cannot remember."

Lord, Pandora gasped, black! Finally she decided this would prove to be a shade better than being a blushing pink standout. And she wouldn't be the only one wearing black—Sarah would be, too.

"And the white powdered wig?" Pandora asked hopefully.

"Yes, the wig . . . but with long love locks, instead of the towering dome of chubby curls. Too oldish for you."

"Thank you, Sarah."

Pandora looked aside to conceal her terrible fear—fear of what the future held in store for her. Now she was startled by her own awakened longings and by the man who had initiated them, the "man" who would follow her and find her.

Where would he find her—at the Millers' party?

Pandora had closed her eyes and rested her head against the swing's back . . . for just a moment, so she thought. But time passed and as she dozed she hadn't noticed Sarah moving back into the house, leaving her alone.

Warm, so warm. Her head began to swim in the beginning of a deep daydream, as she was lulled by the gentle motion of the swing, the softly twittering birds splashing in the birdbaths. She imagined crystal-green eyes smiling. A fringe of thick black lashes, dark eyebrows rising sardonically above them. Above her was a shadowy figure with a lean muscular frame. He came to her now like a warm night wind while a feeling of unreality took hold of her. His head was bending, his lips lowering . . . hers parted in wonder . . . a warm feeling invaded her bones. She heard or only imagined laughter, deep and resonant . . . and exhilarating. A sweet wildness stirred Pandora and she opened wide her arms as though to clasp the male form . . . then her eyes flew open for a shadow had fallen over her.

"What *ever* are you doing?"

Pandora stared, blinking her flaxen lashes. There was no man there with crystal-green eyes. It was only Sarah and she was looking down at Pandora as if she were quite a lunatic.

Chapter Thirteen

"Look at that. If it isn't Harlequin himself!"

"No, silly, he's a wizard!"

Every tongue at the party had been chattering away about the peaceful and unhurried nineties and the century that was fast slipping away to usher in a new era. The question in every heart was "The twentieth century—what will it bring?"

But something else—*someone* else—had diverted their attention. The sound of gossip from their wagging tongues rose to the high ceilings of the ornate room as under the flaring gaslights and below the sparkle of candelabra and chandeliers a black-robed character sporting a wizard hat with moons and stars—matching the sweeping, wide-sleeved domino—made a grand entrance. Rounds of hearty laughter flitted through the crowd that glittered in Paris gowns, high pompadour wigs, and flashing diamonds.

As this wizardly figure bowed gallantly low and brushed his rouged lips against bejeweled fingers, he perused, through the slanting eyeholes of his mask, each and every female's face. Each time, seemingly satisfied with his perusal, he moved on as bemused eyes followed him.

"Was he smiling at me—*especially?*" wondered one woman, her voice caught up in a breathless note.

"No, Amanda," said the dashing, scarlet-coated man suddenly beside his wife. "He was spying beneath your petticoats to check if you're a blue-blood, when he swept a bow before you!" The man chuckled uproariously.

Women in shimmering white paused on stairways, in halls, and in the parlor, whispering to one another. . . .

"Who is he? An actor from the comic theater?"

"A wizard from the Circus Royal?"

"*I'm* not shocked by the black tights peeping beneath the robe," Ma Sissy announced unblushingly.

"No, not since *The Black Crook* introduced tights to San Francisco!"

"He's enchanting, whoever he is—and I'll bet handsome beneath the mask and rouge!"

"*And* under the tights!" a bolder, younger woman dared aloud.

"He doesn't talk much, and in such low tones if he does."

"And why should he? He must remain anonymous!" Young *Lady* Ashe giggled. "It's more fun that way!"

"Pooh!" The banker's wife smirked.

Agnes moved away from this group of the smart set. Some women, she thought annoyedly, will gossip about anything! But still there was a tiny spark in her hooded eye as she shot a discreet glimpse toward the black tights of the man who was fast gaining popularity and the name Romantic Wizard. Finally a smile quirked at the corners of her mouth. She had to admit he was indeed a compelling figure—whoever he was.

In the lofty-ceilinged parlor, Pandora sat stiffly in a high-backed chair of carved walnut. Beside her awed companion, Sarah was seated haughtily in a rocker with a Brussels-carpet back.

An Aubusson rug stretched the length of the huge parlor and everywhere shone elegant cut-glass vases filled to overflowing with La France roses, azaleas, and snowballs. Several overstuffed sofas covered in red plush had been arranged in half circles; and large cheval mirrors with gold frames reflected the polished magnificence of rare inlays, imported woods, and mosaics of generous catholicity. The atmosphere was one of unrestrained splendor. This bedazzlement was the Miller country estate. Pandora wondered for a fleeting moment what their home in San Francisco was like; she knew she had never witnessed such wealth and glitter—and so much delicious food!

Chatterings and low chuckles reached Pandora, as did the music made by the Hungarian orchestra in the ballroom. Mouth-watering odors wafted in from the long, linen-draped tables, and though the men weren't allowed to have a smoke in the parlor, still scent from their Havanas drifted in to annoy Sarah's delicate nose.

White-coated men strolled about bearing cocktail trays held aloft, and drinks were replenished with astonishing speed.

Here were the leaders of the city; merchants,

politicians, bankers, judges, gay young blades, and of course the smart set, all resplendent in scarlet coats and black trousers, fine snowy cravats, and waistcoats all in the same brocade. Who could tell one from another?

The imported gowns, the fine feathers that nodded above white pompadours, belonged to the wives of the Nob Hill millionaires who had shelled out a thousand dollars apiece for a gown of white satin. Sarah's seamstress had let her off easy—five hundred dollars each for the black gowns.

All the guests who drifted into the parlor took a second look at Pandora, demurely sipping her Shasta water. Sarah was just introducing her to Diane Ashe and her husband, Todd, when all tongues about them ceased to wag and the room grew hushed. The wizard had just entered the parlor, trailed by an assemblage of gay women who appeared like so many chickens clucking after a rooster.

"Aha, there he is," Todd Ashe announced. He bent to Pandora, adding, "I was just about to tell you we have a wizard in our midst!" He chuckled much too loudly in her face.

"Show us a clever trick or two, wizard!" Diane called to him through the line of flapping chickens.

He executed a short bow after he had come to stand in the center of those following him about. Pandora and Sarah had a front-row seat while some couples drifted behind their chairs. Pandora blushed, feeling rather than seeing the eyes in the slits sweep her from head to toe.

"May we have your attention!" Diane shouted

needlessly, clapping her jewel-flashing hands together.

Smiling, the wizard pulled from beneath his flowing domino a plain deck of cards and one of court cards. "I will tell a card," he began, "by smelling it. But first, I must have someone assist me." His darkened eyes scanned the milling crowd, and in a low voice he said, "You . . . there, the lovely vision in black."

Pandora flicked her gaze to Sarah, but her heart pounded and her cheeks went beet-red as she realized he meant her. With a nudge of her elbow, Sarah urged Pandora to stand. All eyes were glued to the young beauty gowned in black satin like her elderly companion. She rose slowly, praying that no one could hear the triphammer of her heart. For some reason she couldn't fathom, Pandora was thankful that he didn't touch her when she went to stand beside him.

"Aha—her gown is a dark echo of his domino!" someone called raucously.

Now he did touch her and Pandora shivered from the contact as he led her to a love seat and sat himself beside her. He spoke low into her ear, tickling it with his warm breath as he explained what the others should not and could not hear. He straightened then and pulled a length of heavy dark material from his domino sleeve that draped over his arm hugely.

"A blindfold." He held it up for everyone to see.

Even in this crowded area, Pandora's senses began to reel from the faint masculine scent that was his own. She listened while he began to talk about the

139

strong sense of smell and touch which blind people are said to possess. Then he stated that he could, while blindfolded, distinguish the court cards from the rest. After that, he tied the heavy cloth behind his head; the domino he wore was covered completely.

"My eyes are tightly bound, correct?"

Murmurs and nods passed around the circle. He took the pack in his hands and, holding up one of them in view of the whole company, felt the face of it with long fingers.

"It's a court card," he announced after picking one at random from the deck of cards Pandora fanned out close together.

Murmurs of astonishment arose. Diane smiled smugly; she had seen the young woman in black tread on his toes, right foot. As he proceeded to the next card, a plain card, this time Pandora remained unmoving.

"What is a wizard?" someone new in the room asked, peeping over Diane's shoulder.

Diane tossed back, "A professional fool, but employed back in the Middle Ages to amuse the guests with jokes, tricks, and antics."

"No, that's a jester," Todd corrected, then chuckled. "But that's close enough!" He sloshed a bit of champagne onto his scarlet coat, but paid this no mind.

The wizard announced, "It is *not* a court card this time. A common card." His rouged lips parted in a smile meant only for the young woman aiding him.

The wizard really had the ladies convinced that he possessed the extraordinary power to which he laid claim; that is, all but one with keen eyes.

"Phooey!" Diane exclaimed low to those beside her. "It's only a trick; he has his other fool there step on his toe, and when it was not a court card, she does nothing."

Pandora was about to rise and join Sarah, when he ordered her in a low voice, "Stay." Then to the people, "I will now perform the doll trick."

"Well," Diane snorted, "let's see if he has any believable tricks up his sleeve. This one should prove how good he really is."

He held up a wooden, painted doll, six inches long. "First, I'll pass the little fellow around, so that you can see, folks, that his head is quite intact."

A half circle around the ladies, and then the doll was handed back. They had tried removing the head, but the darling thing wouldn't budge, said one woman.

"I couldn't get it off," added another.

"Neither could I," stated a third.

"I will now place the doll in this bag, and proceed with my story."

He held the bag of very dark material up for all to see. "The little traveler you see before you, ladies and gentlemen, is a wonderful little man who has been all over the world. *Ah*, but he has grown much older and very nervous.

"One evening, just lately, at a small cabaret in the south of France, he was stating just how nervous he was and how very much he dreaded being robbed, when a Jew who sat in a corner of the room undertook to impart to him the means of making himself invisible at any moment—ahem—for a sum to be agreed upon."

The wizard saw that he had captured the crowd's rapt attention, and so went on. "The bargain was struck, the money paid, and the Jew placed at his disposal a small skullcap, which, as soon as it was placed upon his head, rendered him at once invisible.

"And now I shall show you, ladies"—he noticed that more men had gathered around him—"and gentlemen, the power possessed by this cap!"

He then introduced the doll into the bag, which had a small opening at one end sufficiently large to admit the doll's head to pass through it. He showed his audience the little head, and then announced, "And now so that there can be no deception—I will turn the lower part of the bag over the doll." He watched them nod collectively when the doll's body became visible.

Again holding the doll's head above the bag's top, he said, "I will now show you the wonderful cap by which the old gentleman was at once rendered invisible." He produced the cap from his domino, placed it upon the darling head of the doll for a moment, and then removed it just as swiftly. The head disappeared into the bag, which he then turned inside out. No trace of the doll could be seen.

"I can't believe it!"

"This is one of the best sleight-of-hand tricks I've ever seen performed!"

"Why don't you strike it against the table, Wizard!"

The powdered face grinned. "Exactly. I shall do that now," said the tall man.

He struck the bag on the edge of the sofa and then

the floor. A smug look plastered on her ivory-complexioned face, Diane stepped closer.

"All right, Wizard. Let's see if you can bring him back again. Just as fast."

With a bow and a flourishing finish, the wizard placed his hand into the bag, showed the head through the opening—once; and quickly, again tossed the bag onto the floor and trampled hard upon it.

"He's gone again!"

"Well done, Wizard!"

The gathering thinned out then as some preferred to go and dance, some to fill their stomachs; but others trickled into the parlor.

"More! More! Entertainer!" a buxom woman who had stayed crowed.

Now he lifted Pandora from the love seat with a gentle hand beneath her elbow. "Don't shiver like that," he whispered into her ear.

Her gaze flicked off his face and went chasing into the crowd, searching for Sarah to come save her. But Sarah was now surrounded by a flock of clucking elders.

"I—I am not shivering," she shot sideways.

He merely cleared his throat before going on. "Now, what is your name, mademoiselle?"

"Madem—" Pandora stuttered. "D-Dora. Just Dora."

"*Just* . . . Dora." His voice pitched even deeper yet. "Sweet mystery . . . Dora."

Something struck her as familiar when the entertainer spoke that way.

"Ah! Dora. Shall I try to guess your *last* name? We've never before met, correct?"

Pandora blushed. "You may—guess," was all she offered.

"Don't be so nervous, Dora sweet," he murmured, pressing his handsome long fingers to his temples in duplicate arches. "Just concentrate on your last name, please."

After a time of much high tension, he said, "I *am* sorry, folks, I cannot guess her last name!" He inclined his head with a glitter of unfathomable eyes through slanting slits.

He tossed an arm in the air. "The young woman has fooled *me!*" he announced.

Pandora blinked away from the wizard, and frowned.

Now he bent to a suitcase that seemed to have appeared at his feet quite magically, and he brought out a scarlet coat, much like the ones the guests wore, but thinner. He turned the sleeves inside out to show they contained nothing. Discarding his robe, very quickly so as not to appear indecent, he put on the red coat. He looked quite ridiculous in red tails and black tights. But several pairs of female eyes widened at the display of muscled legs.

"Sir . . . there." He asked one elderly gentleman to lend him a large silk handkerchief and, having tossing it over one hand and a part of his arm, with his free hand he quickly withdrew from it a long string of vivid flowers. The silk roses spread out into a huge bouquet of soft, elegant flowers that rustled when they blossomed, leaves and all.

He handed one bouquet to the woman nearest him

on the opposite side from where Pandora stood. Baffled, she exclaimed, "Where could they have come from?" She buried her nose in them and then giggled at herself for sniffing artificial flowers.

He then repeated the process, this time with his other arm. "These are for you"—he bowed to Pandora—"for . . . being here." His voice went lower.

"But they aren't real!" Diane scoffed at the trick.

The woman with the first bouquet came back at Diane. "Ah, real flowers wilt and die, Mrs. Ashe. *Silk* roses are forever!"

"Yes . . . forever," echoed the wizard, directing his gaze upon Pandora.

The crowd began to move then and to circulate to other points of interest, like the ballroom where couples had begun to dance. Although it was nearing midnight, the dancing would last until three, maybe longer.

Pandora was left standing with the wizard. Numbly she held the silk flowers, wondering if she should give them back.

"You will need these again . . . won't you?" she asked shyly, wishing for a moment she could look upon his countenance without the disguise.

"No," he answered in a deep tone, lower, now that they were alone. "I don't do this for a living. In fact, this is the first time—"

"You are not really an entertainer?"

"That's right. Not really." He packed the stuff into the suitcase, even the scarlet coat. He had donned the robe again.

Pandora was baffled by his sudden indifferent

attitude. "You must take them back. I'll feel rather foolish sitting there holding them the remainder of— well, the morning."

"Give them to your employer to hold for you." He snapped the case shut and stood it against the wall. "Would you care to dance—with a wizard?"

"Dora, come here, dear. I want you to meet someone!" Sarah called from somewhere behind Pandora.

Pandora turned and saw Sarah standing next to a man with ash-blond hair. He was exactly her own height, she decided, and had a soft smile curving his pinkish lips. This must be Walter Riddock, she concluded. Sarah's nephew.

"Maybe later—" Pandora was saying as she turned to face the wizard again. But she found herself staring at a mirror that reflected her own baffled image. Where had he vanished to? There was the wall, a couch on either side with groups of gossiping women gathered behind the furniture. Had he gone over the top of one of the sofas? She felt her hackles rise due to the strangely supernatural effect of his disappearance.

He *is* magic! Pandora mumbled to herself as she walked trancelike over to where Sarah and her nephew stood. She heard the groups behind her buzzing about the vanishing act themselves.

"Ha! The wizard has disappeared. Poof! Someone must have popped his magical bubble with one of those rose thorns!"

Sheila Meade, a latecomer to the party, stepped inside the room. "Did someone say Thorn? Has he really come? I'd be thrilled!"

146

"Haven't seen him," Diane said crisply, toying with the rope of pearls trailing down her silk bodice.

"By the way, where *is* Rogan Thorn?" Todd Ashe tipsily wondered out loud.

"Oh!" Sheila tossed back over her shoulder as she stepped back into the hall, "Rogan hardly *ever* attends parties!"

Chapter Fourteen

An hour had passed since the entertainer had chillingly vanished. Pandora had danced with Walter Riddock twice. Afterward he had politely and gallantly ushered her by the arm back to Sarah's side. But now the widow had gone upstairs to retire until teatime tomorrow at two, Ma Sissy had informed Pandora. The older woman had then spent some time conversing with Pandora and Riddock, but had soon moved on, *the* social butterfly always. "Nice," Ma Sissy had exclaimed over the unusual color of Pandora's gown, and then, wagging her fingers— "Toodle-oo!" Ma Sissy had been baffled by Pandora's shyness and mysterious manner.

Pandora's thoughts were serious. She had studied Riddock covertly. For some reason unknown to her he made her feel uneasy. At first she had been wary of him, but because of his charming manner and ready smiles, she soon found herself relaxing. At least a little.

Now Pandora felt as if an icy hand was gripping her heart. Rogan Thorn had just entered the parlor. She warmed, shameless by experiencing the desire she did not want to feel. She sat on pins and needles.

The gaslight behind her hissed and it was all she could do to keep from jumping high off her chair.

Dressed in an elegant black cashmere suit, polished black leather boots, white silk shirt, and a cravat stuck by a splendid ruby—the only red he wore—Rogan strode directly to the love seat where Pandora and Walter were continuing their "getting acquainted" conversation.

All eyes, especially female ones, had turned automatically upon this compelling figure of man. A tempest rose inside Pandora, but she did not dare bat an eyelid even as he took her breath away. She had not seen Rogan Thorn since the night she had fled dazedly from his house with her mysterious "friend" . . . Cara.

Pandora looked aside experiencing a different confusion. She wondered why Cara had not come to the party. She recalled Sarah's words then: only the elite will be invited. You are lucky, Dora, to be going as my companion.

But who had invited the wizard? Pandora sobered. The Millers must have, of course. She had met the Millers earlier and they had been kind and charming, both the husband and wife. Sarah had told her they were childless.

The musicians had begun a soft melody and suddenly Rogan was standing before her. Strange, but the music seemed to have brought him on its lovely notes. As her blue eyes drifted upward, Pandora sensed a barely restrained leash of fury in him. His sweeping, penetrating eyes of green fire swept her from head to waist to ankles and then to feet. Then his eyes swept up again, possessively. He was raking and imprisoning her with his virile gaze.

While Rogan now stared for the most part at the soft curve of Pandora's lips, Riddock cleared his throat. "Rogan, ah, Rogan Thorn, might I introduce—"

Rogan interrupted rudely. "We've already met. Haven't we, Dora? Or don't you remember? You stayed at my home for such a short time, though. I was disappointed. I would have liked your stay to have been much longer—and, perhaps a bit more enjoyable. But, as it was, I found no—ah—displeasure in your company and the moments we did share together."

Pandora tried to blot that picture of intimacy from her mind, but a flush rose in her cheeks, and she turned away. She eyed Riddock sideways, noticing that his jaw was rigidly set. She wondered momentarily why he seemed so nervous and upset. Her own nerves shouted her frustration.

Now Rogan brought her hand to his lips, locking his gaze meaningfully with hers. "Have you recovered, dear Dora? You appear to me worried . . . and you are somewhat thinner than I remember you, and slightly paler." He turned her long, tapered fingers over in his big palm.

Pandora strove to summon the etiquette Sarah had taught her, but everything escaped her mind. He was confusing her, without actually seeming to. He, Rogan, had fired all these questions toward her like an interrogator, and she could not set them in order so as to answer him properly. She chose to reply to what she thought would be the least intimate of them.

"I am fine, Mr. Thorn. Thank you. Sarah has been very kind."

His eyebrow rose. "And—?"

"And—" She faltered. What more could she say with him staring at her that intensely? She decided to make light conversation, but soon launched into meaningless woman chatter.

". . . And the roses, aren't they beautiful!" She went on to separate items in the room, while Rogan's brow darkened with each passing moment.

Riddock fumed. He had to remain silent on what he himself knew of Pandora St. Ives. While in Hawaii he had learned that Pandora had been betrothed to a man named Akoni Nahele, the very same man with whom he had come to do business. But that business had been short-lived. Rogan Thorn had won again. He would think no more on it now, lest his thoughts surface to his countenance and betray him.

Digging out his handkerchief, Walter could be seen to be sweating profusely. This went unnoticed by Pandora, who kept up a stream of chatter about the furnishings, but Rogan eyed Walter's actions closely—like a hawk watched a quivering chicken.

"Is something ailing you, Riddock?" Rogan questioned the man casually.

"I—I think it's become quite stuffy in here. Don't you agree, Pandora?"

Her head swiveled in Walter's direction. *"Pandora?"*

Rogan dipped his head. "Ah, lovely, your whole name?"

"My name is Dora," she almost snapped. "Walter,

I am quite comfortable," she went on to answer the question, "as the other rooms are overly crowded and filled with obnoxious smoke." She did not know why, but she had to keep chattering. "Maybe I will drift into the hall for some of that delicious terrapin, cooked in its own shell, those succulent tidbits served on a dreamy sauce of cream, sweet butter—and, oh, yes, some sherry!"

Rogan peered down at the carpet and grimaced, having just been reminded of Widow Wolfington. The old woman had been busy making Dora over to her liking. Very busy.

"Where did Dora vanish to?" Rogan asked her cryptically.

"What?" She blinked up at him, confused.

"Never mind," he returned tersely.

Pandora let her attention wander, hoping that Rogan Thorn would move off to mingle, but he stayed right beside her chair, as if guarding her every move. She continued, though, to look between the open doors to the hall where waiters carried silver-covered chafing dishes to the already crowded tables. Strawberries with luscious cream, and also several orange layer cakes had been added to the buffet as well as chilled Sauternes for the thirsty couples who had been dancing steady for an hour or more now.

Walter suddenly stood, stuffing his handkerchief carelessly back into his scarlet coat pocket. He ran his gaze over Thorn's elegant black suit, thinking *How unconforming of the man!* Out loud he said to Pandora:

"I'll be back in a few minutes." He was damp with perspiration now. "What would you like me to get you to drink, Dora?"

"Nothing, Mr. Riddock. I've just finished a tall glass of that delicious Shasta mountain water. Thank you, though, for thinking of me." She bestowed a sugary smile on Walter.

Rogan grimaced again, but concealed it by looking aside to a young woman who sat nearby, giving him the eye. Pandora pretending not to notice, folded her hands into the fullness of her skirt.

Walter continued, "We'll go for a stroll in the gardens in a short while; would you like that?" he asked Pandora. She dipped her head slowly, her long sausage curls brushing her shoulders, but Walter could not tell if she had accepted or not. "It will be lovely," he went on nevertheless, "with dawn breaking through the trees, and the birds singing. . . . I'll be back." He took quick notice when Rogan smirked at his prosaic words, but that was all. They avoided each other as much as possible—always.

Rogan laughed low, a sound without amusement. Walter shot through the tightly knit group standing just inside the ballroom. For the moment Pandora and Rogan were the only guests occupying the parlor. Even the demure young woman had risen, giving Rogan a come-hither glance over her shoulder as she went. Lights twinkled, the chandelier coruscated, and the romantic melody took up again.

"Would you care to dance . . . now?"

"Now? I—I—"

But Rogan was already twining his long fingers about her elbow, bringing her to stand before him, their feet just touching, a fold of her gown swirling against his trousers like a satin caress. Then he

153

tucked her arm through his.

"Once . . . only once," Pandora finally found her voice, "and then the walk in the garden with Mr. Riddock." After that, she told herself, she would join Sarah in the safety of their appointed room.

The orchestra played and Pandora danced with Rogan, not once but three times; and during each dance he pulled her closer, closer, while she swayed unconsciously toward him until her bodice touched on his dark coat. The familiar masculine scent of him faintly reminded her of the wizard. But Rogan Thorn would not be the sort to play the entertainer, she concluded.

Pandora had long ago forgotten Walter and the stroll. Dawn was already breaking, and soon there would be bird song, just as Walter had said. The couples danced languidly, the gay young blades yawning over their shoulders, wishing for soft beds to fall upon, and the young ladies looking as if they could go on dancing forever.

Sleepily Pandora leaned against Rogan. Even in her languorous state, she could feel a shiver pass through his tall frame as his hand stroked her back in a slow and sensuous massage. Pandora suddenly realized just how very close they were dancing—if one could call it that. Their feet and legs barely moved. His breath blew warm against her cheek and sent shivers up and down her body. She had no other care; she felt so warm all over, flushed, hot, and happy; and strangely in the next moment bewildered.

Now, like tinder, she caught his ardent flame and she could endure the heat no longer. That same fear was washing over her that she had known before when Rogan had held her tightly, and feverishly kissed her; the time she had shamelessly returned his ardor. His savage kisses had plundered her soul. He had this strange power over her, and yes, a new craving rushed through her body in a savage yearning. He frightened her, as before when he had wanted to possess every inch of her, just as someone else had before . . . before . . .

"Dora." Rogan stiffened. "What is it?"

His ardent gaze, so close, caught hers and held her captive. She could not stand it any longer. No more!

"No!"

With a strangled sob, Pandora tore herself from Rogan's easy embrace and ran, stumbling on her rustling gown's hem. She rushed headlong, weaving in and out of guests who watched her flight with growing frowns. Marble statues rose before her seeming to fill the hallway with giant columns of granite set among shrubs and flowers; she almost toppled one of the lovely statues in her frantic haste.

Frantically she wondered where she could find the stairs. She dared not stop and ask someone. He must not catch up with her, her mind screamed while her heart pounded with a fear she could not name. Her bosom heaved beneath the black satin; she heard him calling, searching. The flame was seeking her out to devour her.

"Dora!"

Where was Walter? She could not see him anywhere. Instead of taking the turn that would bring her to the stairs, she found herself standing outside in the courtyard. It was filled with statuary, too, and scented blossoms, and bubbling fountains.

The cooler air revived her senses a bit and she at once chided herself for being so foolish as to run like a scared ninny. Why be afraid of a mere man? she asked herself. He could not hurt her; so what was she afraid of?

Pandora decided she would not go back inside immediately. Pink streaks of dawn, in a blaze of fantasy were lighting the eastern sky as she wandered down the flagstones of the garden path that led between tall yew hedges. She was safe here in this green and flowered sanctuary where flame-colored flowers nodded in a cool breeze and lifted their dewy heads to greet the coming of another golden morning.

Pandora stood still as a hare, drinking in the earthy smells, the sweet fragrance of flowers, and sounds of awakening birds. Peace washed over her. It was so lovely here. She had nothing to fear after all.

Chapter Fifteen

A brilliant pink blossom floated to the earth between the flower beds.

"Good morning, lovely garden nymph."

Her sense of peacefulness disappeared instantly and Pandora nearly jumped a mile at the rumbling sound of the deep male voice directly behind her. Her hands trembled uncontrollably as she repeated to herself:

I am not afraid, I am not, no matter what, not, not!

But Pandora soon realized that her trembling was far greater than that of the leaves in this garden paradise of the very wealthy. So much was happening in such a short time. However paralyzed with alarm she was, Pandora decided her best course was to play it very cool.

So, with an alluring smile plastered across her face, she turned, having thought up her lines in advance.

"Good morning, Walter. Oh, I am sorry." Pandora acted out her feigned surprise. "I thought—never mind, Mr. Thorn, I was just going back inside. Ohh, my." She yawned wide. "I had not realized how sleepy I was."

His move was quickly initiated. Before she could

go around him, she was brought up hard against Rogan's muscular frame. The sheer power of his manly grip on either side of her shoulders warned her that she hadn't a moment to think further and that she was powerless to act against this assault on her senses. His lips had already swooped down like a bird of prey to cover hers.

"Ah, I am hungry for your sweet flesh, Dora . . . Dora—"

"No!"

The hardness of his grinding kiss returned and was at first brutal, without any tenderness before it changed into a moist caress, followed by tender kisses that plundered her soul, dizzied her already-wearied brain, and assailed her most feminine senses. She snatched her lips away, but was only given a second to speak.

"Are you mad? Stop!"

The oval tips of her fingers clutched his arms but found no yielding spot, no place soft enough to puncture or even to bruise in order to make him halt this ruthless and aggressive attack on her mind and body.

"I am not mad, Dora, just used to having my own way," he murmured with infuriating calm. As he kissed her and nibbled lightly at her lips' corners, he kept her imprisoned with his brute strength.

"You will not have it with this one woman!" Pandora hissed despite his encroaching mouth.

But she soon experienced a rude awakening when his knee rose to press boldly between her softness, and his own hard thigh found the cushion of her womanhood. She cried outrage at this hot intimacy, and flung back her head.

Despite this new arousal, beyond anything she had ever known, she wrenched her burning lips free from his. He imprisoned her harder against him, his hips brushing hers rhythmically, while he murmured and groaned with the heat of desire thick in his male voice.

Rogan sensed a warmth deep within himself; it fanned the fires that had been sleeping in him for so long. This warmth and fire was something new to him and was all it should be. The flames inside were rising, growing hotter until they became an exquisite torture to be endured. He felt as if they were one, breathing in and out, from each other's mouths; each nothing but flesh and matter without the other if he should set her free. But did she truly feel the same way? Her firm, young body spoke to him in a language his lonesome heart had never known existed and all sorts of erotic imaginings flew through his mind, giving him ideas that could have set the whole city of San Francisco ablaze. A long sigh, having come from the depths of his being, escaped from his tingling lips into hers.

"Don't fear me, Dora, please. Ah, you tempt me mindless!" He drew back a little to search her face with a hungry look, his hunger so intense it made him seem to grimace and smirk.

"Stop flattering me, Rogan Thorn. Ohhh," she heard herself moan, wondering at his look that frightened her, sapped her of all will to resist. What was it about him that aroused her maiden's soul so much? "You can't be serious. . . ." she said out loud.

His hands pressed deep into her shoulders. "I have never been more serious . . . you . . . see, Dora. I want you and, damn it, can't you see it!" Again his encroaching lips parted as they forcefully met hers, and he pressed mentally and physically against her renewed struggles of mind and body.

His kisses were savage and demanding, but a sweet anticipation struck her and it was almost too intense to endure. If this was what man did to woman, she wanted nothing more to do with it . . . couldn't allow him to bring this torment to fruition. It was his desire, and not hers. How could she desire this?

She felt her own strength to fight him off slip farther away with every renewed kiss. She took a deep breath and held it as distress widened her eyes. He tossed back his head, feeling her struggles weaken; to Pandora he seemed to take pity on her vulnerability. Though his grip loosened, Pandora could not help but throw a taunt in his face.

"Your mother, poor thing, she must have thought she bore a demon to have such a son as you!"

He considered this, staring stonily into her flushed face. So far, he had a gift for freeing his mind of painful images, but his childhood was nothing to linger over. He stiffened, and Pandora instantly felt this.

"I never knew my mother," he said.

She stammered her next words. "W-well, then, your father must have—"

He cut her short. "My father preferred women, strange women, over his son."

"Oh.".

Now Pandora detected a new sense of urgency in Rogan Thorn, something that had suddenly been unleashed. She must have said the wrong things, dangerous ones for her to have expressed.

He followed her head back and found her already bruised and hurting lips once again. "Nothing can stop what has begun between us, Dora."

Oh no? she thought icily. She decided to let him have his way for a few moments as she stalled for time. She laughed inwardly, planning her next move. She would be in for quite a surprise herself, she was to think later.

Bending her over his arm, his large but slim hand splayed at her slippery bodice while his other hand went to her back to keep her from falling. Pushing aside her bodice, he lowered his face and buried his mouth between her cleavage. However, before his tongue could encircle a nipple hotly, merely touching on the rosy tip, Pandora freed herself once again. But this had taken all the strength her woman's body could muster. Now, surprising him while he was off guard staring down at a half-naked nipple, her hand came up in a rounded fist and dealt him a hearty blow smack on the chin. His teeth crashed together with a startling impact that stunned even this powerful man.

"Oh, dear! I am sorry!" Pandora stammered, seeing the brittleness in his green eyes now frozen over with ice.

Rogan rubbed his chin and winced, indeed surprised at this young woman's force of hand. He appraised her for nearly a minute while she straightened her bodice shakily, then stood frozen, rooted to the spot by what she had done. Long moments found their eyes locked together in combat, green with blue, hers in utter fear, his in black rage. Pandora could scarcely believe that she had planned such a thing and actually carried it out.

But one minute more of that sweet torment and she might have let him lay with her there in the flower beds.

What he said next chilled her blood and would leave her stunned and disbelieving for days and weeks.

"Hard-hearted woman! You have stolen my jewelry, befuddled my brain, and now what would you have—?" he ground out full of sarcasm, but with an underlying fierceness in his tone, too. "What would you have—my heart, also?"

Pandora fumbled in her mind for an answer, but the ferocity of his glare made her wonder what game this could be he was playing with her. He was both hard and soft, both gentle and savage. First he had kissed and embraced her ardently, taken liberties no gentleman would have, under any circumstances, and now he was angered by her physical reproof of his actions.

He reached out to touch a long strand of hair that had escaped from beneath the wig in her struggles, saying, "All that glitters is not pure."

"What do you mean?"

"You are a trap to a man's heart, Dora." His lower lids narrowed his eyes to green slits. "Still, I find myself hungering for more. Perhaps you need some more jewelry? Hmm? To keep you going in whatever it is that you do? Are you perhaps a 'strange woman' . . . Dora?"

"Oh, what do you mean by that?" she demanded to know.

"Just what I said," he replied, sweeping a cold gaze over her that said many men must have had her.

Her eyes were suddenly a wild blue. "Oh, I understand you now, all right!"

He smirked. "But you could deny it . . . is that what you're going to tell me next?"

Pandora suddenly decided to give vent to her most bitter thoughts of this man—to his face!

"Your actions have been most unwelcome, Mr. Thorn. As for your precious jewelry being stolen; *sir*, you have me mixed up with some other woman. Like one of your 'strange women' as you call them. You must know many. You have misjudged me and accused me wrongly several times. I do not steal! Next, I am not a whore; nor do I linger *as a habit* in gardens with—with raping maniacs! And, last, as for your heart, you are welcome to save it for *your* strange women, or, keep it, whichever. It is much too black for my liking! You are a loser, Mr. Thorn!"

Pandora spun from the garden scene like a fuming, spitting shrew, lifting and tossing her skirts and petticoats in an agitated snap of froufrou.

The flame in Rogan's loins had cooled, easing the pressure of his desire that had grown uncomfortable in his tight trousers. Now there was no help for it. He laughed bitterly; there probably never would be.

Rogan eyed her fiery departure with a coolness that spelled danger. So, he was a loser, a blackheart, hmmm?

"Well, Miss Dora Nobody; you, bitch, can go straight to Hades!"

Rogan followed reluctantly in her stormy wake, but promised himself and his male pride that someday, and soon, she would distinguish a loser from a winner. He never lost, *never*, not Rogan Thorn. No, not at any game.

Presleep images began to float behind Pandora's closed lids. She saw a tangle of bodies; two of them began to writhe, to lunge. . . . One was her own! She knew this even in her semiconscious state. With her wildly tossed hair spilling over her back and shoulders . . . she was pressed in an amorous embrace with . . . Rogan Thorn! She came wide-awake.

Enough of that! She punched the pillow with a furious gesture and turned over in her too-soft bed wishing that the tree outside would cease making that scratchy sound against the window so that she could get back to sleep. Sleep! She had had little of that, to be sure.

She moaned. Now the murmur of voices drifted up from the courtyard through the open window and from the hall, too, telling her that the party had livened up once again. When the light in the room had changed, she finally rose to dress. She checked and found Sarah still asleep in the adjoining room. The older woman must have sat for hours at tea, but she, Pandora, must have slept, tossing restlessly, the entire afternoon. What a waste! And now evening . . . What was she going to do? She had no desire to stay up here in this stifling room and be bored to death while downstairs . . . She might as well get dressed in her mauve gown, the one shot with silver threads. She had brought it along for this final day of the Millers' la-di-da gathering.

Pandora sat at the white-and-gold French dressing table in her chemise which was trimmed with eyelet threaded with pink silk ribbon. She had pulled her hair up in back with a pink ribbon, too. It contrasted with the fiery lights in the long curls she had fashioned on the curling tongs Sarah had borrowed from a friend. She'd had to, for the wig had flattened her hair, and she hadn't wanted to wash her hair in the often-occupied bathrooms.

Pandora started at the knock on the door and she turned on the oval-cushioned seat. Before she could bring herself to rise and fetch her frilly robe, the door was being opened. A young woman, not much older than herself, with perfectly coiffed hair of a yellow-blond color, stood there looking just as surprised as she was herself. Later Pandora would think this expression had merely been a ruse employed by this woman with the sickly sweet tone of voice.

"Oh, my . . . *excuse* me! I have the wrong *room*. . . ." She started forward then, raising a dainty hand in the air in an affected manner. "Aren't you . . . why, of *course* you are. How exciting! Dora, the mystery girl, and how lucky I am to have come across you, quite by accident—and *all* alone! Do you *mind* very much if I come in and chat for a while?"

She closed the door behind her, inviting herself in without awaiting an answer. "Damn, I am so bored . . . !" She flounced over to seat herself on the edge of the bed in a languid pose; her arms were stretched behind her, her fingers spread on the mussed bed. "My, you must have had quite a time of it? Or . . ." She stopped, seeing the frown gathering on the other woman's brow.

Pandora slowly eased herself back onto the cushioned seat. Mildly shocked, she watched in the mirror the young woman behind her. This creature seemed to float and sparkle like an effervescent bubble in a glass of champagne. She could just as easily burst like one of those bubbles, Pandora decided. Like a modern-day Cinderella, without her make-up and powder, she would be transformed into a plain simpleton, one with flaws that needed to be concealed in her complexion. But for now Pandora could tell that *she,* whoever she was, had already refreshed her make-up and applied it with a heavy hand. How could a man ever know if she was beautiful or homely, what he was getting for a bride? A groom could, she supposed, on the morning after; of course he could. Pandora decided that this intruder on her privacy—who was still making herself at home—had several flaws to hide and was no natural beauty.

"Bored?" Pandora found herself mouthing the word automatically to her surprise.

"Of course! It is *only* six o'clock, *darling!* Oh, how awful of me to be so remiss. . . . I am Sheila Meade . . . and"—she giggled—"I *know* that *you*

166

cannot tell me your last name because you don't know it. . . . Oh, how terrible not to be able to remember! Is it so bad, darling? I mean . . . not knowing who you *really* are?" She paused to bend her torso down and peep at herself in the mirror.

With her mouth opening and closing wordlessly, beginning to form answers that would have been "I don't know" or "I am not sure," Pandora found herself gazing in the mirror at the smaller reflection behind her own. She automatically moved over a little to allow this Sheila Meade to see herself better.

"My goodness, darling, why don't you turn around so that I can get a better look at you!" Sheila watched her closely, beneath catlike lids, as Pandora turned on the chair to perch on the corner of it. "Oh, you *are* the *dear* who aided that charming wizard. I should've known! I mean I didn't actually *see* you . . . because I hadn't arrived yet. But, oh, let me tell you—I heard *all* about it from Diane Ashe and Ma Sissy—" She paused dramatically. "Do *you* know them?" she asked in a belittling tone.

"I met—*we* met only briefly. . . ."

"*Really*, aren't they the ones with their fine noses in the air. La-di-da! You poor, poor *darling!*"

"I don't think that I really know—"

"Well, let me *tell* you. . . . Oh, do you know what *else?*" she asked, chameleonlike.

Becoming just a little annoyed by now, Pandora breathed out, "No, I do *not* know what else. . . . Why don't you *tell* me?" Pandora said with mocking emphasis, feeling somewhat warm now despite not being fully dressed.

Sheila appeared a bit taken aback, but only for a moment. Then she went on, patting her poufed coiffure, and pulling at a curl now and then while chatting away like a magpie. Finally Sheila arrived at the part about Pandora and Rogan—their sunrise *stroll* in the garden. . . .

"Do you, either of you, know how many pairs of eyes followed you out into the garden . . . ?"

Pandora bristled but cut off the other woman. "No, not unless the hibiscus hedges and blossoms have eyes. . . ."

Sheila blinked her heavily made-up eyes swiftly and stared as if she were seeing something quite odious. She didn't much care for this pretty, long-legged child. Lord! Such shapely and endless legs poking out from that chemise. But this plain girl seemed to be getting the best of her, Sheila Meade! No one did that, least of all this simple creature! Sharpening her claws, the blond woman went on in a waspish tongue.

"Well, no one actually *saw* you together out there *alone*. But tell *me*, darling, did he get you to go out to the gazebo with him . . . ? Ah, that rascal . . . ! And did he only pet? Or did he get you to 'go all the way' with him? Oh, heavens, you aren't a . . . you *weren't* a virgin, were you?" Despite Pandora's audible gasp, Sheila went on as if she hadn't heard it. "Of course, Rogan *does* have his 'problem,' didn't you know? And perhaps he didn't even 'rise' to the occasion. . . . You *do* know what I mean?"

Ever so slowly Pandora came to her feet to tower over this suddenly slightly cowering young woman who was just rising from the bed herself. "You *are* a tall one, aren't you? Now, listen, darling, we *can* be friends. . . . You needn't look at me as if you'd love to scratch my eyes out!'' But Sheila had never witnessed such checked fury in a woman before—a man perhaps, but never a woman. She knew a great urge to be gone from the presence of this supposed-to-be-shy-and-subdued mystery girl. Lord, this Amazon-like woman was a strange one.

"I think you had better leave this room now. Immediately," Pandora warned. "I have to finish dressing. . . ." Pandora, taking long strides, went to the door and flung it wide; then she stood back against the frame, her arm extended in a dismissing fashion.

Sheila couldn't help but toss one last barb over her shoulder as she excited in a sashay of red skirts. "You *are* a simple little *bitch*, and I hope Rogan *used* you well. You see, when he *can*, he *will*, and you would be the very kind he wouldn't give another glimpse. Rogan Thorn plays the game best—*ta-ta!*"

Shaking from head to foot, Pandora, finally vented all the pent-up fury in her by slamming the door. Then she stood staring at it until mirrors all around her began to reflect erotic images of what could have indeed transpired out there in the garden.

After a time she shook off these disturbing illusions. There was a name for a woman like Sheila Meade. Oh, more than one—but they were low names only men found themselves able to pronounce.

Just as she was in the process of climbing into the conveyance that would take her and Sarah and her friends back to the city, Pandora's face went white beneath its light tan. She was crowded into the seat with Sarah and two other elderly ladies, who were chattering away unmercifully loudly; all it seemed at the same time.

"Look there!" a purple-haired crone screeched gratingly into Pandora's ear, poking a pointing finger in front of her nose. "If it isn't Rogan Thorn and that snippet, Sheila Meade! Since when has he taken up with *her?*" Diamonds flashed on her bony fingers as she pulled her arm back to her lap.

The perky one beside the crone croaked, "Heh-heh"—she nudged the other to bump against Pandora—"you should've seen them last night dancing—*clutching* each other in a bear hug, hardly a space between them to stick a pin in. For shame! Did you see 'em, Kathryn?"

"What a *nice* shame it is, too. That Rogan is a handsome devil I would not mind having to warm my bed . . . of course if I was a might bit younger!" the crone rasped in her creaky voice, carefully watching the young woman in her peripheral vision.

"Dora, did you not dance with Thorn the night before last?" It was Sarah this time. "Whatever happened to you last night, anyway?" She gave the young Dora no chance to answer, but went on. "Well, I suppose you were all tuckered out from dancing with him the night before."

Pandora kept her mouth glued shut, but her foot was tapping so agitatedly on the carriage floor that the crone beside her finally noticed; this woman already had noticed where the young woman's gaze was centered. Meanwhile, Rogan Thorn was escorting a laughing Sheila to a waiting carriage into which they both slipped, to be crushed close together with another couple. Rogan looked over just as they were pulling in front of Sarah's carriage and saluted the ladies with a tip of his derby. Pandora surprised everyone by sticking her nose high in the air and looking straight ahead at the driver's back—everyone but the crone who spoke up again.

"Horsefeathers! If Rogan Thorn is enamored of Miss Meade . . . I wonder why he gave our Dora here a solicitous look that said he offered his heart to her?"

Pandora finally voiced her opinion of the man. "He can have his black heart. Ugh! I loathe him. . . . He is disgusting!" But she was upset just the same.

"Heh-heh," the old crone chortled. "He's stink in your nostrils, eh?"

"Oh, my," Sarah muttered. "Such crack-brained talk, ladies! No more of that sardonic man!"

Still, hoisting her witchlike hand in the air, the crone pressed the issue. "He's hot on our Dora's tail, and just wait till he gets in your bloomers, dear. He won't be so disgusting then! That rogue has been around—"

"Kathryn! Please!" Sarah chided, her cheeks highly flushed with embarrassment.

The perky lady piped up, "Kathryn's a soothsayer . . . you know."

"You'll see, dears," Kathryn went on wisely. "There is going to be bells ringing soon . . . for Dora and Rogan. My predictions *always* come true!"

"Never!" Pandora hissed promptly to that.

Kathryn patted the slim knee beside her. "Think better of it, dear. This old woman is never wrong

171

when it comes to love, see."

Pandora's hair seemed to stand on end as she wondered where this Kathryn kept her witch's broomstick. The woman had to be ill-reasoned and unsound, Pandora concluded. She stubbornly refused to say any more all the way back to the city.

Chapter Sixteen

Pandora had lost some of her tan. She had taken to
dusting her face ever so delicately with "complexion
powder," but she needed no rouge—her cheeks
always shone through fresh as roses. Pampered even
more, still by Sarah and now by Walter, she wore
laced boots which were shinier than campaign
buttons. They peeped out from beneath a skirt edged
with velveteen binding. Beneath this outer skirt she
wore others: one of silk, some embroidered and
flounced; and beneath these were other tiny ruffles
. . . but *they* were never mentioned. Skirts were
getting shorter, some flared just above the ankles!

"Shocking!" Walter had snorted. "Just shocking!
What are the women of San Francisco coming to?"

Just last evening Pandora and Walter had joined
the senator in his Orpheum box and society had seen
her in her Paris gown and cartwheel hat manned
with pins. Even more daring—including talking
about it to the senator's wife!—was that she had
borrowed and read the French novels by Émile Zola.
The "third floors" above the private dining rooms in
the city were never, but *never*, mentioned by ladies.
But Pandora, in her curiosity, had almost slipped

and made a faux pas by asking just who went there. *Almost.*

Pandora had seen Rogan, in his Orpheum box, glance at them with sharp annoyance and then glance quickly away to settle his attention on his companion, a frilly little blond with pink pouting lips and batting lashes. Pandora had stared right back at him for a heart-stopping moment that had made her feel suddenly and oddly startled; then she, too, had looked away. The truth had seized her in that awful moment. There is something between Rogan Thorn and me. In that flickering gaze he had been entirely, cruelly aware of her befuddlement, of the stirring in her caused by what had passed between them. She had had the feeling that she was transparent to him. Thank God she was not likely to suffer an encounter with his ravaging clutches ever again!

Despite that thought, she could not help looking over at him just once more. Just once . . . and never again, she promised herself, as she found herself devouring his profile and memorizing his every movement with her starry-eyed gaze. This effort cost her her pride but she was rewarded by no return look from those beautiful green eyes.

Oh God, she had sobbed inwardly, why am I so afraid of him! Why can't I just . . .

Friday took forever to come. Pandora hadn't seen Walter since the night at the Orpheum and now two days later, her hair carefully arranged, she patted her mouth and sighed. Only the two of them were in the parlor; Sarah had been busy all week long with her charities and her church committees and friends.

Suddenly after a long silence, this man, who had seemed withdrawn and bored a moment ago, flew off the couch. Pandora's hands flew to her startled cheeks and her eyes became round blinking saucers.

"Marry me, Dora!" he begged on bended knee.

In Sarah's parlor, Walter Riddock unbosomed his ardor before Pandora who had sat beside him demurely in the stiff-backed chair; she was utterly surprised at the immediacy and the ardency of the words he poured forth. Until this moment, Walter's approaches to her had been respectful, but today, his passion was not to be checked.

Pandora whispered that Walter was to her, as yet, a comparative stranger; and she had tried not to encourage his warmer attentions too much.

Pandora had discovered that a new and delightful sensation had been awakened in her of late. Had she suddenly recognized the most powerful of human passions—what Sarah called the most universal of them—love? Did it exist for her, Pandora? Directed toward *whom?* Surely not Rogan Thorn; he was a horned beast. Oh, yes, it would have been so easy to give in to that man, to submit and allow herself to be carried away. But how far? And to what end?

Now, here, in the parlor, she frowned at Walter's bent head. With his tumble of thick curls he was almost beautiful. Had she been blind, failing to notice the symptoms of growing attachment between her and Walter?

He was quieter now, awaiting her answer while time crept by.

Up to now, Walter had been a little afraid to ask Pandora for her hand, lest he should be refused flatly.

175

Most men would take pause until they felt more confident, that they might be spared the mortification and ridicule that is attached to being rejected, in addition to the pain of disappointed hope. But Walter was not one who possessed too great a timidity of character and he had finally emboldened himself enough to speak of marriage.

Pandora had found comfort and kindness in Walter since the *incident* in the garden had regretfully taken place. She had never asked him where he had gone on the night of the party; nor had she told him of Rogan Thorn's ungentlemanly actions, even though she was sure that Walter would have inclined toward her a very willing ear.

Well, wouldn't he have? Pandora wondered now for a moment.

Suddenly she shot out of the chair, her blue eyes very large and dewy—and shocked. Two weeks ago and now she was just remembering!

Walter rushed to take her hand gently into his, a look of concern mingled with regret plastered on his pale face. "Oh, Dora, I've been too bold and frightened you away. Forgive me, dear heart, I would not hurt you or make you cry for all the world."

Walter rubbed his hand over her shoulder clumsily, feeling and delighting in the texture of a loose silken strand of hair; the gold fire in her hair had never failed to mesmerize him.

"Forgive me?" he repeated, this time a plea.

"Walter, it is not what you think." Her voice was low with emotion. "You have been so very kind, and taken me to such warm exciting places in the city. I am telling you that you have been a wonderful escort and friend and even taught me social graces that good Sarah had overlooked.'' She faltered. ''But . . . it is just that—'' She shook her head, its long fashionable ringlets swinging around.

Walter fawned before Pandora. ''I know you cannot go on. I know, too, you don't love me.'' He shrugged, his voice near to a whimper. ''That can come later, dear heart. But if love is important to you, Pandora dear—''

''What?'' Her warmth was gone in the blinking of an eye and she gripped Walter's arm with a suddenness that halted his speech.

Pandora continued to stare. She had remembered moments ago that he had spoken the very same name at the Millers' party.

A muscle twitched along Walter's jaw. ''Pandora?''

''Again! You called me Pandora!''

Walter, sheepish, laughed a little. ''Oh, yes, you see, it's—after all—it's the same, well, almost, you know.'' He gritted his teeth inwardly, in frustration. ''Dora or Pandora. What does it matter?''

''Not really the same, Walter,'' she argued softly, frowning at him thoughtfully as she so often did of late.

He continued in the same vein. ''What does it matter, as long as you will think over—ah—my proposal and give me an answer soon?''

Her face was a mask of bewilderment. She was hoping that Walter would bring some ray of light into this darkened corner of her brain. Why did Walter sometimes call her Pandora and then halt as if he had made a slip of the tongue?

''Oh, Pandora . . . oh, damn, I mean *Dora*.'' He

heaved a deep sigh, shaking his head. "There, I did it again. I guess it's just that you remind me of the mythical Greek goddess who was searching for her hope; that's all. Dora, I'm not getting any younger, and . . . and I do want you for my wife."

But Walter felt no throbbing in his loins, no turgid growth of his manhood attesting to desire. Instead he eyed a table of onyx and took a moment to admire it; lovely and rich, just like this woman beside him and her . . .

Pandora blinked, frowning. "You were saying?" she said, wondering where Walter had drifted off to suddenly.

He reached out to stroke a curl of her straying hair admiringly. "You're so lovely, Dora. I can't gaze at you long enough. All my friends and associates envy me to the point of turning green."

She tuned in to him again, having drifted away herself, but Walter mistook the faraway mist and the deep blue flecks of passion in her gaze for adoration of himself. He decided that she was beginning to weaken and soon he would have himself a bride—a gorgeous showpiece of womanhood to grace his parlor. For a while, that is. And then . . .

Pandora took a slow, deep breath. "Oh, Walter, I have found such joy in your presence; you are the only man who has not tried to imprison me. I find freedom in being with you and I—I do—I mean I *have* found some men utterly repulsive, those who have taken too many liberties—you—you know." She was becoming nervous and flustered, and she didn't understand why.

"Yes, I know the very sort you describe," Walter

said with a distant gleam in his dark-blue eyes. "If we are to be married, dear Dora, I would be gentle to your slightest denial of my—" He sighed. "I realize that what I say next will not be very proper at this time . . . but I must be—ah—bold for your sake."

"What is it, Walter? Tell me," Pandora asked softly, urging him gently.

"I say *if* we are to be wed, I shall not press my . . . ardor upon you on our wedding night. Though do not be mistaken, Dora; I do want you and need you. But I know—a man can tell these things—that something has happened, something terribly shaking to you in your past—and not too very long ago. It put fear into your heart. Someone has not been gentle with you. Am I correct?"

Indeed a horrible scene flashed before her eyes as Walter spoke, and she stared back, trying to visualize it fully. She nodded quickly in answer to his question.

"It happened"—she gulped with remembered fright—"on the island, yes, where I lived. I can see a man on the beach . . . such an ugly man . . . he was tearing at my clothes . . . and . . . there was someone else—"

Walter snapped his fingers, damning his stupidity at the same time. "Dora, I beg of you, dear, dear, try not to think of it. This will only bring more fear between us—please, don't try so hard to remember the terrible past!"

"Terrible—yes!" Pandora cried out, echoing him. "How— How did *you* know?" She stared past him wildly.

Walter shook her, until, finally, Pandora snapped

out of her horrible fixation with the past. Trembling with fear, she fell into Walter's arms and he stroked her lovely hair in a fatherly fashion. He cooed into her ear and rocked her gently to and fro.

"Think only of the bright future, my pretty doll, my Dora. Oh, how I adore your beauty and grace . . . and more," he added cryptically. "That is all you must think of—for now."

Choking back tears, Pandora nodded fiercely against the rough texture of his coat sleeve. She gazed up at him with reddened eyes and tear-stained cheeks; Walter flinched at her marred beauty.

"Take care of me, Walter! Hold me, closer!"

He chuckled. "I can't hold you any closer than I am already, my dear Dora."

As he said this, Walter, mesmerized, was studying a landscape painting of Thomas Hill. "Lovely," he murmured; Pandora thought he meant her.

It felt so good when someone really cared, someone nice like Walter. It was as if one had received a gift of gold, she told herself, contentment drying her tears. Everything was going to be just fine. With Walter beside her to walk through life's blackest shadows, she had nothing to fear. No, not even the past. The future seemed secure. . . .

"Yes," she said aloud to Walter and then she sighed, glad her decision was made.

But later, after she had seen Walter to the door, Pandora felt a trembling someplace deep inside herself.

She reviewed in her mind the last half-hour. Was she really glad? What did that word mean? It had the same amount of letters as "love." But she had only been *glad* that she finally had committed herself . . . to something. Wasn't love commitment, too? Surrender?

Pandora went upstairs to dwell on that word. Was she only being blind to all that went on around her?

"That's not so!" she chided her conscience. "My eyes aren't shut!"

But even with them open wide did she really see Walter as he was? She wanted to be with him, true. It warmed her when he laughed, delighted her when they talked and teased each other. He had a magnetic smile, handsome features, and his dark-blue eyes sparkled over her . . . adoringly? Was that the word? "You are most novel, Dora, a—" He had paused. "—A lovely female, through and through, without the usual affectation present in so many women nowadays!"

Why wasn't she interested in him in other ways then . . . like physically? Of course, theirs was no love match. . . . Was he a man without passion? Oh, Walter had a passion for life. But then his body had gone absolutely taut the other day when she had brushed his lips with a feathery kiss. Could it be . . . could Walter Riddock be a . . . virgin? A man who has never had a woman? Pandora blushed at where her musings were taking her.

Unbidden, her thoughts drifted to Rogan Thorn. With him, it was as if . . . she were on fire! She had felt a part of him, held in a hot spell as intense as a tropical storm; their short time together had been a tempest of feelings and emotions.

Tears brimmed in Pandora's glacial-blue eyes. She had been afraid of the mockery in that pair of wave-green eyes; and even more, afraid of the power he possessed to make her feel those wild, sweet emotions. Her cheeks were on fire even now thinking of him and what he could . . . do to her. Oh, how she longed to rake her nails across his smirking, self-confident features.

What did it matter what Rogan Thorn wanted of her? What possible thing could he further do to hurt her? Nothing, nothing.

Her cheeks were suddenly, absurdly wet.

"I don't like to think of anything hurting you, Dora," Walter had said the morning before as they had strolled Sacramento Street. But he had laughed then and given the hair hanging down her back another jerk, pulled on her black bandeau, playfully, like a brother would.

They frequently lunched at the Palace together, dined at exclusive restaurants, and explored the curio shops during the afternoons. Sometimes, after he had spent his mornings at his office, they would cross on the paddle-wheeled ferryboat to the newly fashionable San Rafael. Always his manner and speech bespoke a Harvard man. At least, that's what Sarah had said, for Pandora did not know a Harvard man from a rugged sailor. But she was learning . . . fast. To become one of the elite?

Floating between sleep and wakefulness later that night, Pandora punched her pillow and after another restless toss she found herself staring into the dark above her bed.

No, Rogan Thorn could not get to her and hurt her with the sensual power he exerted over her! She ran her hands nervously over the folds of her nightgown.

With Walter she would at least be safe. What more could she want?

What . . . ?

Though Sarah had warned her not to go there alone, under any circumstances, Pandora strolled defiantly through the few blocks of narrow, twisting streets that comprised Chinatown. It was always crowded there at any time of day or night. This Saturday her spirits rose and she had fun just window-shopping along Grant Avenue. Finally, becoming a little hungry, she bought some food from the sidewalk stands, testing dried shark fins—and grimacing—then delighting in tiny fried shrimps with water chestnuts and washing them down with tea. She looked at the penny puzzles, games, and tricks; at the kites that tore in a day (so Sarah had informed her), and the bright paper lanterns: There were also paper flowers that uncurled from tight nubs to bloom magically when floated in a saucer of water—she understood from what the Chinaman was telling her—but she purchased none of these. She was just about to go home, but stopped, fascinated by delicate strips of painted glass, strung on a black silk-tasseled cord, that jingled when there was the slightest stir of air.

She was suddenly aware that a man had been staring at her—actually he hadn't taken his eyes off her—from across the street; he had been watching her for several minutes now, come to think of it. But she hadn't allowed herself to realize this—Sarah had preached often that even if a man stared you were supposed to act normally and as if he were not looking your way.

He was not alone, Pandora realized, as she noticed in her peripheral vision a flash of colorful skirts beside the man. The couple was crossing the street now, coming toward her. A strange expression crossed the man's face, but it went unnoticed by Pandora for when she turned to see them, his face altered to one of sardonic amusement, just for her benefit, Pandora thought.

"Dora, *darling*, my, my, unchaperoned? Don't you know what could hap—"

Rogan Thorn cut her off. "Good day, Dora . . ."

Pandora finally met his gaze and it was as if an electric charge had passed from his green eyes to her blue ones. He almost reached out to touch her arm, but quickly caught himself and pressed his hand along his thigh. She was wise enough to know he would do much more than that, and in broad daylight, if he hadn't had someone along with him. Due to his position slightly behind her, Sheila did not see the bold gaze with which he raked Pandora from neck to toe. Finally, when he was staring her straight in the eyes, Pandora stepped back and smiled brightly.

"And good day . . . to you both."

With that she turned on her heel and left them both staring after her, Sheila blinking quickly and affectedly, Rogan falling afoul with his emotions.

"My, she *is* the rude and curt one, isn't she!" Sheila pursed her lips, lifted her blond eyebrows, and gazed up at Rogan.

Then she frowned. "Why so quiet of a sudden, darling?"

"A dark cloud has passed overhead. . . ."

"Wh*aaat?*" Sheila blinked fast, genuinely this time.

"Come, I'll take you home," he said crossly. "It's going to rain."

"B-But, Rogan . . . there's not a *damned* cloud in the sky!"

Sheila hurried after him as he left her behind with his long strides.

Chapter Seventeen

Although it rained all week in San Francisco, nothing dampened the topic of gossip current in the city—the engagement between Walter Riddock and the mysterious girl from nowhere, the girl with the lion's mane of hair, whose shape combined curvaceousness with slimness, whose diamond-blue eyes seemed to dare the sea to compete with their loveliness.

Even in gay San Francisco the gentlemen with good manners talked in whispers of this love match. The gossip was not an oddity on this occasion; nor was it frowned upon too much, for this was the turn of the century, age of high-spirited romance.

Behind his office door, settled back in his black-leather and oak swivel chair, Rogan sat, dark and brooding. Day by day he had fought back the truth that pressed itself upon him ruthlessly: he wanted Dora. Everything pointed that way. *She* lingered in his thoughts. *His* desire. But just *how* did he want her? And how was he going to realize his desire? Was he going to step up to her and say: "I know you will soon be Mrs. Riddock, but won't you come and be my mistress? What do you say?"

My God, that was laughable! Furthermore, he didn't even know if he could *ever* perform in bed again. To want her and not be able to do something about it—well, that was the problem. His dry chuckle broke the torment of his thoughts. Maybe he was just bored. Then again . . . he had no intention of giving up so easily, even if she was to become Riddock's blushing bride.

If! That was a bigger laugh. She was as good as in Riddock's bridal suite already. He didn't want to dwell further on *that*. . . . He could always put thorns in Riddock's bed. He chuckled wryly—*one* Thorn.

He could always whisk her away the night before the wedding took place, use force— No, that was rotten and he did not relish the idea of rape. Hah! He didn't even know if he *could rape*. . . .

That came under the heading of making love, although it was a bit more crude . . . downright perverted! Damn it, anyway. He shrugged, cursing himself before returning to his work.

Before long Rogan found himself staring across to the window. Damned rain anyway . . . where was the sun? Maybe that morning Wizan had been correct in saying that his boss had a fever; and Bo Gary had added his own opinion. "You look a bit thin and, ah, feverish. Things are not going very good? You should let the doc have a look at you and feel your head to see if you've really got a fever, huh?"

Rogan snapped a pencil in two. Indeed, a fever was just what he had . . . in the butt! A pain there, too, if everyone . . . Ah, hell, forget it. . . .

A heavy frown crept into Rogan's face when a knock sounded at his office door. The knock was familiar, but he couldn't place it exactly. He rubbed his aching head and called:

"Enter."

He did not even glance up when Cara breezed into the room, bringing a storm cloud with her. But he could tell by her strong, exotic perfume who had just entered. A newspaper was slapped onto his desk.

"Look at this!" Cara shouted, pointing. "Here."

"I know, I know," Rogan snarled curtly and shoved the section rudely aside, resuming his reading of a business contract.

"Well," Cara said with a smirk, "have you gotten an invitation, or not?"

"Yes."

"Are you going?" she hissed testily.

Rogan stressed his next words with coldness. "What's the matter, Cara, didn't you rate an invite? Or are you— Never mind. I've got work to do."

"Tell me . . ." Cara almost choked out.

He remained indifferent to her unusual mood. "No—I am not! And you tell me," he ended sarcastically.

"No. I haven't been invited, and what do I care about the stupid old wedding, anyway!" Cara turned to hide her face from him.

Rogan snorted. "My exact thoughts, Cara." His green, marble-hard eyes remained expressionless. He was barely aware of Cara's presence and her sunken mood.

Rogan was oblivious to all the talk; he had shut out the whole bay town that was buzzing with news of the upcoming marriage.

Cara went to stand by the window, her back to him.

"I wasn't even invited," she said softly, inaudibly, "not to my own—" Her words trailed off sadly.

It will be a farce, Rogan continued on his mind's dark path. The young woman, Dora, doesn't even know her own mind. Ha! Walter had fallen for his own lovely thief! Rogan looked out the window, past Cara's hanging head, to the waterfront where the gulls dipped and soared like avenging white spirits. He opened a drawer of his desk with a key, fingered the reticule—Dora's—and then slammed the drawer shut with a bang.

A cynical twist played about his taut lips as he rose from his chair and briskly left his office; a pair of brown eyes turned and followed his broad, stiffly held back.

Broughams and landaus and coupés had been rolling up to the curb steadily. The clock on the landing inside the large white frame house struck five times. Indulging in cigars and brandy, the men waited in the living room with the groom until it was time for the bride to descend the stairs.

In the light from the flaring, hissing gas jets, Riddock's face appeared flushed between the wings of his tall collar. Sarah Wolfington, Walter's only living relative, clucked about him like a mother hen.

It was being bandied about that Widow Wolfington was footing the bill for the entire wedding. But she, too, was reaping the rewards of having had the expensively engraved invitations made up and had not overlooked a single prominent party in the city or the surrounding country: She had invited the elite of Rincon Hill, South Park, Nob Hill, Van Ness

Avenue, and so forth. Sarah had been determined to carry off this wedding in the most approved fashion and had even gone to such lengths as calling in her seamstress to create a lovely satin wedding dress for Dora.

Riddock had reason to fume, though, and Sarah's lips, too, were set in a tight line of grimness—when no one was looking. It had recently been announced in the newspaper that Rogan Thorn was the new Pacific shipping tycoon. Since he had arrived, fawning women had trailed Rogan, and the pretty debutantes rarely left him alone for a moment. He was virtually surrounded by women showing off their newest Paris gowns and high pompadours entwined with diamond- and pearl-decorated ribbons of silk.

The blazing chandelier in the main parlor gleamed down on the mouthwatering wedding supper that had been set up on long tables and was being kept warm by braziers: scalloped oysters, broiled quail, honey-glazed hams, stuffed potatoes, bottles of iced champagne, and a hundred other varieties of food and drink would be consumed, while the music and dancing continued until dawn.

The women "oohed" and "ahed" over the four-foot cake decorated with white sugar bells and doves, while the men gathered below the stairs, as was natural, and began to whisper to one another. What was keeping the bride? they whispered, as the women, too, began to wonder.

The minister from Trinity Church was already there, conversing softly with Sarah Wolfington. She explained to him that the bride-to-be was having a bad time with a hem that had come down and the seamstress was upstairs with her now.

Minister Peck nodded understandingly and excused himself to go and speak to an old friend, one of his parishioners.

Sarah saw the minister heading toward Rogan Thorn. She stuck her fine chin in the air haughtily, but it came down instantly when she overheard the two women gossiping behind her.

"My God, he can last all night!" Diane Ashe was saying, directing her gaze to Rogan Thorn.

Sheila Meade snorted. "Is that *right?* Well, that *must* have been a few years ago, before you were married to Todd. Let me *tell* you the latest. . . ."

Sarah moved hastily away, so as not to hear the rest of it.

Through the open doors, Walter swung his gaze to Rogan; he wondered why the man was looking so self-satisfied. Perhaps Rogan enjoyed flaunting the fact that his shipping empire had pulled far ahead of Walter's. Just then a young man, blond and long-faced, sauntered up to Walter and gave him a big, juicy hug. Diane and Sheila turned their attention to the two men. Sheila nudged her friend.

"The vows haven't even been said and already Eddie Pratt, the second, is congratulating Walter. What do you think about that, Diane?"

"Oh, I have seen *them* together recently—at a restaurant, not to mention other places—uhmm— less respectable!" She hissed low. "Lord, how many of these intimate *friends* do you suppose Walter has hidden?'' She giggled behind her hand.

"Poor Dora—" She shrugged.

"I don't even *know* her. Who does? She won't let anyone get close enough to her—but the Black Widow."

"*I* tried talking to her over tea at Sarah's just the other day, but *she* acts like she's better than *us*. Pretty haughty for a lost soul, if you ask me. Guess Sarah's rubbing off on her."

"Oh, and I hear as long as Dora can't remember her last name, Sarah's using *her* maiden name on the marriage certificate." Diane giggled. "The rate Walter's going now, he won't be able to see straight to sign the thing!"

"Where's the bride?" Everyone was buzzing now.

"Walter is getting drunk." They laughed.

"Look! She's coming down!"

Alexander Moor did a double take, whistling under his breath. Though she looked emotionless, she was still exquisite, a jewel of a bride. "My God, she's gorgeous! No wonder—" Sandy left off, thinking of the scandal it would cause if Rogan's name were linked with the bride's here and now.

Bo Gary glanced around the room. He had been keeping to himself and not mingling with the guests. But he stood stock-still as he watched the bride's descent.

All eyes lifted as the wedding song began. Tall and slim and cool, the bride seemed to float down the stairs, her white train a heavy drag of silk on the red carpet. Her head was high and in her long, slim fingers she carried a small white Bible. Its dangling purple ribbon markers made a startling contrast against the white satin of her dress. Her flushed cheeks, like two feverish spots, showed through the flowing lace veil that was crowned with pink silk roses interwoven with ribbons of a pale-green silk.

Rogan shared his thoughts with no one. To him she looked like a stiff mannequin, emotionless and cold. His eyes met hers in the mirror and this contact seemed to bring them closer. He noticed her eyes were shadow-smudged and blank. When the minister went to take his place on the large platform, Rogan moved closer.

Heart hammering in her breast, Pandora froze at the sight of Rogan; from beneath the shadow of her veil she studied him. All emotion seemed to have been driven from Rogan Thorn and a faint air of dissipation clung to his manliness; she could sense this even from where she stood. His gaze held a reckless glitter that hadn't been there before. He was thinner, which added, it seemed, even more inches to his height. She suppressed a gasp of shock. His lips definitely displayed a cynical twist.

"A beautiful mannequin," Rogan said under his breath, "cold, heartless, and so sad." This was all mad, he thought.

Shivers rippled along Pandora's spine just then, while Rogan continued to gaze at her measuringly. Even through the veil she could see there were shades of deep green moving in his eyes like forest shadows; she had never noticed them before. She felt as if she stood right beside him, instead of twenty feet away.

The music of the solo floated to Pandora, and

Walter suddenly appeared next to the minister, as did Sarah. Pandora experienced mixed emotions and suddenly felt very alone. All she knew was that she wanted to be married and to raise a family so she wouldn't be so alone. Love would come later, she prayed.

"Woman." Rogan breathed the word like a sigh. He quit staring and moved to the fringe of the crowd. His head lifted and he caught himself again. If he didn't stop, he would lose his heart—to a married woman.

Bo Gary glanced about quickly and then slipped unnoticed between the guests whose eyes were glued to the ceremony taking place. Since it was after five o'clock the gas lamps in the pink globes on the tables had been lighted. Bo headed toward one of them, moving furtively.

As the song reached a crescendo, so did Pandora's heart when her gaze found Rogan's again. But she was thoroughly shocked by the wave of sexual desire that rippled through her, nearly making her faint. How could this be—today?

Regrets always come too late, kept drumming in her brain. Suddenly her whole world was tilting upside down. The sprays of flowers appeared ugly to her and brought a sickening, unnatural smell to her nostrils. Beside her, Walter reeked of brandy and stale tobacco, and his face was unnaturally flushed. She was weary, conscious of the day's already having been extraordinarily long.

The minister had been droning on, and now he came to the part:

". . . Let them speak now or forever hold their peace."

There was a short pause and then the nerve-shattering crash of a lamp. First pandemonium broke out with screams and shouts of alarm.

"Fire! Fire!"

The next moment panic.

Chapter Eighteen

While the fire engines stormed along the streets to Summit House, Pandora found herself in a daze, being pulled along by a young man, a total stranger.

The other men had rushed to and fro in search of water, but this young man had stepped gallantly right up to the platform to take her away from the danger.

Pandora had seen the bright flare of yellow-red flames licking at the living room, its curtains already having been consumed when panic had set in. Despite her height, she had almost been trampled, but the young stranger had kept her from falling, while some of the other women tripped on hems and tangled feet. She had seen Sheila Meade and Diane Todd sprawled full face on the floor, screaming.

The men, however, had thought only of being heroes and of putting out the fire and had not bothered to get the screaming women out. The blaze had spread rampantly by the time the young man had pushed and shoved Pandora to the front door; sounds of running feet, and cries of fear were all around them. Pandora could still see and hear the pandemonium: faces, contorted with fear, and shouts, all blurred together. Vaguely she could remember her own voice sobbing and gasping. But why had it been Rogan's name she called out for, and not Walter's?

Her train was proving a hindrance to speedy movement and she was trembling with a new fear as she allowed her young escort to lead her—dazed, numb, and strangely acquiescent—to the foot of the hill where a carriage, shrouded in thick fog, stood. When she tossed a quick look over her shoulder to Summit House, she couldn't see the flames in the windows anymore. It was then that she noticed she was dragging behind her a borrowed cloak. It was fur-edged and very expensive.

Before Pandora could ask where he was taking her, the carriage door slammed shut. He flicked his whip over the horses' ears and they were off.

"Are you all right?" he called back to her.

"Of—of course I am, but where are you taking me, *and why?*" she shouted back, pulling the cloak over her shivering shoulders.

"We'll be there soon," was all he said.

Pandora glowered, but said mostly to herself, "That's *not* what I asked you!"

"Did you say something?" he asked over his broad shoulder, driving the team toward the Embarcadero.

"Never mind!" As Pandora fell back against the seat, she realized she was on the verge of a fit of hysterical giggles. "This is insane!" She was being whisked away by a handsome young stranger, and she didn't mind a bit. She almost felt some relief!

Pandora darted another glance over her shoulder; however, she couldn't see anything but street lamps casting their blurred glow, and cobbles glistening with moisture.

"I just hope and pray that no one was hurt," she murmured, feeling quite silly wearing her wedding dress and speeding toward the Embarcadero. She smiled again, thinking she should not have taken that second glass of champagne to calm her bridal nerves.

She sat up straight as something dawned on her.

"Embarcadero!" She could smell the bay and the wharves.

But the young man didn't seem to have heard her. They came to Pacific Street and then clattered along the Embarcadero until the carriage careened onto the wharves at Battery and Front.

The man who stood there was only a blur as he came out of the fog and loomed at the head of the team. Pandora could only hear snatches of conversation as her driver conversed with the man afoot about the carriage and then came back for her.

Galvanized into action, Pandora slid across the seat and reached for the door. But strong hands caught her around the waist and dragged her back. She could smell the sea damp on him mingling with the after-shave at his throat. Though he wore a fine suit of clothes, he still had the look of a rugged young sailor. He wasn't hurting her, but still she feared his intent in bringing her down here.

"Let me go?" Her eyes begged this too.

"I won't hurt you, Miss Dora. I promise. Just come with me and I won't have to carry you."

Pandora blinked up at him. "You would force me?"

"Yup. Come on now."

"Please, why are we here?" she fired at him as he began to pull her along. "Why aren't *you* back there fighting the blaze? I don't know you. Who are you; please tell me?"

"Don't be scared, Miss Dora," he repeated. "I've only brought you down here because if the fire spreads, it's the only safe place. My name is Bo Gary and I work down here. If the fire reaches the wharves, I'll have to move the *Phantom* out. Fires have been known to spread all the way down here, you see."

Pandora shook her head, unable to make sense of his reckoning. How could the fire spread all the way to the wharves? she wondered.

Ahead, a schooner took shape, and she could hear the lap of the bay water against its oak hull. Suddenly a pair of green eyes sprang up in her mind's eye. They had been sardonic, right before the fire broke out, right before she and Walter had almost exchanged their vows.

Pandora tripped on the long train of her dress. She felt the gentleness of the hands at her elbow when the young man stopped for a moment just as they came up to the pierside berth. He bent, gathered up her satin train, and gave it to her free hand.

"What is the *Phantom*, may I ask—uhhmmm—Bo Gary?" The train was slipping from her hands as she studied his face.

"You'll have to hold this, Dora, otherwise you might trip and fall right into the water. That's cold water this time of night, and we might not find you if you fall in, 'cause the fog's awful thick," he said almost matter-of-factly.

"Is this the *Phantom*?" she asked as they stopped

before a dark schooner.

"Yup. This is her."

The *Phantom* was tied up at her pierside berth, her canvas furled, her deck undulating to the *lap-lap* of the water. They climbed the cleated portside gangplank and walked along the deck. Then Pandora tugged at his arm to halt his long stride. His boyish face rose only a notch above hers.

"How do you know my name, Bo Gary?"

He smiled sheepishly. "Everyone knows *your* name, Miss Dora, your first name that is. Yeah,"—he chuckled at the word—"you *are* still a miss. How do you feel about that? Happy? Or otherwise?" He tilted his head.

"I—I really don't know—yet. Let me tell you, this day has been a nightmare! That I *do* know for certain, Bo Gary. But who does this handsome schooner belong to? Certainly not to *you*. Heavens, you look too young to own a ship, even though it is not quite a windjammer."

Bo canted his head. "Have you been drinking something? Or does your voice always sound mumbly like that?" He didn't wait for an answer, but took her arm again to guide her into the cabin that lay aft.

Bo set out to light the lanterns, and soon their warm yellow glow drove the darkness from the spacious cabin in which she found herself. The bulk of a sea chest took shape, as did the brass-bound portholes. The room was mellow, mahogany paneled with polished brass winking everywhere.

Pandora could see the young man clearer now. His friendly blue eyes posed no harm, but smiled back at her. She found herself strangely unafraid of him, although she should be terrified being alone with a man she didn't know at all.

"You avoided my question, young man. Whose ship is this?" She could see the rippling strength of his muscles as he removed his tailored jacket and rolled up his shirt sleeves, looking more at home like this. He moved about, pulling out a bottle of brandy from a low cabinet. "Well?" she pressed.

"Ah, would you like some?" He waved the bottle in one hand, with the other he scratched beneath the shock of red hair on his forehead. "Now where are those glasses. Ah, they should be right here where the bottle was." He shook his head in a self-deprecating manner.

Pandora held up her hand. "Heavens, no. Nothing to drink, thank you!"

Bo seemed to be looking at her for the first time as he straightened after finding the crystal tumblers. But after her words he took out only the one for himself.

"You *are* tall," Bo commented, whistling under his breath.

"Just three inches short of six feet, to be exact," she proudly replied, wondering why he kept avoiding her question as to the owner of this ship.

"Wow!" Bo exclaimed, his red freckles beaming across a wide nose and ruddy cheeks.

Regally tall, slender, but endowed with soft curves, Bo found himself describing her. He wished his girl, Susie Loo, was here so she could meet Dora. But Susie was working tonight in Chinatown at the restaurant her father owned.

"My girl, Susie, would like you, Dora."

"Susie?"

"Yeah. My girl. Someday I'll introduce her to you."

"I would like that." Pandora looked aside, then back at him with a worried frown. "We really should go back to Summit House now to check if anyone has been hurt. Why, even now Walter could be dying—" She placed a hand over her breast, startled at the sudden wild look that had come across his sweet face. "Oh, did I say something wrong?" she wondered out loud, afraid that she had angered this gentle young man and that he wouldn't take her back.

"I hope the house has been burned to the ground, and with only Riddock in it. God forgive me," he muttered low.

"What was that?" Her eyes flew wide.

"Don't worry, Dora, we'll go back there"—he dropped the mask of anger—"in time."

Pandora frowned at Bo. "Why only me?" she asked.

Bo continued to pour himself a dollop of brandy, but he realized she had been staring at him for several minutes. He knew what she meant, and he had to think up a good enough answer to keep her from becoming too suspicious. He could not reveal to her that it was he himself who had started that fire. He hated Riddock with a passion. The man had tried to make him one of his "boys," even going so far as to intimately touch him. Bo had kept this to himself. If he had but said the word to Rogan, Walter could very well be six feet under by now, and Rogan facing a sentence for murder—at least assault. Bo himself had almost broken the bastard's nose; as it was, he had only bloodied him up a bit.

"I happen to care," was all Bo said.

"C-care?" she stammered, wondering what he meant.

"Yup. Someone else cares, too, but he doesn't know it yet."

"Bo, you are talking in riddles."

"Yup. I know. You'll know the secret I know someday."

Pandora shook her head. Then, "Tell me, Bo Gary, are you in love with Susie?" she inquired.

"You said it! She's a doll, and we're going to be married just as soon as I face her father." He looked sad for a moment. "You see, he's Chinese, and well, their customs are pretty different."

Pandora could see that, but not why this Bo Gary, a total stranger to her, should care what happened to her. She was about to question him on it further when the paneled door swung open.

A glint of satin lining showed beneath a debonair cape swinging from a man's wide shoulders. A scowl darkened his countenance until *his* eyes came to rest on *her* eyes which looked from Bo Gary to him.

"Rogan Thorn," Pandora breathed. "Oh!" she gasped, her cheeks paling with fury. "Now I know. This is *your* ship!" She stared accusingly at Rogan Thorn, but disquieting feelings washed over her. Her eyes moved slowly from Rogan to the burly man standing at Rogan's side. Rogan noticed her glance and he clapped a hand to the man's broad shoulders pulling him forward as he began to introduce him.

"This is Jeremy Cross, the captain of my ship, *Baghdad*. Jeremy, this is Dora—just Dora."

Baghdad. Pandora rolled the name over in her mind, trying to remember where she had heard that. But she told herself not to delve into the past. It was so important for her not to remember just now. She must try to live in the present.

Recognition flared in Jeremy's eyes, but he couldn't quite recall where he had seen this lovely young woman before. The time had not been long ago, but the place evaded him. Nonetheless, his intelligent eyes saw far more than the others who were present.

"Hello, Captain," Pandora answered softly, after he had greeted her warmly. Suddenly she was tearful, without reason, and in the next second she felt that she must explain her presence here, and set forth to do so in short sentences that snagged in her dry throat.

"I—I was to be married today. . . . I wanted to be married today. I don't know why . . . I thought I cared for Walter." She hung her head. "I wanted a family—to call my own. But at the . . . last minute . . . Oh! I just don't know!" She covered her face with her hands. She was so embarrassed now.

His voice came across deep and warm as Jeremy Cross spoke. "Maybe God didn't mean for you to marry Walter Riddock, miss. Could be that you were meant for someone else."

Here her head jerked up suddenly. "God would not do such a thing as to send a catastrophe upon a wedding party!" She was aghast that he, a captain, who had doubtless performed many marriages aboard ship, would even think this.

Jeremy tilted his big head. "God works in

204

mysterious ways, with people, or without, Miss—ah—Dora." He turned to Rogan and laid a hand on his arm. "I'd like a word with you, Rogan. Could we step out to the deck for a minute? Excuse us, miss."

Confusion had risen in Pandora's face, and now she sought Bo's boyish countenance, and asked, "Could I have that drink now, Bo Gary? Suddenly I feel in need of something strong to warm me. Yes, make it strong!"

Bo chuckled. "By the way you look, Dora, I don't think you need much warming up. But I'll get it for you."

Pandora took the glass handed to her and swallowed a healthy gulp of the stuff. Her eyes widened as she gasped and choked, and Bo stepped forward to pat her gently on the back.

She peered up at him with watery eyes. "Thank you." She handed the half-empty glass back to him. "I needed that."

"Which one?" Bo asked, but the reply was never heard as the men stepped back into the cabin.

Immediately Rogan covered the short space between them and put a hand on Pandora's shoulder. Her eyes lifted slowly, and what she saw in his caused her much alarm.

"As you probably know," Rogan began, "I have just come from the fire at Summit House. It did not burn clear through to all the rooms, but . . . some of the people didn't survive. Some were burned pretty badly before the firemen could extinguish the blaze . . . and some, well . . . some didn't make it at all."

Pandora saw his warm gaze rake over her face

consolingly, and a knot of fear settled in the depths of her belly.

"Tell me! Is—is *he* dead?"

"Ah, I'm afraid so," Rogan answered with a softness that was barely heard in the cabin. Then, "I'm sorry, Dora." He tossed a glance over his shoulder to Jeremy Cross and nodded.

Rogan cleared his throat. "I want us to be . . ." he paused, overcome by something close to shyness ". . . to be married."

"What?"

Even though she was shocked to the core by his words, Pandora felt a sort of helplessness. The three men surrounded her, Rogan's look was so forceful and compelling, the set of his strong chin and firm jaw so determined. What could she do? Rogan's mastery of her was almost total this time, and in some strange and frightening way she even desired that to be so. He was possessing her—just like that!

Rogan lifted her chin, and she was vitally aware of his magnetism. His charisma was weaving a spell about her, a web from which she couldn't escape. She nodded. She was trapped; these men afforded her, it seemed, no chance of escape.

This is a fantasy! her mind screamed. But her heart said this is fine and good.

Bo Gary just smiled craftily, his Irish blue eyes lighting up. Tearfully, jerkily, and as if hypnotized, Pandora rose and found herself wrapped in Rogan's willing arm, his fingers going dangerously beneath the tender curve of her breast.

Every nerve in Pandora quivered at his touch; it was imbued with sheer strength.

Bo sighed, Jeremy stepped forward with Bible in hand, and Pandora stared down at the black-leather book of God's word with some awe. Her cheeks flamed as she thought of what would come later.

Rogan was pulling her closer, as if into him, his touch filling her with irresistible pleasure. She had yielded. She could not back down now.

The thing was done.

Chapter Nineteen

Pandora was still in a daze when she removed her wedding dress and held it against her trembling body. Her wide eyes stared at the huge brass bed, the posts of which gleamed dully beneath the gaslights. Her heartbeat was abnormal; she quivered with remembrance.

She recalled that moment in the rented carriage on their way to the mansion, when Rogan's hand had groped for hers in the dark, while his cheek had touched hers just before his warm kiss had moved on her lips and become all-demanding. When she hadn't responded, the inscrutable mask of his face had lifted from hers and sarcasm had edged his tone along with possessiveness.

"Surrender. You're my wife now."

Her temper had flared. "I must have been insane—or quite possibly drunk to have let you have your way and marry me!" She shook, though more with temper than anything else.

"Well, seeing as you are so reluctant to be my willing bride, we'll just have to do something to tear away that icy veneer and temper, won't we?"

His words had not ended questioningly, however,

but emphatically. Strangely, he had let her be, then.

Still the big bed seemed to swim before her weary vision as she tried shutting out the scene which was soon to be enacted there. What a mess she had gotten herself into. She hung her head dispiritedly. Yet, she had to admit that she had no one to blame but herself. She had given in to Rogan's sheer magnetism. Besides, she had gone completely empty inside upon hearing of Walter's untimely death, and somehow that void must be filled.

But must it be Rogan Thorn who filled that emptiness?

Dora Thorn. She tried the name on her lips, and it didn't sound right at all. Mrs. Dora Thorn. No better. At least she had a last name now. Or did she, really? Was this all a dream?

Her color paled as she heard his long and easy strides coming along the hall to the bedroom. Before he entered, Pandora was starkly reminded that she had nothing on but her chemise; here at Thorn Mansion she had no other clothes but her wedding dress. Everything had been left at Sarah's, to have been picked up in the morning and brought to Summit House.

She would sleep in her chemise; that was all there was to it!

With studied motions, Pandora was toying with the pink ribbon running through the eyelets of her button-down chemise when the door was swept wide. He closed it behind him, and Pandora was silent as he stood there, his chestnut hair falling in a careless wave over half his brow, his body clad in nothing but a black-and-red dressing robe.

Pandora swallowed hard. Was that a look of triumph she detected on his ruggedly handsome face—or the arrogance of possession? She decided she saw both. But he did not possess her totally; no, not yet.

His crystal eyes kindled to green fire as they raked over her body in leisurely regard of her woman's form. Slightly breathless and with a twinge of uneasiness she stared back at him but could not find the first proper words to greet her new husband. She smiled a little uncertainly, not knowing exactly what she should do next. It was Rogan who broke the silence.

"I have brought you something to wear to bed," he said softly, his eyes never leaving her parted lips as he walked over to her.

He handed her a diaphanous white nightgown, bridal pure and looking as if it had never been worn before. But Pandora only held the nightgown staring down at it as if dirt instead of purity clung to its fine silken threads.

"Don't you find it to your liking, *Mrs. Thorn?*"

Pandora almost flinched at that last part.

"How did you get . . . the nightgown on such short notice?" she inquired, trying not to think of the woman for whom it might have been purchased.

"I had it." He began to pluck at the ribbons and tiny buttons on her chemise, all the while studying the depths of her blue eyes. "But you won't be needing it for a while," he ended in a low growl.

Rogan moved closer. The nightgown slipped from her shaking fingers to the floor. She hardly noticed that, but dared to peer up at Rogan. Not too far up, for he was only half a head taller.

So close were his lips to hers now, close enough that she could hear the deep breathing through his mouth and nostrils.

So hot was his body moving closer, ever closer.

As if by magic her chemise was floating to the floor to join the other garment. Sparking eyes swept down over her nude torso, went further, and then rose to stop at her petticoat's band; this half slip was the only thing that kept him from seeing and admiring the rest of her long slim beauty.

"Do you want to remove it, or shall I?"

But both his hands had already slid down to her cotton-silk clad hips. They moved in practiced movements, slowly, his long fingers splayed, the tips of them pressing gently into her buttocks.

"Please, Rogan . . ." She couldn't go on with him so close to her.

"Please what?"

"I—I am very tired. Very. Couldn't we wait until tomor—"

"I want you . . . tonight," he broke in.

Her eyes blazed. "It is morning!"

"Morning. Night,"—he shrugged—"whatever. It won't wait. I am fully aroused now just looking at you." He moved to cup one of her firm young breasts. "And soon so will you be, my dear."

With his fingers moving up over one of her nipples, Pandora's quivering frame seemed to catch fire and fill with flames that licked up and down her torso. A grinding ache that was not unpleasant went to her belly and stayed there, sending darts of hot desire between her tender thighs. She had never felt so completely detached from reality, so hot, so trembly, or so very frightened, before. She had never known anyone like Rogan Thorn. He was a man apart. Lusty scenes of love-making flitted through her mind, scenes he was deliberately creating for her by playing more and more with her scorched flesh.

"Rogan," she began with a gasp, "we hardly know each other—" She gripped his wrist to keep his fingers from her tormented nipple.

"And yet we are man and wife," he broke in. "I mean to consummate this marriage, as you shall soon see."

"What will one night matter?" she argued softly. "We are both tired, so what pleasure can be had tonight?"

"Speak for yourself, Mrs. Thorn. I assure you it won't take long. You may sleep till noon then, or longer if you wish, and the next night—tomorrow's —will be for both our pleasures combined."

His growing manhood thrust outward against his robe as it lengthened into readiness and he lost no more time now as he picked her up and carried her slowly to the brass bed. It should have been romantic; instead its dully shining bars looked to Pandora like a gilded prison as he set her down, gently enough, like a loving spouse. She immediately tossed her head about for an avenue of escape. His words were soft and gentle, as he followed her down.

"I know what you are, love, and the end of this, your virginity, will come fast and painlessly. I promise, sweetheart."

"How—how did you know?"

"That you are virgin?"

"Y-Yes."

"Ahhh, let's put an end to the discussion, shall we, while you allow your ardent husband to find out for certain himself?"

Shirking an answer, Pandora tried to roll away from him, but his hard body came up against her side at once, before the roll was completed. She felt his hot mouth descending on hers, at first tender and then teaching her what a man's fierce and possessive kiss was like. Pandora moaned as his well-experienced lips began to steal the reluctance from hers. Beneath his caressing and teasing fingertips, her nipples rose harder than before. Her blood ran hot, though her mind harbored thoughts of a terrible pain to come between her thighs, when he thrust into her honey-warm tenderness.

He took a moment's breather to remove the pins from her hair and that glorious mass spread out on the pillow like a splash of sunshine. Looking at her like this, Rogan groaned from deep within. He fell to kissing her again, her lips, going deeper and ever deeper, plundering with his tongue until her lips felt savaged and bruised.

"You . . . are hurting me, Rogan." She moaned into his lips and plunging tongue.

He lifted his head and his eyes glowed with a fervor that shook her; their emerald greenness was reflected by the one low gaslight above the bed.

"Uhmmm, but this is love's kiss, Dora." As if that accounted for the bruising pain. He wouldn't realize until much later how very hot and hasty and selfish he had been.

Before she could find a muffled rejoinder, Rogan

pressed her into the bed, again with that hot urgency. Fear instilled in her now, with every ounce of strength she could muster in weariness, Pandora struggled as if her very life counted on it, twisting and wrenching away from him.

"Let me go, Rogan. You are not being . . . very nice," she pleaded over her shoulder.

Pandora gasped in the next second as, with his fingers buried in the stuff of her petticoat, he yanked it down over her buttocks. Her position of intended flight was such that it brought her rosy butt high in the air, her petticoat tangled about her knees. Rogan stared hard and silently at the delicious nudity of her backside.

Smiling to himself wickedly, Rogan wasted no time satisfying the urge that came to him and whacked her soundly on the roundest part of her buttocks.

"Oh!" she yelped.

"A love tap," he said with a deep chuckle. A pinch followed and Pandora turned to face him with another yelp and a look of such reproachfulness that he flinched.

"I'm sorry; I forgot myself," he lied, for her look did not stop him from what he had in mind next.

He flipped her unceremoniously onto her back and straddled her with his legs wide apart. As he smiled triumphantly his robe parted.

"Oh, my! Oh!" Pandora cried as she caught her first sight of his inflamed desire. "Oh," she repeated, more softly this time. She shut her eyes against the thick part of him that now throbbed between them, hot and hard and insistent.

When he came down with a leg hooked behind hers, Pandora found her own long legs had become entangled tautly in the bedclothes, imprisoning her thighs in a position dangerously open to a thrust should it come; and that it would she was beginning to see as inevitable.

Her eyes flew open wider because she was shocked at her moistness.

"Dora, Dora, your mind struggles, love, darling, but your body seeps the fluid of desire. Give in to me, my wife. Meet me, dearest." He groaned the words, sliding two fingers over the warmed honey.

"No!" she gasped, turning her face aside.

"Please, for God's love, Dora. Have me now!" A sob caught deep in his throat.

He fumbled with his robe, then turned red with anger when it caught at his shoulder.

"Damn, help me off with this!"

The heaviness in his loins was becoming unbearable. Soon . . .

"No, Dora, stay. Damn, I can't keep you here and do this—"

He thrust forward, but the robe fell as a barrier between them.

Pandora had cried as he did this. "No, no, Rogan, no! Stop! Give me more time!"

"Hell with more time!"

Thinking he was about to enter, she stiffened.

Indeed he was trying, so hard. "Damn it then!" He cursed the robe and let it be. He gritted his teeth, flipping the cursed robe up over his back. He looked like a warlord going into battle half-naked, with his sword out and ready.

"Arrgggh!" he cried in high-pitched torment.

As soon as he moved again the robe's hem slipped back down. Probing against her struggles, he was about to fill her with a plunge finally, when he gave a groan of pure frustration.

"Ahhh, damn! Oh, damn, damn, *damn!*"

Rolling over, Rogan clutched himself as if in pain. *"Ahhh*, ahhh . . ."

He shuddered once, twice, bringing his man's heaviness to an abrupt end.

His brows drew together ominously.

His passion stilled.

Pandora wondered innocently if she had done something in her struggles to hurt him in a bad place. It seemed so to her—the way he was clutching himself.

"Rogan!" she shouted, afraid; then gently, "Rogan . . . ?" She placed a hand tentatively near his back.

He shrugged off the gentle brush of her hand.

"Away, get away from me, bitch!" His words pitched low at the last.

"Oh! What do you mean?"

"You . . . you took too long . . . resisting. It would have been so good. Why?" He groaned out the word. "Am I a man cursed?"

"What?"

"God, you're naïve! I *said*—" Frustration grinding his teeth, he began to blame her. "You put me off too long with your damned icy barricade. I'd have to have a flaming dragon cock to get through to you!"

"Hmm?" Cryptically spoken, she thought. A

puzzled frown rode between her dainty gold brows. She snatched up her petticoat and peered down his long, curved back.

"Why do you speak in riddles, Rogan?"

"Why do you speak in riddles, Rogan?" he mimicked in a mocking tone.

"Don't mock me. Just tell me what is going on?" she asked imperiously.

"You are a woman; how would you know of which I speak?"

"Then don't talk your horny tavern words when you're with me!"

"With!" He almost screamed. "With! You're so far removed from this bed you might as well be in the cellar. Yes, Miss High-and-mighty, let me tell you this then, Dora Good, you're lucky to be safe from me this time," he said in a sardonic tone, "but let me promise you—"

"Oh, stop it! You make no sense at all!"

Furiously he whirled up like a robed dervish from the bed and gripped her hurtfully by the shoulders bending over her. Biting into her flesh, uncaring that she winced, his brows came together in a scowling black band. He seemed to take pleasure from his actions.

"What *are* you hiding from me . . . just what?" he snapped into her face, making her cower and wince from his digging fingers. "Who are you, anyway? *Really?*" he rapped out.

"Wh—What do you *mean?*"

"Maybe"—his eyes narrowed—"you're a scarlet woman, for all I know about you. Maybe a

217

murderess? Would you like me to *pay* you, Mrs. Thorn, is that it? With more jewelry, huh?"

"You *are* mean! I told you—"

"Forget it!" He made a disgusted face, and shoved her away.

Pandora shivered even with the bedclothes swaddled protectively about her. Brusquely Rogan rose and stepped from the bed, seemingly concealing something with his robe tucked between his legs as he went directly to the door. There he turned back to her, glowering, his hands staying over his lower region.

The gaslight hissed eerily in the momentary silence, and she noticed that Rogan's face was red with some strange emotion.

He shook his head, almost sadly. "And I had wanted you in the most passionate way, too. Ever since I'd met you, you've been inside of me. I can't get you out!"

She sat up, tucking her endless legs beneath her derrière. "Rogan,"—softly—"why don't you tell me what hap—"

He cut her off sharply. "Thank you for that, *madam*, but for nothing, my frigid wife."

He grimaced at something she couldn't know of in her naïveté. Then he glowered across to her before he went out, slamming the heavy door hard, leaving her puzzled as she looked down at the stain on the bed in bafflement. Her head jerked back up and she stared at nothing in particular. Just stared.

Enlightenment dawned then as naïveté left her.

"Oh." Pandora clamped a hand over her mouth. "Oh, oh my." She muffled a giggle that bubbled to her throat. Then she let go until her tall frame shook with paroxysms of laughter.

"No wonder he was so angry . . . and embarrassed. Poor Rogan." She halted her laughter, and her glacial-blue eyes at once brooded.

"Rogan." She breathed the name, shakily touching her love-bruised lips.

Chapter Twenty

The smell of rain had hung heavy in the air before the heavens opened up and the deluge began. Outside, the church walls were already slick with it, and inside a man sat alone in the first pew kneeling prayerfully, his face illuminated by low-wavering candles; but his lips remained unmoving.

It was a driving rain that Rogan had ventured out into a few hours before dawn when he had ridden in silence to Trinity Church, leaving the rain-splashed carriage and horse outside to wait with the disgruntled coachman he had awakened rudely to bring him here. He could have driven himself, but after the large amount of brandy he had consumed, Rogan wasn't sure he could have seen his way.

After a long silence, Rogan's brain began to function with some sobriety, his lips to move.

"Dear God, I am a fool. I could not forget her! Why had I seen *her* in every lovely woman who walked along the street? At the theater; in my dreams; on a lacy valentine? Why her and not another?" He moaned low, in distress. "Oh, God, this hurts, whatever it is. Now I have taken her to wife and shamed myself before her! What ugly affliction is this that torments me at every woman's thighs?''

Rogan glanced up sharply when, following a roll of thunder, the cross was illuminated by a flash of jagged fingers of light that thrust in through the tall stained-glass windows. A play of mystical fantasy flickered at the altar and then silence.

Rogan stared with awe, and then found himself chuckling low. ''I guess I said the wrong thing, Lord. Not *every* woman . . . now.''

A tic ran from below his cheekbones to the edge of his unshaven jaw as he stood, stuffing his hands into his trouser pockets.

''Guess I finally received my answer, huh?'' He listened as the rain let up and thunder rolled in the distance.

He stood in silence for a time, as if awaiting an answer from the Almighty. When he spoke again, there was a whimsical quality to his handsome face. ''She's not just any woman, either, my wife, this Dora of mine. Nope, she's pretty damned special, I guess.''

Rogan shook his head, saying, ''I'm a big fool.'' He turned and walked back to the wide doors, then paused to look back to the front of the church. ''Oh, yes, I forgot, Lord, ah, forgive me for the bit about Riddock. She'll learn of it soon, anyway, by the morning paper, if not from some other source.'' He sighed deeply and ended his prayer, ''Just make me man enough again, Lord, to keep Dora. I'll make it up to her. I promise.''

Outside, Rogan turned back to the church doors. The last drops of rain misted his upturned face. ''Dora, she'll understand, I just know it.''

*   *   *

"Oh! Oh! How could he!" Pandora tossed aside the newspaper she had been digging her long nails into, even now scarcely able to believe what she had just read.

But with her own two eyes she had read it.

"Oh! I am going! I am not staying here another minute with that . . . that deceiving . . . that man . . . that conceited . . . oooh! He tricked me! He told me lies and then had the gall to . . . to take me to his bed. Oh . . . almost! Freyda!" Pandora shouted at the top of her lungs.

"I am going, I am going, I am going," Pandora huffed and puffed, striding across the carpet like a steam-engine locomotive.

Freyda suddenly appeared at the threshold, wringing her hands together, knowing what had taken place the day before from the gossiping up and down California Street, throughout the gilded mansions of Nob Hill. Also by the sounds in the house the night before. Oh, such sounds!

"My gootness, vhere are you going, Mrs. Torn?"

"Ahhhh! Don't call me that!" Pandora screeched, as the maid covered her ears from the high-pitched attack.

Freyda glanced down at the shredded newspaper.

"Vhat did you read dat make you so upset?" she asked but knew very well.

"What!" Pandora shouted. "Look there for yourself. Riddock is still alive. Oh, sweet Jesus, I am a dumb, blind fool!"

With her lion's mane of hair streaking out behind her, her bearing that of a warring Amazon, Pandora shot across the room in search of something to wear.

"Pack, pack, *pack!*" she snarled, her wild eyes tossing blue sparks about the room. She halted abruptly before the wardrobe. "What am I doing? Pack! I've no clothes here." She spied the wedding dress in a corner of the wardrobe off by itself, looking very feminine alongside Rogan's manly garments. "Ah! I may look foolish marching out of here in this, but that is exactly what I intend to do!"

"Mr. Torn come home from office soon. Vhy don't you vait?"

But Pandora dressed exactly as she had the day before, minus the flowered headdress, and, in a sweet blur of bridal white, made a beeline for the door.

"Vhere you go? Vhat I tell the mister?"

"Tell him to go straight to blazes!"

Sighing and shaking her head, Freyda picked up the newspaper. Fitting the shreds together, she read out loud, haltingly, barely understanding the words that leaped out at her from the front page:

RIDDOCK'S SUMMIT HOUSE NEARLY UP IN SMOKE

San Francisco roared with laughter early this morning upon learning that multimillionaire tycoon Rogan Thorn duped Walter Riddock, president of Wolfington & Riddock lines, on the very same day his ill-fated wedding should have taken place. The *almost* bride, Dora, the mystery girl who had half the bachelors of San Francisco in love with her, was whisked away to

God-knows-where, but rumor has it "he" took her to his schooner in the wee hours of the morning!

The blaze consumed half of the lower part of Summit House, whose owner is already planning a restoration to be begun by workmen next week. . . . No one was hurt in the blaze. . . . Of course, Mr. Thorn is not being blamed . . . not the king of the shipping empire. . . .

That afternoon was gray with more rain as Cara Kalee leaped down from her rented cab and raced to the door of Thorn Navigation. She wasted no time, but climbed the stairs to rap quickly against the door, impatiently waiting for Rogan's call to enter.

"Come."

Cara burst in, her rain-dampened skirts nearly catching in the closing door which she shut with a firm bang. In high spirits, Rogan grinned from behind his desk. Leaning back in his swivel chair, he laid down the pencil he had been making entries with in a ledger.

"Well, you *have* undergone a change in manner," he said smiling. "Usually you fly in here unannounced. What's up? Ah,"—he held up his hand—"don't tell me. You must have heard."

Cara stared dumbly, before it dawned on her what he meant. "No! I mean yes! I read about the scandal in the newspaper. But that's not—" She quit when Rogan chuckled, his mind in a different frame than hers.

"Cara," Rogan said gently, "why don't you sit. You look terrible—"

"Rogan!" She started all over again. "I'm frightened!"

Rogan went to pull out a chair for her. "Whatever for?" he wondered, but his mind was elsewhere. He was in a hurry to finish his business and head home.

She waved aside the chair and blurted out, "My mother has written me a letter!"

Rogan continued to smile. "That's nice, Cara."

She gritted her teeth at his almost dumb boyish look. She heaved a deep sigh, then went on. "Let me finish. I could hardly read it at first, but I finally made some sense of it all."

"What's that, Cara?"

"The letter, damn it, the letter!"

There was such pain and distress in her face that just looking at Cara made Rogan aware of disaster; he was chilled and alarmed now. For some very strange reason he felt her visit had to do with Dora. Feeling anxious, he went to pour Cara a cup of strong black coffee. But she waved that, too, aside. Rogan stared into the cup. He was stalling himself, afraid of the inevitable, the bad news.

He would have to hear sooner or later, but why should he feel this foreboding included Dora?

He took a sip of the hot coffee himself, then ground out, "Well, let's hear it."

She hung her head shamefully. "Rogan, I should have told you this before." Her voice was like a little girl's.

"Say it, Cara. I'm waiting . . . patiently," he lied.

Her brown eyes turned liquid. She dug into her bag and brought out the pieces of his jewelry.

"First, I have to get this cleared up. Pandora never

stole these." She gulped aloud. *"I did."*

Rogan stared at Cara as if she'd grown ugly warts. "You?" He took the jewelry she handed him, but he barely gave them any notice as he dropped the pieces into his pocket.

"Who is . . . Pandora?" he burst out.

Her eyes flew wide and the room grew strangely quiet.

"Rogan. Pandora is my cousin!"

"Cousin. Pandora," he merely stated woodenly.

"I lied about everything." She hung her brunette head. "Pandora St. Ives . . . and . . ." She shrugged, unable to go on.

But Rogan almost smiled here, thinking that now he could complete the marriage certificate, by adding her maiden name. In fact, he'd decided this very morning after leaving the church that they would be married a second time, a real wedding in the church, in the eyes of God. Now the name would make everything complete. He would be able to perform again. He blamed his guilt for his impotency last night.

But Rogan was in for quite a surprise.

Close to tears now, Cara began to ramble in her near-senseless speech. Rogan, suddenly serious, watched her closely, listening while she blurted the first words out; the rest became a crazy blur.

"Mamma Iola said that at first the islanders thought sharks had been the cause of his death . . . and then Mauli . . . my father . . . found the knife— the one she used for cutting strips of leaves while weaving!"

"What are you talking about?" Rogan gripped

226

Cara by the shoulders hard. Then more slowly, repeated, "My God, what are you trying to tell me?"

Cara's brown eyes widened further, almost bulging from their sockets. "Rogan . . . Pandora has been accused of murdering her husband!"

Rogan went weak all over and had to grip the edge of the desk to prevent the muscles in his legs from giving out.

"Husband?" Rogan croaked out the word.

"Mauli thinks Pandora murdered him," she went on, near to hysteria.

"Who is *him?*" Rogan almost shouted.

"Akoni Nahele!"

"Oh, my God, no," Rogan muttered.

"It's all too horrible, Rogan!" she choked. "Akoni was cut up bad, lying on the beach . . . I mean stabbed to death . . . over and over . . . by Pandora's own knife!" she wailed. "Oh, poor Pandora, my own dear cousin, and I deceived her. I should have been here at her side when she needed me. She hated Akoni with a passion, you see, and I believe Mauli forced the marriage on her. Dear Lord, how selfish of me, Rogan, to have put aside my own flesh and blood." Her nerves were fraying fast and seemed to twitch all over with her next movement.

"Rogan, take me to her! She's at your home, right?"

Rogan's eyes narrowed suspiciously, and then he collected his wits about him, saying, "Not just yet, Cara. We must talk some more first before we bring Dora . . . Pandora into this."

"Oh, Rogan, she needs me! No wonder she doesn't remember anything. She must be so lost, so confused.

God, oh, what a mess!"

Rogan gritted his teeth. "Cara, shut up!" He softened then. "I'm sorry, but I can't think straight. I can't take her—I mean you to her in this condition—both of us."

Rogan strode the length of the room for several minutes, then spun back to stand before her. "Cara, how did Walter know Dora was Pandora? He said the name at Millers' party."

Shame washed over her. "I'm not sure now, but he professed to be in love with her. I—I guess when he found her reticule it happened. I don't know. . . . He must have seen her that day. I lied about her stealing from him . . . and you. I just don't know the whole story, Rogan."

This time there was gentleness to his grip as he took her by the hand. "I have done something very crazy, Cara. I wasn't thinking straight after the fire; all I wanted was to make Pandora mine."

Cara inclined her head. "You stole the bride away and—and made love to her?"

"May God forgive me," he said with a shake of his head. Then, "No, I didn't do either. Bo Gary snatched her away to the *Phantom. I* married her." Something seemed to snap in him then. He murmured under his breath, "And I thought she was a virgin. I'm a bigger fool than I thought." But to Cara he said, "Yes, she's my wife. Cara? Do you understand what I am saying?" He shook her, trying to wipe out her dazed look.

"Oh, I see," she finally said; then shook her head. "No, I really don't understand any of this. Ohhh," she groaned.

Too much was happening too fast. Rogan shook his own head to clear it, but he could not.

The door burst open suddenly. Together Cara and Rogan stared at Wizan who slid into the room on his felt-soled slippers. He tossed up dainty, fluttering hands.

"Oh, golly! Dora girl is gone again—*poof!*"

Chapter Twenty-one

Her mood matching the gray weather outside, Pandora wrapped herself securely in a blanket on the overstuffed sofa after Sarah had gone upstairs for a nap.

Pandora had arrived at Sarah's, completely soaked, her wedding dress a total ruin. She had walked, not having any cab fare. But the walk had taken only several blocks.

The stately clock in the hall chimed another half-hour, making it four-thirty. Pandora poked out of the cocoon of her warm blanket and stretched, then wrinkled her nose. The ever-present peppermint smell in the house surrounded her. It seemed to be exuded from the elaborately carved furnishings, and permeated even the silk brocades.

Every house had its own smell. Summit House smelled like orris root; Rogan's like . . . old books and leather and lemon wax. Enough of that!

The lace-curtained windows were shuttered against the gray sky and slanting rain. A gaslight hissed in the corner, even at this early hour before suppertime.

Sarah had been upset, but more over the ruined

gown than anything else. Even the fire that had devastated part of her nephew's house hadn't seemed to matter all that much to Sarah. And it was a small miracle that Sarah had welcomed Pandora back into her home.

"Well," Sarah had sighed, after helping Pandora off with the drenched dress, clucking her tongue, "Walter is ruined. Rogan Thorn the victor again. It's Walter's own fault and I wouldn't see you married to that dunce now for all the tea in China, even though he is my nephew. All he did after the fire was put out was to go off with his pasty-faced friends. Drunker than a lord with his fluffy companions tagging along. Huh! Giggling they were, with their scented handkerchiefs blowing in the breeze! Now I know all about Walter! His behavior was and still is unforgivable! I could not even begin to tell you.

"But let me say this: Walter used to like women. In fact . . . one of his old flames is here right now." Sarah bent to whisper in the younger woman's ear. "Her name is Pilar, Walter's young Spanish cook. She's been with him for seven years. She couldn't stand the fumes of charred wood, and so is staying here for a time. She's busy in the kitchen already, ugh, making tortillas and beans!"

Pandora wore a troubled look. "Walter must be *terribly* angry," she said to change the subject before Sarah could go on concerning Walter and his friends.

"Huh, I'm the one who should be fuming! If he doesn't shape up I shall totally wipe him out, cut him out of his share in Wolfington & Riddock lines." Sarah looked about the Victorian living room a bit sadly, avoiding Pandora's bright eyes. "You must

231

know that all Walter wanted you for was a show-piece, a lovely possession to grace his parlor and wait on his"—she shuddered—"friends. I am sorry now that love never entered the picture. Poor Walter . . . he's very ill."

Pandora shrugged that off, patting Sarah's hand consolingly. "He will be all right, Sarah." Then she fiddled with a tasseled pillow, looking aside. "What about Pilar?" she asked of the Spanish woman.

"Oh, she'll probably go back to Mexico City someday. She has a son, a darling black-haired, blue-eyed lad." Sarah yawned wide. "Oh dear, I am— What is it, Dora darling? You look a bit shocked all of a sudden."

"Oh, Sarah, I have made a horrible mistake." She stared down at the carpet, embarrassed to go on.

"What could be more terrible than if you had married my limp-wristed nephew? Pray tell!"

"Marrying Rogan Thorn."

Sarah almost glowered at Pandora, before she heaved a deep sigh that lifted her bosom even higher in her chambray housedress. She looked defeated, once and for all, but she was not a sore loser.

"Oh, dear, is that what took place last night? Married to Rogan Thorn. Oh, that *is* bad. My dearest enemy. But at least he has his brains in the right place. Walter, I'm afraid, sits on his!" She smiled genuinely then. "So, it's Rogan Thorn I had the wedding dress made up for, hmm?"

"It seems that way, Sarah, but I believe he must have hypnotized me . . . or something near to it. I had been drawn by those deceptive green eyes, like shallow pools that run deep. Just as I had been fooled by Walter's charm and kindness!"

"Well, Dora dear,"—Sarah chuckled—"with Rogan's winning smile and deep dimples, he could make any woman go weak in the knees, just looking at him, couldn't he?" Sarah's eyes twinkled mischievously.

"Sarah! How could you be deceived by mere looks, you of all people? I thought you despised the man as much as I do."

"Did you?" Sarah lifted a gray eyebrow, wondering out loud. She watched Pandora's reaction closely.

The young woman blushed crimson. "Yes," she replied in a soft voice, the shakiness in it belying the word.

"Well, dear, this conversation and the past week's events have thoroughly drained this old woman. I'm going upstairs to lie down. The house is yours for as long as you want to stay."

Sarah lifted herself heavily from the stiff-backed, horsehair-upholstered chair, and reached over to pat Pandora on the head. "Don't be too surprised if your—ah—husband comes and whisks you back to Thorn Mansion."

"Never! I am never going anywhere with him, even if he owned a castle in Spain!" she spewed forth like a volcano.

"Don't be too sure about that, Dora. Rogan Thorn always takes what he wants!" She chuckled while walking with heavy tread to the door. Suddenly she was not the sprightly woman she used to be.

Sarah left Pandora with those disturbing words to mull over. It had sounded to her as if Sarah had actually delighted in her marriage to Rogan Thorn. Those damnable green eyes—and his charisma. She had even forgotten that she had had a problem this last week, and that her past was still shrouded in a misty veil.

But at times like the present when she was alone, Pandora had time to dwell on what could have been. A place flitted in and out of her imagination. Sand and green cliffs. Wicker chairs and bamboo lattice. White-capped mountains with steam rising above one kingly peak.

Leaving her blanket, Pandora rose and found herself minutes later standing in the small library down the hall. Here sets of books crammed the shelves, gold letters embossed their cracked leather bindings. Sir Walter Scott novels; one titled *Daughter of an Empress*. She chose one, a geography volume.

Seating herself in a stiff-backed chair, she began leafing through the book. Words leaped out at her. California. Georgia. Minnesota. New York. On page 420 she stopped.

Pacific Islands. She scanned down the page. Pearl Harbor. Diamond Head. Waikiki. Her eyes drifted back up. Hawaii. Mind bells began to ring.

Oahu! She was from this Hawaii in the Pacific. That was it!

Remembrance pulsated through her as she caught a fleeting glimpse of a young woman, copper-and-sun hair blowing lightly over her shoulder, running barefoot and squealing, toward the turquoise waters of a sleepy lagoon inside the coral reefs.

It was she, Dora . . . Dora . . . what? What was her

last name? She began to giggle then, but there was a touch of irony in it.

"My name is Dora Thorn!"

"I am Adrian."

Pandora spun about on the chair to find herself staring directly into the beautiful eyes of a small, willowy boy. His eyes were the darkest shade of blue she had ever encountered. Midnight blue they could be called—and expressionless. Cold, came to her mind, for one so young. His spiky black lashes never blinked, not even once as he continued to stare at her oddly, seeming to pick out her innermost thoughts.

Pandora shifted in her chair uncomfortably, before she spoke. "How old are you, Adrian?" She felt rather strange talking to this lad who had appeared suddenly, startling her out of her reflections.

"Almost seven. How old are you?"

"I—uh—I am twenty." Pandora smiled at her recall. Had she known this before? She went on. "Do *you* have a last name, Adrian?"

"Yes. Don't you?"

Her smile vanished unconsciously as those unfeeling eyes kept studying her, wisely, awaiting an answer. He had immediately caught the inflection in her voice, she noticed, and squirmed.

"I didn't, but I do now," she found herself replying automatically. She realized she had said the name "Thorn" when he had first entered the room, but she also knew he was going to ask her to say it again.

"Well—" He shrugged wide shoulders for a little boy. "What is it?"

"Thorn." She laughed, beginning to enjoy herself. "Now you must tell me yours."

"Dancer."

"*Dancer?*" Pandora repeated, thinking the name odd.

"It's Mamma's last name. I don't have a papa. He would not marry Mamma."

He kept piercing her with his gaze; it almost had a tinge of hatred, she decided. But why? she wondered. A little uneasy over his quick reply and revelation, Pandora decided it best not to press him about his father. There was another question foremost in her mind, though, that needed answering.

"Why don't you like me, Adrian?" She wondered if he would evade her again by turning the question aside. He did just that.

The deep blue eyes narrowed with a dark sparkle. "You are pretty. But *not* as pretty as Mamma."

Pandora started and flinched inwardly at that. She was bewildered all over again. He still hadn't blinked, and she wondered why his eyes didn't look away, except when he had let them drop once to take in her slim form, and to rest impudently on the V in her robe before drifting back up to rest on her face.

The usual blushing shyness and nervousness of boys his age was lacking in this lad. She was startled, too, to think that he was almost like a grown man, one with a deep-seated hatred in his little heart. But directed toward whom? Surely not herself?

Now Pandora took in the wooden cross that hung suspended from his neck on a leather thong. The lad was all jutting bones and sharp angles, and the cross appeared overly large on his thin chest, giving him the look of a glowering puppet. She shivered with some unknown premonition.

"Where did you come from, Adrian, and who is your mamma?" she questioned all at once.

"Adrian. There you are. Come here!"

Pandora lifted her gaze past the boy's wide, bony shoulders and saw a stern-faced woman. She wore a white apron over a black chambray uniform. Flour smeared her skirts here and there, revealing she had been in the kitchen cooking. Tortillas and beans, as Sarah said. Her stature was stiff, haughty, and stately; her demeanor that of a Spanish duenna. Unlike the boy whose skin was naturally and gently tan, hers bore a copperish hue.

Tingles of recollection sped along Pandora's spine. This would be the lad's mother, Pilar, the cook from Summit House. She had been with Walter . . . seven years. . . .

"I said *come!*" Pilar repeated harshly to the boy as she shot Pandora a look of pure hatred and withering contempt.

Pilar took her son by the elbow and ushered him out of the room without further ado. Pandora shivered. She would never, but never forget the narrowed look of hatred in Adrian Dancer's dark eyes as he backed up and fled to his mother's skirts.

It somehow smacked of revenge. The lad and his midnight-blue eyes would haunt her for weeks to come. Perhaps even years.

Yes, she decided, *years*.

Chapter Twenty-two

Looking lovely, Pandora was just descending the stairs; she had changed from the faille robe into a velvet dove-gray skirt that reached her ankles, and topped that with a silk blouse with mauve-gray and green stripes with a white flower pattern adorning its shoulders and sleeves. The ruffed collar band was snug at her neck with gray and mauve slim ribbons trailing down over the shy split bodice. Her rounded breasts rolled sensually, straining against the silk when she moved.

Having decided to bathe later, she had soaped and rinsed herself off in the flowered washbowl. Though dressed and refreshed, her nerves were still stretched taut by the disturbing scene with the lad in the library.

Anna, just traversing the hall, started at the sound of slick carriage wheels in the drive. With feather duster in hand, she noticed Pandora when she looked up and their eyes met. The maid had knowledge of all the gossip that had been filtering through the neighborhood.

"Wait a moment, Anna, before you see who that is. Hopefully that's not for me, but I'll be in the parlor."

The kindly maid, Anna, waited until her employer's former companion had hurried off and shut the parlor door. Shaking her head, Anna reached the front door just as the knocker sounded.

Unable to resist the temptation, Pandora listened with her ear close to the crack. It was a man and a woman, she could tell by the high and the low mutterings. She stiffened.

They were coming toward the parlor!

All afternoon at the back of her mind she had feared this would happen and there was a feeling in her now that this man was none other than Rogan come to fetch her. But could this really be since there was a strange woman with the man?

She took a position on the settee, a hastily snatched book in her hand. When the door opened it was as if her most fearful thoughts had conjured him up. There he stood framed on the threshold, the tall ferns flanking him on either side. Anna moved away after peeping in and shrugging helplessly, and Pandora was afforded a full view of the dark-haired woman standing next to Rogan.

She was small, but sensually curved. Pandora could only gape at the sultry beauty of this woman. With glowering brow, Rogan moved into the room, his greeting deceptively soft.

"Pandora."

Pandora hardly saw him or heard him. Her eyes remained glued to the young woman in the plum velvet town costume; as if fascinated Pandora watched as she leaned her closed umbrella against the table leg.

Cara. The woman who had brought her here!

Her heart leapt with joy this time, for she knew by instinct this woman was kin. She had not been able to identify her in the dark that night when Cara had whisked her away from Thorn Mansion. Not quite sure of herself or the other woman's intent—for after all, Cara Kalee had made no effort before this to visit her again—Pandora began shyly.

"Cara, it has been a long time."

Pandora went to place the book on the table beside her, but it fell with a thud to the floor; she never noticed this in her nervous anticipation.

"You remember?" Rogan was saying at the same time the book fell.

"Is that so hard to believe?" Pandora said, trancelike, never looking up at him once.

Shyly, Cara came to stand before her cousin. "Oh, Pandora!" She broke down, rushing to pull the other woman into her arms.

Her damp cheek pressed to Pandora's, Cara stroked her silken drawn-up braids, like a mother reunited with her lost child. Sniffing loudly now, Pandora glanced up with misted eyes to find Rogan hovering, hawklike, watching them intently.

"Are you my . . . cousin?" Pandora asked Cara shyly.

"Yes, of course!" Cara cried.

The unusual happened next. Warmth and understanding flowed into Rogan's soft green eyes, and Pandora saw him in a new light.

"Pandora . . . *why?*" was all he said.

Rogan knelt down beside the two women, but took Pandora by the hand, quietly lifting her. He guided her to the sofa and beckoned Cara to come sit beside her cousin. He cleared his throat to speak.

"We have to talk, Pandora."

"Why that name again . . . ? I'm . . . Dora." Wildly she studied them both. "Aren't I?"

Cara took the long-fingered hand into her smaller one. "Why do you think that you are Dora and not Pandora?" she questioned, a gentle smile curving her lovely lips.

Pandora thought the question odd, and frowned her confusion. "That is as far as my memory serves me. When I thought deeply in order to answer Rogan . . . as I lay in his bed the first time—" She blushed here and Cara urged her with a smile to go on. "As I lay in his bed . . . no, I mean after the carriage accident, my mind stuck on that name and would go no further." She glanced up at Rogan and then back to her cousin, and shrugged helplessly.

"What is wrong with me . . . am I always to be without remembrance of . . . the past?" Pandora shook her head.

Cara sat straighter and Rogan, his head bent attentively, stepped a little closer.

"Tell us what you do remember, Pandora St. Ives . . . Thorn," he said at last.

Pandora spun to face him. "Why didn't you tell me before?" She looked at him with accusation in her eyes.

"I wanted to, when Walter said you were in San Francisco."

But it was Cara who had answered and Pandora swung back to her, asking, ' What kept you from helping me . . . Cara?" Her voice queried pitifully.

Cara let a smile slip to Rogan; a look of

remembered fire and new affection clouded her eyes momentarily. Then something else replaced that look and Pandora clearly saw friendship on her countenance. Merely a cover-up? Pandora looked down at her lap, remembering something, and she spoke of it now.

"I guessed that Rogan—I mean I realized he had a woman . . . somehow I could tell—"

Cara interjected. "Men like Rogan always have a woman," she ended with a smile, but Pandora was not so inclined.

Rogan blushed handsomely. But then he, too, had cause to frown.

"But I had no idea that it was you," Pandora went on. "When Sarah Wolfington loosed the gossip, well . . . now I know for certain it was you she spoke of."

But Pandora decided not to add the bit of Sarah's that Rogan had *several* new ladies. She sighed inwardly. Her memory had slipped so often she wondered if she was sane at times.

Now Rogan realized why Pandora had seemed so cold toward him. He silently cursed the Black Widow. He guessed there was more to it than that, though. There was the fear of man's touch in and about Pandora. It had happened long before *he* ever kissed and caressed her, and tried to make her his. Damn! If he had completed the act the night before, things might have been different between them now. If he could have just broken that icy barrier, surely she would have melted. Thinking this, a powerful tide of desire surged through him and he ran a finger beneath his collar.

Cara noticed his discomfort and mistaking it, said, "Lord, it's close in here."

She went at once to open the doors wide, permitting the air from the hall to circulate in the parlor. Rogan hunkered down in front of Pandora, taking her hands into his.

"We are going to try to help you remember, Pandora," he said softly. "Try to get used to the name—it belongs to you. Trust me?"

She smiled sweetly into his eyes. "Pandora Thorn does sound"—she blushed hotly—"nicer."

"And so it does," he agreed wholeheartedly. He turned aside with a thoughtful frown. "But for a while I think you should go by your maiden name. I deceived you, Pandora, and have no right to call you wife."

"The ceremony *was* a little primitive," she added. "And hasty."

Disappointment washed over Pandora. He was stroking her hand methodically, but he was gazing up at Cara now. Did he have regrets about what had taken place on shipboard and had he just now realized his love for Cara? He is just being nice to me, and doesn't really want me for his wife, Pandora decided. She had been prepared to do battle with him, believing he would drag her back to his home by the hair like a caveman with his catch. She should really be feeling relief that he had not, but she was indeed sadly disappointed.

Rogan studied Pandora with hooded eyes. How virginal she looked in her sweet braids, like a maid still waiting to be led into womanhood. This could not be; she had been a married woman once before.

Had she left a child behind in her haste to flee the island? Not even Cara had knowledge of that. Pandora must have had a sound reason to have murdered her husband—if indeed that was true. Looking at her now, it was very hard to believe. For all her height, she looked suddenly small and very helpless.

Out in the hall, Rogan noticed the furtive blur of a black chambray uniform and white apron. This was the third time Rogan had noticed the dark-haired maid lurking about like that. Where had he seen her before? he wondered.

Pandora had seen this, too, and had been aware that Pilar had caught Rogan's eye. Cara was deep in thought, staring at the pendulum of the clock on the mantel, so she hadn't noticed.

Rogan unbent and stood. "Would you like to come to my office, where we can talk in private?" he asked Pandora.

For a moment she was stunned, before she collected herself. He did not even want her back at his house, and somehow this hurt. She thought how embarrassed he must be after what had taken place in his bedroom, how silly and inexperienced she had appeared. She was aware, too, that Rogan had something of a problem, one she didn't quite understand yet. But then, she might never have a chance to understand it.

"Do you have a wrap?" he asked, taking her silence for assent.

"Yes," she answered before she could think further. "The gray one in the hall closet."

While Rogan went to fetch her three-tiered cape,

Pandora sat nibbling on a fingernail. Cara had not spoken in such a long while that Pandora wondered what could be troubling her. There was something bothering both Cara and Rogan, she guessed. But what could make them look at her with something close to pity?

When Rogan appeared in the doorway, Pandora stood. She recalled something he had said earlier, before he had guided her to the sofa. He had said: "Pandora, why?"

What, she wondered now, had he meant by that? Could he have been feeling badly that she had left him?

"Coming?" Rogan held out the cape to slip around her shoulders.

Pandora walked toward him, but she had missed his wandering gaze that had swept her from head to foot as she rose, the stark-naked look of desire that had glinted in his eyes momentarily before he spoke.

Now he was wishing again that he had been able to go all the way with her the night before.

Chapter Twenty-three

Despite the rain-slicked streets and the stealthy mist, the Thorn coachman reached the building at the foot of the hill in fifteen minutes. Pandora was the last to step from the carriage to where Cara waited with opened umbrella. Huddling together, arms wrapping Pandora securely in the middle, they sped beneath the pelting drops to the door.

All was quiet in the office on the second floor when Rogan bent to his task of lighting a fire in the grate and then flamed the gaslights with matchsticks. Cara bustled in a corner niche, making coffee that soon permeated the warming air with its fragrant bean odor.

It didn't skip Pandora's notice that her cousin was well acquainted with the whereabouts of everything in Rogan's office. Wondering and waiting, Pandora sat silently.

Not standing on ceremony, Rogan finished his tasks and went to slide his buttocks onto the corner of his massive desk. Letting one foot dangle to the floor, he faced Pandora who had sat waiting patiently for several minutes. He wasted no time, but came right to the point.

"Pandora, what do you remember of someone by the name of Akoni Nahele?"

She barely saw the mug of steaming coffee that was placed into her hands, scarcely heard the word of caution from Cara that it was hot. Rogan regarded Pandora as Cara came to stand beside him. With a delicate frown, Pandora tried the name on her lips.

"Akoni Nahele," she said slowly. Her head shook furiously then and she nearly spilled the hot coffee on herself.

"No!" she said vehemently, after noting that Rogan had been studying her curiously.

Slipping from the desk easily, Rogan bent to whisk the mug from her hands because they had begun to shake. He put it aside and took up her hand, staring deeply as he searched her eyes for pictures of what must have been a terrible scene.

"The eyes are the windows of the soul, Pandora, and yours show fright all of a sudden. Why?" he ground out, showing her no mercy.

"No, don't ask me any more—please! I do not like that name you said!" she cried angrily.

"You said it, too!" he shot back.

"I do not care what I said. Take me back to Sarah's immediately!" Her eyes narrowed and tossed blue sparks at Rogan. "You brought me here merely to interrogate me. I won't have it, I'm not a criminal!"

"Maybe that's just what you are," Rogan gritted out between his teeth, egging her on.

"Oh! What do you mean!" She clenched her hands, her long nails digging into the flesh of her palms. A fingernail snapped off and she stared at its ragged tip, an odd expression growing in her gaze.

Rogan uncurled her long fingers and then reached up to shake her by the shoulders, his breath hot on her face as he pressed her to remember.

"Think, Pandora, think of what that name means to you, damn it!" he began to rap out. "I'd say the accident by my carriage added to your forgetfulness. Did you have one before that?"

"Did I have *one what?*" She spat the words into his close face.

"Accident, damn it, what the hell did I just say!"

"Bastard, take your hands off me!"

With great effort, Pandora pushed herself up and out from beneath his arms. She briskly shoved him away, and, surprised, Rogan watched her go and stand at the window. Rogan and Cara exchanged frowns, then looked back collectively to Pandora who was shivering noticeably.

"Cara . . ." Rogan began, but Cara caught on before he completed his sentence, and held her hand up.

"I—uh—left my reticule in the carriage. I'll be back shortly, Pandora," Cara said, carrying the mug to Pandora.

Before Pandora could find a place to set the mug down, Cara was already going out the door. She decided to stay at the window. She looked askance at Rogan as he bent to his desk and rattled a drawer with a key. From the corner of her eye she continued to watch, seeing him take something out. When he began to move toward her, she snatched her head straight up, bracing herself for his next move. Her flesh tingled in anticipation of his touch. She wanted it. She wanted his warm hands caressing her flesh,

248

not his harsh words that made her feel like a witless little girl.

Before he reached her, she began to speak, and her voice shook with indignation. "I am not naïve, not the child you seem to think. I find it inexcusable for you to question me so!"

"Do you?" he drawled.

He had stepped up behind her. His hand suddenly slid up Pandora's arm and she was pulled back against his hard chest. A long moment passed and she began to sway on her feet, the coffee mug clenched hard in her fingers. Coffee sloshed over the rim and onto the floor. He snatched it from her grip, tossing it, coffee and all, into the flames where the liquid hissed and the mug shattered. At the same time he spoke at her back.

"Pandora, loose your flame from within. It's there; I can feel it trying to surface," he whispered urgently.

Now her temperature rose and her pulse quickened from his nearness; yet she hadn't heard his words fully.

"What did you say?" she murmured, feeling his hardness at her back.

"I said you should let Cara and me help you, otherwise you just might find yourself . . . behind bars."

She frowned deeply. "Prison?"

He made no reply, but encircled her waist and gave something into her hands. Looking down, her face went white with strained emotion.

"Oh, I do . . . remember this!" she gasped and fumbled inside the reticule to take out the comb with her hair still woven between the teeth.

"Remember more!" he ordered harshly into her ear.

"I cannot! I am afraid to!"

He spun from her as if she were suddenly repugnant to him. "Coward," he hissed.

Pandora whirled to face his back. "Stop nagging me with your questions. It is so easy for you to shout 'Remember, you coward' when you are not in my shoes! Mr. Thorn!"

His lips curled with the curse, "Damn you!"

He reappeared at her side, snatching the reticule from her madly clutching fingers and tossing the thing across the room. He turned back to shake her roughly before his lips claimed hers. Pandora struggled beneath the brutal but strangely tender kiss; but it was no good, for he kissed her all the harder, all the deeper, bruisingly, lips to lips, chest to breast. Now his hands took her hips to pull her against his desire. Growing, enflamed, his wanting pressed and lifted to seek the place his lustful mind had craved since he had looked upon her the very first time. Nothing mattered for now but his need to possess, to mate, to ease the growing fire and pain in his lower region. But she held back, when he wanted her to yield.

"Just let whatever happens happen. Give in to the fire in your lips and your thighs." He breathed harshly into her ear. "Pandora, you are mine!"

Shameless, hot, aching desire ran through her, while at the same time her mind hurled about madly for means of escape. She begged him to stop, to be gentler, and hissed with a nip at his searching lips. She finally escaped from his next full kiss, her eyes and head rolling back as she clawed at his shirt.

"Stop it, Akoni! You hurt me! Be gentle . . . not yet . . . not here . . . They will come and see us!" Her eyes widened as if in horrible fascination and surprise. "Akoni! No! He . . . oh, stop!"

Shivering with heat, Rogan shook himself from his driving passion long enough to see what was happening. His gentle ravishment had brought this scene to her mind and to help her now he must continue, he realized, sinking his face to the gentle rise above her bodice where he found a tender spot for his tongue.

"No more!"

She continued on her mind's frightful path backward in time.

"Blood . . . there is so much . . . much blood. . . ."

Rogan took this for the deflowering—Akoni Nahele taking Pandora. But now there was more, a method to Rogan's madness.

". . . No, I did not want this! It is my knife . . . my knife stabbing! Oh, stop, please . . . stop," she ended with a whimper.

Rogan lifted his mouth from the slim column of her neck, nearly shouting, "Knife! Yes, Pandora, tell me about the knife!"

"No . . . more . . ."

Standing there, Rogan had all but made love to Pandora. His hands had taken possession of her flesh, going inside her bodice, cupping the sweet-nippled breasts, then going beneath her skirts, taking hold of her softly rounded small buttocks, his pressing need grinding against her. He had to put a halt to it, or else he would surely shame himself once

251

again. His breathing was labored when he finally let down her skirts, and loosened his hold on her.

Pandora had not blinked or done anything for several minutes. Then her horror-filled vision cleared and she saw Rogan, not Akoni.

Her staring eyes finally blinked and she fainted.

When Cara entered, her eyes opened wide. She found that Pandora had swooned in Rogan's arms and she flew to his side to help.

"Oh, Rogan, what happened!" Cara cried.

"She was having flashbacks; I guess that I brought them on," he answered with a soft blush of sheepishness.

"Here, carry her over, and I'll prop her feet up on a chair while you sit with her, Rogan."

Now across his lap, her feet propped on another chair while Cara rubbed her slim ankles for circulation, Pandora's dark gold lashes fluttered half-open.

"I'm bringing her home with me, Rogan."

"To the boardinghouse?"

"No, Rogan, to Hawaii!"

Rogan jerked his head up in alarm. "Won't that be dangerous? I mean your own father has accused Pandora, hasn't he?" he asked while stroking back the sunshine hair from her sweat-curded forehead.

Cara's face dropped sadly. "I forgot to mention one thing. My father has passed away, another reason Mamma Iola wrote to me. *She* has not accused Pandora; she has always loved Pandora. And, Rogan, only the three of us know the dark secret."

Cara handed Rogan a handkerchief and he dabbed at the moisture on Pandora's brow.

Rogan fixed his gaze on Cara. "She doesn't know

anything. Only when she's in a trance, I've discovered. It would be too stressful for her to talk of it now."

Pandora moaned. "Talk of what, Rogan?"

"To Hawaii, Rogan," Cara repeated, having made up her mind firmly.

"Very well. The *Baghdad* is leaving in two days and you both will be on it. Pandora will stay with you at the apartment until then." He noticed Cara's worry. "I'll see that no one else finds out where . . . Wait a minute, are you sure that the police know nothing of this in Hawaii?"

"No one . . . but us, I said, and Mamma Iola."

Rogan took a deep breath. "We're worrying over nothing, I guess. Remember, she might have it all come back to her once she's back home."

"Rogan, this is worse for Pandora, *not* remembering. She'll never be able to live a full life, free from worries of the sordid past. We have decided to help her, and Iola will be a balm for Pandora." Cara shook her head then. "Rogan, how could you have married her in her state of mind?"

Rogan snorted. "How did I know her mind? As for my bad actions, someday I'll explain, Cara. But right now we have to get her to your apartment."

"Take me home," Pandora murmured weakly, too wearied and drained to think straight.

"Yes, Pandora love," Cara softly whispered, "I'll take you home."

Chapter Twenty-four

The tall, dark figure, his narrowed gossamer eyes seemingly devoid of all color, stood alone and watched the *Baghdad*'s spread white canvas catch a brisk sea wind which carried her out of the harbor. But Rogan Thorn was not waving good-by.

He stared until the billowy sails grew smaller and smaller in the distance, until no trace of foamy wake marked where the ship's prow had sliced through the bay's waters. He stared, his eyes beginning to burn from not having blinked often enough, until the dot that was the ship had disappeared. It was as if the mighty hand of God had reached down to wipe the vessel from the sea's surface.

Rogan shrugged his shoulders, thrust his hands deeper into his trouser pockets, and turned to make his way back to his office. Seagulls screamed their mournful *eeees* as they circled the empty berth where the *Baghdad* had been moored. Their cries tugged at Rogan's heart; he stopped to turn and watch the gulls for a moment as they dipped to scavenge for a morsel in the refuse dumped from the ship, and then he continued on his way.

* * *

Days passed into weeks before the *Baghdad*'s siren figurehead thrust her breasts proudly through a veil of mist and the gently beckoning beauty of the island lay before her like an emerald gem born from the sea.

The minute Pandora had stepped from her cabin, she felt the humidity of the tradewinds. At first the island was a mere blur to her as she gazed at it from the ship's rail. But now as Capt. Jeremy Cross came to stand beside her—Pandora gazing so intently ahead that she was oblivious to his presence—the gentle rise of Diamond Head became visible.

Ships lazing in the harbor came into view; mists shrouded their holystoned decks, their masts pierced the heavens. Behind all was the lush green island as a backdrop. Sand beaches sparkled and cliffs loomed. The housetops beyond the bustling harbor appeared dull gold in the pure colors of sunrise.

"Honolulu," Pandora said wistfully, "I remember . . . some."

Remembering? Yes, she was!

As in San Francisco, here, too, were hills near the sea, blue shadows on green swale, and a city. But instead of mists and fog that lingered, here mere puffs of clouds rode a sparkling sky and the sea was clean and gorgeous. Even the shadows bore light, and every color took on a new and special hue.

"Mrs. Thorn—uh—I mean Pandora," Captain Cross corrected, for he'd discovered early in the voyage that she disliked being addressed in the former manner. "When we land, would you like the mate sent out with your baggage immediately?"

Like a fresh summer breeze, Cara swept up behind them. "Yes, we are all packed and ready to go."

"Yes, a carriage right away," Pandora murmured, still staring out at the approaching island, wondering, dreaming back to the not distant past. "The green in the distance," she breathed, "just like Rogan's eyes."

Cara and Jeremy exchanged happy glances. At last, this was a good omen.

The carriage was ready, the baggage stacked aboard. Pandora had donned a cornflower muslin dress with pale blue ribbons threaded throughout its bodice of cotton eyelet. She wore no bonnet, and her hair shimmered with health and gold highlights in the sunshine.

"Mahalo," Pandora thanked the boy who had loaded the baggage.

The almost-black eyes of the boy smiled into Pandora's. She had spoken Hawaiian with musical softness, the vowels and liquids predominating. He was Hawaiian, one of the blooded rarities, and he did not wonder why the pale-skinned wahini spoke his language so well, as there were many people of different races here, but mostly *haole*-Hawaiian, Chinese, and Portuguese; here the customs and traditions of many cultures were blended into a dynamic composition of East and West.

The year of annexation had brought more Portuguese from Madeira and the Azores. These people proved to be industrious, thrifty, and law-abiding. Most of them had remained and multiplied, having brought their families from their homelands.

Pandora had felt like a stranger instead of like the

kamaaina she was when a Hawaiian woman with heavy smiling features stepped up and greeted her with a lei of plumeria. She looked out at canoe loads of flower-decked folks who were singing and shouting, "*Aloha.*"

Pandora said in English, "Love to you." Yes, she thought, *Aloha* means hello, and it means I love you. . . .

Pandora turned to her cousin, who was wistfully fingering her own lei. Cara smiled reminiscently.

"Here flowers are a favorite expression of affection," Pandora said, remembering as she brought the lei up to her nose and smelled its delicious fragrance.

Every island had its own lei. Maui preferred the rose. On Oahu, home of kings, they claimed the *ilima,* but they used leis, for greeting, of several different flowers. On Kauai, the *mokihana,* a perfumed berry, was threaded with *maile.* Hawaii had always favored the *maile* vine, and *lehua.* And on Molokai pungent and enduring necklaces were strung from *kukui* nuts. Pandora recalled that her favorite—maybe not by recollection but by her senses—was the wild lavender orchid. One dark-skinned girl gaily passed by with the flower in her piled-up hair and Pandora caught herself staring wistfully at it.

"Yes," Cara said softly. "We are home." Cara smiled jubilantly; she never wanted to leave again.

They left the wharf and wound through the bustling city of Honolulu, where planters strolled the streets with their ladies, the men wore wide-banded white hats and sported colorful scarves at their golden-tanned throats. The women in flowery hats or gay bonnets often wore dresses from the mainland. Some of the men wore their sombreros at a jaunty angle. These rakish-looking plantation owners in white tropical suits, busy and arrogant, reminded Pandora painfully of Rogan.

Rogan. Her husband. When would she see him again?

But Pandora was content just now to look around as they drove north through the city, toward windward Oahu. She could think of Rogan later.

In the city, the tiny shacks, smothered in bougainvillaea, gold, and hibiscus, despite their ricketiness, had a special charm. As did the battered carts along the street by which Hawaiian women and children stood stringing leis as varied and intricate as jeweled necklaces.

The road led to Nuuanu Valley where the affluent summered; and beyond the last plantation, it wound upward through a forest of *koa* trees from whose branches big-leafed vines trailed. The essence of ginger blossoms spiced the cool damp air where *ti* plants marched tall. Here the sheer cliff of Nuuanu Pali commanded the wide sweep of the windward shore. Kaneohe and the Punaluu. Farther on, scrub grass ran into the surf almost, and the waves foamed so near that salt spray was carried on the brisk wind. When Pandora lifted her face to catch it, she was haloed in gold beneath the sun.

The sea was mildly green in the breakers, and was decoratively enhanced by a silver filigree of foaming wave crests. Beyond the swells were patches of lavender in the water, as though flowers floated just beneath its surface. Farther out the water deepened into clear jade, reminiscent to Pandora of a pair of familiar eyes.

The women continued to ride in silence, each lost in her own thoughts, drinking all the beauty in. On the *mauka* side, away from the sea, rose the green jagged-backed mountains, while on the *makai* side, where dark lava had cascaded down into the water, the ocean was cobalt, aquamarine, and purple over the coral. Pandora saw Hawaiian boys fishing, their catches lying among the lovely shaped, pink-mouthed shells strewn along the beach. The Koolau mountain range towered beside the dusty road, as they skirted miles of cane fields.

"It's not far now," Cara commented, breaking the silence and watching Pandora closely for her reaction.

"You mean it is not far in comparison to the long journey by boat we just completed!" Pandora giggled happily, glad to be alive for the first time in a long while.

Indeed the sun was setting by the time they drew near their destination. Pandora's eyes lit up. She was remembering, and it actually felt good. The island's tropical arms welcomed her and she did not experience the horror she had expected. Ahead were the glittering, sea-splashed shores and the waters where she had played and swum—yes, she could swim like a fish! Pandora remembered the blue secrets of the lagoon that perfectly matched her eyes. She welcomed the sight of the familiar thatched lean-tos beside the ocean, with poincianas growing near their doors in huge pots, these flowers like ballerinas on fire in the sunset.

"Look!"

Cara had squealed with pleasure. Set back a little way from the beach road was a small white bungalow; a dark-haired woman of squat countenance stood on the veranda as if she had been awaiting their coming.

Iola's brown eyes lit up as the carriage drew closer and she dumped the pineapple and knife with which she had been working. She rushed down from the veranda, holding the skirt of her muumuu high. The carriage hadn't even completely come to a halt when Cara leaped from it and ran to throw herself against the woman who had tossed her arms wide in joyous welcome.

"Mamma, Mamma," Cara was crying.

"My baby!" Iola crooned, rocking her daughter in her arms.

Soon seeing Pandora over her daughter's shoulder, Iola beckoned her niece with one arm that she freed from Cara's tight embrace. "Pandora, you come, too," Iola cried happily.

Her niece stepped from the carriage as the driver began to unload the heavy chests of *koa* wood. He smiled and nodded while the young woman went, at first tentatively, and then faster, until all three women were wrapped in a loving embrace. Iola brought up her muumuu to dab at her happy wet eyes.

"You think I not want you, too?" Iola studied Pandora's bright eyes that threatened to cry. "Why you not remember me? Been not so long, niece."

Pandora stretched out a cool slim hand to Iola's plump, tear-stained cheek. "Oh, I do; I remember you very well. Oh, I love you, Aunty Iola!"

The tears finally fell, but Pandora was not ashamed to shed them. She was home with those who loved her. She was not afraid.

Chapter Twenty-five

Before leaving San Francisco, Cara had carefully packed a lamp with orange- and green-ruffled shade; it now cast its mellow glow over the cozy atmosphere of the good-sized living room which was the main room and the largest, the rest being tiny, curtained bedrooms, and a kitchen. This lamp now stood on Iola's small sandalwood table where she could admire it; the table was one of the many gifts Pandora's father had brought his sister from the mainland. When alive, Colter St. Ives had gone away on business, to North or South America for several years at a time. Colter had traveled extensively, but Iola had lived on the island all her life, and no one could tell her that she was not completely Hawaiian, though such was not the case.

"Mmmm, that was delicious," Pandora murmured, patting her full stomach after their supper of fresh vegetables, coconut milk, fruit, and fish that Iola had caught herself that very day.

"I shall grow fat!" Pandora exclaimed, wrinkling her nose as she remembered Sarah's dislike for obesity.

"Good, you need fat," Iola joked.

"What a relief to be home again and take off my clothes!" Pandora ended with a sigh, sticking out her bare legs and feet from her muumuu.

Pandora had pulled her freshly washed, squeaky-clean hair up in back and held it in place with a beaded clasp, into which she had tucked a white ginger bloom. Its long mass tumbled in sparkling abandonment down the middle of her back. While she had taken her turn bathing in the back room where the huge wooden tub was set up, Cara had talked in hushed tones with Mamma Iola in the living room.

"Her eyes look sad, beautiful still as watercolor behind surf. But sad deep inside." Iola shook her sleek-haired head, shrugging with a deep-felt sigh.

"Yes, it's true, Mamma. But we must not treat Pandora like an invalid."

Iola leaned forward, ever eager for new words. "What is 'invalid'?" she asked, checking her mental storehouse for the meaning.

"You know, like she is sick and helpless. She is not, and we must not act like nurses; nor should we pamper her too much. Some, I know you can't help it, but she has to remember what happened herself. We can't push her; that could be dangerous."

"I hope it is not bad, to remember," Iola said, staring back in time.

"So—" Cara moved closer, scraping up the wicker chair. "Tell me what you know, Mamma. Quietly."

Iola heaved an even deeper sigh. "She wanted to run away from wedding, before it happened, though Mauli say no! I beg with Pandora to understand uncle, she might come to love Akoni Nahele. She say,

'No, I could never love Akoni! I rather die!'" She emphasized this with an exact shake of Pandora's head. "Pandora tell me before wedding—when Mauli force her to be Akoni's bride, *or else*—that she never let Akoni touch her! She cook, she sew, she wash dirty clothes, but never make baby with big, fat Akoni. I laugh, it so funny, then I was sad at her look. She know why I laugh; Akoni very hot for woman, and most for Pandora." Iola had to chuckle, even now.

Cara spread her hands wide. "What then? Did the wedding really take place? Did Pandora finally agree?"

Iola slapped her well-padded knee. "Not happily, never! She see my fighting with your father, she do it I think for me. She love me, and Mauli use this knowing like fisherman use his spear and net to sneak up and catch fish. Women fish!"

Cara stopped chewing her fingernail long enough to add, "I see. Papa played both ends against the middle, and Pandora was in there."

"Oh, I love Mauli, my husband, still do, even though he dead. He sly man, and it is sad now, he wanted for Pandora to make family more babies. Pandora will make beautiful babies someday. Mauli was wanting that."

Cara smiled sadly, but a frown soon followed. "What about the wedding, Mamma? Tell me about that now."

Iola became animated. "Oh, was big wedding, and luau afterward! Many folks come from Kailua and Honolulu, from way up north shore, and even from other islands. Sailboats and steamers full of happy children and grown-ups. You know, Mauli knew many, and he like big families. Some poor, some rich, all welcome. Your old boyfriend come—Joe Bane—and sister Leilani."

Iola recognized that Cara's eyes had lit up at the mention of Joe, but she went on as if she hadn't noticed. "Akoni was happy and drunk as *kalua* pig in sauce; bride Pandora sad but, oh, so beautiful in white angel *holoku*, flowers of white ginger and gold plumeria in her sunshine hair. I cry so much for her when Akoni take her to honeymoon on old plantation, Akoni meaning to live in smaller house out back far from big one, keep some land, and fix up from money all come in from big sale of house. See, Akoni he know nothing of planting sugar like his grandfather. Him lazy—Akoni *was* lazy. Now Akoni very dead."

The brown eyes of the large woman stared searchingly into the mellow glow of the fuel lamp, as if answers to many dark secrets lay in its ruffles.

"But—who does the plantation belong to now?" Cara wanted to know.

"He—Akoni—sold to very rich man come from America before wedding took place. No! *Two* men wanted Nahele plantation, but only one could buy. Of course, richer man win!"

Now Cara stared, frowning. "Is the new owner there now? Has he come to claim his land?"

"No one there; not even now!" Iola exclaimed her own surprise over the new owner's absence. "No one fix up broken house, no one take care of pretty garden flowers that weeds choke—and not even begin to plant taro or sugar!"

"Well then, the plantation belongs to Pandora—I

mean she can live there if she wants, for the time being, can't she?" Cara wondered.

"Is her place until he comes. Someday owner come; then he might not let her stay. Huh! She always has home here with us." Iola shrugged.

Cara brightened. "She could work at the plantation, if the owner has children. A governess, or something of that sort. Pandora's very well educated, her mother taught at the Mission School, and Pandora also knows her books, religion of the Christians, and Latin and Greek. It could even be enjoyable for her; she loves children."

"Maybe." Iola bent her head.

"Mamma, what's the matter, is there something more you haven't told me?"

"Maybe. I tell you later—someday when I know whole story myself."

Cara shuddered visibly. "Mamma, I know Pandora didn't do it. I mean she couldn't have—killed Akoni!" Next her eyes flew wide. "Where, oh where is Pandora's—uh—you know, the knife?"

Iola leaned back heavily, her pudgy hands on her knees. "I hide them good. Knife and bloody dress. No one find, ever. When Pandora run away before morning, and Mauli find body, only him and me know. I hide all. Mauli never ask, him too sick from stomach disease, drink too much; you know it long ago, and Mauli die. He die, yes, but shut his eyes first and say with last breath Pandora not do it, not kill Akoni Nahele. She too good person. Someone bad do it, very bad. We have to be careful, bad one might come back. Him try to hurt anyone here, I kill *him* first!"

Cara had questions but kept them to herself: what if this new owner of Nahele plantation could be the murderer himself? Possibly, for something in the puzzle did not fit together. She had a shaky feeling this was the reason for the absentee owner. She swallowed her fear next, but with great difficulty. Pandora may very well be the missing link—*he* might have been waiting for her return all this time. But why?

Now the three women lazed together in the living room, the sun no longer peeping through the bamboo lattice. They had cheerfully put away the washed plates and cleaned up; then the room grew silent. They had ceased to chatter, as they had while busy over the meal. The younger women grew drowsy after the delicious fare; they had just managed to finish a desert plate of chunky, sweet pineapple with shredded coconut. Pandora moved silently out of the room and onto the veranda. Cara's eyes followed her cousin, then closed in weariness while Iola watched on.

Farther up along the beach, spears of flickering firelight danced. People, neighbors perhaps, were holding a luau. She could smell the *kalua* pig roasting, cooked to delicious tenderness in a fire pit. From the veranda Pandora could see the illumined faces, all happy ones, some distance away, gaily moving about, small figures that danced and ate while their Hawaiian songs drifted to her. Men and women who would probably go to make love later, on the beach, or in their homes. Husbands and wives. Happy couples.

Pandora was wrenched into loneliness. She could

also smell the cool lagoon waters not far off; she remembered that in places the shallows matched the color of a pair of iridescent eyes.

Green eyes. A man dangerously masculine.

Her body tingled, young and vibrantly alive, then went afire from head to foot. Her arms ached, telling her she had been foolish not to let him make love to her. She wanted him now—Rogan—with a feverish wanting that bloomed in her heart and flamed between her long limbs.

Rogan Thorn, so far away, the man whose savage passions were making her a woman, who knew, finally, what it was like to desire a man.

But would she feel this way when again they came face to face? Or would the fire be greater? She blushed, placing a hand over her thudding heart at the thought.

She was so far from San Francisco now. The tall buildings, the cobbled misty hills, the mournful foghorns. Houses, brilliantly lit. What was the matter with her, anyway? She had been so happy to be home again—and now, foolishly, she wished to be back . . . back with *him*.

Pandora went quietly back to the small bedroom. She heard Iola already sawing logs across the way, and Cara making the sounds of preparation for retiring. She drew the mosquito net across her window, but still could pick out the huge stars twinkling. Tropical stars; they seemed so much bigger here. A full tropical moon, riding high, so bright . . . so romantic. Perhaps the gods here were romantic, too.

Pandora hugged the fluffy pillow close, her eyes

beginning to close. The manly image slipped into her tired mind unbidden.

Rogan.

Dearest, darling.

She wistfully removed the white flower and set it on the bedside table. She recalled that all red, purple, white, and orange flowers stood for passion. Her flower, lonely little blossom. By morning it would be found wilted there where she had placed it.

Chapter Twenty-six

In the morning, Iola softly told Pandora that she was a widow; her husband, Akoni Nahele, was dead.

A flicker of pain and horror moved like a shadow across her face and was gone. Iola did not mention the wedding night. But Pandora listened quietly as it was revealed to her that Akoni, her deceased husband, had no living relatives to claim his earthly possessions. Much to her surprise, Pandora learned that a huge tract of land behind the house belonged solely to her; this land hadn't been included in the sale of Nahele plantation. It was very rich land for planting sugar cane; and there was a vast grove of coconut palms—hers too.

"Very much money come to you, Pandora, if you have men to work sugar land for you," Iola was telling her niece as they breakfasted on the veranda.

Unceremoniously Iola dug into a huge pocket, then handed her niece an envelope. "This money yours, from sale of coconuts. Our neighbors, they sad, think white shark take Akoni's life, leave you poor young widow. You remember them soon. They pick and sell coconuts for you at wharf to merchants. They keep some for the work, rest is yours."

"Oh, no, Aunty, you keep it. I owe you so much; you've been so good to me!" Pandora protested, her wet eyes sparkling.

"My girl owe me nothing! You keep, or I be mad as spitting volcano!" Iola shoved the envelope back into her niece's hands.

All through the conversation Cara had been frowning thoughtfully, listening while she seemed to watch the Hawaiian boys fishing farther up the beach. No one else knew of their secret, kept going through Cara's mind. No one, that is, but the murderer. Was he, this already-wealthy American, greedily waiting to snatch the land that now was solely Pandora's? Would he stop at nothing to obtain it?

Cara shot to her feet, saying, "I'm going for a walk along the beach, Mamma. Is Joe Bane still at home, or has he gone to the mainland on business again?"

Iola finished up her last bit of pancakes smothered with coconut syrup. Surprised, she smiled, remembering that Joe was an old flame of her daughter's. In fact, Joe had been the first of many suitors who had come to court her daughter. But Mauli had found his daughter with Joe Bane on the beach, in broad daylight, both stripped of their wet clothing after a swim. Locked together, they had been vigorously making love in the sand. Joe had just finished when the blow caught him full on his jaw. Not put down by this attack from Cara's father, Joe had returned countless times to court Cara, even after she had long gone to the mainland. He finally discovered where Cara had run off to, but he never followed, even though he loved her with a fierce, unending passion.

271

"Joe is home," Iola said cheerfully. She liked Joe, always had, he was so big and handsome, and mostly Hawaiian, with a smidgeon of Irish. "I see him in Kailua just other day. I think he was mailing another love letter"—brown eyes twinkled mischievously—"to some lucky girl in San Francisco."

"In—!" Cara bit off, her face flushed as she remembered all the letters Joe had written in vain; those that she had not answered.

"Are you taking Patsy?" Iola asked her red-faced daughter. "She still best horse around, even though she old. You used to like riding Patsy."

"I'll walk today," Cara announced. "I sure need the exercise!"

Pandora flew into animation. "Oh, Aunty, I would love to ride Patsy! The beach looks wonderful to me this morning and the sun is not too high yet."

Worriedly Cara spun about. "Pandora, don't ride too far—it could be—uhmm—dangerous." She shot her mother a significant look. Pandora seemed to be remembering things more quickly now.

"Pooh!" Iola expelled the word. "Pandora and Patsy old friends. Horse be happy to take her, like old times! I make Patsy ready. Pandora, you go put on old breeches and baggy blouse you used to wear to ride. Look in trunk in your room."

Pandora squealed in delight, then took her dish to the kitchen to wash and put away. Feeling girlish all over again, she rushed off to her bedroom and rummaged through the trunk for the boyish garb.

"See you later!" Cara called back in high spirits as she left the veranda and touched the sand with her

272

grass slippers.

Iola waved, dabbing at her plump, happy tears with a fold of her huge muumuu. My girls are home again, she sighed to herself, and went to prepare Patsy for the ride.

Palm fronds rustled in a slow dance to the mild sea breezes. Nudging Patsy with her bare knees, Pandora started up the path toward the house. Dismounting, Pandora left Patsy nibbling the patches of grass that spread along the hill's edge alongside the mansion. She entered the wind-blown courtyard, darting glances over her shoulder as she stood indecisive.

Several hundred yards along a barely visible path which led to the private dock, she could see the long stretch of sand, the beach that posed a threat to her somehow. She would not venture there yet; she could not bring herself to brave the walk there for she sensed some memory that lay waiting like a beast behind some black rock.

The three-storied house was in poor repair, the vegetable garden to the right neglected and over-grown with thick-leafed weeds. Everything appeared wind-blown; there must have been many storms, and no one had been about to clean up after them. Luckily the house had been built high enough to be safe from the tidal waves.

Pandora stepped into the vine-shaded lanai; a board creaked ominously. She darted another nervous glance over her shoulder, but saw only Patsy still nibbling the spindly grass contentedly. A small grin of relief crept over her face. The horse would have signaled with a whinny if a stranger had approached. This faithful, old brown horse was like a great friend to her. They had had many special outings together, riding out before the sun climbed too high in the azure sky. Yes, she remembered *that*.

Wraithlike, Pandora moved through the big, airy rooms. She threw open a few musty windows to the sunshine and sea breeze. Nahele plantation. She had spent one terrifying night here alone, upstairs, while out on the beach . . .

"No! Not yet . . . must not think of that now. Easy, Pandora, let it come back easy," she scolded herself softly. Now was not the time to recall the worst that had happened. One thing at a time must be taken, let it fall into place . . . easy.

She had remembered enough for one day; so much had filtered through her mind already . . . that she could almost picture Akoni Nahele in her mind's eye. His image was growing clearer with each step she took in the huge house.

Pandora returned when the air was just turning hot, the breezes balmy no longer. The jacaranda trees were in bloom, their petals, a delicate shower of blue, puddled about their trunks, and their fragrance reached her as she jogged along on Patsy's high back. She pondered on what she had seen at Nahele plantation. To whom did the place belong now?

As frightening as the thought was, she wanted to move into the old house and fix it up. Indeed someone should! It must have been a grand show-place, with gardeners tending the grounds, housemaids bustling inside with dusters and lemon wax, and visitors in from the mainland during the winter months. A *haole* family had even lived here for several years. She could remember the girl, blond and pretty, dainty but mean-tempered. She had had a haughty nose forever in the air.

"Now I remember Akela too. Akela, the old woman who lived there before Akoni took over." Pandora surprised herself by talking out loud. Akela Nahele, her deceased husband's grandmother. Her face had been amiable, brown, and wrinkled, so sweet, so unlike that of . . . Akoni. Of course, Akoni's black eyes had permitted Pandora no peace when she had visited Akela.

Why did all the good people have to die? Like . . . Mamma. Not now! Later she would reminisce about her parents.

Yes, she would love to clean that old house. Iola had said she could get men to work for her, those who had sold the coconuts. She could still see the long, stretching hallways in the house, the Persian rugs, and smell the mixture of sandalwood with mold and mildew. The rosewood and teak furniture had been covered with huge white cloths; protected little though, since no polish had been applied for years. What sort of man could this owner be to leave the plantation in such poor repair? She decided he must be an uncaring soul; he must have more than he needed of worldly goods. The thought made her tremble with anger.

Pandora had not dared to venture to the third floor; for some reason there was something up there for which she was not yet prepared. Tomorrow she would visit the wind-blown plantation again. With each visit she would gain strength and the past would be easier to remember.

God is my strength.

Pandora looked to the sky; what her Christian mother had taught her was coming back to her now.

Chapter Twenty-seven

Joe Bane entered the lanai of his modest, two-story home. Red dust from the cane fields dotted his white trousers and he wore a ragged straw hat that shaded his bronzed countenance. He wore high boots and a shirt of brilliant print. A big man, Joe's presence at once filled the small porch. Joe knew his sister, Leilani, would have a cool glass of lime juice waiting for him.

The juice was there on the table, in the lanai, but so was something else—*someone* else.

He removed his hat and his dark-velvet eyes shone.

"Cara." Joe caressed the name softly. He had the fine, chiseled face of those of Hawaiian blood. It was set off by straight shining black hair; the auburn highlights marked the Irish in him. And he possessed the strong broad shoulders and back of his seafaring father.

Cara shivered with remembered passion and pleasure, a streak of incredible sweetness washing over her. She realized quite suddenly that Joe had always done this to her, made her feel the complete woman. Of course, Joe was not nearly as handsome and arrogant as Rogan Thorn, but Joe had always wanted her. Big and bold and demanding. Lusty. His blood ran hot and his passions flared readily. He never wasted time with preliminaries. He reminded Cara again of a young bull, horns and all. In fact, Joe did see red very often and had to blow off steam.

"*Aloha*, Joe. Won't you say the same?" Cara asked shyly.

Almost three years had passed. Joe just stared as if he were seeing a ghost, a very lovely ghost from out of the past, who had haunted him since she had gone.

"*Aloha*, Cara." He glanced around the room then. "Where is my sister?" He twirled the battered hat. "Has she left you to talk to yourself?" His eyes were burning with intensity and the remembered heat welled up in his strong loins.

Cara flushed nearly down to her grass slippers. "No, we talked. But you know Leilani. She is like a pretty butterfly; she doesn't stay long in one place."

Cara gulped loudly, watching Joe's huge muscles flex in his arm as he tossed his hat onto a wicker chair and picked up the lime juice to sip it.

"True." Joe eased his huge frame onto a bamboo lounge. "My letters, didn't you get them, Cara? I wrote so many. Did you burn them?"

Cara smiled prettily but guiltily, setting her round cheeks aglow with red patches. He kept staring deeply into her eyes and a trembling began deep within her.

"No. I mean no, I didn't burn them." Cara shivered in anticipation.

They were going to make love soon; it was inevitable. It was in their blood.

"What then? Why no answer?" Joe took her small

hand into his, squeezing, dwarfing her dainty fingers with his big, strong ones.

"I—was embarrassed. I ran away after Mauli found us—us making love on the beach," she murmured, breathing deeply, smelling his manly scent.

"I know that! Think I was not embarrassed, too? My cheek still bears the imprint of your father's wrathful knuckles, I think." He chuckled deeply and his chest rumbled.

Shyly Cara peered down at the mat floor. "I've had many lovers, Joe; you know that is why father didn't stop me when I wanted to leave the island. In fact he pushed me out of the house with his biting words."

Joe grinned. "Where did you learn to talk so fine, Cara? You used to be my wild, little *wahine*."

"A woman by the name of Sarah Wolfington . . . taught me." She looked down at his hand buried in her lap, she felt the heat there. "Joe, even in San Francisco I couldn't seem to get enough of—different men." She would not say that she had once loved Rogan Thorn. No, not now . . . not ever.

"I always knew that, too. But still I loved you. You are different now?" His dark eyes searched her paler brown eyes imploringly.

"Slowly, Joe, go slowly. I'm changing; I promise you that. I guess I'm just getting older . . . maturity, you know." Cara shrugged.

"Cara," Joe began with a crack in his voice, "I've been faithful to you. *Cara*," he ended with a note of caress.

Cara blinked incredulously. "How—Joe, you've not taken a woman—all these years?"

"Celibate, yes, for you. I love you."

It was that simple. Joe pulled her gently up from the chair, his eyes fervently aglow. It was obvious to Cara what Joe wanted as he took her hand and led her upstairs. He wasn't one to waste time, ever.

From a vase in the hall Joe took a red hibiscus flower and tucked it behind her left ear. Cara knew what this signified—a woman had a lover.

As soon as he had firmly shut the heavy door to his bedroom, Joe reached out, his bold touch tingling through every nerve in Cara's small frame. It was the same ritual, and Cara wanted this as much as Joe did.

"Joe," Cara faltered, taking up his hand to her cheek, "I think I'm going to be afraid—this time."

Joe lowered his bronze face. "You think that is going to happen? Fear not, Cara. There is something new between us. On your part. Love is washing over us, coming strong and mighty as a tidal wave. Feel it. Cara, come, hold me."

Indeed it was akin to a great wave of love and desire. But Cara begged in an odd little voice, "Joe, go slowly; it has been a long time."

Her gorgeous dark hair, released by capable hands, spread and tumbled about her shoulders when Joe worked the mass from the bun at the nape of her neck. They kissed then, with him probing her soft mouth with his big tongue. Both trembled with desire, still Joe tried to check his urgency to make love to Cara; to go slower as she said. But Joe was like a hot volcano about to erupt.

"Cara," he groaned, "it has been so long for me. Oh, love, I must have you now!"

Joe lifted her and, kissing her throat as he went,

carried her to the mahogany bed. She moaned little-girl sounds at the touch of his big hot hands and gasped with pleasure when his throbbing length came hard against her thighs as he came down beside her. Cara's sarong was unceremoniously swept aside and Joe laughed softly, a deep, manly triumphant sound rumbling from his wide chest, when she moved against him with sudden impatience.

"You *lie*, Cara mine; you cannot wait. It has been a long time!" Joe said over her.

His sensual lips began to nibble at an auburn-tipped breast, his hard, callused fingers purposefully moved along her inner thigh, arousing, setting her secret places on fire. Eagerly Cara helped him shed his dusty clothes, until they both lay naked, close and trembling, wanting to discover each other's deepest secrets all over again.

"Cara, Cara!" Joe groaned into her neck. "Love me, love me, Cara!"

The time was now. She opened up to Joe shakily then and his ready maleness plunged between her thighs to enter her warm honey. Cara whimpered in painful but lovely ecstasy when his heavy thrusts stabbed even deeper, to the hilt, into her tender flesh. He couldn't get far enough inside her, it seemed. Their hips met, drew apart, then came together with love-sounds; expert lovers straining wildly, madly to become one.

The tidal wave washed over them as Joe brought Cara with him to trembling, spiraling heights; again, again, and again they made love, tasting the sweet end together finally.

"Joe!"

"Cara . . . perfect love . . ."

They slept then, as if the world, too, had come to an end for these entwined lovers. Content, Joe murmured in his half-sleep.

"Cara, marry me. Be my woman alone. I love you, Cara, Cara. . . ."

"Yes, Joe, yes. I love you, too!" Cara knew he meant every word he said. Joe always had.

Chapter Twenty-eight

The contours of the island were indiscernible in swirls of morning mist. But soon the jagged mountains, set back from the sea, would be seen to poke green fingers into the yellow sunshine. The mynah birds high in the hills were already calling with hoarse throats to their mates. The bird-of-paradise flowers dripped dew, as did the fragrant plumeria and frangipani. There was no sign of life on the beach yet, no sound but the lazy lapping of the crystal surf on the shore.

A cooling breeze coming through the window brought Pandora to wakefulness. She sighed, at once deciding she would set aside all fears this day. No matter what, she would steel herself to whatever hidden menace lay in her path.

Today Pandora was not tormented with anxiety. It was going to be a grand day, she thought, humming the melody of a waltz from the Millers' party as she rose to wash in the blue-specked basin. She felt that invigorating joy that comes to early risers.

A plan came to her as she splashed her face with cool water and grabbed for a tapa towel. Her spirits soared high by the time she padded into the kitchen to help Iola with breakfast.

"Aunty, I am going to move into the old house and fix it up!"

Iola gasped and nearly jumped out of her tan skin. Then she continued to lazily slice the pineapple into strips, an expression of suspicion replacing the surprise on her face.

"I'm sorry I surprised you like that, Aunty."

Pandora twirled in her rose-flowered muumuu.

"But I feel so good! I must have slept off my tiredness; I feel like a new woman!"

Iola chuckled deeply. She decoratively arranged the spears of pineapple on a plate, setting them around a whole, sliced avocado and wedges of papaya.

"Like 'look of love' on woman's face, eyes deep as water seen from cliff." Yes, her niece seemed to be back to normal. She smiled. Like a balm, the island worked its own cure on a person.

Pandora set about to scramble eggs and Cara entered, humming too, looking fresh and lovely in a flowered sarong, coffee cup in hand. Iola beamed, nodding toward the browned sausage that Cara could now put on the plate.

"My girls sure look good this morning! Both be whole again." Iola grinned, nodding wisely. "Island gods make well. Uhmm-hmmm!"

Although she'd been brought up in the Christian faith, for this day Pandora went along with that. The Hawaiian gods were shining down on them, as was the Almighty. She slid the scrambled eggs onto a huge platter and set the freshly baked biscuits in a circle about them. The food was then laid out on the table on the veranda; they sat down on the bench to eat heartily.

Pandora licked her fingers clean after consuming another tasty sausage. Cara mimicked her cousin, nudging Pandora while they giggled like little girls together. Iola sighed in contentment. The world sure looked good and bright this morning.

"Just like old times when Pandora and parents come to visit," Iola began happily. "Girls make grass skirts and white-ginger leis and do hula. Giggle all the time and ride the waves, lay in the sun and turn brown as them sausages!"

Despite the mention of her parents, Pandora brightened. "Oh, I would love to do all that again! Let's ride the surf tomorrow. I remember—I have a sarong especially cut for swimming. I know I can still hula, too!" She weaved her torso and upheld arms sinuously where she sat.

"And *how* you hula!" Iola cheered, remembering Pandora's expert movements. "Ah! Lono come with drums later. I invite, and we make fire on the beach and girls hula again under moon. I go out to run in back and catch chickens—kill. I know girls like cooked chicken with rice!"

Lono. The name rang a bell, Pandora thought as the vision of a very old man with a dark face and white hair popped into her mind.

Cara clapped her small hands together. "I'll invite Joe!" She blushed at once, something her mother hadn't seen her daughter do in ages. Cara went on quickly to add, "And Leilani, she loves to dance, too!"

"All our friends!" Iola put in. "I invite many

neighbors. We make it luau. Though have to be later," she added after a moment's thought, "maybe in two—three days."

In her excitement over the coming luau, Pandora forgot completely her plans to clean up Nahele plantation. But now, as Iola turned serious, she was reminded of them. Her aunt leaned forward, her voice turning soft.

"We all help you fix up old house, huh?" She nudged her niece. "Pandora, you like after luau we go there?"

Cara looked from one to the other, wondering what the mystery was that she didn't know about. Pandora caught her cousin's bewilderment and spoke up.

"I'm moving into the house on Nahele plantation!" She chuckled warmly then. "At least until the absentee owner comes to boot me off his land!"

Cara set her teeth. "He can't do that! Whoever the old goat is, he has no right! After all, you practically own the whole backyard to the place." Cara had a thought then, and brightened. "It's terrible to say, but maybe the old geezer had a heart attack or something while he was counting all his money. He may never come to claim his land."

"Maybe he all alone, have no relatives, too," Iola put in.

"Those are awful things to say, Iola, Cara. Maybe he's a kindly old gent." Pandora cocked a flaxen eyebrow next. "Maybe he's even—young! Who knows, though, what he is?" She shrugged at the last.

"What if"—Cara began suspensefully—"'he' is a 'she'?"

Iola roared in mirth, rolling her round belly. "That be a hard nut to crack!"

Cara and Pandora fell to giggling at the incongruous statement. Serious again, Iola held up her meaty hand to put a halt to the laughter. The girls dried their eyes and leaned forward expectantly.

"If *he* . . . maybe the man not stay if he come. Huh?"

Cara and Pandora exchanged glances and shrugged, completely lost to the older woman's meaning. There was something *more* significant implied in those few words.

Wickedly, Iola went on. "Hawaiian, like big Joe, too, make it maybe hard—uh—for him to live here? Maybe him sell back house to Pandora? Maybe *give* even? Huh?"

Cara and her mother watched Pandora for a reaction to this naughty scheme to oust the new landlord. But Pandora would have none of this. She shook her bright head, chiding them for their wicked thoughts—Iola's mainly.

"He may have children." Pandora tossed out her palms. "I *love* children!"

Iola saw the wisdom of Pandora's declaration; she then brought up something that surprised the younger women, and gave their speculations a new twist.

"Maybe him bachelor. Handsome, strong, need a woman?" Iola sat still, twiddling only her brown pudgy fingers over her muumuu.

"Count *me* out!" Cara expostulated. She said no more for now; not until Joe came would she make the announcement that they were to wed.

The round head of the older woman swiveled toward Pandora, she for whom Iola's cunning inquiry had actually been intended.

"I have a husband," Pandora murmured, her eyes lifting to gaze out to sea.

"No, niece, you a widow. No have husband," Iola corrected.

Cara swept her eyes toward the beach when her cousin's eyes pleaded for aid in this. Cara wondered how Pandora would handle this one.

"I—yes, I am a widow," was all Pandora said, low.

Well, Cara decided, at least that was the truth!

That night Cara and Pandora performed as they had when small girls growing into teens. They had worked on their grass skirts and white-ginger leis all afternoon. Pandora was mildly shocked that Cara wanted to let her hair hang loose over her naked, bouncing breasts. Cara did have beautiful breasts, heavy for a small woman. In the end, though, they had fashioned bits of tops from colorful scraps of material. It was easy enough to create the modest clothes still worn here by the natives.

Feeling small beside her cousin, Cara peered up at Pandora. "I sure hope you have finished growing. If you don't, your pretty head will be in the clouds!"

"Really, Cara." Pandora giggled in fun. "I am not *that* tall!"

The tropical moon shone down as the girls, Iola, and Lono had their own private party on the beach. To practice, Cara had said. The toothless old man grinned, pattering on the tapa-cloth drums set between his knees as he squatted in the sand, and the girls began a rotation of their bellies. The gentle night-scented breezes lifted long strands of hair from Pandora's high round breasts; her loosened hair alight with red streaks from the firelight, seemed to fly as she danced. Seated next to Lono, Iola chuckled occasionally, rocked in rhythm, and sipped rice wine.

Pandora tossed the grass skirt wildly, her slim, boyish hips rolling in erotically suggestive movements, both sensual and innocent at the same time. She danced with joyous abandon, her most passionate thoughts centering on a tall, handsome man. As she rocked her hips faster, her eyes slipped to Cara whose movements were just as wickedly sensual, maybe more so. But Cara's dark eyes were dreamy in the firelight, and Pandora began to wonder on whom her most intimate thoughts rested. What man created that intense look of desire?

Erotic imaginings entered Pandora's mind. In her mind's eye she saw Cara and Rogan, lying together as they often must have, making love with abandon. She imagined those gracefully gesturing arms clutching Rogan in a fierce embrace, saw them locked together, mating—those suggestive circles of Cara's hips, in time to the rhythm of the drums. . . .

The dance mounted to a frenetic beat and the hula ended suddenly. Pandora was bathed in perspiration, her heart thudding and jumping wildly, as strange sensations darted in her belly. She felt moist and hot. Cara appeared as if she had been transported to heaven. Pandora lightly frowned at her as her cousin dropped to the sand.

"That was wonderful!" Cara exclaimed, out of breath.

"I see—you were having fun," Pandora said softly, her eyes glowing magenta in the firelight.

Cara caught her breath which had been labored. "Why, Pandora, weren't you?"

Indeed Pandora had become aware of every inch of her woman's body during her most sensual movements. She had felt desire so intense that she had thought she must surely explode from the excitement. She wanted to learn every secret of her womanhood. What she really desired was to relive that night in Rogan's arms, but live it all the way, until her whole being pulsed with . . . with what? She was yet ignorant as to what end she sought.

"Pandora?" Cara finally quit panting. "Do you—ever think of Rogan?" But she looked beyond the firelight.

Pandora started. *"Me?"* She peered around the beach and saw that Iola and Lono had gone back to the house for more rice wine.

"Of course you—who else?"

"I should have asked *you* that!" Pandora tried to keep down the sudden jealous anger she felt.

Yet, Iola had announced just that afternoon, away from her daughter, that Cara was seeing Joe Bane again. He had never forgotten that he was Cara's first sweetheart, Iola had added, and she had a strong feeling they would soon marry.

"I am content." Cara sighed the words. "I am here to stay. There is nothing back in San Francisco for me anymore. Remember, I sold all my furniture."

She waited for a response. "You didn't? Of course not. Well, it was enough to get us here—it wasn't a free ride." Cara wouldn't add, though, that she'd gotten a little financial help and spending money for their clothes from Rogan. She went on, "And all my personal belongings in the world, I packed and brought back with me."

"You won't go back ever? Ever?" Pandora asked, surprised at this.

"No," Cara said and sighed. "I am very happy here. This is my home."

"Well," Pandora began, licking her lips wet. "What about Rogan Thorn? I thought you and he were . . . lovers."

For now, Cara paused and smiled thoughtfully.

Pandora hardly ever thought of herself as Rogan's wife; not legally that is. Married yes, but not truly in the eyes of God. Again she wondered what had compelled her to become Rogan's wife. Lord, they were not even friends, but rather acquaintances— warm acquaintances.

Cara quit her pondering. "I was in love with Rogan. Was, I say. He—" She shrugged. "Well, that's all behind me now. Pandora, you still look puzzled over something. You shouldn't be! You see, Joe and I are going to be married. But let that be a secret between us for now."

"Oh . . . yes," Pandora murmured thoughtfully.

Of course, Joe and Cara were in love! Pandora almost kicked herself for a fool. Cara had never glowed like this around Rogan, at least not as far as she knew; not when they departed from San Francisco.

"And Pandora, as for you and Rogan, all you have to do is add your maiden name to the paper made up by Captain Cross. Then you and Rogan will be truly man and wife, making the document legal and binding. That is, if that is what you want."

Pandora looked shocked momentarily. "You mean if Rogan wanted it so, he could just tear up that paper, and it would be something like a divorce? Like nothing had ever taken place between us, no marriage vows, nothing?"

Cara shrugged. "Really, I don't know if it's just that simple. Captain Cross and Bo Gary were witnesses. Rogan *could* tear it up. . . ." Cara let it hang, suspensefully.

"What do you mean? Is there something else that binds the marriage?" Pandora's mind whirled back to that night.

"Y-Yes. Nothing is more binding than when the marriage is consummated." Cara turned so as to gaze into the fire, away from her cousin and her troubled frown.

Pandora chewed her lower lip, murmuring, "I see." She was surprised to find that the remembrance of their wedding night brought a painful lump to her throat.

Chapter Twenty-nine

Through a morning mist of golden hue, the *Phantom* had sailed like a graceful apparition past Molokai and put in at Kailua. Cara had received the letter from Rogan not long ago and now he was here.

Secretively, Cara had kept the letter to herself, not knowing how Pandora would react to his coming. In fact, it was Rogan's idea that Pandora should not learn of this; he wanted to surprise her.

Cara had never thought to see the handsome San Franciscan here in this setting. But as he had said himself, he had been here on business several times before, but never for pleasure. The multimillionaire tycoon fitted well with the wild beauty of her island home. He was dressed in a dark flowered shirt; his white trousers flapped in the breeze about his long, lean legs while, barefoot too, he strolled on the beach with her. He carried a pair of soft-heeled shoes.

"You look wonderful, Rogan; just like a handsome plantation lord!" Cara complimented profusely.

Having been on shipboard for several weeks, Rogan's countenance already had a golden-brown shade, which enhanced his eyes, gossamer green as the palest underwater plant seen through a misted waterfall. Oddly, he appeared taller, leaner, of longer face, and reminded Cara somewhat of a dark-skinned pirate. He looked relaxed away from his shipping empire, but there were new crinkle lines at the corners of his eyes that hadn't been there before. They only added to his virility, she decided.

"Mahalo," Rogan returned with a dip of his sable-brown head. His hair, burnished with golden glints here and there, framed his sun-tanned face that seemed to have acquired a spattering of freckles across the bridge of his nose.

"Ah!" Cara blurted. "You know Hawaiian!"

"Indeed I do, *wahine.*"

"You *would* know the word for girl, wicked man!"

Rogan grinned, flashing white teeth beneath a sun-bleached mustache. "So, tell me, why don't you look Hawaiian like Mamma Iola?"

"You've met her?" Cara was surprised.

"Just. She introduced herself, offered me some lemonade after the hot ride here. I was just about to return to Kailua when I noticed you coming along the beach. Well, is Iola really your mother?"

"Oh, yes! But Mamma is not full-blooded Hawaiian; she just looks it. Don't remind her she is not, though! She thinks of herself as total native Hawaiian."

Rogan kicked at the sand with his bare feet, his voice going softer. "Where does Pandora come in? Is she your mother's niece?"

"Colter St. Ives is—*was*—Iola's brother. Swiss blood I think. Whatever, we are all mountain-island folk. Half-warm-blooded, the other half cold-blooded." She laughed at her joke.

"What about Pandora's parents?" Rogan eagerly wanted to know.

"Linda was a schoolteacher. She was a Christian, but Greek myths were her favorite subject."

"Greek myths, hmm?" Rogan murmured. "So that's where Pandora got her name," he added as an afterthought, recalling a tale in Greek mythology about "Pandora's Box."

Cara turned serious. "I will tell you later how Colter and Linda perished in a shipwreck. But later—yes! For now, tell me: You said you've been here before." She let her cheerful brown eyes roam over his cool and clean attire.

"Of course. I've been to every port that the *Baghdad* has seen—and more—well, nearer to home—with the *Phantom*. This is her second time here; she's my private schooner. But, you know that. I've taken her as far as New York and up into the Chesapeake. Virginia is beautiful, but I favor these islands. This one in particular takes my breath away."

Cara peered up at him. Speaking of breathless, she wondered if he'd seen Pandora. She must not have returned from Nahele plantation, Cara decided.

Cara, shielding her eyes from the sun, sighted a young woman just coming down off the veranda. "Oh-oh, be prepared, here comes Leilani, Joe Bane's little sister. She has been dying to meet you ever since she overheard me telling Joe of your coming." Cara felt guilty then, for everyone knew this but Pandora.

"Joe, hmm? Is he the guy who puts those stars in your eyes lately?"

"Yes." Cara blushed.

Rogan let out a low whistle then. "You said *little sister*, didn't you?"

An exotic girl with upswept black hair was sauntering toward them. Small and lovely, sensuous, Rogan noticed at once. All bashfulness aside, she stepped right up to him and placed a white-ginger lei around his shoulders. When she leaned to give him a kiss, she giggled from the tickling of his thick mustache.

"Aloha, Mr. Thorn!" Her eyes swept him with incredible sultriness.

"*Aloha,*" Rogan returned softly, her audacious flirting making him catch his breath. This young woman hid nothing!

Leilani tilted her dark head to one side, continuing to scour him from head to foot. "There is luau tomorrow at our home, Mr. Thorn. You are coming?"

He chuckled. "I guess. If I'm invited."

"Of course!" Leilani and Cara chimed together.

Iola waved from the veranda just then, but Rogan was captivated by the pretty Hawaiian girl, so he didn't see. Cara waved back, noticing that her mother was looking the other way now, in the direction Pandora had taken on Patsy. Iola stared back at Rogan Thorn, a pondering expression lining her heavy features as she put a thoughtful finger to her lips. Cara shrugged and Iola went back into the house to finish preparing her favorite Hawaiian dishes for the luau.

"Well," Rogan muttered, finally returning to earth. "I'll have to get back to Kailua now. Pleasure to meet you, Leilani."

"Mmm-hmmm. Later, Rogan Thorn, at luau."

Leilani sauntered away then, swaying her hips in a practiced manner, knowing that the American was watching. She pursed her lips. All men watch Leilani, she thought.

"You just got here!" Cara complained.

Rogan finally tore his stare from the swaying, twitching buttocks. But he knew the dark eyes had held promise of pleasure—if one was so inclined.

Cara watched Rogan go, wondering at his strange attitude. Had he had a change of heart? No word about Pandora? Leilani's charm must have gotten to him. Cara tossed up her hands and went into the house. Whoever began the fiction that women were the fickle sex must have been a fool!

Cara smiled to herself then. All men but Joe, her love.

The blue-green sea rolled in foaming breakers to the white sand. Mesmerized by its action, Pandora stood on the top floor in the east wing, staring out the window. Gradually she became aware that something else, a nameless horror, held her in a trancelike state.

A knife was held loosely at her side. It was her knife.

A few minutes ago Pandora had discovered that and a bloodstained wedding dress concealed at the bottom of an old trunk shoved far back into a corner. The dress was hers, too. This she knew.

Pandora's sun-tanned face had gone pale at her discovery of these items. Her heart had quickened. But now it seemed as if there were no life in her at all and the last shred of sanity had seeped from her mind.

Earlier in the day, Iola had gone to the trading store for material to create more muumuus and sarongs, plus the new gowns for the luau, for her girls. So Pandora had headed north. Patsy had been fresh and anxious to stretch out her legs as Pandora had urged the mare along the beach road. Arriving at the plantation, Pandora had roamed the upper rooms of the shadowed and silent house. In the hall she had found a hodgepodge of old furniture, old matting, and a stained feather mattress; all had been piled against the faded blue walls.

She had felt as gay and light-hearted as when she had awakened that morning. She had donned a new, aqua-colored muumuu that Iola had made for her; it had taken the older woman no time at all to fashion it.

As she had wandered through the house, her eyes had fallen on the old trunk. Pandora had rummaged happily through the contents in the hope of discovering some treasure that had belonged to Nahele's grandmother. She had loved the dear old Hawaiian woman and the plantation was all very reminiscent of Akela.

Fear had seized her as her hand touched a cold object at the bottom of the trunk. Then she had seen the white dress, washed several times she could tell, but still obviously bloodstained.

How Pandora had ever made it to the window, she'd never know. Now emerging from her trance and beginning to tremble, Pandora took the knife back to the trunk and, kneeling on a straw mat, she lifted it. The blade glinted, catching the light streaming through the window. She held it for a little longer, trying fiercely to remember; then she opened the lid of the trunk and hastily stuffed the sharp knife back into its hiding place.

Who had hidden these? she wondered. Who, and most important, why?

The lid shut with a muffled sound after she had let it down. But Pandora stayed where she sat, wavering uncertainly.

"My knife; my wedding dress," she muttered. Just that morning Iola had said that Pandora was a widow, namely Akoni Nahele's widow.

All at once, Pandora started as from a dream . . . a nightmare. She shuddered. Talons of fear pawed fiercely up and down her back. With a wild cry she thought she knew how Akoni had died. It was no sickness or shark that had taken her husband's life.

He had been slain—oh, God—by her own hand!

Loathsome shapes of horror and murder crouched before her, and with a cry she turned aside, not wanting to see the visions, her mind trying to flee from them. But wherever she looked the shapes were before her.

Blood, a knife slashing flesh. Someone running— her?

She reeled backward and sprawled on the floor, striking her head on the edge of the trunk.

Gathering gloom spun about her, faster than a whirlwind in an endless night. It seemed as if a black breeze bore her on its wings, and the island gods cried angrily to her through the murk settling in her brain.

"Pandora, leave this place. We must bid you farewell."

A great sob rose in her throat. "No, not yet!" She rolled her head on the hardwood floor. The Hawaiian gods were angry with her for—for murdering one of their own people?

"No, I did not do it!" Pandora sobbed.

The gods seemed to laugh at her then. "Woman, you have many dangers to go through before the truth be known. But through a sad and happy time you will find it. You have opened the trunk and loosed the past, curious one. We would give you precious hope; what will you do with it?"

"I would take it and keep it."

"First you must free yourself, or else feel a murderess forever. Your heart is locked within your own hopelessness and despair. You must search for the one with the hero's heart. Promise."

"I promise!"

"He is here. . . . He is here. . . ."

From the misty darkness in which Pandora had lain down to sleep, she rose up and pushed herself to her elbows. She crouched for a moment, listening. Then she shook her head to clear it. She did not believe in Iola's island gods!

Such lovely hopes and dreams? Pandora laughed aloud at the dream. She had been ready to promise anything in her fear. But now suddenly the world seemed right again.

"There is some magic spell at work here," she said with a deep chuckle, feeling for the tender spot on her head where she had bumped it.

Keeping her eyes averted from the trunk, Pandora sped down the stairs and out the door. Patsy whinnied when she approached and, turning her big head, the horse rubbed her long nose tenderly against Pandora's flushed cheek.

Pandora rode back, peace-filled, to her aunt's home. She spied a dark schooner riding far out in the waters, but paid it no mind. Men were always fishing these waters beyond the dock. As the horse jogged along, Pandora thought she had experienced a very strange thing indeed. Nothing like it had ever happened to her. But miraculously her mind had cleared; she was untroubled again. The afternoon had been like a fantasy.

But this was nothing compared to the events that would follow.

Chapter Thirty

After bedding Patsy down in the shed, Pandora walked the short distance to the house. She smiled, thinking over the strange day she had spent at the Nahele plantation. Slipping into the house, she found that all was quiet. She remembered that Iola would be taking food to the Banes's for the luau. But her cousin should have returned by now; perhaps she was just napping in her room.

"Cara?" she called softly.

Pandora received no response. She started out of the room to go into the lanai, but her hand froze on the louvered door. Through the slats she could see two people, moving slowly, close together. She gulped at the intimate scene and began to back away. Cara and Joe were locked in a lovers' embrace.

"Joe! Joe! I love you."

"Cara, my *lovely* woman, how I want you now. I cannot wait for *honi-ipu.*"

His huge hand slipped into her muumuu capturing the fullness of a round breast. Pandora's eyes were like twin blue moths drawn to a flame as Joe's hand moved to the front of his trousers. Pandora caught her breath at the size of him.

He wasn't going to . . .

Pandora's muscles betrayed her and her feet would not budge to take her away from this erotic scene. She wanted to run. . . . She had to be gone from here.

"Here, Joe? Like this?" Cara was asking him softly, breathlessly.

Joe answered by slipping his hands behind Cara, lifting her gently to him, cupping her small buttocks, almost letting her feet touch the floor.

"No one is home, Cara darling."

She was lifted off the floor now, her legs brought up to entwine about his waist. She moaned, "Yes Joe, we are alone. Love, give me all!"

Her thighs were parted wide and with one forward motion Joe was in her. Pandora tried shutting out the scene, but her eyes flew open as if with a will of their own. Cara was tossing back her head, mewling softly in her throat. He pressed slowly, then faster and faster, his ragged breathing harsh as he lifted her higher to bring them closer yet.

Pandora stuffed a fist into her mouth to keep them from hearing the whimper that escaped her throat. Joe was muttering endearments and Cara was writhing and crying out loud as she answered his need.

Pandora's blood pounded and coursed hot and she felt the flames rising up between her own limbs. It was as if she were bound to a burning stake that held her prisoner. The pair were shuddering together now as Pandora finally backed from the door, her cheeks flaming.

Pandora strove to be free of the intense excitement that had built up inside her like a live thing. But hearing a shuffling behind her, she started. She spun about wildly and found herself facing Iola. Her aunt took in Pandora's shocked white expression and the bright red spots flaming her cheeks. Iola peeked through the louvered door and chuckled softly.

"Huh, my girl needs man, too." She took Pandora by the hand to lead her away from the loving.

Pandora choked back a sob and freed herself from the woman's gentle grip. Tears made hot trails down her cheeks as she flew through the house and outside. She headed toward the beach, not caring where she went, just wanting to get away from the lovers she would have to face if she stayed.

On the beach now, Pandora slowed. The sound of the waves lapping the shore soothed her jangled nerves somewhat and the breeze fanned her hot cheeks. But her heart still beat a rapid tattoo.

She should not have spied on them, Pandora chided herself; that had not been decent. But the love and desire that had flamed between the two had held her spellbound. There were no secrets between Cara and Joe, she found herself thinking a little jealously.

Pandora slumped to the sand, folding her long legs beneath her. Oh, to have a love like that would be heavenly, someone to sit beside her now while the sun set plunging into the sea like a red ball of fire. To be held in his arms. She looked across the sea, sighing dreamily now.

The sun seemed to hiss in the water as it left the rim of the world, and Pandora sat alone bathed in lavender and pink, wishing, just wishing that her man was here.

*　　　*　　　*

A full moon rode high. Folks had already come from Kailua and Honolulu and even from the other islands in the chain; sailboats and the island-hopping steamer had brought them. The announcement of the forthcoming wedding would be made later, but for now some guests roamed about mingling while others sat on floor mats or long benches, nibbling at their leisure from the sumptuous feast laid on *ti* leaves spread on tapa mats.

The musical accompaniment to the feast was played on ancient instruments. There were drums of many sizes; the jumping bug (ukulele), gourd rattles, and bamboo flutes. A most beautiful tone came from the fluted conch shell; it produced a haunting sound—a mellow call that floated over the grounds and could carry over miles of ocean or lea. A small Hawaiian woman carried a tiny drum which lay in her lap as she sat back on her heels. Her voice was old, but she managed it so well that its effect was pure sweetness.

Tables and chairs had been provided for the *haole malahinis,* the white strangers, but the young and limber were encouraged to sit on the floor. *Ti*-leaf tablecloths were scattered with flowers and there was an array of curious little bundles of soaked and soggy leaves. *Laulau,* the leaf bundles, disclosed soft and savory meats of pork and beef when unfolded. Roast pork from the *imu* was the *pièce de résistance.* Small rubbed *koa* dishes held the relishes of turmeric, tiny dried shrimps, and chopped *kukui* nuts. Throughout the feast the hula girls had been dancing and tantalizing aromas filled the night-scented air.

There was a mingling of blood here that included

some Oriental and some Hawaiian, but mostly *haole*-Hawaiian like Joe Bane. The faces were all richly hued. Lono's dark eyes were calm, speculative, as they came to rest on his grandson's *haole* guest from America. He wisely nodded as if they shared a secret when he caught Rogan's eye. Rogan was looking over the crowd when Cara came up behind him.

"Don't worry; she is coming," Cara said, latching her arm into his.

In taupe-colored trousers and a green-leafed shirt which matched his eyes perfectly, Rogan was darkly handsome. He dragged his eyes away from Joe's grandfather, the very old man with the dark face and white hair, to acknowledge Cara's presence.

Rogan cleared his throat. "Uh, I was only looking for Leilani."

"Sure," was all Cara replied.

He went on as if he hadn't heard her. "She promised to dance for me. Who else did you think?" he asked, smiling.

"Well, Rogan, you are very lucky suddenly. Here she comes," Cara wore a sly grin.

Rogan spun about, almost spilling his drink on Cara's new *holoku*. He had joked to Joe that the drink had floating garbage in it. Joe had laughed at that, never having heard it put quite that way. Floating fruit, maybe. But Bane had chuckled.

"Well, well, if it isn't—uhmm—hello, Leilani," Rogan greeted the exotic female, his eyes still weaving throughout the colorful groups of people, standing and sitting and just-arriving.

"Oh, Joe is looking for me," Cara said, already

moving away. "See you later; don't get lost now, you two." She winked an eye at Rogan, and received a slight narrowing of the eye from him.

Now it was Leilani who latched on to Rogan and she was much like a tree-clinging vine for the next quarter of an hour. She led him to a table that had coconut shells of *poi* on it, along with pineapple juice, lime juice, papaya, and the curious bundles of soaked and soggy leaves.

"Try it, Thorn," Leilani said, giggling. "You like *poi*."

She dipped her fingers in, gave them a quick swirl and carried the pale purplish ball quickly to her mouth. She opened her mouth to laugh when he only stared and shuddered a little, and the stuff could be seen sticking to her tiny teeth.

"Ah, I think I'll try something else, Leilani," Rogan begin. "I don't think I care for *poi* enough to learn that trick."

"Ha-ha-ha; oh, Rogan Thorn, someday I get you to eat *poi*, hmm?" She looked up at him over her hunched-up, bare shoulder.

"Leilani, do me a favor, will you, and get me another drink? But this next one without the colorful bits of fruit?"

"Oh, yes, Thorn. I get you drink, and make it very strong for you. All right? You stay here, wait for Leilani?"

Rogan hunched his shoulders and sighed in boredom when she had gone to a far table at the side of the veranda. The symbolism of the native dances was lost on him, but still he stood, mesmerized for a time by the whirling and swirling of the red- and yellow-feathered gourds.

Rogan began to wonder if he should have come to this luau. So far it was damnably dull and boring, and even the hula girls could not hold his attention for long. He brought a huge, cut blossom up to his nose to smell its fragrance; then something caught his eye and his gaze froze. A man, a very dangerous sort by the looks of him, was scanning the crowd carefully. He seemed to be on an important mission and he puffed at length on a long fragrant cheroot. His eyes narrowed as the smoke drifted up into them. He was indeed after someone, raking through the guests like that, like a spy or the secret police.

Rogan decided that the man might very well be searching for his wayward wife, nothing else. Why would the police be pursuing a criminal here, anyway? This was an engagement party, and no one here could be under investigation. Not that he knew of, that is. He shrugged, letting it go for now.

Rogan didn't notice Leilani's approach, lost as he was in his own thoughts, until she stepped right before him and placed the drink into his hands. She flashed up at him an almost unhappy smile.

"Would you like me to hula for you, Mr. Thorn?"

"Well,"—he laughed softly—"maybe a little later. I'm trying to put some fire in my blood right now"— he held up the potent libation she had brought— "and it takes all my concentration."

"Fire?" Leilani swayed her rounded hips in time to the drums beating for the other hula girls. Shamelessly she moved closer to him. "Oh, yes! I know how to make bigger and better fire in Thorn," she purred, brushing the front of his trousers with the sexual movement.

Rogan held her away from him and looked down at Leilani with a little smile. Undaunted, her brown arms came up to snake and hook about his neck. He held the drink out stiffly with one hand to keep it from sloshing on either of them. Suddenly his jaw squared and he was not smiling anymore.

"What are you looking at, Mr. Green Eyes?" Leilani tilted her head provocatively. Following his line of vision, she turned slowly, still clasping her hands at his neck.

Wise Lono nodded again to Rogan just as a tall, golden vision of beauty stood directly across from Leilani and Rogan. She had come like the morning sun up over a hill. Her sunshine-streaked hair was caught up in a silver net strung thick with tiny pearls and smoothly falling down her back midway. She wore a pink-and-turquoise, princess-style *holoku*, a striking silk creation that trailed behind her in back and clung to her high round breasts in front. One huge flower had been tucked behind her right ear, signifying she had a lover. She was haloed in gold beneath a tiki-torch.

"Oh. It is only Pandora," Leilani said with disinterest after she caught the direction of his eyes.

"Yes. Only," was all Rogan muttered.

"Why you shiver, Rogan Thorn? Is not cold, but very hot night," she said meaningfully, trying to capture his attention.

Entranced by the sudden appearance of Pandora, Rogan stood speechless. Leilani caught her breath,

309

and let her arms fall to her sides. This man was staring at Pandora as if she were a queen or something just as magnificent. She pouted. Haughty Pandora. How come Rogan Thorn did not look at Leilani like that? Leilani was annoyed by his obvious appreciation of the *haole* woman. She decided she could make Thorn desire her just as much, if not more. All she needed was time.

"She is a widow. No fun." Leilani added another barb.

"I know." Rogan watched Pandora walk over to Cara and Joe Bane, her silk dress revealing a graceful shimmer of movement as it molded against her slim curves.

"Ahem. Excuse me, Leilani."

Before Rogan could gain full stride, Leilani caught up with him to enlace her fingers around his newly tanned ones. There was nothing he could do, no gesture or word or phrase that would not appear impolite; and so he was compelled to walk with Leilani by his side, a superfluous smile plastered across his face.

Between the slanting curtain of her lashes, Pandora saw them come her way. She was not surprised to see Rogan, for she had known beforehand that he had come to Hawaii. Earlier, she had seen him walking the beach with Cara and she had watched them covertly. But now her cousin had eyes only for Joe Bane. Strangely, she had felt pangs of jealousy at the first glimpse of Leilani with Rogan. Maybe not so strange, she deduced, considering how lonesome she had been without him. Still, the beautiful Hawaiian girl followed him everywhere, Cara had said on a trip back to the bungalow. Then there had been the twinkle of mystery in Cara's eyes, and Pandora had wondered why.

Now Pandora pondered on it no more: philanderer Rogan Thorn had found himself yet another love. He was nothing but a wicked, wicked man! But for now Pandora could see that Rogan was enjoying himself immensely, and, Leilani was known to be free with favors where men were concerned. He would certainly find himself well-entertained this night, to be sure.

Pandora felt him drawn to her, and held there, before he even reached her. If he so much as touched her, she would fall apart right here in front of everyone. That she could not allow to happen.

"*Aloha*," Rogan said smoothly and smiled down into her ice-blue eyes; eyes that appeared longer with the upsweep of the hairdo. She wore only one flower—love's flower. A brilliant red, as if full of young blood, it seemed to be leaning toward him with its wide mouth flaring, breathing on him with a heavy, exotic perfume. Her gaze fastened on his mouth and seemed to melt before lifting.

He was, he realized, embarrassingly disturbed.

"*Aloha*, Rogan Thorn," Pandora answered with a false bright smile, but the little catch in her voice betrayed the quickening of her pulse.

How handsome and dark he looks, Pandora thought, her perusal carefully sweeping his bright chestnut hair, its fullness curling slightly. One of his rare sweet smiles curved his lips. Impulsively, her eyes lowered to take all of him in, and then widened to fly away at once.

311

Rogan did not bat an eyelid; he looked so composed and cool that she kept herself from perusing him further. But her heart seemed to stand still and wait.

The slow moments added up. The sea blew in on a westerly wind that shifted and ruffled his hair. All the stars blurred and seemed to be trembling, but Pandora knew it was she herself who trembled with taut desire.

"Are you enjoying your . . . vacation?" Pandora blurted and the words sounded all wrong and stupid to her burning ears.

"*Now* I am," he said, never glancing away from her.

Leilani leaned heavily and possessively against Rogan and smiled cattily up at the taller woman. Pandora's fingers itched to slap her oval face and to tear at her silky jet hair that flowed in a straight arrow down Leilani's back. They had never cared much for each other, and this time was no exception. And Rogan—his manner was infuriatingly calm, while she felt tossed about inside.

"Come with me, Mr. Thorn. Leilani wants to show you something now. I have a special dance for you. Come on. Ha-ha-ha, come!"

"Go ahead, Mr. Thorn," Pandora mimicked Leilani. "You are ambitious, and Leilani's hula *is* something you should not miss," she added, tossing her head in that special way of hers.

Rogan's eyes flashed. "You're ambitious, too, aren't you?"

"What are you getting at?"

"I admire women who know what they want out of

life and go after it."

Pandora flicked a glance over Leilani and then back to him. "As you do?" she asked.

With that, Pandora, not awaiting his answer, tossed her head and walked away with a grace that a queen would envy.

All right, Rogan thought, go away, haughty Pandora, and we shall see who will be the winner of this foolish game you play tonight.

The *bom-bom* of the drumbeat pulled Leilani into her hip-swaying and arm-waving movements. They told a story of spring flowers that rose from the earth and swayed; rain fell on the thirsty blooms; they lived, they died; they blew away withering in the wind.

Rogan wore an inscrutable expression while watching Leilani dance to the beat of the drum that pounded in his blood, pulsated. His blood began to heat, and his sensuality quickened to a feverish pitch. As young men pressed closer in the circle about Leilani, she tried to see over their heads to Rogan Thorn. But he let himself drift farther back and finally he stood outside the thick ring. He tossed a sweeping glance over his shoulder. Then the crowd parted a little where Leilani danced and with sign language Rogan showed her that he was going for another drink.

Rogan took the opposite direction from where the drinks were set up and darted his eyes this way and that. He scowled darkly. There he was again, the cloak-and-dagger man. Rogan felt his irritation rise and, purposely avoiding the smoking man, went off the veranda.

"Cara, have you seen Pandora?" he called to her and Joe in the garden.

"Sure, Rogan Thorn," Joe answered for his woman. "She went that way."

Joe pointed in the direction of the beach. Rogan's step quickened.

Chapter Thirty-one

Where the stately columns of flowers thinned out to scattered blooms along the path to the beach, a lonely figure moved slowly. The tropical moon bathed Pandora's face as she paused momentarily, darting glances over her shoulder.

The moon-touched palms swayed and shook their fronds a little uneasily. The breeze off the sea seemed to wait, a part of it held in sultry suspension.

Freeing her hair of the pearled net, she stepped out from under a tree-clinging vine, stopping just long enough to disentangle a tendril from the clutches of the vine. With her chin resting on her shoulder she glanced back again and, holding up the trailing skirt of her *holoku*, Pandora moved a little faster now, going through the trees toward the beach. Her heartbeat quickened and her legs moved more rapidly. The beat of the drum became distant, but still pounded in her pulse, mingling with the whooshing surf and the swaying swish of palms. Breathless now, she reached the lagoon where the sand sparkled like diamonds in the moonlight.

She knew this secluded spot; she had come here before. . . .

Rogan's thoughts raced ahead to Pandora. The night game she played was at hand, its outcome predetermined. Even if it was one-sided, he was sure to be the winner. His groin turned tumid, desire increasing with each long stride he took. He felt the thrill of the hunting cat on the heels of a fine quarry.

Pandora kicked off her dainty wood-heeled slippers to better her own long stride in the deep sand. She resumed her former speed, and her breath now came in short little gasps that pained her chest. Then, between one breath and the next, the inevitable hand clamped hard on her shoulder. She cried out a whimper and tried to keep moving.

He gritted his teeth and tried jerking her to a standstill. The hands, the grip, wonderful and warm and strong, finally spun Pandora about.

Trembling with a violent shudder, a sob lifted from her throat and his name slipped involuntarily from her lips.

"Rogan!"

In the moonlight he gazed down at her, tall as one of the legendary Hawaiian chiefs.

"Yes, don't be afraid, Pandora; it's only me."

She was encircled in his viselike arms at once.

"Here alone," he continued against her ear. "Just the two of us with the moon meant for lovers."

Pandora said nothing, but swayed in his arms, the softest part of her figure against the thigh that was bent to keep her from falling. He held her securely, bending her far back, and brushing her lips with kiss after kiss before deepening their desire with the insertion of his tongue. He drew her closer and they exchanged kisses again and again. Pandora felt the

316

treacherous currents in her flow toward him while his lips lowered to her neck, then lower yet, touching upon each breast that he swiftly bared. The vision of Leilani brushing up against Rogan loomed before Pandora. Her lips, parted fresh from his kisses, formed the biting words she unleashed now.

"Damn you, you have no right!"

His head came up sharply. "No right?" he asked incredulously.

"Let me go, Rogan!"

He shook his head firmly.

"No! No!"

Pandora put her hands flatly against his chest and shoved, but instead of breaking contact, he only tightened his hold. She bent back from him, her hair flowing straight to her buttocks, swaying sinuously. But he gathered her chest back to press against his, crushing his mouth this time over hers until she tasted blood. Rogan seized now what he had desired ever since he had first taken her in his arms in his home. Even as she struggled against his rocklike hardness, he lifted her none too gently and proceeded to carry her to drier sand, away from the surf that had licked at their bare feet. Her hands balled into two slim fists to beat against his chest, and he let her play herself out. He stood there, rigid and unmoving, while she continued to fight a one-sided battle desperately. Finally he laid her down on the sand and followed her, his long frame close.

Forgetting himself in the heat of passion, Rogan moved over her, his length pressing so hard between her thighs that she cried out in pain. He was not going to be gentle, she feared.

"You . . . are being too rough. . . . Oh, *please* . . ."

"I do not have it in mind to hurt you, sweet . . . but the night is not over yet. Trust me . . . God, how I want you!"

"I—I forgot something," she fibbed, suddenly the coward.

He lifted his head. "What is it now?" he ground out, impatient to know the secrets of her perfect body that tormented him into madness.

"The luau . . . the announcement, Cara and Joe . . . I . . . we cannot miss it!"

"Oh, God, Pandora, is that all?"

"No . . . suddenly I do not feel so well . . . something I ate maybe."

He almost snapped apart inside. "Hell!" he grumbled. "You haven't eaten a thing!"

"Earlier—before I arrived."

"You are a tease, Pandora, and damned if you don't blow hot, then cold!" He moved quickly beneath the shimmering dress and began to probe, bunching the skirt up to her thighs with a knee.

"Oh!" She started, suddenly gone rigid. "What . . . ?"

"Don't worry . . . yet. It's only a caress. . . ." He showed her what he was doing to her by pushing her skirt higher; she stared down to see it was nothing more frightening than his hand gently exploring the outer secrets of her honeyed thighs.

"Does that feel good?" He murmured the question hoarsely. "Lay back, Pandora, relax."

She caught her breath in a gasp.

"Easy, sweet, you've been this way before." He probed a bit further and found himself frowning over the unexpected barrier that he had come up against. "No, it couldn't be. . . ." He shook his head.

"That . . . hurts a little, Rogan." She quivered all over like a startled fawn, and she was becoming truly alarmed now.

He chuckled, sliding a knee over hers. "It must have been hard for you . . . did it hurt much?"

Pandora frowned under his shadow that kept the moon from finding her face. What did he mean . . . ? Did *what* hurt much?

"I promise not to hurt you. You're so incredibly lovely . . . how could I?" His burning gaze traveled slowly down her slim body, then up again, knowing her resistance was disappearing. "I'll be gentle, sweet, but you must trust me right to the end. . . ." He frowned to himself, at his own words. She couldn't know his damnable tormenting thoughts. What an awful path they traversed. I must make good this first act, he thought; another night like this might not come. . . . Oh, Lord, to end too soon . . .

Rogan positioned himself over her, then brought his lower half only down to thrust and roll gently this time, rhythmically. Pandora moaned beginning to wish he would remove his clothes. She was as good as naked herself, she thought, with her breasts half-bared, her skirts bunched up to her waist. Her heels dug into the sand, her back arched naturally to press close to his demanding thighs, her own seeking to get closer to the hardness grinding between them. Her eyes widened when his mouth came down to close over a coral-tipped nipple that swiftly hardened when his tongue flicked it lightly. Without her even being aware of it, her fingers went around his neck

319

and threaded through his thick brown hair. He left the nub he had made moist. Now he knew her desire matched his.

As she lay vulnerable beside him on the beach, her dream became reality, his conquest was complete. She knew this; so did he.

He drew her close, his leg entwined with hers, and buried his head in her shining hair that had tumbled and spread itself in a fan about her head. A quick joy surged through her blood when he finally spoke.

"The stars are yours this night, dear love," he murmured, nuzzling her moist neck, her throbbing pulse there. "No more denials?" he asked to reassure himself.

"No," she said in a shy little voice, defeated, but glad.

Fearing the worst would happen, as before, Rogan groaned near her ear, "It must be now, Pandora. Now!"

After removing their clothes in a rush, Pandora felt the tumescence of his manhood nudge her quivering thighs. No more pieces of clothing were between them now and they began to kiss and nibble at the hot places on each other, gasping, lunging, trying to get closer. They strained together, and she spread her thighs for him in readiness.

He plunged deeply, once.

"Oh, God! Ohhhh," she cried, and he stopped, staring down at her in surprise and some shock at the pain she had experienced.

"No, Rogan, do not stop. . . . Oh, please, keep on . . . keep on . . ."

He moved himself slowly, still frowning down at

her, almost out, and then forward again. Deep. Once more. No more.

"Damn! *Damn!*" Rogan groaned with a deep sob.

"What . . . ?" Pandora's eyes flew wide to stare at the moon.

The flame threatened to consume her, too, but when she arched her back for more, she was disappointed because his delicious fullness had receded.

Rogan gritted his teeth in frustration. Surly and cursing, he rolled heavily from her and seemed to be burrowing himself into the sand.

Pandora's star plunged to the earth.

She wondered painfully if this was all there was to it. Was this *honi-ipu?* as the Hawaiians called love-making. But no, it could not be. Cara and Joe had made love long and hard, striving to an end that seemed to be a mutual ecstasy. Their loving had appeared so natural and wonderful, not like this pain followed by sudden emptiness. She still felt the throbbing between her thighs and wondered why he should be the one so angered. It was not her fault!

"You were a virgin!" Rogan muttered darkly.

She gritted her teeth, then spat, "What did you expect—a whore?"

"Damned if I didn't take your virginity," he repeated in a dumbfounded gasp.

His words echoed, shattering the magic that had been alive between them so short a time ago. She even had to force a bitter laugh now as she moved to stand, brushing sand from her nakedness with frustrated movements.

"And you act as if it was I who took yours!" she

spat back in his moon-drenched face that rolled toward her. "Why don't you go back and find Leilani, Rogan Thorn?" she said in that woman's sing-song voice. "She certainly is not a virgin! You would like that better—a whore!"

Uttering more unkind words that drove barbs deep into where a man lived, Pandora gathered her clothes.

"Rest assured, I will then," he shouted up at her, but a new strong wind tore his words to pieces.

"You made me miss the announcement for the wedding!" she shouted, too, into the breeze.

"You made yourself!"

Fast as lightning she was up and away, speeding naked along the beach, her clothes flying out behind her. She stopped long enough to pick up a slipper she had dropped. It was then she noticed the rent in her dress.

"You ruined my dress, you beast, you bodice-ripper!" she screamed back over her shoulder.

"Stupid virgin!" he returned.

"Animal! Philanderer!"

"Dizzy bitch!"

"Oh! Oh!"

Rogan watched her silvered figure race up the beach, her dress halfway on, her loosened flipping hair a moon streak behind her.

"Damn! Damn!" Rogan muttered, snatching up his clothes. He noticed his ruined fly, and shouted to the disappearing woman, "You ruined my pants, you trouser-ripper!"

He cursed his inadequacy again. His head hung low; his taut face seemed to sag.

The haloed moon moved restlessly, blown adrift into its own dark sea. The tarnished green eyes of the man were glazed over, full of anguish. He crushed the red love blossom with his heel as he rose brusquely, then slowed, and stared down to where he had lain with Pandora.

She had been a virgin. Her blood on the sand. Given freely. Why not? Wasn't he her husband? Wasn't he a . . . man?"

"Oh . . . God!" he shouted and gave a cynical laugh that was worse than crying.

"Oh, God—why?"

Half-naked, his shirttail flapping against his taut buttocks, he plunged off the beach and struck for the trees.

The wind strengthened. The red petals lifted and blew away.

Chapter Thirty-two

The chattering of the wild mynah birds had wakened Pandora before the first rays of sun had arisen over the island. With haste she dressed for the day and quickly gulped down the glass of chilled coconut milk Iola had drained from shells yesterday. Cara and Iola had not yet returned from the Bane plantation. They must have spent the night there, she suddenly realized. She was grateful for this time alone because she sorely needed to iron out her problems. But later. For now, the Pacific beating on the shore beckoned to her.

After a few quick strokes of her hairbrush, she snatched up a turquoise sarong with white-printed leaves, left the bungalow, and made for the beach. Tucked under her other arm, she carried a surfboard.

The morning had dawned beautiful and balmy, but later the cruel heat of the sun would beat down. Summer had come in its full flowering glory, and a floppy hat would be needed for many weeks to come.

Pandora, as in the past, rode her board far out to the breakers where the sea shimmered deep blue and purple. The rolling Pacific was blue and mighty. She welcomed the sun, already hot on her bare head as her golden arms stroked the water. Each day had seen her grow more bronzed from lying on the beach near Nahele plantation.

Now! Having waited for the perfect breaker, Pandora stood up. She was an expert surfer, she knew, and like the native Hawaiians she used a sleek board. Slim and straight as a candle, she rode a big wave in to shore, skimming in as smoothly as a duck, and repeated the ancient process all over again, paddling out and riding back in. Finally, mildly exhausted, Pandora chose a spot where she could position her top half beneath the cool shade of a palm. She wanted to tan her legs a bit. Indeed it was growing hotter, and her colorful sarong was quickly drying in the heat.

A high feminine giggle drifted down the beach and reached Pandora's ears. She rose at once to her elbows. She tensed all over when she saw them. Rogan and Leilani were walking toward the bungalow.

"How nice; they must have spent the night together," Pandora hissed softly. They stood not far from the bungalow now. "Well, they won't find anyone at home! Too bad!" Pandora tossed damp strands over a glistening tanned shoulder.

About to stretch back out, something caught Pandora's attention again. Rogan, his green eyes discernible even from this distance, was scanning the beach. Once, swiftly, toward the palm grove, then back to Leilani.

What do I care if he has seen me, Pandora thought haughtily. She tossed her head again, hoping he was looking. The twinge of pain between her legs returned and she damned Rogan Thorn all over again.

Pandora lifted her eyes, took in the scene, and pursed her lips. He was bending his head toward Leilani and the slut was lifting her lips for his kiss! Her sensual woman's body molded to his, Leilani seemed eager for more than just kisses.

"Huh! Too bad he can't do anything about it!" Pandora said, thinking that Rogan Thorn was not man enough to do even that slut justice!

With a sniff of disdain, she stretched back out and missed the firm gesture Rogan made when he set Leilani from him. Leilani pouted childishly, but there remained a look of determination about her.

But Rogan had caught Pandora's movement. He'd seen her all this time, yes, but he didn't have any desire to meet her face to face this morning. He set his teeth, a muscle twitching along his jawline.

"Why did I come this way then?" he said aloud.

"What is the matter, Rogan Thorn?" Leilani questioned impishly. "You do not want to go inside? It is cool in there," she added tantalizingly. She had spied Pandora, too, riding the surf. Coyly she tried once more. "No one home, we go inside, huh?" She tugged at his arm insistently.

"Ahhh, not now, Leilani. I have to get back to Kailua. Bo Gary is waiting for me; he wants to take the *Phantom* out and do some fishing," he added, almost to himself.

"Bo Gary?" Leilani frowned. "Who is *he?*"

A smile quirked Rogan's full mouth. Leilani certainly had a short memory, for Bo had been at the luau the night before. Sure, Bo had stayed only a short time, wanting to return to the ship. But who could miss the lad, with his mop of red hair, and golden sprinkling of freckles? There were not many countenances like his about these parts.

"Well, you wouldn't want to meet him," Rogan said just the same. "He already has a woman, dear," he lied, knowing he and Susie were through.

"Oh, she is with him on your ship? I don't care; I meet him anyway, and your ship!"

Rogan flinched at her manner of speech, wondering why it wasn't cultivated like her brother Joe's. "Haven't you ever been to school, Leilani?" he asked, merely to make light conversation before he walked away.

"No like school," she purred provocatively. "Better things to do. Like make love," she added boldly.

Rogan had to chuckle at that. "There is more to life than just making love, Leilani." He caught himself up then, his own words ironic to his ear. Damned if he hadn't thought of nothing else of late. He might just as well lead a celibate life, though, for all the good it did him.

Leilani did a shocking thing then. She put her hand on him. It stayed for a second before Rogan gently lifted her hand from himself and met her disgruntled frown with a pasted smile.

Leilani turned surprised round eyes on him. "You do not want to make love, Rogan Thorn. I can tell. I can *feel*. Why?" Her dark eyes hardened like black pearls. Leilani was unable to fathom his refusal. Every man wanted Leilani.

"Really, no," was all Rogan could get out. Then, "Leilani, I'm a married man. Hasn't anyone told you?"

Dark eyes grew larger. "So what? Many men with wives have Leilani. I can make love better than they. Men say Leilani is best!" She puffed up her chest. "What more man want?" She shrugged with affected airs.

A woman who is not an educated whore, Rogan thought to himself.

Now Rogan saw Pandora striding gracefully up the beach toward the house, her sarong clinging to her curves enticingly. She hadn't bothered to change back into her muumuu, and it now trailed on the sand behind her. Her shimmering hair had dried into a halo of sunshine. Its waves rippled down almost to her waist. Her round breasts deliciously outlined, strained against the taut material of the sarong. Tall. Womanly.

"Dear Lord," Rogan muttered, catching his breath.

Leilani ignored his gaping green eyes, and gorgeous Pandora, who walked in a line that would take her not far from where they stood. Leilani danced sideways, her voice going softly sing-song.

"Mr. Rogan, come walk on beach with Leilani and play. Leilani is bored. You can kiss me again? Ha-ha-ha!"

But Rogan kept gazing at Pandora's haughty profile as he muttered, "Oh, Leilani, go and play by yourself. I have to get back now."

Yet, his feet betrayed his words and he could not budge from the spot. She looks like a tanned island goddess. How gorgeous her lips, like sweet cherries, full and curving. He felt his desire harden blatantly in his trousers and he stuffed his hands in his pockets to ease his predicament somewhat. But with her practiced eye, Leilani had sighted the turgid display and she set out to taunt him.

"Huh! I know what you and *haole* Pandora did on beach last night. I know you make love to her." She went on despite his intake of breath, and she giggled nervously on a high note. "I tell your wife. Ha-ha-ha!"

Placing her arms akimbo, Pandora halted, her ears having perked up at Leilani's last statement. She tossed her bright head and canted it. With a mocking expression on her full lips, she stared Leilani up and down until the girl flinched under her piercing blue daggers and stepped back. Pandora advanced, like a hunting tigress, her gaze challenging, her height formidable, while Leilani shivered noticeably.

Pandora's eyes flashed coolly, not betraying the fire within her. "How dare you—you slut!"

Beneath Rogan's amused scrutiny, Pandora turned on her bare heel and made her way arrogantly to the house. Rogan's eyes glinted with humor, his mouth quirked rakishly.

"I'm not surprised her temper has a short fuse." He looked quickly to Leilani, whose pouting mouth and frowning brow played havoc with her delicate features. Poor thing, she had melted like butter beneath Pandora's glare.

"Good-by." Rogan shrugged, stuffed his hands into his trousers, and strode along the beach to where his horse, cropping patches of grass, avoided the cactus spears with her soft muzzle.

Leilani was left alone, staring after Rogan, and wishing she had not lent him one of their finest horses. Her fury turned to childish tears.

"Every man want Leilani," she said. "Why not Rogan Thorn? Huh! *Haole!*" She shrieked then when the powdered sand she'd kicked up drifted into her eyes.

Pandora entered the house, its coolness a delight, her smile smug. But she wasn't upset. No; in fact she was quite pleased with herself. More than she would have thought.

But later when the starry heavens twinkled and sultry breezes tossed palms softly, that night found Pandora first tearful and then sobbing. Cara had stayed on at Bane plantation, but Iola had returned. She sat beside the bed and stroked Pandora's long, tangled hair. Pandora had calmed down somewhat because of the big, loving hands that soothed her, just as they had during storms when she had visited her aunt as a child. Pandora sniffled.

Later, after they had conversed softly for a time, she asked, "Are they like my God?" They had been discussing the forces of nature and Pandora was curious about what had taken place the day before when she had discovered her knife.

"The wind and sea and mountain gods, yes," Iola said. "They, too, are all one. Pele, she is the biggest goddess, of wind and fire, on big island. My ancestors—yours, too—they could read skies and make meaning of the clouds and the rainbow and way the rains fall. They read the sea and wind and thunder and way birds fly. Ku, he is shark god, to sacrifice humans." She watched in the half-gloom for Pandora's reaction to this.

But Pandora was thinking of her grandparents. The original missionaries and some of their children had done well, but most had died poor. They had inherited the boldness of spirit it had taken to sail around the Horn in small ships. She had inherited it, too, supposedly, but sometimes she wondered where this bold spirit of hers had flown.

Iola went on. "But I like your Christian God, too. My gods only worship nature, but have power, too. I learn about your God, Him, in mission church in Kailua, long ago."

"My mother, was she very pretty?" Pandora asked in a voice thick with drying tears.

"Linda was schoolteacher and, yes, very pretty. Tall; long legs, long hair, just like my baby," she crooned. Iola frowned lightly now, and tried again, for the fifth time. "Now, why my girl cry? Someone make you sad? You tell, I make it better."

Pandora wasted no time now, but revealed everything, right up to this morning when her husband had been flirting and kissing with Leilani. Iola, taking all in with rapt attention, now held up her hand to halt the flow of words.

"Handsome American my girl's husband?" She felt rather than saw Pandora's nod. "How nice, you make big, strong babies together, huh?"

"Ohhh!" Pandora wailed. "You don't understand. Rogan, he . . . he . . . has a problem!" she finally blurted out.

"*Big* problem?" Iola tried to think of what that could mean.

"Very big. He—he doesn't function properly—his most intimate part!" She rushed the words together in total embarrassment, sounding foolish even to herself. "How else can I tell you, so you'll understand!" She groaned.

"Oh!" Iola brightened. "Man part wiggles like soft worm, gets nowhere fast, huh?" She waited expectantly.

Pandora was thankful the room was dark. Her face had turned three shades of bright red. She tried to think of what to say next; that had not been exactly the way it was.

"Yes, he's what you might call fast." She groaned. How could she explain to Iola that Rogan consummated prematurely.

"Oh." But Iola frowned her puzzlement.

"I mean"—Pandora chose her words carefully—"he cannot carry through! Iola, what I'm saying is—" She remembered a certain Chinaman. "Poof! It's gone!"

"Oh, yes!" Iola clapped her hands. "He made good stiff erection, good thrust, and then he comes! Sometimes before thrust, huh?"

Pandora gasped. She couldn't have said it better! Aghast at her aunt's hidden wisdom, Pandora laid back on the pillow, as weariness seeped into her bones. Now what? Her head was drumming in anticipation of a solution from Iola.

Iola said nothing more but patted Pandora's shoulder as she rose, with amazing speed and strength after a full day of being busy at Bane plantation cleaning up.

"Go to sleep, Pandora. I fix everything tomorrow.

I give something to Rogan Thorn. I grind up seeds for your husband tonight, make very powerful stuff to make good and hard, long, long time."

Her hands flew to her cheeks as Pandora gasped, "Oh, no!"

"Oh, yes!"

Part Two

Passion Flower

Chapter Thirty-three

After two days of waiting for Rogan Thorn to appear, Iola gave up looking down the beach road for him.

Pandora continued to visit Nahele plantation, but never stayed there overnight, or came home too near dark. But on the third day, Iola packed a big basket, hitched Patsy up to the old plantation carriage and drove the several miles with Pandora to the sprawling house. Iola had summoned several Hawaiian boys, who were neighbors, and the dark-skinned lads were now busy as bees. They worked only in the cooler morning hours, tidying the overgrown patio and weeding out the vegetable garden for new plantings. These were the first of the tasks to be done at the run-down plantation.

The most troublesome vines having been cleared from the living-room windows, the light revealed an odd mixture of well-worn rattan furniture and carved teakwood. Delicate watercolors had once decorated the walls, but were now faded blue; the only cheerful bit of color was a Chinese vase that now held peacock feathers. The furniture in the house was all antique now. It looked as if some pieces might have come from Boston around the Horn with the help of the missionaries.

From a room on the third floor the cloud-shrouded mountain far inland could be seen, and from another window at the other wing, the bright magnificence of the Pacific far below. A small island to the southeast shone like dull gold in the morning sun.

Pandora busied herself scrubbing out the porcelain tub in the bathroom, while in another room Iola hummed at her task of polishing the cherrywood sofa and the rosewood chairs, all with quite threadbare upholstery. An old brass bed shone from recent polishing. The smell of must and damp wood pervaded the house, but now mingled with beeswax and lemon polish, it was not unpleasant. Too, all the windows and the louvered doors had been thrown wide, allowing the sweet odor of the wild flowering vines to enter.

Pandora was not so sure her spirit of adventure was going to be strong enough to make her think of spending a night here. But that's just what Iola had in mind.

Iola dusted off her hands now after heaving the trunk into a nearby closet. Slyly she peered over her shoulder to see if Pandora had been watching, but her niece was still working at the other end of the hall. It was better for now that Pandora did not see the mystery items she had stashed away, Iola decided cleverly. Someday, maybe soon.

Passing another room, Iola opened the door and with dismay stared about her. The floor felt gritty underfoot, as if it needed much sweeping. Shuttered windows had been fastened shut, closing in the smell of damp. She went to throw them wide. As she was about to turn from the window, she did a double take. Outside beyond the dock a white-hulled ship was coming closer. She was rakish, set low in the sparkling blue water, and totally exposed to the hot rays of sun that baked her clean decks. Iola strained her gaze, a puzzled expression growing on her chubby face.

"Who might that be?" she asked herself.

Shouts from below interrupted her thoughts and Iola looked down to see the boys running from the patio. As they caught sight of Iola leaning out the window, they gathered together and shouted more, waving their brown arms in excitement.

"Pretty white boat comes!" one yelled, jumping up and down.

"Ship is coming!" another youngster called up, as if Iola could not see this for herself.

"Just like black ship come the other day, but this one all white!" the third put in.

A board creaked as Pandora entered. Her hair was tucked back with a colorful strip of aqua material that matched her slim sarong. Iola turned round brown eyes on her niece.

"What is all the shouting about? Iola, what were you staring at like that? I thought you might fall out the window. My, what is it? Can I see, too?" She came up behind her aunt.

"Ship." Iola shrugged. "Never see before."

"Move over," Pandora said, so she could see, too.

"Must be just men fishing, or diving for pearls, come to new water from one of other islands," Iola guessed out loud, watching the ship growing larger by the minute.

"Or . . ." Pandora licked her lips, mulling this over as she watched the ship tie up at the end of the long dock. "Oh, she is beautiful, just like a white-winged dove!"

"Or"—Iola began to finish for her niece—"owner now come to claim his land? Huh! Why he come now when we make plantation house pretty!"

Still, Pandora could not contain her bubbling excitement, just like the boys.

"Let's go down and meet the ship!" she cried.

But the curious boys, groaning with disappointment, were whisked back to their tasks. Iola stood with arms akimbo to make certain they were working. If this was the new owner, she didn't want the boys to hear her, just in case there was some old-fashioned swearing going on. She intended to give him a piece of her mind. To not have come to even see the house before this! She clucked her tongue noisily.

"Maybe him just some panjandrum," Iola said, snorting.

"Wh*aaat?* Oh, Iola, your big words. Sometimes you certainly surprise me with them!" Pandora laughed gaily. "Well? What's a panjan—ah—drum?"

"You know, big shot. Some come from Honolulu sometimes, try to buy plantation. Don't know how they know of empty house from miles away, must have big long eyes!" She giggled then, hiking up the hem of her yellow-flowered muumuu to walk faster.

"Or spies," Pandora said, wiggling her fingers in the air.

340

"Hee-hee-hee." Iola's plump bosom jiggled in mirth.

"Maybe someone like that Candice Randall who used to live here with her uppity folks," Iola said as an afterthought.

"Ugh!" Pandora grimaced. "Candy, I remember her well."

"You do?" Iola's face came about incredulously.

"Uhhmm-hmmm. She was sugary sweet—and mean!"

"Bitch!" Iola added with a deep chuckle. "She been here, too. Try to claim she own half the house."

"Really?" Pandora shrugged. "Well, let's not spoil the day with further talk of her!"

"Look! Big shot stepping onto dock. Ho!" she exclaimed then, her eyes widening.

"Rogan Thorn!" Pandora said incredulously.

"Good morning" Rogan called, looking chipper as he strode along the dock toward the shore.

Pandora gripped Iola's meaty arm. She was suddenly terrified. "Iola, don't you *dare*," she hissed into the woman's ear.

"Rogan Thorn, *aloha!*" Iola called back, then grumbled aside to Pandora. "You worry for nothing, girl; what's the matter?"

"You know very well what I mean! If you give that stuff you brewed up the other night to him, why, I'll never speak to you again! I'd die—"

"*Aloha,*" Rogan said to them both, noticing the high flush on Pandora's cheekbones. His glowing eyes took her in from head to grass-slippered feet. "Looks like you've been hard at work this morning."

341

His gaze drifted up to the speck of dirt on her forehead. "Here, let me get that for you."

He pulled out a handkerchief to dab at it.

"Wha—?" Pandora instinctively stepped back, but Iola nudged her forward so suddenly that she almost bumped Rogan's knee.

As it was, Pandora had to throw out her arms to catch Rogan's wrists to keep her breasts from meeting his chest. Though Pandora glowered at Iola, she couldn't help but experience a pleasant shock from the contact. It stirred her emotions, and her blood pounded more hotly in her veins. She shivered. What she didn't know was that Rogan felt her excitement, although at the moment he only smiled into her eyes.

"There, it's gone," he said, stuffing the handkerchief back into his buff breeches.

"Hi there!" Bo Gary, with a seaman's canvas bag slung over his strong shoulders, was sauntering up behind Rogan. He blushed. "I mean *Aloha*."

Pandora beamed at the lad. "Bo! I've missed you. Why didn't you come and visit after the luau. Shame on you; I expected—" She stared at the slight rolling of the ship, and frowned not at this but something else.

Rogan caught her perusal of the ship. "Iola, why don't you take Bo Gary up to the house." He nudged Bo. "He told me how very thirsty he is—just a few minutes ago."

Bo Gary blinked his Irish blue eyes. "I did?"

Rogan gritted aside to the younger man, "Don't you *remember*? You said you were dying of thirst."

Bo affected absent-mindedness, scratching under his cap. "Oh. Oh yeah!"

Iola literally dragged the lad by the arm, saying, "I have cool lime juice, greens, and papaya. You like?" she asked in a you-had-better tone.

"Oh . . . *sure.*"

Rogan watched until Iola had passed the overhanging monkeypod and had herded the lad into the house, then he turned to Pandora who was still staring at the ship.

"You had a question, about my ship?"

"Yours?"

"Uhmmm, yes."

He kept his eyes trained on her slim hips as she moved closer to get a better look.

"She's freshly painted!" she exclaimed. Then she saw the curlicued name in bold black letters on the side.

Pandora's Promise, they spelled out, seemed to shout the name at her.

"She's the *Phantom!*"

He came to stand behind her, very near.

"*Was* the *Phantom.* But the same ship, the very same one we got married on."

"Rogan," she began very softly, "why did you name her that?"

She turned so abruptly that at the movement her nose nearly brushed his chin. She stepped back then as a queer shiver shot through her.

"Because it's reminiscent of the promise you made to honor and obey," he said cryptically.

"You left something out," she blurted without thinking.

"No," he murmured, stroking her bare arm, "you did."

"You just baited me!"

His eyes narrowed. "So I did."

Several phrases had come to her mind in retort, but none of them seemed appropriate. She was trying to be nice, but he was making it very hard for her. She felt shy, very, all of a sudden. Her lashes dropped to softly brush her pinkened cheeks. She went giddy again from his nearness, his touch that had heated her flesh. She peeked up at him and smiled, drawing her dimples upward. He smiled back at her. He, too, had dimples, manly ones. Then he did something she hadn't seen him do for a long time.

"Rogan! You're blushing!"

He cleared his throat and said, "Men don't blush."

"But you do! I've seen it before."

He looked away and now it was she who took the initiative and stroked his arm. "What's wrong, Rogan; why do you look so peeved all of a sudden?"

He gripped her arms hard. "Do you think I can make it with you?" he ground out.

"What kind of a—question is that?"

"Answer me!"

He shook her with a sudden jerk. She muttered, but no sensible words would come. All at once his lips covered hers, opening her mouth to his probing tongue. As if it were the natural thing to do, her hands slipped behind him and clung to his back. He thrust a knee between her legs and unconsciously she responded by moving her hips.

"I want to know everything about you," he groaned against her lips, then found and kissed the sensitive spot behind her ear. "Help me, Pandora. Lord, I need you—all the way!"

She tossed her head provocatively. "Did Leilani

help you, Rogan Thorn?''

Hot with sudden jealousy, she squirmed from his embrace, and left him standing there, shocked, while he watched her stride to the house.

When Pandora walked in, marched straight up the stairs, and slammed the bedroom door in the southeast wing, Iola stood staring up the staircase. She slowly turned her head then, and seeing Rogan in Pandora's wake, watched him make his way to the stairs. Suddenly Iola shook herself and moved to catch up with the man.

"Wait, Rogan Thorn. I have something for you!"

Her arms folded across her chest as if she were cold, Pandora stood at the window watching Bo Gary take his cool lime drink out to the patio where the washed wicker chairs squatted. The Hawaiian boys were resting, sharing a huge bowl of sweet cherries that Iola had set out. Behind her, Pandora heard the door click open. She knew Rogan had followed. Is this what she had wanted, to be alone with him, without prying eyes?

"You are jealous," he clipped.

The words were suddenly close at her back, and Pandora whirled with chin held high to confront his blazing green eyes. She tried to form a smart answer, but no words to that effect would issue forth.

"When do you plan on going back to San Francisco?"

She knew her question sounded casual, but it was plain that she had ignored his statement. He stepped around her, to the window where he could look out to the water on which he saw his ship resting like a landed dove.

"Why did you choose this room? You could have slipped into the drawing room, the study, anywhere but here?" His gaze swept the high bed with its dully gleaming posts and then he took in the rest of the room.

A huge Turkish rug in the center had recently been swept; the wood floors surrounding it were blond and polished. Tropical flowers sweetly freshened the room; there were pink, orange, yellow, and red blossoms, floating in huge rose porcelain bowls along with a few *tiare* flowers of virgin white. The bed wore fresh linen, its posts hung with mosquito netting, as if in expectation of a guest tonight. Or perhaps more than one.

"Have you been staying over? Or is this your— going to be your first night here?" he fired at her, after studying the room closely, slowly.

His glance measured her as she walked about the room, appearing at ease as her fingers touched a colorful bloom here or there, then trailed in the water. Her sensuous sarong clung to her slim almost boyish hips and molded her high bust. Its hem was short; and endless, tanned legs poked out as she walked, as if she were modeling the delicious bit of garment. She turned to face Rogan, her pretty mouth compressed.

"First—I am not jealous. Second—I slipped into this room knowing you would follow, yes, because other ears would hear if we were downstairs now."

Rogan toyed absently with a flower, but his gaze roamed up her long legs to her full, curving lips.

"Did you expect an argument? Because of your jealousy?"

"I already told you, I—"

He cut her off with this: "Why were you a virgin?"

"I do not remember! Anyway, it is none of your business!"

He remained cool to her hot reply. "You could not have been Nahele's wife for very long. Have you thought about that?"

She bent her head so that a thick strand of golden hair fell across her profile, hiding her expression. After a stifling silence she spoke.

"One night, I—I think."

Pandora frowned, disliking the turn the conversation had taken. What he said next caused her to stiffen, her blood to run cold.

"The murder had to take place that night then—" He ran his fingers through a chestnut wave of hair. "If murder it was."

"You"—she sputtered—"you are half-accusing me!"

"Don't be stupid! I said that . . . meaning you merely might have been protecting your precious damned virginity!"

"That is still accusing me!"

"He might have been forcing you." He looked to the bed.

"Oh, what do you mean? Why in heaven's name would I want to . . . keep my own husband from . . ."

His lips curled. "Why not? You do the same with me. *I* am your husband." He flicked a long finger at a delicate white blossom, so sweet, so pure.

"Show me the marriage contract! Only then shall I believe you. Tell me this, Mr. Thorn, how can it be legal when you did not even know my name?"

Rogan strode to the door, drawling over his shoulder, "I have the contract, and your maiden name *is* there, my dear wife! I mean to fetch it now, from my ship."

"Tell, oh, do tell me, you think you are so almighty wise, what is it then?" she snapped, at once sorry for her defiance.

"St. Ives." He made a mock bow. *"Was."*

Her mouth gaped two inches, but that was all she could do for all her shaking.

"Don't you remember *anything?*" he asked with a taunt. "You may do well to remember more from now on."

She stared after the closing door. Rogan was still trying to tell her something. She shivered, hugging herself again. But memory would not come to her until much later.

Strange, but Rogan must have changed his mind about fetching the marriage contract. Pandora mulled over this.

From the window in the east wing where she had been cleaning and straightening up, she could see *Pandora's Promise* pulling away from the dock, into the sun-striped sea. The sun would set soon, but for now the air was muggy with the wind from the south. Why had Rogan left like that, without a word?

Pandora turned quickly away from the window, went along the hall and entered her own room. Her room? Yes, she would stay the night, maybe several in fact.

It was hot here and the walls seemed to close in on her. A great weariness washed over her, just looking at the fresh, inviting bed. She had labored to clean the house most of the day, but the confrontation with Rogan in the afternoon had sapped her strength. Iola was busy down in the kitchen, her favorite place—in any house. Pandora would not be missed, so she decided to lie down awhile.

Pandora woke slowly, her sarong sticking to her limbs. A rosy glow filtered into the room. She could see out the window from her bed. Across the waters the sun was sending its last light of the day, as long purple steamers flung upward against a gray-white sky and southward on the horizon a pale golden haze hung over the ocean. Still no ship in sight beyond the dock.

She could hear sounds below, a pounding. Perhaps Iola was making *poi*. She could smell meat cooking, so it was close to dinnertime.

In the fitful dream she had just had, Rogan tipped her face up to his and his smile was tender. The dream was all very sweet and in it she wanted his manly, sensual passion. She fostered the false hope that her desires could all come true someday, she suddenly realized. But did she truly want him? She was still uncertain if it were lustful desire or—or love she felt for Rogan.

He had left so suddenly, without any explanation as to where he was going, or why. Well then, why did he always have to be so mysterious? He had told her to help him and, finally angered by her jealousy, had said coldly that he had the marriage contract with her maiden name on it.

You may do well to remember more from now on, he had said. And before that: *Your precious damned virginity . . . You do the same with me. I am your husband!*

Remembering Cara's words, she sat bolt upright in bed: Nothing is more binding than when the marriage is consummated.

But that meant the wedding night and only then, didn't it?

Chapter Thirty-four

The sun rose blood-red to splash against the waters of the Pacific. Pandora had stretched and yawned, waking to the busy house. She had run to the window to see the steamer unloading the surprises. Then it had hit her—upon seeing Candice Randall strolling along the dock with her pretty pink parasol and ruffled froufrous—that Candy's father was the new owner of the plantation.

Nahele plantation was surely turning into a popular place. But of all the people that Pandora could do without at this time, Candice Randall was at the top of her list.

Along with the arrival of the unwanted guest, the island steamer unloaded its cargo of furnishings. Not only that, but a passel of household servants and a few gardeners.

Candice Randall, here to take over and give orders? Oh, God, please let this not be so! But this was exactly the way it appeared to Pandora.

The gardeners wasted no time, but took the plants that had been shipped out of their earth boxes, and busied themselves planting beds of roses about the patio. Dressed, and wearing a large hibiscus blossom in her well-brushed hair, Pandora stepped from the house to watch all the activity. Candy must have gone inside to make herself comfortable, Pandora decided, for she was nowhere to be seen. She was probably giving orders to the servants she had brought with her. Well, why not? This was the Randall house now.

"I could fare worse, I suppose," Pandora mumbled, stepping around the side of the house.

One gardener worked at the arbor, already training purple bougainvillaea to climb upward. Colorful pansies peeked from the earth boxes, and fresh hibiscus bushes waited in burlap wraps to be planted near the house. All these flowers! Bright fuchsia would bloom with the ferns; they would need a lot of water until they got a good start. One of the gardeners was ecstatic over the wild lavender orchids and shyly picked one to hand it to Pandora when she stopped to watch him work.

"Thank you," Pandora said. "They are my favorite." She smiled, tucking it behind her other ear. "What is your name?"

"George. And you are Pandora Thorn, I can tell." The man smiled through the dirt smudges on his cheeks.

"What! Who has told you about me, George?"

He seemed to be recalling something important and looked sheepish over it. He shuffled his dirty shoes. "I'm not just a gardener, ma'am. I can mend broken furniture and do just about everything about the house, see."

"That's nice, George. But who has told you how to recognize Pandora . . . Thorn if you met her?"

"Why, Mr. Thorn, your husband."

"Thank you, George. I'll talk to you again later."

She left him with that curt reply. George scratched his head beneath his oily cap as he watched her go.

"Yer very kind, ma'am," he said belatedly.

Going in search of Candice Randall, Pandora slipped in the back way entering the kitchen. Iola had been scrubbing vegetables, but now she stared around at the bustling, interfering kitchen maids. Pandora and Iola exchanged shrugs of bewilderment. All this activity—this was so sudden.

"Aha, there you are!"

Pandora cringed before she turned slowly. She knew that silvery tone. It was sugary sweet too, with an underlying note of steel. It came to Pandora then—Candy had acted as if she had owned the place when she had stayed here with Donald Randall, her father. Now she actually did. Pandora suddenly felt weary and defeated. Just when she had been feeling at home here. What would happen to her now? She could not stay with Iola the rest of her life. And now Rogan would not take her to San Francisco; he hated her.

"*Aloha*, Candy," Pandora greeted as she turned. "Did you have a nice journey?"

"Nice!" Candy snorted. "With all that furniture, so that one could hardly turn around? And all the stuffy servants; packed in every cabin, so that I had to share one with a maid? Ugh! I'll never do that again!" She swaggered about, inspecting the kitchen and grimaced. "What a mess! This place will take months to clean up! What has happened while I was away? It looks as if some dirty Hawaiians have been living here!"

"Huh!" Iola heaved her chest and snorted her offense. She tossed the carrot that she had been scrubbing into a refuse pile and went out with her back straight and proud. "Huh!" she went again.

Candy tossed her yellow-blond head. "God, and I thought I was bored with Papa and his mistress. Whatever shall I do now that I'm here?"

"Maybe you could help clean up your—" Pandora bit off, hearing a familiar voice behind her.

"Well, here you are." Rogan popped his head in the door.

"Well," Candy said, brightening. "Did I mention being bored?"

Pandora was about to answer, but Rogan beat her to it.

"Bored? With all that has to be done around here?" Rogan said with a cluck of his tongue, shaking his head and causing a chestnut wave to fall boyishly over his forehead.

"Oh, my!" Candy exclaimed, all flustered. "Let's get busy! Where should I start?" She peered at Rogan sideways. "Oh, I've never cleaned house before." Then she giggled with affected embarrassment. "Pandora, you haven't introduced me!" She stared at Pandora who was looking at her strangely. "Oh, you *are* she, aren't you? You look so different!"

"Candice Randall, this is Rogan Thorn. He . . ."

"Yes? Go on, Pandora." Rogan waited.

"He is visiting—" Pandora began, looking straight into those gossamer-green eyes. "A vacation."

His eyes glittering strangely, Rogan looked at the

blond woman. "Candice Randall, are *you* staying long?"

"Of course!" she said breathlessly. "Forever!"

And wasn't that the truth, Pandora thought to herself dismally.

For the remainder of the day, Candy trailed Rogan about, but she never once dirtied her hands. Pandora was with the maids in the kitchen; they wanted to learn all there was to know about Hawaiian cooking, and were thrilled that Pandora knew how to make *poi*, the paste made by pounding the dampened taro root. She promised to teach them later how to make *laulau*—soft and savory pork and beef folded into leaf bundles. But roast pork from the *imu* was the *pièce de résistance* and they wanted to taste that for sure when they had a luau.

The kitchen was suddenly stocked with everything they needed. More was coming, one of the maids had said, on the next steamer in the morning. Pandora was saddened. Iola had disappeared, no doubt gone back home after Candy's horrible rudeness.

Pandora was prepared to do the same. She had taught the kitchen cooks all they needed to know, for now. Why should she stay? If Iola was not welcome, then she was going, too! She had done enough; the rest was up to Candice Randall. As for Rogan, he could do whatever he saw fit!

"Where are you going?" Rogan demanded, grabbing hold of her arm as she descended the stairs, bags in hands.

"What do you mean? I have done my share, and now I am leaving. Iola is gone, why should I stay?"

"I'm staying, and you belong here, with me," he said softly.

"Oh-ho, not in someone else's house I don't. Especially when I am not wanted!"

"You *are* wanted!" he shot back.

And with that, Rogan set down her bags and pulled her up the stairs and into the bedroom Pandora had stayed in the night before. She struggled, but he was stronger. She cried her outrage, but his words were deeper and more forceful. He released her then, bowing as he swept his hand wide, daring her to do his bidding.

"Come in," he offered with a devilish grin.

"Why, thank you for welcoming me into *your* bedchamber!" She spun about to face him when the door was closed. "What now, Mr. Thorn?" she snapped.

"Why do you persist in calling me that? I have a first name and I rather like being addressed as such. My employees and acquaintances call me Mr. Thorn."

Keeping his eye trained on Pandora, Rogan began to peel off his white linen shirt, not making any attempt to conceal his desire when he touched on the fastening of his trousers and led her gaze there. She gasped in surprise at his readiness that was plain to see, and when she looked into his face, white teeth gleamed in the sun-darkened countenance. It was all Pandora could do to check her urge to fly from him. But the better part of wisdom restrained her. He would only catch her and make things worse for her. Like rape.

Still half-dressed, he came to her slowly. Her face

flushed, her pulses quickened, and her knees went rubbery. She could sense his intense hunger for her, and that he restrained himself from lifting her up and bearing her to the bed. A sweet ache was beginning inside and she began to wish that he would do just that and claim her body. Even if it was only lustful desire and nothing else. Love had never come into their conversations once.

"The sun is setting again," he murmured, quite unexpectedly.

She peered up at him shyly. "It does every day at this time." She wondered momentarily where she would be when the sky had darkened and the stars came out.

Minutes passed and she grew even more confused and tormented. He continued to scrutinize her with those wild green eyes. What was his game? She had to admit it; she wanted his arms embracing her. Was he merely waiting for her to make the next move?

"Two of them this time?"

Rogan reached out and fingered the wild lavender orchid and then the hibiscus blossom in her hair. His fingertip brushed her ear when he plucked the hibiscus and tossed it over onto the bed. She shivered when his hand returned and she laid her flushed cheek on it. The sweet warm look in her eyes sent tremors through Rogan.

"The wild lavender must have been fashioned just for you. It's most becoming tucked there behind your shell-like ear, complimenting your golden complexion and making the sea come alive in your eyes. Yes, the sea has lavender in it here, not far out from the sands. You appear to be part of everything here, like a goddess of paradise. A passion flower," he ended deeply.

"Oh, Rogan, that's beautiful, what you just said," she murmured against his large hand, caressing it now with her cheek.

Their eyes met and froze, locked in an almost physical embrace. The ardor of the chase was over and both were prepared to meet halfway. To and fro their emotions raged, with her clinging to denial, him playing hide-and-seek. The moment was here, to share, to give. Rogan had dreaded this moment, though, had feared that he would not be able to carry through. He needed assurance from her and he sought it. The truth of the matter would be known now.

Rogan and Pandora met and kissed simultaneously. Her hands roamed over his back like the touch of a butterfly and she brazenly rubbed herself against him. They embraced deeply, came apart. She removed her sarong and he finished stepping out of his clothes. The sunset cast its reddish glow through the window and glistened over both their desirous bodies. Rogan's breath caught deep in his throat at her unadorned beauty, and she swept a gaze downward to the magnificence of his rigid manhood. He was all man; no one could deny this. Her senses fully awakened and aroused, she backed slowly to the bed while he pursued in the manner of a stalking panther, his green eyes pantherlike, too.

Another embrace, and they slid down to the bed together, their legs like endless limbs entwined, their hot bellies meeting and quivering in anticipation of being joined in the deepest lovers' embrace. Getting her hair tangled in his fist, he pushed the tresses back carefully and found and kissed the sensitive spot behind her ear. He lay above her now, moving carefully, sensuously, sliding one hand over the glorious length of her from the sweet curve of breast beneath her arm down to her nipped-in waist, slim hips, and then over to the secret place of which he would soon take possession.

"Rogan . . . Rogan . . . love me! Don't ever let go; I need you, always and forever."

Rogan breathed deeply, rasping. "Pretty strong words, sweetheart. Will you mean them when we are done?"

"I-I'll try, Rogan, I promise."

"I hope you do," was all he muttered.

"Rogan?"

"No more questions now, sweetheart. Just let love come now."

"Yes, now. Rogan, now!" she begged shamelessly, lifting her hips to meet his.

"Easy, *kuu ipu!*"

He knew the Hawaiian word for sweetheart and this utterly thrilled her. She let him take the lead in the love-making now, as he made free with his hands, his burning lips, every part of himself to arouse her to a screaming, feverish pitch.

"Oh, you lovely passion flower," he muttered low, unconsciously crushing the wild lavender orchid with his cupping hand.

What Pandora did not know was that he felt more than a little unsure of his ability to bring the act to fruition. Unable to ease his fear of failure, the torment of the unknown that lay just ahead, he rose suddenly from the bed and went from her without a word as to what he was about.

Surprised, Pandora watched Rogan with passion's lazy-lidded eyes, half-open sapphires. With his back to her, he was doing something, seemingly looking down at something, but what? She heard him furiously curse then and saw him set something down on the chair beneath his shirt as if hiding it; then he turned and walked slowly back to the bed. His tall form, back to the window, was cast in shadow since the light of the red sunset was nearly gone now and lent only a purplish hue to the room.

She felt again the pressure of his weight as he once more lowered his head to torture her saucy nipple with his tongue. An intense sexual hunger grew and she writhed and opened her long legs when he touched her there.

My God, why was he torturing her this way? She was near to sobbing out loud from the throbbing ache in her belly. She did so softly then and clutched his neck when he caressed the peak of a pink nipple and then took it into his mouth, sucking gently. Sliding her hand down over his tautly muscled belly, Pandora boldly fondled him, finding him ready as her hand closed over him. Her heart gave a little lurch. Rogan groaned and immediately pushed her hand aside to position himself over her. Through slitted eyes she studied him. He smiled almost a painful smile when she opened her thighs, a natural movement of love, and arched her back to better receive him. He moved over her, lowering now, and she cried out when his manhood pushed between her yielding thighs.

"Rogan, have me now! Please!" She thought she would die from wanting him.

He did not go deep, not at first.

"Oh, yes. Yes!" she cried as he moved slowly, teasing her.

Pandora felt the tears smart in her eyes. This was so wonderful! She could hardly believe this glorious thing was happening to her. She rocked her hips while learning what he wanted of her.

"This is beautiful, Rogan," she murmured, seeing him in a haze.

"Stay. Stay," Rogan mumbled several times, as if sending up a prayer.

A sea-borne breeze stirred the tapa-cloth drapings at the edge of the window. The murmurings from the bed were becoming louder, more insistent, more passionate. Longing for an end to sweep her up and away, Pandora was making mewling sounds in her throat, arching her back higher, higher. She saw the beads of sweat begin on his brow and felt her own begin on her upper lip.

"Rogan. Rogan," she cried over and over, pleading with him to take her to the plateau where love's bliss reigned.

Her eyes lifted to his and widened slightly. She was immediately sure that this ecstasy was soon to end. Moisture kept beading above her lips and she parted them to speak.

"No . . ." Her voice held a pleading whisper in the twilight encompassing the bed. "No, Rogan, not . . . yet!"

But Rogan jerked his head back as if he'd been stabbed and plunged deeply, once more, his ecstatic murmuring rising to a howl that he quickly stifled by nuzzling Pandora's neck.

"Ah—" he sighed deeply into her ear, "but you are a passionate woman! Woman! Woman!" He bit into her neck gently.

Moments passed while she caught the breath that had seemed to have left her during their lusty tumbling and straining.

"You are not so bad yourself, Thorn!" she finally said, and there was still a breathless little catch in her voice.

He growled low. "Thorn again, eh! What must I do to teach you a lesson? Make love to you endlessly, hmm?"

She chuckled provocatively in his ear and played, tugging and teasing him into a new rigidity. "Thorn! Thorn!" She tempted him to carry on.

"Ah, you sweet piece. Surrender and offer your secret to me again, woman!" he groaned against the slim column of her neck.

The incredible heat grew in her again and sang in her veins. Obediently, surely, Pandora spread herself for him once again. When he reentered her this time, he plunged, so big, filling her with a new burning ache so that she yielded totally to the pleasure that was almost like pain. Up to the hilt this time, he made his way like a young stallion and her thighs lifted when he rose, following him, then driving her back to the bed. At times, he almost left her completely, but stayed her hips with his hands. She was so eager in her new-found womanhood, that he wanted to cry for the sweetness of it.

Something blossomed in her body then that she

had never felt before. They soared on the silver-tipped wings of unending passion; climbing, grinding their hips together, away, together, mounting the highest mountain of pleasure, soaring, man joined to woman, straining to complete the joyful ecstasy.

They trembled at the top. Pandora's star soared, brightened, expanded, then exploded into a million sparkling shards of rapture that had gathered in her body. They trembled to a close. A perfect end, in body, soul, and mind. Bliss. And even more.

Rogan smiled. His whole world that earlier had tilted upside down had now righted itself. He was a man content in his woman.

Chapter Thirty-five

"Well, where did everyone go off to, and leave me here all alone?" Candy wondered out loud.

But to go and check would have taken too much effort. Candy even missed the glare of the maid who had just entered the room where she continued to work on her tapestry. She poked her needle deftly into the square to complete a pansy of purple and blue. She sighed, cocking her head as she surveyed her work. Jane went back to the kitchen, shaking her head at the girl's laziness. She would get no help here, she decided.

The night was warmly tropical, but a stiff wind circulated, drifting in with the smell of roses and orchids from where the doors and windows stood open. Outside the rose mallow had turned a deep rose color at dusk. Now it had closed its petals tightly to greet evening and would not reopen until the next morning when it would begin the day as a white flower.

Candy had already decided that she would stitch the rose mallow into one of her patterns; she adored the flowers of the island. But she did not care much for the boredom that reigned here. At least for now.

Candice Randall had donned an electric-blue dress with a white lace insert near the throat. But who was there to see her in this luscious creation? Damn, suddenly she missed the elegant balls, the splendid carriages, and the mansions and country estates of San Francisco. There was no one place she could really call home. Her "home" had always been the road, for as long as she could remember. The longest they had stayed anywhere was here with the Naheles. Akela, what an ugly wrinkled old woman she had been! And her grandson, Akoni, wherever the devil he was.

Her papa was a rover, a merchant and a wealthy one at that; but Donald had gone on to Paris with his latest French whore to visit her homeland. The lazy, red-headed twit would no doubt hang on Donald's arm during the entire journey, even when they arrived in Paris. Why couldn't Donald see that she herself could entertain him better than any mistress he was with at the time?

How boring! Candy grimaced. The fragrance of exotic blossoms wafted in to her. Romantic and spellbinding—this could put one to sleep, with the right partner, the perfect lover, that is. There was probably a huge yellow moon hanging outside, too, and here she sat with only her tapestry for company!

"Ugh! I should have gone on to Paris, and the devil take Papa's French whore!" Candy snapped irately to herself, then rose from the deep chair, and flounced down the hall.

She walked along, smirking with distaste. The paneling must be *koa* wood cut from the trees on the plantation more than fifty or more years ago, and the very long rug she remembered went all the way to the other staircase at the end of the hall. The tattered runner must have come from China. Everything looked so old and worn in the hallway, but the rooms up and down had been newly decorated with fine furnishings.

"Well, what do I care, as long as I can find some fun to have here?" It better be pretty soon, too, she told herself, or else she would be packing up and taking the next island steamer to Honolulu. Better than bouncing over the rough roads in an open carriage; that would only give her fair complexion freckles.

"I'm starving," Candy announced, stepping into the kitchen. "Have you seen Thorn?" she asked Jane hopefully, in the next breath.

"Nope," Jane muttered. But she knew where Rogan Thorn was at this very minute. He was with his woman. The lie was all right, because she realized that Thorn did not wish to be disturbed. And why should he be by this empty-headed chit?

"What's that you're making? Some Hawaiian garbage?" Candy sniffed to Jane, wrinkling her nose in distaste at the papaya and greens she was chopping up and arranging neatly in a bowl with juicy guava.

The gardeners, George and Fred, who had entered by the back door, widened their eyes when they saw Candy, for she looked like a delicious frothy desert. She tossed a blond wave over her shoulder and postured in a provocative manner. Daring, but she realized that they would not come within an inch of touching her with their grubby, green-stained fingers. They could gape all they wanted, but dared not touch. But Fred was kind of big and handsome, part Hawaiian, she guessed, and she tucked him away in her mind for use later, perhaps, when she could not take the boredom any longer. Of course, Fred would have to clean himself up first before he ever made love to her. But for now, there was Rogan Thorn to play with and tantalize, until he departed for his home in San Francisco. Now when had he told her that? she wondered.

"Have you boys seen Mr. Thorn?" she asked, holding a white hand up in a feminine manner while brushing a strand of yellow hair back.

"Nope," George stated succinctly.

"Uh-uh," said Fred with a grunt, his black eyes gleaming over her with dangerous, unconcealed lust. "Don' know where he is," he, too, lied. This blond *haole* must be deaf, he was thinking, if she hadn't caught the cries of love-making coming from above. But then he had been outside where the sounds had drifted down strongly.

"What did you say?" Candy snapped. Then, "Never mind, he'll find me when he wants a bit of feminine company! He certainly won't find it with Pandora; she looks like a copper-haired Hawaiian herself. Lord, the way she dresses, you'd think she was a native! Ha, she probably followed that ugly Iola home to eat *poi*. Ugh!"

Fred stiffened. "I like *poi*. It is good."

Candy paid the man no mind, saying, "Tell Thorn I'll be waiting in the dining room if he should want me!"

They watched her twitch from the room in a blue

swirl of silk. The men nudged each other, grinning, while pointing upstairs. Jane caught their exchange and her ready smile emerged.

Jane visualized Pandora's bronzed bareness, the flowers adorning her rippling hair. She had ceased to marvel at the young woman's unself-consciousness. Here on the island naturalness was the ticket. Candice Randall, who prissed along with her well-coifed head, fully clothed in her finery, was out of place.

Now Jane glanced at Fred with his *aloha* shirt wide open over his hairy chest, and she blushed. Fred had brought in tiny dried shrimps, slabs of pineapple, and watermelon and set them whole onto the worktable. Jane boiled the coconut milk with cornstarch, as Pandora had instructed, and Fred cut up the pineapple to add to the confection. The banana bread had been baked, the chicken roasted. The girls were setting the table in the dining room, and one had gone up to knock quietly on the bedroom door to announce that dinner would soon be served. Jane had ordered the girl to leave the message and then come away hastily. Thorn had been hungry before, but now he would be ravenous; Jane chuckled at this thought.

A short time later, Pandora and Rogan entered the dining room, their arms wrapped about each other's waists. Curiously, Pandora dragged Rogan to a halt as she stared at the colossal dining table that replaced the old one. She noticed that even the ceiling fan above the table was working again. Long Persian rugs graced the once-bare hallways upstairs; on the lanai was new, lacy whitewashed wicker furniture. And there were marble topped tables and stands for every imaginable purpose.

"I wonder when Mr. Randall will move in, now that his daughter and all this new furniture has been shipped in," she whispered to Rogan.

"Hmm? Oh, I wouldn't know about that," Rogan answered casually, his face a dark-tan glow in the low-burning lights.

Candy brightened considerably, patting the chair beside hers. "Thorn! Come and sit by me, I've been looking all over for you!"

"Really?" was all he returned; he gazed fondly aside to Pandora. "Shall we sit, my dear? It sounds as though dinner is ready to be served."

"Yes, I am famished!"

Candy pouted when Rogan continued to ignore her as if she weren't even there. Then she noticed how different Pandora appeared. Her head was held high and she looked poised and radiant. She was wearing a fresh muumuu with short ruffled sleeves. Candy studied the muumuu with its red and turquoise flowers stamped on a white background, then she gazed down to Pandora's white sandals. Candy felt the discomfort of her own high-heeled slippers and wanted to spit at the other woman, wishing she could look this good in such simple clothing. How handsome Rogan and Pandora seem together, she thought enviously, both tall and good-looking. It was almost as if they were related, like sister and brother. They seemed unreal to her, in a sense, yet so perfect, that she sat enthralled. A goddess and a god, she added to herself.

In his white tropical suit, Rogan's eyes looked even

greener, more luminous, if that was possible. He pulled out a chair for Pandora and then one for himself next to hers. Candy bit the inside corner of her mouth in vexation. Just looking at the still-warm expression on Rogan's face convinced her that he had been spending some time with Pandora.

Even though Rogan graciously included Candy in the conversation, by looking at her now and then, she could not understand who or what they were discussing.

"I've received a letter from Alexander Moor, my man in charge while I'm away."

Pandora smiled. "I remember the place, your office, but not the man I am afraid." Then something he had said suddenly made her pause. "You received a letter, addressed here?" she inquired, with a puzzled lifting of a tawny eyebrow.

"Well, actually the letter was transferred off the last ship into Honolulu," was all he offered.

An indirect answer, Pandora thought. But she let it drop for now. The night, the perfumed air, and the afterglow of their love-making was making her feel a bit heady.

"Here." Rogan lifted a decanter Pandora had never noticed in the house before. "Let's have some wine."

He began to pour into her glass, but Pandora placed a hand over the rim, peering up at him from beneath lazy lashes. "I really do not need any, Rogan." She looked at him meaningfully and he caught the message.

"I don't either, really, but I'll have one to quench my thirst." He looked across the table. "Candice?"

"Yes, Thorn. Pour me some; I could use some warming up." She tried to steal his attention from the woman beside him, but it was no use. He seemed to have eyes only for Pandora. She told herself it was just because Pandora was still a novelty to him. Later, her own time would come, she told herself confidently.

"Where is Bo Gary?" Pandora wanted to know all of a sudden.

"He took the *Promise*"—his eyes twinkled here as he shortened the name of his ship to avoid curious questioning from Candice—"to Kailua for a few repairs. There is also a luau there he wanted to attend tonight. Seems that he has found himself some new friends."

Pandora was just about to ask him about Bo's girl, Susie, when Jane and a small Chinese girl carried the food in on huge trays. Gallantly Rogan helped the younger one set down her tray. Pandora was becoming increasingly curious about all the new servants popping up seemingly from nowhere and all of a sudden. Very romantically Fred entered just then to pass out flowers, reserving a red one especially for Pandora. All but Candy chuckled over this flower that signified a woman had a lover. The secret was lost on Candy, and she frowned, not liking to be left out of the fun. She sat back, tapping her long painted fingernails on the table. Her time was coming. Soon.

"Fred. Won't you join us?"

"Me?" Fred pointed to his large hairy chest.

"Yes, you." Rogan chuckled at the man's pause. Fred appeared overjoyed and chose a seat next to

Candy's. She bristled, smothering a gasp of disapproval. Pandora had noticed Candy's behavior and wondered why Candy did not speak up. After all, this was her father's house, wasn't it?

The meal progressed in silence as all but one attacked the colorful fare with hearty appetite. Candy grimaced as, with her fingers, Pandora daintily ate the *limu*, an edible seaweed.

"It's not bad," Rogan announced, popping the *limu* into his mouth. "Have some, Candice?"

"Ah, I'll pass," she said, sniffing with distaste and snatching up a bit of mango to munch. Soon she pushed that away, too.

Just like a native girl, Candy was thinking again, while Pandora handled the strange food without forks. Pandora was watching Jane closely. The woman seemed more intent on pleasing Rogan than Candice as she shuffled in and out, awaiting orders from Rogan for this or that. And there seemed to be an atmosphere of tension, she noticed suddenly, coming from whom she couldn't quite tell. Or was this only her imagination?

Pandora caught Rogan studying Candy from beneath hooded eyes. What was this? She bit her lower lip, worrying. No, she must be mistaken. Why would he now be desiring Candy after their wonderful two hours of love-making. No, it had to be something else about the woman that bothered him. But what?

Suddenly Rogan pushed back his chair. The brusque movement startled Pandora, but she continued to sip her lime juice as if he hadn't even moved from her side.

"Excuse me, but I have some unfinished business to take care of."

With that he strode from the room. Pandora watched him go, wondering why the sudden odd behavior. Her heart sank when Candy laid her napkin next to her plate and pushed her chair away from the table.

"I think I'll get a breath of fresh air," Candy announced and then swept from the room.

Fred's eyes went blacker and he, too, stood up to follow in Candy's wake. Pandora stared across the table and a puzzled frown puckered her brow. She sat alone for a few more minutes, and then she, too, pushed back her chair.

Chapter Thirty-six

Inside the bedroom, Rogan handled with much loving care the two Lafoucheux dueling pistols, notorious for firing at the slightest touch. He held one up in the lamplight; then after cleaning the barrel with a rod and oiling the chamber, he put it back in the finely tooled case, reloaded another, and peered along the barrel while aiming the pistol toward the wood.

The door swung open just then.

"Oh! Oh, no!" Pandora splayed herself back against the jamb, her hand over her heaving breast.

His green eyes glittered oddly for a moment, the gun still pointed at Pandora's heart. Then as he caught the sweeping terror in her eyes, his hand shook before he lowered the dangerous weapon to his side. Her staring eyes followed the bore down and then leaped wildly to his face. His countenance was strained taut, like tapa cloth stretched over a drum, and sweat beaded his forehead and upper lip.

"You gave me quite a fright, Rogan, d-darling." She spoke in a quavery voice.

"I—oh, God, I wasn't aiming at you, sweetheart. I mean that—I—" He faltered, realizing just how easy it would have been for the pistol to go off in a second.

She laughed shakily. "It certainly appeared that way—at first. But now I understand. . . ."

His eyes, the color of a turbulent green sea, glittered over to her. They were filled with unreadable emotion. "Come in; close the door," he muttered.

She continued to stare while he continued to clutch the pistol. "I—uh—I was just cleaning them, and checking to see if my aim is as steady as it used to be." He peered down at the pistol, then placed it back into the case.

Her heart beat fast as she sat gingerly on the edge of the bed, still watching him strangely as he strode across the room. Her blue eyes glittered as if tears threatened to spill at any moment.

"You didn't close the door," he said gently, and turned to face her after he had. "Why so nervous, Pandora? You make me that way, too." He waved his hand toward the pistol case. "You don't believe for one moment I would actually want to hurt you?"

He came to stand by the bed and gazed down at her with a pained expression. He reached out to brush his hard knuckles against her cheek that was warm and flushed.

"Lord, sweet, I'd never hurt you—never in a million years!" He pushed the words out with some difficulty.

"I know that now, Rogan." She laid her dewy cheek upon his hand and smiled up at him tenderly, with adoration. But the promise of passion still stirred between them.

"You are feverish, love. Can I get you something,

like a cooling drink of lime?"

"No, Rogan. But thank you . . . anyway." The troubled lines were beginning to melt off her countenance.

She swept her gaze from his concerned face to look at the room as it was now. All his luggage and clothes had been moved in. He had been busy with that task when she had been . . . She had been a silly fool to think he had gone out to meet Candy in a darkened corner somewhere.

She spied a kimono-style robe of aqua silk, and a question arose on her features.

Rogan met Pandora's eyes, and he smiled warmly. "It's yours. I bought it for you yesterday from a Chinese silk merchant who stopped off in Kailua. Do you like it?" He lifted her from the edge of the bed and led her over to it.

"*Kuu ipu*," Rogan murmured, "sweetheart," into Pandora's scented hair as she fingered the fine garment almost reverently.

He stood at her back, his arms wrapped about her waist possessively as his lips and teeth in turn kissed and nibbled with a feathery touch at a tender spot at the nape of her neck. With childlike simplicity and submissiveness, she allowed him to help her take off the muumuu and slip into the slippery robe. The sensuous feel of it sent quivers of delight up her spine and down into her now-bare toes that stood in the folds of her muumuu which had floated to the floor.

Rogan's expertly arousing hands, splayed over the material and caressing every curve beneath, also had something to do with the sensations she was experiencing. He stepped back, and soon his shirt followed the muumuu to the floor; then his boots and his trousers. Pandora bent to him and was gently smoothed against his length in a passionate embrace. When she stood on her toes slightly to reach his height, their tall forms were fitted in all the intimate places.

Rogan nibbled at the cherry-sweet corner of her mouth, then slid to her slender neck where he whispered a question: "Are you tender?"

Her answer stirred against his ear; the "Not so" sent shivers through him.

"God, how beautiful you are."

Kneading gently now, her nipples stood out like blossoms unfolding beneath his manly touch. He was so hot he could scarcely breathe out the question.

"Ah, sweet beauty, do you want it again as much as I do?" Her answer came quickly and he pulled her closer against the throbbing length of his thighs.

She pushed away from him a bit and lowered her eyes to take in the sight of his bold manhood stabbing against her thigh. He smiled at her curiosity and reached out to stroke and probe between her thighs until she thought she could no longer endure it. She remembered something then and felt an intense fire spreading downward. She was seeing the erotic scene all over again—Joe and Cara making love. She reached around his neck to lace her slender fingers in his hair, looking deeply into his eyes, meaningfully. Moisture beaded her upper lip as she waited. He nodded finally.

"Yes, Pandora. I want you, dearest, right here. But I'll have to be careful not to hurt you—like this," he said, already dropping his gaze measuringly.

He slid his hands to her buttocks and tugged her closer, until his manhood touched her cleft and lingered there like a moist kiss. He lifted her only slightly by the roundness of her buttocks and she arched her hips to meet him sliding into the first of the warm honey. He bent to tease her lips with his tongue then, and she responded by slipping hers between his teeth as deep as she could go while he sucked and blew.

"Oh, Rogan, please, please . . . now . . ." she pleaded brokenly, panting into his mouth with her sweet breath. She gasped as he opened her thighs even more and watched the muscles strain in his arms and shoulders when he turned her hips slightly.

Then he was in, driving far up inside her and lifting her to stand on her toes. With his sheer strength he moved easily, rhythmically, sliding himself in and out while Pandora braced herself against his chest. Rogan began shaking so badly, with such unbearable sensation that he was finding it hard to remain standing. He lifted her legs to wind them about his waist and carried her like that, to the bed. He came down with her, murmuring love words into her ear. They made love tenderly now, their eyes meeting and holding; a darting heat shot through Pandora again and again. And he was experiencing the same feeling, she knew. It seemed impossible that he had taken her earlier, because the ecstasy between them now drove on to a new height that captured her body and soul. They met gloriously again and again and their mutual passion soon became explosive pleasure pain, hips grinding harder and harder, his manhood continuing to swell until every thrust melded and became like one. His hand slipped beneath her buttocks and their pleasure pain hurled them together into a shattering culmination to their love-making.

Pandora's head lolled over the edge of the bed. She had fainted.

When Pandora stepped out onto the lanai the next morning, the thought of Rogan ever desiring Candice Randall had been swept from her mind like so many filthy cobwebs before a broom. She embraced the deep summer day and hugged the soft sea breeze to her breast. The blue-shadowed island surrounded her in all its glorious beauty—blue sky, blue sea, even the blue of her eyes glowed more brightly.

"Blue, blue, blue. True, true, true," she shouted happily, tossing her arms toward the sky.

"Pandora is drunk, huh?"

"Iola!" Pandora swept down the broad steps, her short muumuu displaying a shapely turn of leg.

"You have shore-whoopee time last night, huh?"

Pandora tossed her slim arms about her aunt and hugged her fiercely. Iola rocked back and forth with her big girl and gave her a bear hug.

"Oooof!" Pandora let out her breath after the woman released her. They giggled like schoolgirls just out the door.

Over her shoulder Pandora spied Patsy and ran to pat the mare and pucker her sweet lips at the huge muzzle. "What have you got there?" she asked Iola then, spying the immense hamper bulging with foodstuffs.

"Goodies! *Mahimahi* macadamia pie and passion fruit!" Iola beamed, thrilled for her joyful and radiant girl.

"Passion fruit!" Pandora squealed, and the older woman lifted an eyebrow wondering what could be so humorous about that food.

"Boy!" Iola shouted and clapped her hands to her stout Hawaiian neighbor lad. "Put horse in shelter, then go fetch some plantains. *Wikiwiki!*" she called for him to be quick about it and he smilingly complied.

"Now, *wahini*, where's that skinny-nosed Jane who almost push me out of kitchen when she come like she own whole darn' place!" She flexed one arm hugely, giggling, "Hee-hee-hee."

"Oh, no, Aunty. Jane is very nice. Come on, I want you to get to know her. She is so excited about learning how to cook Hawaiian, that she's like a happy puppy!"

"Huh? Oh, that be good. I teach." Iola plumped up her bosom proudly.

"*E mai*," Pandora invited, "come in, Aunty." She giggled again. "Even if Candice's father owns the place, come and be welcome. I love you even if she does not! I'll give her a swift kick in the shins if she mutters another nasty word to my aunty!"

"Good girl! You let her have it, huh?"

"Of course!"

Inside, Iola spied Rogan just traversing the hall. He stopped, turned to look at them, and did a most amazing thing, Iola noticed.

"Your man, he blushes like woman," she whispered to Pandora.

Pandora lowered her lashes when Rogan gazed across the space into her eyes. She looked up again, and her heart turned over. He hadn't moved a muscle, but stood mesmerized at her presence. He appeared so boyishly handsome that she wanted to run and throw her arms about his neck, to smooth back that forelock from his blushing face.

"I know," Pandora murmured; "that is what I love about him." That he was a man, in every sense of the word, she kept to herself, wishing she could spend the entire day wrapped in his arms.

"You stay here, my girl. I like to talk to Thorn by myself. Huh? You mind?"

Pandora could only smile at that, and Iola went to Rogan before her niece could answer. Pandora noticed vaguely that Rogan appeared sheepish over something Iola was saying to him. Now she wondered: what could her aunt want to discuss with Rogan in private?

The conversation was held in low tones that did not carry to Pandora. But Rogan shook his head every time that Iola seemingly put a question to him. At last, Iola beamed and shook Rogan's hand *haole* fashion. He chuckled warmly, nodding to her aunt; then a brown eyebrow lifted in a humorous fashion.

Iola was sighing happily as she returned to Pandora who was still puzzled about their hushed conversation. She opened her mouth to ask, but caught Rogan putting a finger to his lips, silencing the older woman. Rogan then blew Pandora a kiss and continued to wherever he had been going when they entered.

Pandora, determined to shake Iola down, followed the woman closely. At the kitchen door, Iola halted abruptly and Pandora bumped into the woman's bulk. Pandora again opened her mouth, but Iola put a finger to the young woman's lips.

"Shh, no ask. Come, let's go make something good to eat in kitchen. Basket of goodies is waiting."

Pandora pouted, but followed her aunt into the veritable hot box.

Rogan's thoughts deepened as the days sped by. Pandora. His passion flower. She had gotten over being a timid virgin finally. He had always known she would be the lusty type of woman who likes her man to be unique in sexual adventures with her. A walk along the ocean's edge just after twilight, making love on their private spot of sand where she removed her sarong, the delicious movement of her perfect breasts, dancing up and down, free of any encumbrance, luxuriating in the feel of them moving freely beneath his touch. She had made him a complete man again. How could he ever stand to lose her?

Too bad it all had to end soon, he told himself as he walked the strip of beach for some time alone. Paradise had never seemed more wonderful and glorious to him, but business waited for him in San Francisco and so did other matters. She would have to come willingly; he would dislike having to force her but this time he must do it, if it came to that. There were no two ways about it.

"Rogan Thorn. *Aloha!*" Fred shouted, coming

toward him on the beach.

"Fred. You are just the man I want to see. Jane told me you have been admiring something of mine. Come along; I'd like to give it to you."

Fred beamed. "You really give it to me? I never see one like it before. Don' have them like that here."

"Well, Fred, it is all yours."

Chapter Thirty-seven

Pandora lingered over steaming coffee and banana bread with Bo Gary and Candice. Rogan had excused himself to go and do something after he had whispered an aside to her. She had blushingly avoided him, unable to tell him why she could not go to his bed at this time. She sat after he had gone, cursing her time of month that stayed so long with her.

When Candy excused herself to go for her "walk," this time Pandora was prepared to pay it no mind, even though this night seemed a reenactment of the other.

When Rogan had not returned an hour later, Pandora excused herself and left the table. Bo Gary had watched them all leave, one at a time. He sat staring around the empty table.

"I might as well excuse myself, too. There's no one left." He chuckled as he went out to spend some time with the comforting lady—*Pandora's Promise.*

On her way up the stairs, Pandora felt the delicious warm breeze. Because of it the huge leaves on the old gnarled tree that reached toward the house whispered, panting on the rise and fall of the night wind, and the tapa hangings billowed softly. From her angle of vision on the stairs it looked as if someone— maybe more than one—sat on the broad lanai in front, but with all the clinging vines and thick shrubbery she could not be certain.

She decided then that the person or persons were only Fred, or possibly George with him, if indeed it was not only shadows she saw.

In the half-gloom, Pandora found the door. Thinking of Rogan and another time, she turned the knob expectantly, then stepped inside. She swept a gaze about the dark room. The lamps had not been lighted. There was not a soul here.

Biting her lip, Pandora retraced her steps, but then headed toward the lanai. Empty. Outside when she reached the sand, the wind lifted her hair and blew it back sinuously from her shoulders; the hem of her muumuu rippled along her long legs. She froze. Yellow-blond hair caught her wide gaze.

There. Two people were walking close together in the moonlight. A pain squeezed over the region of her heart. Her eyes strained to see them better, and she stared and stared, waiting for the terrible answer.

Candice Randall had snatched up a hibiscus blossom and tucked it behind her ear, in essence aping Pandora, unconsciously desiring to be like her rival. She had been playing with and teasing the man with her, tormenting his sensuality until he began to feel he must have her. Her hand dropped now to his leg, then moved slowly upward to torture him further.

"You should not be out here with me. Why did you

follow?" he asked, deeply annoyed and excited at the same time.

"Oh my, you are so strong. You really want me, don't you?" she purred provocatively, running her palm down the front of him. She stopped the movement. "My goodness, you *are* great!"

"Yes, and I will have you now."

But Candy was suddenly afraid and cried out when he pushed her unceremoniously to the ground, crushing the hibiscus blossom into the sand. She began to whimper and plead with him, but he murmured that he had warned her long ago to quit teasing him. Now it was too late.

"You are far from help."

Moving fast, his big hands bunched her skirts up to her waist. He pinioned her under his arms, despite her obvious fright.

"Oh, no, I was only flirting a little. Please don't hurt me. Damn! You are too big for me, you bastard!" she hissed like a spitting cat close to his face.

"You ask for it, woman."

"No, Fred, please. It will hurt too much."

"You easy woman. It not hurt you. Heah, now!"

Without undressing, only unbuttoning the shirt Rogan had given him, Fred released his turgid manhood. Candy dared to look down as he shifted above her and her eyes fastened incredibly on his size. He growled deep in his throat, shoved her back into position, and before she could struggle, he thrust and entered her quickly; despite his goodly size he slipped into her warm honey sheath easily.

"I know you open good," Fred groaned and

plunged far into her, and she arched against him naturally. "You big for little woman." He grunted in her ear harshly.

"You ass! Ohhh," Candy cried low then as he already began to pulsate within her. She shivered and rose with him.

"Pau!" he cried out in a rasp against her damp neck spiraled with tendrils of disheveled hair.

Like creatures rutting in the wild they came together more fiercely this time, until finally, they lay bathed in sweat side by side and panting heavily.

Pandora stood stunned, waiting for the nausea to leave her. Their voices had carried the other way on the wind, but she had visually made something out— a bit of cloth, so familiar, as the tall man lowered himself onto Candy.

Pandora stuffed her fist into her mouth. "No, oh no, no, no, this cannot be true." But she knew she was not dreaming.

Bare feet churning up puffs of powdery sand, she whirled and ran before they could rise and see her. *Their* sand, *their* flowers, gone forever due to a lusty interlude here in her own special place—the place of her heart.

Damn them! Damn them all to hell!

She ran, her hair streaking out behind when she wasn't tripping, fleeing the scene that had sickened her to the core of her womanly being. Candice and Rogan. Over and over their names combined and crashed through her brain until there remained no corner free of *Candice and Rogan.*

She sobbed. Oh, God, how could he do this thing

to her? Her heart was breaking into a million pieces, just as their ecstasy had at the height of their love-making.

Finally she dropped to her trembling knees. Her hair hung over her face in moist tendrils that seemed to have lost their healthy shine.

The wild abandon of tropical nights was no more. He had broken her heart. She had seen the green-leafed shirt fluttering behind him as he drove into Candice Randall. The very same shirt Rogan had worn so many days here.

Pandora lifted herself from the sand with strained effort, walked doggedly into the house with her chin held high, and went up and locked herself in the bedroom. After she had tossed Rogan's personal effects out into the hall, after she had finished sobbing herself into a streak-faced wretch, after she was all dried up and angry; only after that she slept.

Rogan was rocking her gently, murmuring sooth-ing words into her ear. To comfort her. She had seen visions reaching from the dark tunnel of her past. He unwrapped her sarong. They made love on the sand, her bare buttocks making a soft impression as he crushed her and her flowers into . . . flowers . . . flowers . . .

Pandora woke with a start. She was bathed in sweat and she could hear no heart beating next to hers. Only the wind outside and the lonely breathing of her own soul.

Offshore the island was mauve-tinted in the shadows beneath the fierce glory of orange morning clouds. Fred was on his way back to his family in Kailua, and Iola had returned with Patsy and the rickety carriage. She wondered at the man's haste to be away. Fred, she noticed, appeared angry and frustrated, at the same time shamefaced about something. Iola could not give a name to the mixed emotions playing about his dark countenance. Not until she spied Candice Randall studying flowers out back beside the lanai. Iola saw that Pandora was not on the front lanai as usual. But that dainty slip, Candice, had an air about her that indicated she was very pleased over something.

"Aha!" Iola exclaimed to herself softly. The girl had gotten what she wanted most, for a while anyway. "Who she be after next? She big floozy, no doubt have one heck of good time with big Fred. I hope he give it to her good, one big one to keep her skirts down for a while! Bad bitch!"

Rogan came up quietly behind Iola. "Talking to yourself, so early in the morning?" But his smile did not reach all the way to his eyes. There was pain in them. He had found Pandora still cold and close-mouthed. This made him more confused than the night before when she would not speak to him, would not even allow him into the room when he knocked . . . he should have pushed his way in right through all the furniture he knew she had piled against the door.

"She has to come out sometime. To eat, to go to the bathroom," he muttered to himself now.

"Huh? Oh, Thorn, where you come from?" Iola blinked up at him in surprise. She had been pondering just as deeply as he had.

"I have been here most of the night—well, part of it, anyway." He frowned up at the house, wondering if she would see him off this time. He had to return to Kailua to meet the island steamer from the big island.

"You having trouble with Pandora, huh, Thorn? She not be talking to you?"

"How did you know?"

Iola appeared sheepish. "I guess, that's all." She would not embarrass him further by letting him know she had seen him the night before hauling his things from the hall into another room beside the one in which Pandora had locked herself.

"Well, I must be on my way. Try to talk some sense into your niece for me, will you? I'm at a loss as to what is eating away at her." He tried hiding his weariness from the older woman, but she had very keen eyes.

"You have to do that yourself, Thorn. You look pretty tired. You been up all night, huh?" Not awaiting an answer, she went on. "Candice Randall make much trouble; you keep an eye on her, else that one make Pandora jealous over you."

Rogan started. "Trouble? I hardly think the blond woman has anything to do with us, and the immediate problem." But he had kept an eye out for her, he wouldn't confess now. "Just to put your mind at ease, though, the woman doesn't interest me one bit. Only Pandora does."

"Oh, I know. But Missah Randall got her horny eyes on all mens around here. She make things seem what they not. Watch out, Thorn."

"Maybe," was all Rogan muttered as he strode toward the dock.

Iola stood in indecision for a moment looking up in the direction of the second floor. She shook her head then. Nope, she decided. Let this man and woman figure things out for themselves. This aunty will stay out of Pandora's hair for a while. She would go see what Jane was doing in the kitchen. That is, if the skinny woman was even up at this ungodly hour.

Pandora searched each corner of her heart and mind. She was so troubled in both that the pain was becoming unbearable to withstand. Whatever strange fate had brought her and Rogan together she would always be happy for one thing: that she had had the chance to know him. And yes, oh yes, his passion.

She was falling in love with him; that was for certain.

But now, he would never hear it from her lips. She did have some pride, after all, however lonely. She fluctuated somewhere between anger and hurt and love. Oh! The pain of loving! The price one paid!

For the next half-hour she perched on her sunny windowsill, drying her long hair, the door in back of her open so she could be sure to hear if Rogan returned. But no, he would not return. She could see the ship, *Pandora's Promise*, pulling away from the dock. She had been washing her hair down the hall and had not seen him board, but something told her he was aboard with Bo Gary.

There was nothing Rogan could do or say to make her understand why his passions had gotten the best of him. He had hidden the fact quite well. Why should he tell her, anyway? It was just that she had hoped and prayed he would have confessed his unfaithfulness. This hurt so much.

So soon after their perfect passion he had gone on to another woman's arms. Was that the way it was with Rogan? Once he had conquered one and proven himself a man, not consummating prematurely, to move on and on and on . . . ?

Rogan. Candice. Damn them. She tore at her hair with a brush, glad for the pain it brought. She then slammed the brush down on the small table beside the window.

Go ahead. Cry! Because, woman, you are almost as ignorant and blind as those two think you are! What a fool!

For now, no ships were visible far below on the sea; no carriages or carts moved on the road above the house or the one below it. No one seemed to be stirring downstairs.

No. I am not a fool. I know everything now. But the sad part of it was, just what was she going to do about the situation?

Well, one thing was certain; she was not going to sit here and tear her hair out over those two. In fact, there might be more than two women with whom Rogan was pleasuring himself. Of course, he was most certainly proving himself to that whore Leilani right now. Hadn't Iola said the young woman was going to Kailua this morning?

Bored, she stared about the room feeling the walls close in on her. She needed to be outside in the fresh air, out of this old musty house while she still owned the morning.

Shedding her tapa robe, Pandora hurried to the monkeypod wardrobe to put on a blue sarong decorated with gold birds perched on delicate branches in front and back; then she added a string of limpet shells about her slender neck. How she wished for a flower to tuck in her hair, but at a glance around the room she found the vases empty. On her walk to the lagoon she would discover one to go with her sarong, to cheer her up. Hopefully.

But, truly, now that she had caught Rogan with another woman, would she ever enjoy anything as much again as the love they had shared? Oh, her heart was breaking, hurting. All that was good seemed to have vanished into thin air. Nothing would ever again be good enough, for she had known the best of love and joy, and for such a very short time, too.

The breeze outside lifted her hair and finished drying the longest golden strands as Pandora started back down the slope, by a different route this time. She did not want anyone to see her; she needed some hours by herself to think.

She rounded a curve and began to climb. Now the path turned narrow. Higher up rose groves of eucalyptus trees with their ragged bark. An occasional tree bore masses of orange and green fruits clustered close to the main trunk. Papaya. At all times of the year a few were ripe enough for eating.

Almost no light penetrated here halfway up; the rank growth of still more vines and flowering trees almost shut out the vast blue of the sky. The air was thick and still, heavy enough to taste, and scented with the cloying sweetness of an overabundance of flowers that forever bloomed and withered. Just like love and its death, she thought forlornly.

As she proceeded into an area where the dark green trees curved gracefully upward, the sun broke through here and there. A small red bird perched in one of the thick trees that were flowered with identical red. She reached the rocky cliffs a little breathless. Beyond the lagoon below her the waves broke on the rocks in a ceaseless ebb and flow. At her feet were fern fronds, wild orchids, and birds-of-paradise. Sheer cliffs made heart-stopping drops to the lagoon on her left, but on her right there was a spot where she could climb safely down.

The cooler air here had a fresh, clean smell. She stood a moment beneath the uncluttered sky, then she made her way down carefully, hanging on to thick vines till she dropped finally onto the damp sand. The water was like a thin sheet of crystal over the dark lava rocks that shadowed the lagoon. At the bottom more ferns uncoiled their graceful fronds, growing high like green tatted lace. Fuchsias and flowers with thick glossy leaves leaned over the clear mirror of the aqua-tinted pool.

Pandora could see her sad face reflected as she knelt at the edge of the water, drank, and bathed her warm face free of perspiration. In the green-and-blue silence surrounding her, with bright flower faces nodding here and there, there was the merest sibilance of leaves, like a vibrating curiosity that reached out to her. It was almost—she whirled about—almost as if someone were watching her every move.

There is no one here, the vegetation gods seemed to say. She relaxed and sighed. Such a lovely place to be. Flowers bloomed with a spicy fragrance in the thick, springy humus wedged into the rocks by nature's hand.

Pandora tucked into her hair a wild lavender orchid that she had unconsciously picked on her way down the rocks. Rogan liked this flower; it suited her, he had said. Which one fit Candice? she wondered with sudden fury at the remembrance of them in their special place in the sand, entwined, making lusty love.

Hope, Mamma had said; there was always hope when all else disappeared or failed. A tear slid down her cheek. *Hope for what when all was gone?*

As Pandora left the sleepy lagoon, someone walked not far behind her, keeping to tree shadows, and she never noticed the stealthy presence.

Chapter Thirty-eight

When Pandora reached the house her step slowed, for Rogan was standing there leaning against the porch, smiling narrowly at her approach.

The totally male smell of him reached her in a drift of sensuality before she came completely to a standstill before him. An appreciative smile curved his lips as he took in her revealing sarong with its bright colors. He marveled at her cool beauty. She fought the urge to go to him and melt against his hard body, knowing he could turn her own body into jelly. He was viewing her with lazy eyes when he pushed away from the support to move toward her. She backed away, praying he would not touch her.

"Have a nice walk?" His voice was deceptively soft.

"I am not in the mood for an argument again. I am thirsty and hot, so if you would move aside?"

Irritation crossed his features. "I only asked you if you had a nice walk."

Suddenly he tugged at her hand, pulling her off balance. Pandora closed her eyes and felt desire for him shiver through her. Though she was not by any means small, she felt so beside him. Lazily he was sliding his hand down to her waist, finally letting it go down along her hip.

"Let me go, Rogan."

"You know you don't mean that."

"Yes, yes I do. You are biting your fingers into my hip. Stop!"

His eyes became crystal pools. "I meant to hurt you, and I'll do it again if you don't stop this game you're playing with me. You won't win, you know."

Pandora could sense the sexual aura he emitted, and it seemed to come from every pore of his body.

"You have no right to—"

"We've been through this once before, if I recall right. Pandora, I'm your husband, and I have every right to put my hands on you."

She attacked him verbally. "Not to hurt me you don't!" She tried twisting away, but she was confused by her own sudden weakness toward him.

"It is only that I long for your willingness." A bitter smile lifted one corner of his mouth. "We're married, Pandora, and I want you. I have tried to be patient and understanding, to leave you alone for a time with your thoughts. You told me you were confused about your feelings for me. But you haven't explained."

Gently his hands stroked her hips in a seductive caress, and she looked away, trembling with the usual awareness of him. She could see his tanned fingers and she tried to find the courage to tell him that she loved him, but her courage broke. Her lips formed his name, yet no sound escaped her mouth. She blinked up at the man who was calling himself her husband, and suddenly she realized she did not know him at all. Would she ever?

"Why me, *today*, Rogan Thorn? What is wrong with Candice Randall's company today? Oh, is she perhaps busy with someone else?"

Pandora pushed at his hard chest, this motion slipping her hips away from his fingers. His eyes darkened, and a frown gathered on his brow.

"What in hell are you babbling about?"

"Please, Rogan, I'm too tired to fight with you," she snapped, noticing the pain in her palms as her long nails bit into them.

"Please . . . explain," he bit out harshly, fury tightening his jaw.

Blue flames darted in her eyes as she lifted her chin and met his. "Do you deny that you were with Candice on the beach last night?" Tears welled up and blurred her vision.

Rogan had to laugh at that. "You're saying that I bedded her there, I take it?"

"Yes. You had sex with her!"

"Caught me, hmm?" His amused voice reached out to her.

Pandora flinched inwardly while Rogan tossed back his chestnut head and laughed. She looked up at him and felt her lips begin to tremble, but her hurt turned quickly to anger that deepened with intensity. She must never let him see how deeply hurt she was inside.

His countenance hardened then. "Now that you think you've found me out, why don't we go see just how right you are." He tugged at her arm, but she would not budge.

Her eyes widened, questioning his intent. "What do you mean? Where are you wanting to take me? If it is to the bedroom, I'm not moving from this spot!"

"No, not there, not yet anyway. We'll discuss this with Candice, and then in *our* bedroom you can apologize over and over for your hasty accusations."

Iola popped her head out the window as they passed, with Rogan dragging Pandora along with him. Iola smiled, wishing she were young again.

"*Aloha,* Pandora," she called. "Have a nice walk?"

"Ooooh!" Pandora seethed. "Why don't you all just leave me alone."

"Come along, love; I am not going to leave you alone. Not ever again, not with your silly little jealousies. Come on."

Candy dropped her tapestry and needle onto the table beside her in the lanai. She tilted her head, watching Rogan and Pandora approach, and licked her lips. Pandora, looking down from her height onto Candy's smirk, gave the other woman a murderous glance before she peered sideways at Rogan to catch his reaction at having them all meet together after the scene she had witnessed the night before.

Now would come the telling, to be sure. Already, Pandora told herself, they both looked guilty enough to be strung up by their heels.

Pandora had a hard time swallowing her fury, but she waited impatiently for the act to unfold.

"Rogan, darling, where have you been?" Candy drawled, avoiding Pandora's presence completely.

"That doesn't matter right now, Candice. But what does is we've something important to discuss with you."

Candice's brittle blue eyes swept over Pandora, then moved to focus on Rogan's lips. "Both of you, darling?" Her question slid off her tongue like poisoned honey.

"Of course, both of us," he almost snapped into her cosmetically enhanced face. He caught the biting glance Candice flashed his wife. Indeed, he deduced, Candice is a jealous woman. If she kept this up, the bitch was going to spoil all his plans. He gritted his teeth inside his mouth, thinking that frustration would make him ripe to commit murder.

Rogan's warm fingers crushed Pandora's arm in a painful grip. Her heart was pounding thunderously, partly from wanting passionately to believe Rogan, and partly from fear at what Candice would reveal. Rogan wasted no more time, but came right to the point.

"Candice, tell me, why did Fred leave in such a rush this morning? Was it something you said, or—did?" His hand moved to Pandora's back, to the bare spot there, and brushed against her soft skin until he felt her shiver.

Goose bumps raced along Pandora's spine. She glanced down at his other hand and saw that his fist was clenched so hard that the bones showed white beneath the tan. Rogan watched Candice and waited with visible impatience for her response.

"Fred? He left this morning?" She looked at one and then the other, curling her pink mouth. "Why, no one told me," she added, licking a corner of her lips.

Rogan cleared his throat exasperatedly. "Well, let me ask you this then: gossip from the *kanakes* has it that you were seen walking on the beach with—ah—Fred. True?"

Candice had been staring at the colorful birds darting across the branches on Pandora's sarong. Now she studied the large one at her midriff.

"Pandora, I would love to stitch that design onto my tapestry. Would you lend the thing you're wearing to me for a few days?"

Pandora shook with anger and glared at Candice. "I will not! This happens to be one of my favorites. Iola gave it to me, and I'll not let it out of my sight."

Now, Pandora chided herself, Rogan was probably laughing inwardly all the while at her insane jealousy. The walls and columns of the lanai seemed to be closing in on her. The hand splayed at her back moved slightly and a tingle set fire to her spine. She looked up at Rogan, but he was all business. No doubt he had thought he would come out the winner in this game he played with Candice, and herself. To bring some control to her emotions, she quickly stepped away from Rogan.

"Don't leave," he ordered over his shoulder.

She stared at his darkened eyes fringed by even darker lashes. His whole countenance seemed to scowl blackly, but she would not yield him the satisfaction of besting her at this deceitful game he played. She had already decided guilt was the verdict, so why in the world was she standing here being made a fool of?

"Rogan, darling." Candice broke the stifling silence with a deep purr, for a moment keeping her eyes trained on Pandora, then as she went on shifting her softened gaze to Rogan. "Why don't we take that walk on the beach you promised me?"

"What?" he ground out furiously.

"Of course, don't you remember, dar—"

"Oh!" Pandora cut off the rest of the sickening endearment.

"Lousy bitch!" Rogan growled down to Candice, but she remained unruffled by the curse.

Pandora backed away from Rogan. "Don't you touch me!" she choked with rage. Her emotions were spinning wildly and she had to get away from them both.

Furious beyond belief, Rogan whirled on Candice and she shrank back at the feral look of him. She bit her bottom lip, stood shakily as if to run, and he shoved her back down into the wicker lounge. He looked ready to explode, but before that happened, Pandora backed farther away and spun about to run back into the house.

"Damn it, Pandora, come back here!" Rogan called after her in a thunderous voice. Then to Candice, "Leave here," he said softly, dangerously.

"Here? You mean this spot?" Candice asked in a quavery tone of voice.

"No, I mean this house. Immediately."

She snickered at the wide back he kept turned to her. "What do you want me to do—walk on water?"

"I don't care if you have to walk on horse crap; pack your bags and leave."

She settled back into the chair smugly. "You can't order me around, Thorn. You don't own this house!"

He whirled on her, his face a dark mask of fury. "Who says I don't?" he growled so close to her that his breath stirred her blond hair.

"I—I—" She only shrugged.

"Good. I'll expect you to be on the next island steamer that stops. If you are not, I'll bodily remove you myself, slut!"

Candy wiggled in the chair, as if to settle herself more firmly into it as she watched him eat up the distance to the beaded curtain. He flicked it aside, turned back to glare at her, and then disappeared into the house. Candy curled her pink mouth. She snatched up her tapestry and continued to work on the rose mallow, stabbing the needle into the flower's heart, wishing it were someone's flesh. One woman's in particular. Rogan Thorn she could handle. Given time, she would worm her way under his skin, very thick skin at that, but Candice Randall wasn't born yesterday. She knew his type. She had had much experience with men like Rogan. How like her father he was, she told herself, gazing down appreciatively at the flower that was beginning to take life. A flower, in the sand, with the sea waving in the background.

"I am staying right here. Ohhh yes," she hummed to herself softly. In fact, the excitement was just beginning to pick up. She wouldn't miss it for the world.

*　　*　　*

Hurriedly tearing off her sarong as if she found the thing distasteful, Pandora stepped into the porcelain tub she had filled to near overflowing. The water she had ordered one of the boys to heat on the stove downstairs was hot and soothed the muscles that ached from her long walk. She scrubbed herself until she felt raw, as if the strong soap could wash away the degrading scene she had just been forced to go through. She felt dejected.

Damn Rogan Thorn! He had been forcing himself into her blood ever since that fated day when Wizan had struck her down with Rogan's carriage. Of course, she did have something to do with it; she had walked blindly into the path of the speeding carriage. Yet he had been traveling quite fast, so it had not been all her fault.

Rogan had been bent on conquering her will ever since, for he had tracked her down everywhere she went. Or had it merely been coincidence that he had seemed to pop up here and there? Whatever, she shrugged in the water, he was here now, too, and damn, to remove him from her heart and mind now would take a miracle.

Well, she was clean now, feeling less defiled by "their" presence. Stepping from the tub, she slipped into her tapa robe, and wrapped her hair turban-style in an old towel.

Just then the door to the bathroom flew open and banged hard against the wall. Pandora started and jumped back with a squeak. Darkened green eyes locked with hers for a moment. She pretended not to fear the scathing gaze that flicked her from head to toe.

"Are you finished?" he inquired harshly.

"Quite."

"Well then, come into the bedroom," he invited huskily, taking in her freshly scrubbed flesh, her long legs that peeped out from the split in the robe. When she hadn't moved a muscle he demanded that she do so.

"You do not have to rush me, Rogan," she replied tartly. "I was on my way there before you barged in on my privacy."

"You gave that up long ago, *Mrs*. Thorn."

She almost laughed with derision. "You mean my mind, of course. I had to have been insane to become involved with you, *Mr*. Thorn!"

Ceremoniously he splayed his long body against the door frame, and bowed slightly for her to proceed him out of the steaming perfumed room. She swept by him with such a grand air, the high towel giving her the look of a tall, aggressive, Amazon woman. She knew she threw caution to the winds by behaving in such a haughty manner, but what did she care, really; he could not hurt her more than he had already by bedding that slut downstairs.

Once in the room, with the door shut firmly by Rogan to ward off intruders, Pandora stood adamant, unmoving and unmoved while he proceeded to peel off his shirt and moved to the buttons at his trousers.

Silly, but she could not help noticing his hair again. Its rich chestnut thickness was burnished with sun streaks, and it was styled back from his tight face.

In or out of doors it looked windswept, but the curls at the nape of his neck were always kept firmly in check. She loved running her long fingers through those curls.

His fingers hovered over the last remaining buttons. "Well," he said, "what are you waiting for? We'll be out before dawn, Bo Gary and I, so I must get to bed early." His scrutiny narrowed then and his voice went lower, demanding. "We're going to make love, Pandora, so you might begin by peeling off that homely robe you're wearing again."

"Homely! If you think so, why don't you find me a better one," she snapped, running her hands down over her hips and thighs provocatively. She would not remind him that he had given her one.

"I already have. I mean to pick it up, along with some other items, tomorrow." He had forgotten about the Chinese silk one.

"Do you want me to have to fight you?" she said suddenly.

An eyebrow rose. "Fight? You mean that I'll have to rape you?" He popped another button from its hole, slowly, maddeningly.

"Yes, exactly."

"If that is your desire, Mrs. Thorn, I'll gladly accommodate you."

She took a full step backward, then stepped sideways. But a table met the cold back of her legs and she was halted from going anywhere but toward the bed. She stayed.

"I am hungry. I have not eaten anything but a banana today," she announced suddenly.

He shook his head and had to smile at that. "A banana," he repeated, chuckling. "A banana for a mischievous monkey. You look just as ridiculous, too, Pandora, in that getup."

Licking her dry lips, Pandora stared as the last button yielded beneath his two fingers and the dark V of curling manhood hairs became visible between the gape in his trousers.

"Pandora?" His husky query brought her eyes darting back to his face. "We'll eat later."

He flung a hand toward the window where the tapa curtains flirted with a curling sea breeze. "I've made a mistake, sweetheart; it's still quite early, and the sun has not even set. You'll have time for dinner."

"I am hungry now!" she said with a flick of her turbaned head.

"We'll eat later," he repeated, moving toward her, his desire visible.

Much later. Very much later, the darkened room and the blurred gray shadows pulsated with the sounds and movements of ecstatic love-making.

They had come together twice now, tenderly, and were beginning to make love again. There had been no cause for rape, and Rogan was glad. Misty-eyed, she had allowed him to peel off the robe and unwind the towel from her hair. The urgent need she knew for him had set her on fire once again. Their passion had blossomed into full bloom. It was love for now— pure love. The faces of the other women melted into nothingness, and she had danced to his tune of passion, standing there, inching closer and closer to him, while she raised her trembling lips for his kiss. Her breast had been cupped in his palm; his other had sought out her lower curves, probing, finding, sinking then into moisture, melting her resistance.

But that was before.

Now they moved as one, savagely, straining, each thrust and pull more beautiful than the one before. Tension was beginning to build inside her again, hotter, deeper, darting, a new pleasure of a kind she had never before experienced. Shimmering with sweat, the male beauty of his naked form labored and groaned huskily over her. As he moaned deeply from his own pleasure, he lowered his head and his tongue gave her an intense sensation as it flicked her already bruised and hardened nipples.

All that mattered was now. She indulged herself for a moment in thinking tonight was exceptional. Her eyes were shining like two great stars.

"Pandora," he groaned through the flames of passion. "Say the words, my love!"

She felt now as if she were being torn into bits. She knew perfectly well what he wanted.

"Kuu ipu. Do you love me, Pandora?"

Pandora bit her lip as he ground his hips into hers hard and fast, faster, faster . . .

"Do you?" he persisted, rotating his loins hot and harder.

"Yes," she murmured through the cloud of joy next to pain.

"Then . . . then say it," he demanded.

"I—I—" she merely ended with a whimper.

"Must . . . must I use force to . . . to get you to tell me?"

He began to spurt hot and heavy inside of her.

"I love you.... Oh! I love you very much, Rogan!"

"Ahhhh, and I love you, Pandora! My passion flower forever!"

He finished.

And so did she. Knowing sweet death.

Chapter Thirty-nine

Time passed. In the sand the flowers that had not been buried blew away on the wind's breath, only to be replaced by new blossoms where they made love.

In her new-found joy, Pandora locked away that part of her past that still remained a mystery. She never ventured into the dark closet where Iola had stashed the trunk, and never questioned the older woman about why she had put it there.

As he had promised, Rogan brought her a lovely lavender negligee and peignoir purchased on the island-hopping steamer that had carried a merchant whose best selling merchandise consisted of women's lacy and silk undergarments.

Her heart brimmed with love, but she had never spoken of it again since that night, two weeks ago, when they had confessed their love at the height of passion. But Pandora continued to blush intensely whenever Rogan was near, or when he approached her, surprising her from behind. When he seemed to take pleasure in doing this to her, she flushed even harder.

The weather was of a changeless temper so the

steamers regularly traversed back and forth between the islands and brought more furniture. Several new pieces had been added to the living room; they were covered with colorful chintzes stamped with bright bouquets of blossoms in rose and mauve. One showpiece, a blue velvet overstuffed armchair, wore a lace and tasseled antimacassar. Pandora exclaimed over the Victorian "witch's globe" filled with mauve and pink sand, much like a soft tropical sunset. Chinese porcelain lamps and smooth sandalwood tables had also been added to the room.

The *kanes* were at work out back beginning to clear the fields for the next planting, actually the first in a very long while. Had Candy ordered them to this task herself, without her father's permission? Just who was the manager? Pandora wondered about this.

One day she was out walking the beach by herself. Rogan had gone off with Bo somewhere. It was hot for early June so she wore her straw hat with streaming ribbons, and her white- and cream-embroidered skirt. This ensemble was another gift from her generous husband. She had come to think of herself as truly Rogan's bride. She smiled. Sometimes, though, thinking of his name, she felt that he, too, was a thorn in her side. She giggled softly. Bride of Thorn's.

When would Candy's father come to take over? But could she leave? Pandora had come to love the old house; it was like a second home to her. Then where was her first home? She often wondered, too, of late: would Rogan be taking her back with him when he sailed (soon, he had said, he must return) or would he

411

leave her behind—like a sailor, promising his woman he would come back for her, and never returning?

She came to stand beneath the monkeypod tree now and looked up at the house. Weathered gray shutters had been replaced by painted green ones, and the lanai roof had been repaired and now provided a wider shelter. The essence of orchids carried on a sea-borne breeze and the restless tossing of the trees foretold possible rain for the evening hours.

She glanced over her shoulder to the beach. Her footprints in the sand—and his. From the night before when she had again throbbed from his every caress that had again led her to the heights of fulfillment. She had given herself to him wantonly, and had clung to him unashamedly. She gazed up at the sun now, remembering. . . She had been running playfully away.

"Pandora! Come here, moon-witch!"

"No! No! No!" she had called over her shoulder, the wind catching up her shrieks and giggles, tossing them back like a taunt into his face. "Catch me if you can . . . but you can't . . . I am too fast for you!"

She whirled around the bole of a palm as his words just caught up with her: "That's what you think, my long-legged Amazon!" He sounded out of breath and this made her laugh even louder, more carelessly.

She pretended to hide now, but peeped out from behind the palm while he advanced with the lazy stride of a panther; under the moonbeams that bewitched the island, his eyes were golden-green. He kept coming, stealthily, slowly, while she led him in a gay carousel about the palm until she broke free to run in a zigzag pattern along the moon-sparked beach. But the soft tufts of sand slowed her and she found it harder to keep her distance from Rogan. Again she was losing wind.

"Ah! I've got you!" He snatched at her streaking hair that shimmered like moon dust and starlight, and pulled her up shortly. "Lady, you are in trouble now because I'm a lecherous ogre and I am going to take you down on the sand, tear that bitty thing from you, and ravish the hell out of you!" he said without a single catch in his breath.

"Rogan!" Pandora whirled and splayed her hands over the naked mounds of his chest that rose and fell normally, showing no signs of exertion. "You cad . . . you aren't even . . . out of breath . . . look, I am panting. Why you! You have been playing me out like a hound on the tail of a fox!" She sensed rather than saw something then. "Rogan, why you are naked!"

"Hmmm, yes, I've noticed . . . and you are such a fox—foxy lady, come here and let me love you until you scream for mercy."

"Oh, no you don't!" Pandora gave him a backward shove while he was off guard and turned to flee again.

"Hah! You won't get far this time!"

He caught her just as she completed the turn. "Who did you say was fast before?" He chuckled low in his throat.

Even though he had her by the arms she kicked out her legs to be free, but only succeeded in bringing him down to the sand with her while he crouched behind her backside, his hands coming away to splay in the sand on either side of hers. She shrieked and struggled, but he held her fast, not in any frame of mind to let her go. This tantalizing position sent strange sensations through him. He experienced wild imaginings of what he could do to her now.

"Relax, love, I'd like to get to know you better—" He chuckled over her left ear. "Mmmm, like this, we've never . . . loved like this before. . . ."

"And only creatures do, Rogan," she said shakily.

"I'm afraid you are wrong there, sweet," he murmured hoarsely.

"Rogan, let me up. I don't think I would like . . ." She tried to twist her neck up and see him, but the effort made a painful crick there.

He moved his loins closer and her palms went deeper into the sand. She heard him whisper above her, something erotic, while at the same time he nibbled her shoulder blade, causing her to feel even more breathless and hot than when she had been running and playing . . . but this was not playful.

"I want you." He reached up to cup a breast made pendulous from the crouched position.

Pandora tried to lower herself to the sand, but an arm wrapped around her belly to keep her from breaking the delicious position. He whispered "Please" into her ear. . . .

"I don't know . . . Rogan . . . I—"

"Shh. Just let me show you . . . God, you have the most perfect body . . . my passion flower. Always virginal . . . tight."

Rogan moved against Pandora in an exploratory way, letting her feel his hardness, a taste of what she could expect . . . before he had freed her sarong in the

414

back. Her starry world began to rock and sway when he tugged with one hand to finally free the sarong. . . . It fell away. He bent over her to kiss her moist nape, carefully, so as not to give all his weight onto her back. She began to shake uncontrollably before he eased his weight from her arms by lifting her for several moments and then setting her back in the former position.

"Better?"

"Rogan . . . let me up now?"

"No."

The gently pounding surf mingled with the blood coursing wildly through her veins. In her lower body there was a pulling and tugging that she already recognized as desire. . . . Maybe desire was only one part of love. . . .

"Why?" she begged him softly.

He gave her his answer by straightening and slipping his hands along her ribcage; they lingered a moment, then slid down to her hips. He made a lifting movement gripping her there, but then he did nothing more erotic than to playfully excite her. . . . Now his finger probing until she was making little cries and moans in her throat. "Love, pure and sweet, any *way*," he said.

"I am going to swoon, Rogan!"

He chuckled. "You wouldn't have very far to fall, love." He moved all the way to her. "I'm glad you're ready, because . . ."

That last tiny bit and he lost himself in her with a push that joined them as man and woman. He did it all. She screamed softly as ripples folded over ripples inside her while he drove even deeper. She felt as if she were floating over the waves of the sea while the foaming surf pounded in her, out, in; it played white about her feet and thighs and . . . the melody of his rhythm touched her much-beating heart, and she was lifted bodily with the music rising sheer out of the sea. He came to her like a love song; a sonnet, that filled her tenderly, that rode her heartstrings. . . . He put fresh life and strength into her limbs, her slippery wet flesh. Her torso stretched and her face lifted to gaze for a moment at a star . . . the stabs of pleasure lifting her ever higher . . . and she saw a great starburst rise out of the sea making her look at the wonderment of passion as she had never seen it before. But this was more than mere lust. . . .

"Ohhh . . . Rogan!"

He gripped her hipbones harder as she swayed to and fro with the rhythm of his love music and she felt a strange new power gathering in her loins. His sweat trickled onto her like sweet rain; she turned her head to look at him over her shoulder. For a long moment their moon-drenched gazes locked together. His voice dipped lower—she hadn't known he'd been speaking—till it became but whispers of love words in her ear. He slackened his speed for a minute and felt her trembling from head to foot. She arched her hips, begging him to renew his rhythm.

"Pandora . . ."

"Rogan . . ."

In the next vigorous second there came one explosion, then another, one tumbling over the other. The island seemed to rumble, the sea to crash over them like a tidal wave. The massive erotic explosion shook them both. They tumbled to the sand; they kissed, stroked, hugged, paused to drink in each other's countenance. And Pandora knew more was coming. Much, oh, much, much more . . . love, pure and sweet, and any *way*. . . .

The sun blazed from a blue sky when she made her way back to the house. Voices drifted down to her from the lanai as she stepped onto the broad steps. Cara and Joe sat in chairs around the new Victorian oval wicker table. They were sipping fruit concoctions Jane had made up.

Cara brightened. "Pandora! We've been looking for you for an hour. Where have you been hiding yourself?"

"She has been taking her usual walk on her favorite strip of beach," a deep voice answered.

All eyes turned to Rogan as he walked out onto the lanai from the house. His expression was hard to fathom as it had been of late. Pandora's heartbeat quickened as she looked up to meet his gaze. In white trousers and Hawaiian shirt that opened halfway down his broad chest, he was compelling. His clothing lent him the look of a handsome plantation lord. Pandora wondered briefly about this; he certainly looked as if he belonged here, not like the dashing shipping tycoon whose carriage had crashed into her in San Francisco.

This thought brought a hard lump to her throat. He would soon be leaving—without her; she just knew it.

"Hello, Pandora," Joe greeted warmly.

"*Aloha*, Joe. Cara," she returned softly.

Rogan pulled out a chair for her and she sat,

looking up at him from between the curtains of her lashes. *"Mahalo,"* she thanked him.

Joe chuckled. "Pandora is going Hawaiian all the way, I see."

Rogan surprised them all next by bending down close to Pandora and speaking close to her lips. *"Honi kana wikiwiki,"* he said in perfect Hawaiian.

Pandora blinked into his face. "What was that?"

Cara turned to Joe. "I don't even know what he said. Fill me in, please."

Joe smiled down to his woman. "We will see if she does as he asks." He grinned up at Rogan, as if they shared a secret.

With one arm draped over the top of her chair, Rogan leaned a little closer and kissed her, once, quickly. Her blue eyes narrowed playfully as she caught on to his words, and did as he had asked in Hawaiian.

"Mmm, that was nice," Rogan murmured, "for a beginning. Should we pick up later where we left off?"

Pandora blushed and pushed him back into a chair. Joe did the same with Cara, kissing her once, quickly.

"Aha," Cara said, enlightened. *"Honi kana wiki-wiki.* Kiss me quick!"

Rogan stretched out like a cat, his eyes going around the table. "What game should we play next?" he asked, feeling alive and grand.

But he lost his smile suddenly and Pandora stiffened when Candice entered the lanai. Half through the beaded curtain, she paused to take in the comfortable scene with the couples enjoying each other's presence. Her eyes glinted ice-blue.

"Excuse, please," a tiny voice came from behind Candice.

The blond woman continued to pause, one arm stretched up and clutching the beaded curtain lightly. Her tight bodice displayed the rounded curve of one breast and Joe stared, wondering just what she was after, posing invitingly like that. Joe curled his arm about Cara's shoulder, possessively, squeezing, telling his woman she was all he needed, despite the open invitation of the other woman.

Rogan's countenance darkened and Pandora could feel the sudden tension in his arm which rested alongside hers on their chair backs. The voice begged again, but still Candice hadn't budged to allow the woman behind her to enter. Pandora spoke up, clenching her hand into a fist.

"Come in, Kolina."

"Move please," squeaked the tiny voice.

"Candice," Pandora snapped crisply, "are you deaf? Kolina would like to come in."

Rogan half-rose out of his seat, but Candice caught the warning and moved aside. She plopped into a chair, wearily, as if she had labored hard at some task all morning. Avoiding all the stares that threw visible dislike her way, she picked up her tapestry and needle. Rogan sat back down, but all the fun had drained from him. He had ordered her to leave countless times, but she had always come up with the excuse that she was ill, and would go when she had recovered. Now she said she would take the island steamer after the luau.

The Chinese-Hawaiian girl finally entered. Her

heritage was displayed in her brown-gold skin, smooth and taut, her long pretty lashes, and her diminutive feet which attested to her Chinese blood. She spoke seldom, and always with downcast eyes.

"Oh, excuse please!" Kolina bowed shortly before Pandora. "You like I clean room with big brassy bed now? I try yesterday, but . . ." The mixture of pidgin halted its flow as she bravely peeked from Pandora to Rogan and blushed pink-gold.

Pandora, too, reddened beneath her golden tan. It hit her again: just who was giving orders around here? Why did all the maids and *kanakes* constantly come to her for their tasks? She glanced over to Candy, but that slightly befuddled girl now had her eyes glued on Joe's large hands which rested on his thighs, bare and brown below his tapa shorts, thighs that resembled the bole of a small live oak. Pandora's smile curved at his naturalness; Joe was never modest, even in the company of women from the mainland. Her gaze drifted back to Kolina just as Rogan was saying something to the small woman.

"Kolina, yes, you may clean and straighten *our* bedroom." He casually leaned back then and poured two drinks from the fruit pitcher, one of which he handed to Pandora; his eyes rested on her lips which formed the words "Thank you." For her only, he smiled.

"What!" Candy shouted belatedly, as if she did not have knowledge of them sleeping together all this time.

"Why, of course, we rather enjoy sleeping together," Rogan said laconically, as if reading Candice's thoughts perfectly. She was easy to read, he told himself.

I despise you, bitch, his look seemed to be saying. Candice started, as if he had said the words aloud.

Pandora began to ponder something. The Hawaiian boys, the *kanes,* whispered louder than they should have with Jane in earshot, that the fair lady was meeting a *malihini,* a stranger, out back at one of the grass-and-wood shacks that had been vacant for several years now. Pandora bit her lip in thought, wondering if Bo Gary could be the one she now met. Now that . . . She could not continue with the thought. The lad was on the rebound; Susie's father had turned down his offer of marriage to his daughter. Rogan had chuckled while telling this story to Pandora, for Bo was young and there were certainly plenty of pretty *wahinis* on the island. Hearing that, Pandora had only kept silent.

Setting down her merely sipped drink, Pandora rose.

"I'm going into the kitchen to see if I can help Jane and Iola with dinner."

Rogan watched her walk gracefully through the beaded curtain. He rose, stretched high, and then, too, excused himself, but only for Cara's and Joe's benefit; Kolina shuffled after him. Candy snorted haughtily. She reminded Joe very much of his sister, Leilani, though they were of very different backgrounds.

"Why does Rogan constantly trail after *her?*" Candy said with a sniff of disdain.

Joe leaned forward, bringing Cara's arm along with his to rest against the length of his thigh. Candy stared, then allowed herself the pleasure of a peek at

421

his bulging crotch. Joe brought his knees together, and Cara smiled at this action that was so unlike him.

A moment later, Joe asked, "You mean Pandora?"

"Yes, *her*. Is she Rogan's mistress or something?"

Cara leaned forward, too, but to drop the bomb in Candice's lap. "Rogan and Pandora are man and wife. Didn't you know?"

Smiling with pure satisfaction, Cara took Joe's big hand in hers and together they rose.

"What! Pandora is—Thorn's bride? Oh, I don't believe a word of that!" Candy exclaimed with a shake of her blond head.

Joe grinned widely, as he squeezed Cara's small hand affectionately, but his next words were for Candice's ears only.

"She never fools anyone, my Cara; you better believe it, woman!"

Later that evening Rogan lingered downstairs, deep in male conversation with Bo Gary and a few men who had suddenly appeared about the place. Candice, as usual after dinner, had gone out for an evening stroll. Not one person wondered what the woman was up to; nor did they much care.

Pandora had gone upstairs early, to bathe and tidy up the drawers that had lately become cluttered with all kinds of fancy gifts Rogan had purchased from the traveling merchants. She came upon something in a lower drawer that caused her heart to stop for a second—a flacon of salve concocted from exotic blossoms that, once applied, could make a man last all night.

Iola! The sneaky woman had given the stuff to

Rogan despite her warning that she had better not. No wonder Rogan had performed like an expert lover, keeping them both satisfied for long hours into the night. Suddenly their love-making became a farce in her eyes; devices, he needed this to love her! Her and other women, naturally!

So that was what he had been doing the first time they had made love in the bedroom and he had left the bed suddenly and turned his back on her!

She tossed the flacon across the room and it scooted beneath the bed. Let it stay there; then see how well he performs! Damn him! Liar! Cheat!

Chapter Forty

Pandora quickly left the room, closing the door quietly. Where was this all going to take her? she wondered. Her heart was sick and sad. The sound of tinkling laughter brought her up short. Candice had returned, no doubt, from wherever she had been roaming. She took a deep breath, then started walking once again, her steps quick, going to the stairs.

Tears came to her eyes as she thought of the glorious past several weeks; then back further in time. Destiny had taken her to Rogan Thorn in San Francisco. Had she never left here, she might never have known him. Now, troubled, she began to wonder again why she had left. And again, who had murdered Akoni Nahele? Questions flew at her like quick bats in the night. Just who really owned the plantation? Donald Randall? If so, why wasn't he here to manage things?

Upstairs, on the third floor, she moved gingerly down the hall praying that the wider floorboards up here wouldn't creak and alarm someone downstairs. She stepped inside the room where she knew the mystery awaited her.

Finding some matches, she was about to light the oil lamp when a board out in the hall creaked. The sound made her jump and lose her matches. Though she hadn't lighted a match, darkness seemed to come closer, reaching out to her, black, inklike. She cringed instinctively when she saw the outline of a man standing just outside the door. Then she saw the light; the lantern floated eerily into the room and stopped before her. She flattened her palms against her skirt, her eyes going wider as the lamp was lifted higher and Rogan's face became visible.

"I thought I heard something as I came up the second flight."

His all-too-familiar voice came down around her burning ears and his masculine brow arched in question. Her gaze was drawn momentarily to the low storage door; swiftly then, she pulled it back to his burnished countenance.

"Pandora?" He had noticed where she had glanced, but now he was watching her face closely. "What are you doing up in the dark here?"

"I was just going to light a match, but—but I dropped them."

A frown flickered across his handsome face. "That's not what I asked you." He set the lamp down on a table, then turned back to her.

"Just . . . nothing."

"Nothing? Why do you appear so guilty? I can feel you trembling from here."

He closed the short distance between them and pulled her into his embrace. She wanted to melt and be swept away into forgetfulness, but he had fooled her twice now. And she was falling, falling, utterly,

425

always, madly in love with him. She began to think that he could beat her, step on her, kick her, and she would forgive him. Yes! Yes! Always forgive!

"Rogan, let's go back down," she murmured against his throat. "I have forgotten what I came up here for."

Now that was a lie, she realized, but what else could she say? She'd rather he did not know where her secrets were hidden. As for her heart, well, that was an entirely different matter. She could always conceal that.

Holding the lantern in the room as they stood on the threshold, Rogan kept his back to Pandora while he stared across the room to the low door. He squinted thoughtfully before pulling the knob to click shut.

Liar! Cheat! Dear love! Pandora cried inwardly as they descended the stairs, while her anger mingled with love mounted, as the lantern tossing eerie spirals of dull white over the cracked paint of the walls.

He flung her on the bed as if she were nothing but a rag doll. Biting her lip, she peered up at him through the disheveled curtain of sun-streaked hair falling over her brow like a lion's mane.

"You change colors just like a chameleon, Pandora!"

She rolled over and scooted to the edge of the bed, and then stood before he could reach her. She faced him defiantly across the bed, feeling safe for now, with her arms akimbo.

"Colors? What do you mean?" she hissed over

to him.

"You know. Moods." He began to inch around the big brass bed. "What the hell did you slap me for a minute ago?"

She began to back away. "I was forgiving you," she said simply.

"Forgiving me! I'll be damned if I understand you, ever, woman. If *that* was forgiving, I'd hate to cross you," he said, but he couldn't help smiling a bit.

"You have, damn you!" She danced away from the bed and went to stand at the window where a warm breeze somewhat cooled her flaming cheeks.

Running his fingers through his mussed forelock, Rogan sat heavily down on the edge of the bed. He watched her at the window, but made no move to rise and go to her. He became aware of something amiss. The drawer; it was sagging open, a mess of spilling items. His eyes raced across to Pandora and riveted to her bare, slim back.

"Aha! So you've found the loathsome stuff!" he exclaimed, and rose to begin a search of the room, knowing without looking that the flacon wasn't even in the drawer.

She peered at him over her shoulder. "Are you by any chance looking for something, Rogan?" she asked in a petulant voice. Then she went on to taunt. "Do you think you will be needing it tonight, or can you go without it?"

Suddenly his fury mounted that she would ever believe that he had needed that junk, the evil-smelling concoction her aunt had brewed especially for the *man with a problem!*

"Well?" she tossed over her shoulder. "Did you

find it, *lover?*"

The half-smile on his lips disappeared, and he went striding to the door and flung the wood wide. He removed something from his belt, and she turned to gasp as she saw the knife's blade gleaming in the lamplight.

"No, dear love, but I found this earlier today," he said softly, almost threateningly as he slipped the knife, her knife, back into his belt.

"You—" she stammered. "That—that is mine."

"I know," he said, beginning to close the door while he stepped out. "But, that stuff under the bed was never mine."

"You—you never used it?" she squeaked out the question. "Wait!"

He lifted dark sardonic eyebrows in a listening expression. "I'm waiting . . ." he said across to her, civilly enough.

"Tell me, what else was I supposed to believe when at first you . . . and then you . . ." She could not bring herself to ask him how it was that suddenly— after the first two misfires, one after the wedding, the other during the luau—he had become an expert lover. Experience did not have to tell her that he was this.

"That is a mystery that I . . ." Now he could not find the proper words to describe his sudden return to youthful, red-blooded virility. But his eyes narrowed in the next instant; he heard himself saying, "Tell me this: without Iola's mishmash of exotic love potion, *lover power,* how do you suppose I made it then on the sand with you—uhmm—was it three or four very *satisfying* sessions?" He paused. "Without the flower-bud junk?"

Red blotches of embarrassment appeared across her cheeks, but Pandora's eyes pricked up and she blinked wide. She hadn't thought of *that*. Then . . .

"No. Not once."

He shut the door in her dumstruck face.

The tables had been painfully turned on Pandora. It was she who now searched out that tall frame, and watched, and waited, while he avoided her at all turns.

It rained finally, hard and fast. The wind blew and the sky overhead was dark, moonless, starless. A single light shone from the ship *Pandora's Promise*. Every night, for four wet days now, Rogan had slept with Bo Gary in his cabin. Pandora seethed with anger when Candy skipped out to visit them every day. . . . Oh, and Rogan even welcomed her!

"The slut!" Pandora hissed while with a vengeance she sliced pineapple in the kitchen with Jane and Iola for the luau that night.

Iola rolled her eyes heavenward, for two reasons, but said, "She hopes no rain come tonight to spoil luau, huh, Pandora?"

Pandora whirled, the long-bladed knife turning with her. "She! Don't ever mention her again! I would like very much to slice off that blond bitch's hair and stuff it all down her throat."

Iola stared down at the wicked blade and backed up a step. "Tsk, tsk, not very Christianlike, Pandora. I was talking about my girl Cara, not who you think."

The cluster of golden-shower trees dripped the last of the raindrops outside the tiny window and Pandora paused, her knife on the pineapples, to stare mesmerized by one sun-struck droplet clinging to a bare sprig. She popped more macadamia nuts into her mouth to tide her over until the feast.

Her father had known Jordan, the man who had first brought the macadamia nuts from Tasmania to Hawaii and had planted them beside his home on Wyllie Street in Honolulu. She remembered seeing the first trees, having thorny, hollylike leaves—so her father said, for she had never seen holly—and oh, how she had loved her first taste of the delicious nuts.

Remembered!

Still starry-eyed, Pandora turned to Iola. "Aunty, was my father's name Colter?"

"Oh, yes!" she exclaimed as she continued to make up the many coconut-shell dishes. "That was him. Colter and Linda, very beautiful man and woman together. Colter was very handsome man just like Thorn."

"Tell me about them, please."

Iola shrugged off her niece's plea. "You remember his name. This be good. You keep cutting pineapple, Pandora, my girl, and look out window sometimes. You remember all soon, by your own self."

Slicing deftly, Pandora expertly removed the hard core of the pineapple and tossed it into the refuse pail. She tried hard to remember, but the noise and excitement of the coming luau pulsed in her veins in time to the drummers's practicing out on the patio. Youngsters ran in and out of rooms, getting into mischief wherever they could find it. Cara and Joe, strangely enough along with Rogan, had decided to throw the luau here at Nahele plantation. Already the house was swarming with guests, and every room was filled, right up to the top floor of the house, with men, women, and gaily laughing children.

Cara and Joe had been married earlier that morning at the mission church in Kailua. Cara had been radiant in her gay and lovely *holuku*, brightened up with creamy embroidery by Iola's expert stitching. It had been shaped to the body and given a longer than usual train.

She herself had donned the bright muumuu Iola had fashioned for her the night before. She had not changed out of it yet, but later she would surprise them all and put on her old grass skirt, topless, and let her flowered hair stream over her breasts temptingly. Concealing . . . up to a point . . . when she moved . . . to hula. . . .

Rogan had commented on the muumuu she had worn to the church. It had a print of star jasmine stamped over a dove-gray background.

"Very bewitching," he had drawled, then tossed over his shoulder, "if not—uhmm—a bit flowery."

Bewitching, eh? Pandora smiled slyly to herself now. *Just wait till he sees what I'll wear—or won't—later!*

Chapter Forty-one

Pandora stood indecisive over the colors.

Fresh-cut flowers, many leis, and her grass skirt were spread out in a rainbow on the bed. She chewed her lower lip, hearing behind her the two giggling *haole*-Hawaiian girls in their teens with whom she shared her room. Pandora felt nervous as she wondered if she could go through with this thing she had planned to capture Rogan's attention away from Candice; and oh, yes, Leilani was here, too, sharpening her claws against Candice's. She looked out the window, pondering the outcome of her plan.

Then her heart took a dive right down to her bare feet. There in the yard, filled with Hawaiian and white guests and *haole malahinis*, stood Rogan, startlingly handsome, compelling, all in tropical white, with Candice and Leilani, both gazing up at him in a sickening way that Pandora loathed with every fiber in her. Rogan looked up to catch her watching, and he winked with a broad smile. Pandora whirled away from the window, her cheeks flaming with a furious passion that threatened to choke her.

Malia and Luka were giggling again, and Pandora, trying not to show her irritation, shooed them from her room. After the door had shut on their high-pitched giggles, Pandora crossed barefoot to the window and dropped the tapa cloth over the whole square.

Easing the muumuu down over her slim hips, she let it fall to her feet; then she raised her hands to thread slim fingers through the copper-and-gold mass of her hair; when she let go, the long strands fell shimmering to her waist. She smiled wickedly, delighted that she had allowed her hair to grow this long and wild.

Like a lion's mane, Rogan had said to her since his arrival.

As though submissive to some soft-spoken command, she cupped her breasts, one in each hand. Her flesh tingled as she did this and her nerve endings prickled. Another thrill of delicious wickedness shuddered down her spine. Little wonder the full-blooded Hawaiian hula girls went naked on the upper half.

She tentatively touched the tip of a round breast, something she had never done with conscious thought. Lovely, she told herself with a little conceit. Why not? They were perfectly formed. Her slim fingers slipped down to her hips. Well, she told herself, a little shy there, but they would do; in fact, her hips appeared just fine in a hula skirt. She swayed those slim hips now in a seductive circle and chuckled softly.

She would lure him with her feminine wiles and the alluring smile she had practiced all morning with her back turned to the other busy women in the kitchen.

Her body began to writhe and weave a sensual pattern while she floated her hands and beckoned to the handsome man.

"Come to me, Rogan Thorn, my beautiful man. Know that I love you."

It took all day to prepare the luau. The main dish was a whole big pig roasted and left to tenderize for hours in the earth oven—an *imu*—placed in stones, preheated, that soon became red-hot. When done, the meat was so tender that it melted in the mouth. Between the thick banyan trees in the yard, trestle tables had been set up, laden with tapa mats bearing bowls of colorful fruit, mango salads with papaya and pineapple; bowls of *poi* for those with the stomachs for it; *haupia*, a coconut pudding; steamed breadfruit, and yams from Iola's year-round garden; salmon and tomato, and much, much more.

The older Hawaiian women sat back relaxing in their old-fashioned muumuus, gowns modeled on the Mother Hubbard style that had been made for the natives long ago by missionary women. Around their parchmentlike necks were different types of leis, some formed of flowers, some of seeds, coral, shells, nuts, or pieces of ivory. They slowly sipped rice wine or fermented coconut milk.

For now, Pandora wore another fresh *holoku*, white, with short ruffled sleeves and rose hibiscus flowers printed on it. A fragrant frangipani flower was tucked into her upswept hair on one side; on the other she had allowed her hair to wave seductively close to her face. She trembled with excited anticipation during the whole feast. Now Rogan, looking cool and poised, stood at the end of the long table from her, his eyes ever mocking when they came in contact with hers. She had brushed by him earlier, too close for comfort really, her flanks meeting his leanly muscled legs for a breath-taking moment.

Pandora gritted her teeth, almost biting her tongue. There they were, different as night and day in countenance, Candice and Leilani, shadowing Rogan wherever he would light, even for a few minutes. Pandora wondered which one he had chosen to end up amusing himself with this night. But she smiled inwardly at that, her plans for seduction burning inside of her.

Actually, discounting Leilani as a silly, empty-headed fool, it was Candy whose eyes Pandora was prepared to scratch. The cheap slut!

He could not fool this girl, Pandora sniffed; she had seen that green-leafed shirt, like no other she had ever seen before on the islands (he must have purchased it in Chinatown before departure), and that was one item he couldn't convince her she had been wrong about—like the stuff under the bed. Well, it was no more; she had taken care of that!

Pandora tried to concentrate on the delicious food, but her thoughts kept racing ahead to when the young girls and women would rise to dance. She sighed, impatient, tired of all the chatter and mingling she had been through most of the after-noon. Joe and Cara had gone off for a while, to be alone, as was natural for a bride and groom.

Suddenly she was aware of someone behind her, someone who had come slowly from beneath the tree shadows. She risked a swift glance over her shoulder, knowing instinctively who was there.

"How long have you been creeping up on me?" She turned back to her plate.

"About five seconds now," Rogan said with a smile in his voice. "You've managed to elude me all afternoon, Pandora."

"Me?" She gasped then, choking on a bite of breadfruit she had been chewing for several minutes now. *He* was the one who had been eluding her all *week*.

He laughed with a throaty chuckle and patted her on the back until the food unstuck. His green glance touched on her hair and face briefly. She could feel his breath stirring the waving strands at her cheeks. But his manner told her nothing of his innermost feelings. Instead, he seemed to be mocking her with his sudden presence, for he had stayed away from her for what to her had seemed ages. There was raw hunger inside her for him, but she would not look into his eyes and allow him to see the love shining from her own.

"Where are your thoughts?" he demanded with sudden softness in his tone.

"Thinking how different you act all of a sudden," she blurted, wishing she were elsewhere now.

"Look at me," he said softly close to her face.

When she did not comply, he straightened a bit, and then she lifted her head, pretending to scowl at him to conceal her true emotions. He stared into her face for several seconds, eying her lazily. In a hot flood of emotion, desire surged like a torrent through her. Rogan brushed the tip of a brown finger across her cheek; then, without another word, turned on his heels and melted into the crowd.

Pandora was totally bewildered by his actions and the tension that had vibrated from him. Had it been desire? Or something more that to which she was afraid to give a name? Now she was feeling a strange blend of sweet anticipation and apprehension.

When the young, half-naked girls rose to dance, Pandora pushed her plate aside and slipped away to her room. Iola had lifted a questioning brow at Pandora's hasty retreat up the stairs, but then had shrugged, feeling that what was between her girl and Rogan Thorn was none of her business.

Pandora had grabbed a tall glass of rice wine on her way up. Now choked on the strong stuff, her cheeks aflame, as she had downed half of it in a hasty gulp. She clutched at her throat, took another gulp just the same, and smiled as it went down easier this time. She had never drunk very much, but tonight, she told herself, she would make an exception to her rule.

"Please, God, forgive me," she muttered, her usually full, pink mouth a taut white line. Nothing in her life had prepared her for what she was determined to do this night. Her temples throbbed, and her feeling of uneasiness grew.

"I am going through with it. Oh yes, sir!"

Half-dressed as she would stay, she went in search of yet another tall glass—of something stronger this time.

A low murmur ran through the crowd circled about the dancers as she approached. Rogan caught his breath in surprise when this slender and graceful *haole* woman neared, swishing her grass skirt as she walked barefoot to the line of hula girls.

"Pandora," he exclaimed softly then, as the torches lit up her hair, adorned with white tiare flowers, and set fire to her glorious figure.

My God, he had never seen her quite like this. He was even more tense than before, and watchful, knowing that she was on a dangerous route this night. But as to exactly why, he wasn't sure.

Pandora's heart thudded and her blood pounded in her ears as the drums began. She would have to do her best; Leilani was at the other end of the line. The torchlight caught the gold in her hair and the loose strands danced like curling tongues of red-and-gold flame. Pandora couldn't see Rogan's face in the darkness beyond the torches, but she knew he was there, watching intensely and wondering at her game.

Rogan stood perfectly still. His ardent gaze never left Pandora. Down the line Leilani's hula was stationary, undulant quivering. Her olive-tan body weaved and writhed, accompanied by the rhythms of drumbeats and the strange music of nose flute and *hokeo*. Rogan never noticed Leilani; he was so spellbound by another.

Iola came to stand by Rogan; a middle-aged Hawaiian stood on the other side of him. Iola nudged Rogan as he watched Pandora float her long, tapered hands and sway her hips seductively while laughing softly.

"Boy, she some gorgeous woman," Kamuela from Maui exclaimed.

438

"Believe me, I've noticed," Rogan uttered unconsciously.

"Now that's a good hula!" Iola shouted merrily, eyes bright on her girl.

Just looking at her caused Rogan to tingle hotly from head to toe. In the past he had considered the obscenity of the dance; now he saw there was a gentle innocence in it as well, as she told a story with her lovely hands. She danced with her beautiful feet always flat to the ground, her knees bent as she shifted her tall form back and forth. The rippling motion of her hands and arms indicated the waves of the sea; then a ship bobbing on the ocean; then, at the end, her fingertips met in a point, picturing a star. The star of hope, everyone realized who read her motions and had knowledge of the dance.

The hula ended suddenly; then just as quickly picked up again, with a faster drum tempo now, a Tahitian beat enriched by tapping sticks together, to which hips and bellies seemed to move faster than was entirely possible.

"My God," Rogan breathed, feeling a huge lump slide halfway down his throat and stick there. "I never— How does she do that? It's damned suggestive, too—with all these men gaping and leering—"

"A special dance," Kamuela interrupted suddenly. "There be my woman in the middle. Oh, there is a gentleness about her that I love!"

Rogan cleared his throat. "I'll bet," he muttered, seeing that the older woman kept up with the younger. He believed his eyes were beginning to cross from trying to watch the many fast hips.

Pandora throbbed with the love she felt for Rogan. She put a beautiful smile on her face, her body reaching out to him, aching, wanting the void filled, desiring him to capture her, make love to her on the sand, the flowers, always . . .

Rogan went wild-eyed then. Pandora had turned, so damned suggestively he wanted to break her fool neck in front of all these other men ogling and leering at her. Her breasts were sharply outlined when she raised her arms, exposing their white curves and part of a rosy nipple pushed through the plumeria lei and long strands of hair. She was naked on top!

"Ah," Kamuela murmured. "Pretty *haole wahine* shows what lovelee bubbles she has." His lips parted to display yellowed teeth; he began to clap his hands.

Iola gasped at her niece's show, staring round-eyed. "Oh-oh. Thorn get mad, very much now," she muttered to herself, inching back through the crowd, not wanting to be too close when the sparks flew.

"Pandora!"

Rogan seemed to leap like lightning toward the line of dancers. There was an insanely wild expression in his eyes, like threatening green fire lit with white sparks from the crackling torches. The drum-beats rolled away into the dark over the waters, and the women and girls came to a standstill with a dying swish of grass skirts and disappointed sighs from the men.

Rogan put his hand around the back of her neck and began to usher Pandora through the now-chuckling, murmuring crowd. Joe and Cara, who had returned, were standing now at the fringe of the excitement, searching for the cause of the sudden commotion and the lack of music. Then they saw what all the others—including the puffing constable from Honolulu—were watching with such rapt attention.

"Good way to end dance!" one *malahini* shouted. "Just like old times, drag woman down beach for some *honi-ipu!*"

Lusty cheers followed them as Rogan propelled Pandora into the dark, but no utterance of protest came from her lips; she only smiled secretively to herself.

Yes, it was this for which she had been aiming.

Chapter Forty-two

On the beach Rogan whirled her around just as the effects of the inebriants hit her. She hiccuped loudly in his furious face, and her plans of seduction were shattered in an instant. How foolish she felt. How ashamed. But she was going to hide this fact, she told herself.

The moon was hidden by the palms flanking them and the darkness shrouded the expression on his face. But she knew he was incensed by her actions when he shook her roughly.

"Well, Pandora, let's get on with it!" he demanded with clenched jaw.

"Get—get on with *what?*" She blinked into the dark outline of his face, having an inkling of what he was driving at.

"Your clever scheme of seduction, that's what. Aren't you woman enough to see it through now that you've gotten this far?"

Methodically he ran his hand up her naked torso and beneath the plumeria lei to cup a breast that quivered from his manly touch. He teased a peaked nipple erect. She fleetingly felt a shiver of desire pass through her, but it was the wrong time for it because of his anger. Yet try as she might to resist, she couldn't with him fondling her so carelessly.

"I believe, without the slightest doubt, that you are jealous." He dropped his hand to his side.

"I am not—"

"And half-drunk!"

"I am not—*hic-cup.*"

He snorted. "I never thought I'd see the day when you'd act the tease. Well, my dear, it's time you paid off."

"You—you talk like I am some whore—like Leilani—or Candice," she stammered, beginning to sway dizzily.

"Act like a whore, Pandora, and you get treated like one. Damn it, Pandora, how many other men back there do you suppose entertained the same thoughts of bedding you as I did?"

"You are jealous!"

"Damned right I am! You are my woman, and better begin acting like it. A woman, I said, not a cheap, scheming whore!" His voice was tight with anger and she was suddenly afraid.

She twisted free of his grip. "You—you hate me, you just use me, and then go—go prancing after Candice—and Leilani!"

Her befuddled mind cleared a little to think. He hadn't said he loved her since . . . that night. Had it only been his passion speaking? Could he even remember the words that professed his love, and demanded the same from her own lips at the height of passion?

"I'm afraid your plan has failed, Pandora. Truly I don't want you like this, because I just might break your damned fool neck, and don't trust myself not to do it."

There! He did not deny that he hated her, or that he'd rather bed down with one of the two sluts.

"I am not your woman—and don't you ever, but every say so again!"

She tried slapping his face, but he caught her arm in mid-swing. He twisted it back and brought his face close to hers.

"You're very desirable tonight, Pandora; in a conniving way, though, that I find cheap. I could lay you right here, but I've concluded it wouldn't be any good for either of us." His jaw tightened as he simply looked into her face, his expression close but totally unfathomable. He went on. "I'm not a man to play foolish games with, Pandora."

"Oh!" She stepped back, stunned. "You play games—with the other two. What about them, hmmm?"

"That makes two of us, you're saying?"

"Of course!" she snapped back.

"They mean absolutely nothing to me, Pandora. With you I play for keeps, no foolish game."

"Oh, you are saying you love me?" she challenged him, but wishfully.

"I'm saying nothing tonight. Only that we're leaving for San Francisco in the morning."

"Oh." She hung her head, feeling shame washing over her. Now he would leave her and never return. She would simply die of a broken heart.

He took her by the arm, sweeping her into a walk. "I'll take you up to your room now; then I'll leave you."

"You—" she stammered. "You and Bo Gary are leaving . . . so soon . . . just like that?"

She felt herself dying inside, slowly, piece by piece.

"I'll see you early in the morning, very early."

She swallowed the heavy lump in her throat. "Fine, Rogan."

"Be packed, and ready to sail with us."

She dragged him to a halt, gazing at his moonlit face intently.

"M-Me, too?"

He chuckled. "You, too. Did you think I'd leave my heart behind?"

Pandora barely slept a wink she was so excited. She sailed through the hours just before dawn feeling like a blushing bride and just as nervous, too. But that was before the nausea hit her. It slowed the packing of her luggage and she plodded along wearily. Biting her bottom lip, she sat down on the edge of the bed. Where was Rogan? she wondered.

Perhaps in her befuddled state, she had misunderstood him the night before. Her gaze traveled out the window to Rogan's ship, and there she saw Bo Gary licking her into shape for the journey. But where was Rogan?

Just then she caught sight of him stepping out of his cabin, stretching wide and high to embrace the morning. Shielding his eyes from the sun, he looked up toward the house. She raced to the window and was just about to wave to him when he turned on his heel and reentered the cabin.

She went back to her bed as the nausea returned. Her stomach growled, but food was out of the question. There was nothing more to do now but wait.

"Pandora! Are you ready?"

She bolted upright, shaking herself from her troubled dream as his second knock sounded. Smoothing her wrinkled blue skirt and white blouse, she rose and went to answer.

"Pandora—ah! I see you are packed and ready to go."

There was an aura of excitement emanating from him. He looked the sailor in a pair of buff pantaloons and a worn seaman's loose blue shirt. He had stuck his head in the door and now he straightened to call down the hall for the boys to come and haul down the luggage.

"The rest is aboard already," he said.

She decided this meant he had taken all of his belongings from the room, because his drawers were empty.

Iola swept past Rogan and threw herself into her niece's waiting arms. After they had hugged and kissed for several minutes, while Rogan shouted orders to the lads in the back hall, Iola drew back and took in her niece's countenance with a frown. Her brown eyes fell to Pandora's flat belly, concerned.

"You are not feeling well, I can see. You are going to have a *keiki*, huh?"

Pandora gulped, knowing what this Hawaiian word meant. Then she shook her head. No, it couldn't be.

"Aunty, no, I am not going to have a—a baby. I think I just had too much to drink last night."

Iola nodded with reassurance. "No, not what you say, Pandora. Your face tells me you are going to have a *keiki*. I know this."

One of the boys hauling a trunk with another announced, "The *wahine* Pandora is going to have a *keiki!*"

Rogan stepped back into the room, his eyes sweeping over both women with question. "What the hell is a *keiki?*"

Hiding her trembling hands in her full skirts, Pandora swept past him to lift her rattan suitcase. Iola chuckled, going back downstairs to finish packing her hamper full of goodies for them. After she was out of earshot, Rogan put the question to Pandora once again.

"Just tell me, what is a *keiki?* What's all the mystery about?" He followed Pandora about while she gathered last-minute items. His eyes suddenly narrowed when she clutched at her stomach. "Something is wrong, Pandora, just what the hell is it?" he growled over her shoulder as she stuffed hairbrush and combs into her little suitcase.

She faced his wide stare. "Yes, Rogan, I've got a *keiki.*"

"Well, damn it, what is it then!"

"A hangover!" she lied, going past him and out into the hall.

Rogan shrugged, standing alone in the room now. "Why does she act like it's my fault?" he asked himself.

Cara and Joe walked Pandora to the waiting ship, but Iola pulled Rogan back into the house when she remembered something, and she showed him the item in the hamper she had packed.

"I almost forget, Thorn. Fred tell me to give shirt back to you. He does not like it; too many memories. If you know what I mean?"

His thoughts were elsewhere, but he nodded absent-mindedly. "Oh, yes, the shirt. Thank you, Iola."

She grinned widely. "You never use *stuff*, huh?"

He tore his gaze from watching Pandora through the window he had wandered over to while Iola stuffed the shirt back inside the loaded hamper. He turned back to the woman with her head cocked to one side, waiting but already knowing the answer to her question.

"Stuff? Oh, that." He gave a low, husky laugh then. "With a woman like Pandora in his arms, even the most impotent man wouldn't find much use for it!"

"You said it, Thorn!" Iola rolled her belly in merriment.

Pandora's Promise pulled away from the dock, and sailed out into the aqua water like a full-winged dove. The rhythmic creak of her deck planks was familiar to Rogan as the ship rode with the gentle rise and fall of the sea's waves.

The lump in Pandora's throat was made worse when Iola, waving her chubby arms, tossed a plumeria lei into the water, and threw kisses wide into the air. Cara stood with her man's arms wrapped about her tiny waist and he held her high in the air

448

when the ship grew smaller. Finally Pandora had to squint to see them in the glaring light of late morning.

Quietly Rogan came up behind Pandora where she stood still waving at the rail. "We'll return, sweetheart; then the plantation should be flourishing and everything in order."

"Yes, I would like that," she murmured with wet cheeks.

But Donald Randall owned it now, she thought to herself sadly. Would he welcome them back? Donald never stayed in one place long, though, and neither did his daughter. She had proven that by being absent during the farewells. Where had Candice gone off to? she wondered—but not for long.

I do have part claim in the place, Pandora said to herself, thinking that if Donald should want to plant the back field he would have to get permission from her. The land grant from the deceased Hawaiian king was hers now; no one could argue that. Yes, she would persevere. Part of her would forever belong here. That land belonged to her, and no one was going to take the plot. She would fight for it, to her death if need be.

She slanted her lashes up at Rogan now. "What is Briar Rose, Rogan? I heard you tell George to take care of that, whatever it is."

He gazed into her eyes. "We'll return," was all he said.

"Rogan," she insisted. "What is Briar Rose?"

"My plantation, love; didn't you know?"

He studied her for a long moment. She pulled her

eyes away from his barely long enough to make out the dot of a house sprawled atop the rise. Then she looked back to Rogan who only smiled and nodded toward his plantation—Briar Rose.

Candice Randall almost had to jog to keep up with the man's long stride. Her *haole malahini*, white just like herself, the Hawaiian lads said of Candice's lover, the man with the pale-blue eyes.

"Where are they going?" the *malahini* demanded, indicating the ship that gained distance by the minute. "Tell me!" he snarled, slapping Candy hard across her pasty-white face.

"Oh, damn! You are hurting me; you never did that before," Candy whined up at the tall man. "What is the matter with you? You said you loved me!"

"Tell, or I'll break that skinny neck of yours!"

"San Francisco, back to Thorn's home. Who cares anyway? You didn't before!" she screamed.

"Come back to the hut with me, bitch!"

The huge banyan trees at the edge of the field spread shade over the small house. He passed through the main room and plunged through the curtain into a musty bedroom. There he began to pull a battered suitcase out from beneath a sagging cot and to toss in the few articles of clothing he had brought to the island with him several weeks ago.

"Get a carriage hitched up for me. You know your way around here!" he ordered while continuing to toss everything about, and glaring at her when she hadn't moved.

"I—I don't know if there is one," Candy snapped back.

"If there isn't, steal one. When I first arrived, I seen that fat Hawaiian woman with one. Get hers if she's here. Anything—a horse, a donkey and a cart!"

"Well, how in the hell did you get here?" she tossed at him.

"Never mind that; do as I say."

"I'm coming with you; I hate it here," she wailed.

"No, stay and watch the house. It may all be yours someday, if you're a good girl and do as I say."

He grabbed her by the arm, but her temper rose and she twisted away. He stared down into her ice-blue eyes, and with a queer smile on his lips, he went on.

"I'll return in a few months, if all goes well—this time." But he wore a cold, indifferent expression that gave nothing of his secrets away.

In the end, Candy had to send a boy to Kailua for a carriage. But before it could arrive, a steamer had come around the shore, and by that time the *malahihi* was fuming. Candy pouted as he stepped onto the dock with not even a farewell and boarded the steamer hurriedly. Standing on the dock, her hair blowing, Candy shouted over the water to him, not caring if anyone heard her.

"I know you now. You don't like women; you like anything in pants. Boys! I saw you with that young Hawaiian, going into the hills, just yesterday! You were patting his—"

"Shut up!" he yelled back to her, darting a glance around to see if anyone had heard. "Stay at the house; it's all going to be yours someday!"

Angered by his indifferent treatment, Candy whirled and flounced back to the house. What did she want to stay here for? She needed a house and a hanky freak like she needed a hole in her head! Like hell!

"I'm going home," Candy snorted, stomping into the quiet house. She stood stock-still then. Just where was home?

Chapter Forty-three

Rogan led the way to a heavy paneled door, and when he lifted its latch, she stepped over a sill into the captain's cabin. There were charts, binoculars, and all the other seafaring treasures that belonged to this man who seemed stranger to her each passing minute. She stood as one in a trance, looking about her, remembering more than she cared to. This was the wood and brass-bright cabin where it seemed like only yesterday they had been married. The ship's log was open, as if Rogan had been writing in it earlier.

When the ship moved into the open sea and the first great swells seemed to be lifting the rakish schooner right up into the low-hanging clouds, she suppressed the feeling that she would be sick again. In the closeness of the cabin she experienced a feeling of faintness. In addition to possible pregnancy, it had something to do with what Rogan had revealed to her a short time ago. Fear nibbled at the corners of her mind. Why had he held out from her so long, and not told her he was the new owner? Just what was he trying to hide from her?

"Why don't you sit, Pandora? You look a little pale and weary." He continued to dig through some papers on his corner desk, pushing atlases aside.

Pandora obediently agreed that she was tired and sat on the edge of the bed that was big enough for two. There were chairs, of course, but she wanted something softer to sit on as she fought her nausea. The nagging thought flashed again through her mind.

"You have visited Hawaii before, Rogan?" she asked softly.

He stopped fiddling with some charts to look up at her. 'Yes. I thought you knew."

She tried to ignore the tremors beginning within her. "How about the last time you were in Hawaii, was it then that you purchased Nahele plantation?"

"Yes. Walter Riddock was there, too, at the office of Allen and Stone in Honolulu. But Walter invests in plantations only to provide cargoes for his ships. I was inclined to do the same, but all that changed. I wanted to have a home on that lovely island, a home away from home." He chuckled here once. "Very far away from home. I have several now, you know. No, how could you?" He looked at her sharply then. "Why are you holding your head, Pandora, a headache?"

She ignored that. "You said Walter Riddock. He was the other man seeking to purchase Nahele plantation?" She remembered her aunt telling her something about this other one.

"Again, yes. But I always win anyway when we are pitted against each other . . . with anyone for that matter." He glanced up from the open logbook that gleamed whitely and shot her a meaningful look. "I always, but always, get what I am after," he went on, not looking at her now, but showing her his profile as he reached for a tumbler of brandy. "Want some?"

She grimaced and shook her head furiously.

"I didn't think so."

She barely heard him, for she was thinking about the grant from King Kalakaua to Nahele. Rogan must have paid a tidy sum for the place then. To be sure, the plantation was valuable land, worth a fortune in sugar. A chill settled in the pit of her already tumbling stomach. Rogan must have been in Hawaii at the time she had married Akoni Nahele. Someone had to have murdered Akoni. But, with a conviction stronger than any emotion, she knew that Rogan was not a murderer; yet, what evidence did she possess, concrete evidence? And why would Rogan want to dispose of Akoni anyway? He had all he wanted . . . even her . . . unless . . .

He settled his gaze on her. It was penetrating, and she wondered if he could invade her mind. Was it her imagination, or was he really looking at her as if he would enjoy strangling her?

"Do you also know who owns the land out back of the house?" she asked very softly, unconsciously twisting a fold in her skirt.

"Of course. You do, my sweet Pandora. But now it belongs to both of us, as man and wife." He had gone back to looking through the papers and ledgers.

She swiftly went on to reply in her nervousness, "We have not been properly wed, if you remember, Rogan."

The green eyes came up dark as emeralds. "We will

be. It will be a church wedding, but a small one. This time we shall do it right, Pandora, love."

He kept calling her by that endearment. How much truth entered into the small word? she wondered grimly. Suddenly she realized he frightened her. It had something to do with the land and ownership. Was he one of the many men who lusted over land? Why hadn't he told her before now that Nahele—Briar Rose was his? Why was he always so secretive? Just now she had learned to fear him; and too, she realized how very much he meant to her. Was this—could love be ingrained with fear, without turning into hate? With that thought, she grew more uncomfortable than ever.

Her eyes flew to a sea chest against the bulkhead and then slid to her rattan suitcase beside it. The grant to her land was there, and now his gaze followed where hers had gone moments before. The green narrowed in his eyes; then he stood brusquely.

"I must go and relieve Bo at the helm. Sam is preparing our dinner, and will take over later so that we three can dine together. Do you mind taking our meal with Bo Gary tonight, Pandora?" He moved from behind his desk.

He had taken on, she knew, another mate to speed their voyage to California. He was a small, squat man, part-Hawaiian, but wiry as an ape—and just as homely, she decided at first look at him.

"I don't mind, Rogan," she returned meekly, and his brow shot up.

"Sam is a great cook, and the delicious meals he prepares will speak for themselves."

"That is nice, Rogan." Embarrassed, her gaze chased off to the hamper Iola had packed, hoping that the "goodies" could be added to their dinner. She would hate to waste the Hawaiian fare.

"I read your mind, Pandora." He went to lift the heavy hamper. "I'll see that Sam gets this, and we'll have a feast if I know Iola."

Take what you want from life, but pay for it. . . . Pandora pondered those lines, unable to recall just where she'd heard them. And another: The more you give in life, the more you gain. . . . Wasn't that one from Linda's philosophy?

Dreading she knew not what, Pandora picked at her food on the pewter plate with detached interest. She had chosen a simple white-laced blouse, Victorian style, shirred at the shoulder caps, and a dark-red rose skirt of English challis. Before sitting down at the table across from her and Bo Gary, Rogan noticed at once that her hair was not hanging loose down her back as often it did on the island, but was pulled back and coiled in a heavy knot. A red ribbon trailed down and wisps of loose curls escaped at her temples and the nape of her neck.

"I like that . . . when you put up that mane of yours."

"Do you, Rogan?" She turned her eyes on him; they shone like China-blue saucers. "I thought that I looked an absolute fright. . . . I didn't know what to do with . . . my hair. . . ."

"You are learning . . . that is all," he said tersely.

Pandora frowned at his hidden meaning. Bo Gary

457

intercepted her look of puzzlement, and as long as Rogan appeared to be in one of his "quiet moods," not giving a measure more than an exchange of pleasantries, he took up where the cool remark had left off. But Pandora had already erased any hurt in her eyes almost before Rogan could glimpse it; her lashes were lowered to her quickly flushing cheeks.

"Ah, Rogan's family has always been one of the most influential in San Francisco . . . so you can see why . . ."

Slowly, Rogan lifted his head, chewing the forkful of beef he had just stabbed from his plate. He washed the meat down with a swallow of watered rum and lime juice. He waved his hand in the air nonchalantly.

"Go on . . ." Rogan continued with his meal, sliding buttered peas and tiny pearl onions onto his fork now. But he kept an eye on Pandora who was rolling a pea around on her plate with her fork.

"I mean—uh—" Bo Gary faltered, then went on more quickly, knowing it was up to him to carry on the conversation. "Like you said, she's learning. Pandora's had a pretty good teacher to initiate her into the—uh—exclusive set. She knows how to pour tea from fine old Sheffield and should do well at giving stately dinners. . . . She wasn't born loving a gay social life, you know. . . ."

Pandora was beginning to see what Rogan had first been driving at—very much. "Do many of the elite . . . the women of San Francisco bathe while wearing nightgowns? I've heard they do."

Rogan coughed, almost choking on a bite of

458

laulau meat before he washed it down with a huge swallow of liquid.

"Yeah," Bo Gary picked up, not meeting Rogan's sudden glare across at him. "Some of them have never been all the way undressed since the day they were born—unlike your island women in Hawaii." He chuckled, warming to this subject.

"Myself included!" Pandora said with animation, remembering how she couldn't wait to get her clothes off and slip into a muumuu or a sarong, after having draped herself in so much clothing while in San Francisco.

Pandora sipped her lime juice now; then set her glass down. Rogan hadn't spoken two more civil words to her, even though he had come to the cabin to change for dinner. She was lonesome, having left behind those she loved, and her birthplace. Why did people in San Francisco have to wear so many clothes . . . ? Why couldn't folks there be more *au naturel?* Even now she felt stifled in so much clothing.

Pandora emboldened herself further, despite Rogan's quiet mood that spelled danger. She was throwing caution to the wind, but what did she care?

"Sarah said that women there boast that no matter how many children they have borne, their doctors never have seen their bodies in complete undress!" She ended with a small giggle behind her hand.

"Damn!" Rogan cussed, slapping his napkin down after swiping it across his lips in a vicious gesture. He leaned across the table, glowering at Pandora. "Those so-called *women* would be better

459

off dead and buried! But, my dear wife, if you ever speak of such as you've done here this night . . . in the company of my friends and associates, along with their wives, I'll take you across my knee and beat you then and there! I despise scandal. Everyone there in San Francisco knows what everyone else knows, and scandal might be suppressed but never hidden!" he hissed into her face. "You would do well to remember that!"

Tears brimmed in her suddenly pale blue eyes. "Oh, you think *I* would be shocking to the prudish? Is that it?" She laid down her fork with shaking hand.

"You had better not be. And no *lady* reads Émile Zola . . . !"

"Oh . . . who told you that?" Her face went white beneath its tan.

"The senator's wife—a very good friend of mine . . . you do remember at the Orpheum when you sat gossiping with your husband-to-be?"

"So?" she snapped. "I am going to get myself a divided skirt . . . and some of those new-fangled *bloomers*. What do you think of that, Mr. Smug-and-Proper?"

Bo Gary softly excused himself and slipped from the cabin, on tiptoe, closing the door carefully in going out. But neither of them noticed, for they sat glaring across to each other, the air crackling with anger and tension.

"Over my dead body!" Rogan slammed his fist onto the table; the peas and onions jumped like Mexican jumping beans.

"I might even pose in the *altogether* like that French model—or Little Egypt—in the Poodle Dog!" She lifted a shoulder in the manner of a coquette.

"That did it!"

He gave her a wilting look before rising, flinging back his heavy chair, and going to the door to viciously slam from the cabin. The slow, bewildered realization of what he had been driving at hit her full force.

"I will even wear a diamond-studded garter . . . for you only, Mr. . . . . Arrogant . . . *Hypocrite!*"

Pandora hissed these things while she snatched peas off the plate one by one to aim them at the door. "You taught me all the randy rutting you know . . . there on the beach and now . . . now you, mister, have the nerve to preach to *me!*" Her voice rose.

A pea was just sailing toward the door when it was flung wide with a jerk, and Rogan stood there framed ominously. The green thing struck him right below his right eye. He looked down at all the peas scattered on the floor, some squashed beneath his boot onto the polished wood, some rolling to and fro with the gently rocking motion of the *Promise*. He strode right through the mess. After the first murderous glare elicited when he had been struck with the bit of their dinner, he never gave her a second look. He crossed the cabin, snatched up his sextant and binoculars and, without further ado, was gone.

Pandora had not moved a muscle. She was still wearing the startled waiting look that she had had on her face when he had barged in, looking fit to kill.

461

Nausea claimed her again and she stumbled to the bed to sink on it in a miserable heap. The hurt was as real as if he had stabbed her or stoned her. She sobbed softly into the feather-tick pillow. *He never loved me. He . . . he only brought me back with him because he wants me to suffer.* Was it because she had danced without a stitch on top? She sniffed loudly, pitifully. *Oh . . . how will I ever understand him! Is he jealous of something . . . ? But what . . . ? Is he insane? Oh, God, I'm so afraid and alone!* She rose from the gently swaying mattress and dried her eyes. Someone had to clean up the mess she had made. She began to do just that, but soon found herself sobbing wretchedly once more, the handful of peas she had picked up smashed inside her fist. She squatted there, for how long she couldn't know, before she decided she must be brave.

I love him.

Was Rogan *taking* or *giving?* There had to be a way to find out the truth. But how was she to deal with this new and frightening and arrogant man with whom she had fallen desperately in love? Oh, God, how . . . ?

Over the next week and a half, Pandora became flustered and tense at Rogan's slightest touch; even their most fleeting eye contact shook her emotions. His wind-tossed forelock when he returned to the cabin late at night made her want desperately to reach out and smooth it away from his high forehead. But there was no time for intimacy. Twice heavy rains had plagued their progress, despite the third

462

man. She longed for Rogan's touch and his intimate, passionate caresses. Her desire rocked her, even more than the swells of the ship.

She loved him, desired him, and feared him.

Hero, search for him, her dream had said that morning at the plantation. Or had the dream signified something else—like a prophetic dream? What did she have to be afraid of?

Certainly not Rogan.

There was a squeak as taut lines were made fast to mooring bits when the *Promise* berthed. The smell of the bay and wharves drifted through the brass-bound portholes to Pandora. San Francisco. The scream of gulls, and the many creaks of deck planks, and the hawser's straining squeak. On the waterfront there was loud ribald laughter; the smell of beer and whiskey radiated from the swinging doors of saloons.

But the gull's scream was something by itself, lonely, echoing along the fog-shrouded bay and the dark mass of wharves. She was drawn irresistibly, poignantly, as on her first day here, to the sound of the gulls crying out.

To please Rogan and his household, she had taken time to dress carefully and brush her hair till it shone like apricot-colored silk. She wore a peach-colored dress with a pleated skirt, one that Rogan had purchased for her in Hawaii along with all the other gifts he had lavished upon her. She had never worn it before now. She was glad that the color picked up the pink in her cheeks; she hadn't had much color lately. She couldn't understand why the nausea had not left her yet. Perhaps it was because Rogan was always so frightfully stern. She did not dare think there could be another reason for her clinging morning sickness.

But were she pregnant, it just might make an enormous difference in their already shaky relationship. They had had a terrible argument after she had discovered that he had brought along her trunk without her knowing. She had come across it by accident only a week ago, a rug thrown over the top.

"Rather curious that you won't even open it up," Rogan had shot back when she had verbally attacked him for taking it upon himself to remove the trunk from the house. A slow anger had kindled in his eyes then. "I believe you are a coward, Pandora."

Having spoken with infinite pity and yet with something of contempt, he left her staring at the closed door of the cabin.

Alone, she had covered her face with her hands, sobbing. "He does hate me. He does!" Then: "He won't even sleep with me!"

He had seemed bored with her presence after that and the remainder of the journey found them almost total strangers to each other. With her eyes on the handkerchief she was almost shredding now, she waited for Rogan to come to get her.

"Ready?"

The door flew open at the same time the question was asked. His face wore a cold, closed look which led her deeper into a morass of fearful doubts and unspeakable suspicions.

"Yes."

She rose, feeling unnatural anxiety, and at his

nearness her skin tingled when he put a cape around her shoulders. He was studying her appearance, and only the merest hint of off-guard surprise crossed his face before he raised a protesting eyebrow.

"You could have worn something a bit warmer and not so pale in color. There is mud from the rain and you'll ruin your dress." Without another word of kindness, he went to his desk.

"How was I to know about the weather!" she tossed at his back.

He looked up once, swept her rudely from head to foot and then lowered his head busily. She felt her legs trembling beneath her pale-peach skirt, and she was dizzy and sickened by the jumble of her disordered thoughts. She studied him surreptitiously while he gathered some charts and things from his desk.

Silence again. That eternal, damnable silence between them. Her heart began to plunge into an unfamiliar sadness mingled with fear. Dear Lord, she thought in anguish, what awaited her at Thorn Mansion?

The rain-splashed, mud-spattered carriage had drawn up to the gangplank. The fog was in tonight and the occasional streetlight was surrounded by a pale, blurred nimbus. Pandora waited in the carriage into which she had hurried wordlessly while Rogan gave her a hand. That briefest touch had made her tingle, but he seemed not to notice for he strode away to converse with Bo Gary for several minutes before returning.

Curtly addressing the driver, he climbed in without a word to her. She wanted to scream at him to notice that she was alive. But when the carriage lurched suddenly as the horses and wheels clattered along the planks, she was thrown against him. He put a steadying arm around her, however, he voiced no regret for his curtness, or anything else for that matter; all the way up the cobbled hill to the house time seemed suspended. How wretchedly troubled she was, how lonely, even while grateful for his silent presence beside her.

When the carriage finally drew up to the house, the gaslights shone a welcome from between the lace curtains and half-drawn drapes, but Pandora felt her stomach give a lurch. Would they all welcome her back after she had stomped off so ungraciously?

"All right?" Rogan barely whispered, squeezing her hand once.

"Fine," she lied, wetting her dry lips in the shadows.

Actually she was filled with panic, and Rogan's cool attitude only added to her uneasiness. Alighting, he covered her hand with his own and said nothing.

Wizan poked his head through the mere crack to which he had opened the door, so that he could see who had arrived. Then his slanted eyes widened and the door was flung wide. He ducked back in for a moment to holler for Freyda before he came hurrying down the few stairs with quick little steps.

"Oh, golly, by golly, why you not let me know!"

Freyda stuck her head out the door, "What is going on?" she wondered. "Vell, for gootness sake! Th mister and his lady are home."

Pandora shot an odd glance to Freyda, as if she didn't quite know how to take the woman's last remark. Rogan was instantly beside her, taking her arm to guide her toward the staircase while he corrected the maid.

"Mr. and *Mrs.* Thorn are home."

Chapter Forty-four

Already the bedroom held a hint of evening shadows. Pandora felt chill, and dreaded the coming night. Another night alone, two now since coming . . . home . . . She wondered where Rogan put down his head at night?

"On Sheila's bosom or some other slut's, no doubt!"

She felt a lump that heralded tears rise in her throat. With a tired hand she reached for the tortoise-shell brush and then, reflecting back over the horrible day and what she had overheard, Pandora whipped the brush angrily through her hair, lifting the long strands.

"Oh, how could he bring me all the way here, and do this to me! The lecherous cad!"

She had filled the better—worse!—part of the day with fittings at the dressmaker's. Clothes, he said, you need beautiful clothes. You live in a big house now, own a carriage and pair. You will entertain, must know about food and wine and flowers and music.

"You will have everything," he went on, after they had dined in stifled silence for a time. "The ambitions for Thorn Navigation are unbounded. You are married to a shipping tycoon, you know."

She narrowed her eyes as if she would spit at him. "You have never once since we've arrived allowed me to think anything less!"

A possession. That was all she had become to him. This brought her to thinking that he only had wanted her because of the land to which she held the title. He *is* greedy!

She had provoked him and he had left the table brusquely. Sitting alone at the long table with the gasolier above it twinkling brightly over the rich, deep carpet beneath her feet, she had thought—Yes most women would envy me.

Now Pandora wandered over to look out the window from the stately mansion on Nob Hill. Her room, her silks and velvets, everything a woman would desire and more.

Sheila and Rogan. Was it true what she had heard while she occupied a dressing room, next to two gossiping females?

"Have you heard the latest?"

"What's that, Amanda?"

"Well, the whole bay town is buzzing, and it doesn't take long for this sort of thing to get around!"

"Amanda, don't keep me in suspense. What sort?"

"Rogan Thorn. He has his father's weakness, evidently."

"What's that?"

"Women!" the woman Amanda hissed aloud. After a pause she went on. "Elijah kept many woman, you know. He could practically pull one out of his hat; you know he was a magician?" Her voice rose.

Pandora had gasped into her hand, but had willed her heart to be calm while she listened to the rest.

"So who does Rogan Thorn keep? You know he had brought his supposed-to-be wife back from that island in the Pacific?"

"Oh, that won't stop him! He's like a candle burning at both ends." Amanda sighed, *as if* she cared.

"Who is the special woman he keeps?" the smaller, chirping voice persisted.

"Sheila Meade. But she's only one in a barrel of sweet peas, I've heard. Like I said, he's a candle, and we can guess which end will burn out first!"

They had launched into a fit of giggles then, and Pandora could just imagine them falling against each other, putting their faces close to see which one could open her mouth the widest in a homely scandalized O. With pins tearing at her tender flesh, Pandora had ripped off the lovely gown Rogan had ordered to be made for her, and had fled the dressmaker's as fast as she could.

The door to her bedroom had barely closed after her when she had thrown herself down on the bed and sobbed. She had been sick with revulsion, sick with terror. Sick! Sick! *Sick of him!*

"He is heartless and cruel! He must have murdered Akoni thinking he would get that land!" She had muffled the screaming words into her pillow. Much later she had sat up to dry her eyes, hiccuping loud. "He will not have me, not my land, and not"—she felt her breasts; uncomfortably they had begun to swell—"and not my baby!" She pounded the pillow

470

afresh. "Bastard! I hate him! He has murdered my heart," she ended softly, hiccuping again, "too."

Seeming to drift on a lonely cloud from the window, Pandora walked back to her dressing table. It was new, of course, with a white- and black-upholstered chair. The white French table, itself, was dressed with tiers of white ruffles. She removed the blue dress she had come to hate because of this day, and stepped out of her ribbon-trimmed petticoats, and finally the chemise. She made a face at her glowing nakedness in the mirror.

"Soon I shall be fat and ugly. He will hate me even more then. What have I done to make him despise me?" It must have begun the night she tried to seduce him away from Candice and Leilani, she told herself, swallowing a little cry.

A knock sounded at the door. She knew by the tentative sound that it was only Nan, and called for the maid to come in. Nan entered, quiet as usual, to brush her hair some more and tie it back with a slim pink ribbon. When the woman continued to frown lightly and look aside, Pandora realized suddenly that she was still naked!

"Nan, you can go now," Pandora said, trying to hide her embarrassment. What must the woman think of her, sitting forlornly, with misted eyes, not even caring she was naked?

I am not a queen, Pandora wanted to shout at the woman's back as she went out. *I am only* . . . She did not know what she was anymore!

She slipped the nightgown over her head, tied the satin ribbons of the peignoir, and sank wearily into a plush, dusty-rose armchair. She picked up a magazine and made a pretense of reading by the hearth while dozing fitfully and waiting for Rogan. She did not want him to catch her feeling sorry for herself.

But as usual, he never came to their bedroom.

Sleep would not come to Rogan, and he slipped from the mussed covers of the couch he had been using as a bed for two nights in his study. Two by two he took the stairs up to the master bedroom and entered by the hearth's low light. He searched the bed and his heart dropped to see that it was vacant; then his gaze found her asleep in the chair. He went there quietly, careful not to wake her.

The blue ribbon twined in hair that rippled its richness to the floor, sinuously; and her cheek rested on her forearms bent over the arm of the chair. Her lashes were still damp, as if she had been crying softly in her sleep. He cursed low when she murmured and a sad smile lifted her lips gently and then was gone.

Rogan felt a lump appear in his throat. He was ashamed of his ridiculous, brooding moods of the last several weeks, and now especially for having allowed Sheila Meade to visit him at the office. He had taken her home twice to get her out of his hair. Nothing else. He should have had the sense to say something, tell her to get lost. Had he wanted Pandora to hear the gossip? No doubt she had already, by now.

His gaze slipped lower. He had noticed the slightly thickened look to her waistline. In fact, earlier this night Nan had congratulated him on the coming baby. He had merely stood stunned. Actually, on the ship he had known all along she was different. Even now, everything he did seemed to make her irritable and angry. Had he noticed some fear, too? But why . . . why was she afraid of him? God, he needed some answers.

He had taken a perverse pleasure in avoiding her and the simple truth she carried.

His eyes were hard and cold now.

His mother had denied him even before he was born, and he had grown up scarred by parental rejection. His father had been too busy being a magician, and a philanderer. He had needed something—or someone—to supply the lack in his life. Riches. The company to be the best. His home. More, always more. And then this woman had come stealing softly into his lonely life.

And now this! A surging wave of untold anger and pity for himself coursed through his veins. Lifting her gently, he carried her to the bed and placed her down beneath the covers; then turning without another look at her, he left the bedroom.

Sometime in the wee hours a fog bell tolled mournfully, and instantly Pandora was awake, bathed in sweat that had soaked through her nightgown.

There is no hope, no hope, the bell seemed to be taunting.

She could smell of the rain-soaked streets drifting sweet and steamy in through the open window. She looked down over herself then. How and when had she climbed into bed? She hadn't remembered doing

473

so. She stared at the vacant pillow beside her and sighed in loneliness.

An hour passed, then another, and she found herself yet unable to go back to sleep. She rose from between the mussed sheets and went to stand at the window. The street below was hidden by thick, swirling fog, a gray fuzz that blotted out even the shape of lampposts. The contour of the cobbled hills could be vaguely seen. The clock below struck two. She listened for sounds of Rogan's footfalls. Again, there were none. She was so abominably lonely and all that she loved on her island paradise was such a long way away.

It was a quietly pleasant morning. On the street all along the block Chinese houseboys swept sidewalks or scrubbed marble steps. Soon the grocery boys, and the icemen, and the vegetable vendors would pull their carts along the curbs.

Pandora had again allowed Nan to brush her long hair and to tie it back with a pink velvet bow. She had donned a matching dress, velvet, with the same velvet but of a darker rose-pink running through the beading of its square yoke and ruffled wristbands. Her hair was carefully waved in the back—Nan had done it on the curling tongs—and she looked quite in fashion.

Pandora was in the parlor unpacking the Oriental objets d'art that Rogan had packed carefully in elaborately carved Hawaiian chests of *koa* and monkeypod. She was just lifting some masterpieces of Chinese jade out of their paper wrappings and straw and placing them carefully in a glass cabinet when Wizan entered the room bearing a tray of chicken sandwiches and little cakes and lemonade.

"You should eat something now, Missus Thorn. You only have black coffee and orange for breakfast." He watched as she lifted a porcelain figure of a goddess out of its wrappings.

"Oh, isn't it beautiful!" Pandora exclaimed, turning the slim figure around in her hand.

"Velly—oh, I mean verry," he corrected. She had been helping him pronounce his r's and he could say Thorn now instead of Thol'n. "She is goddess of hope. I do not remember her name, but there is another of her there in the cabinet."

Pandora bent to see the exquisite *blanc de chine* figure, and lovingly placed the one she held inside the cabinet next to the other one.

Wizan beamed. "Like sisters, they are two of hope beside the other. Just like your Christian God, he is hope, too."

Pandora looked surprised at that. "Yes, Wizan, Jesus is our hope. I believe that very much."

"I pray all the time to him," he announced with a big smile.

Pandora looked up from the jade and ivory figurines she had unpacked. "You do? That is wonderful, Wizan," she said softly, getting a warm feeling from just talking to this little Chinaman.

"I have to go now, and pick up Mr. Thorn at office. You eat something please?" He bowed curtly with the tray.

"Oh, yes." She laughed. "I will, Wizan. Just leave

it there on the table and I will nibble at my leisure."

After he had gone, Pandora stared unblinkingly at the two figures side by side. Pearls of wisdom from the Chinaman, she thought to herself. He had been a godsend this day, and she would not soon forget how very much he had helped her to realize there was always hope. Pray, her mother had taught her, and the door will open. A ripple of excitement went through her as she completed the unpacking and hummed a tune she had learned in the missionary school.

When Rogan returned from the office he flourished two tickets for a sophisticated Sardou comedy about which everyone in the bay city was buzzing. She was instantly animated, her heart hammering erratically.

"Oh, Rogan, what shall I wear?" She had been sitting in front of the bay window on a beautifully upholstered sofa, and she looked like a dream in her pink velvet dress.

He chuckled. "You look good enough to eat right now. But I have picked up your new dress from Mme. Daphne's. You will have to look your best, for the very elite of San Francisco will attend and we'll promenade in the lobby between acts with the most distinguished of families."

Pandora turned aside to conceal her disappointment, murmuring, "Oh." Her animation dwindled.

Rogan noticed that her enthusiasm had diminished, but he said nothing to voice his regret over his announcement. Instead, leaving her with the word that she should be ready by seven, he strode broodingly from the room.

Pandora arranged her hair in a most provocative style, but somehow her heart just wasn't in the fun she would ordinarily have had in doing her toilette. Her feelings were a mixture of joy and dread. She wished Rogan hadn't spoiled it all with his act of snobbery. Was this the true Rogan Thorn? Arrogant and conceited? Or was he merely hiding some hurt she had no knowledge of behind that façade he put up so often of late? She just did not know enough about his background. On the other hand, there was as much mystery in hers as there was in his. But just how far back did Rogan's hurt go? she wondered as a new knot of apprehension settled in the pit of her stomach.

The play was daringly risqué, but entertaining just the same, and when they promenaded in the lobby between acts Pandora lifted her chin proudly, knowing she was stunning in her electric-blue dress with shoulder poufs of *gros de Londres*. Her diamond ear-drops glinted as they swung from her ears while she walked beneath the sparkling chandeliers. Rogan wore a swinging, debonair Inverness cape which he had flung carelessly over his shoulders; a glint of satin showed under its broadcloth. They both wore immaculate white kid gloves, hers reaching all the way to her elbows. The cut of his evening clothes and his pearl studs were handsome, and he carried a top hat that he twirled in his fingers roguishly.

Then, with a sinking heart, Pandora caught sight of Sheila Meade approaching them. Her yellow hair was piled elegantly high on her head, and the cream satin gown she wore looked as if she had been poured into it. Pandora wondered briefly how the woman had gotten a chemise between her flesh and the gown; there probably wasn't any underclothing to speak of, she decided as Sheila halted before them.

"Rogan, *darling*," Sheila purred provocatively, her eyes flying over Pandora briefly. She pulled something from her pearl-studded reticule. "I missed you today, but you know how busy a girl must be on a day like *this*. Here is your handkerchief, Rogan dear; you dropped it in front of my place yesterday."

Rogan blinked as she dropped the initialed square of cloth into his automatically outstretched hand. He stared down as if she had deposited a frog into his immacuately gloved palm. Pandora regarded him with an unwavering stare for several moments, her eyes not the blue of the sun-dappled sea any longer, but rather stormy.

Sheila puckered her rouged lips and then sailed off through the crowd, tossing over her shoulder, "Ta-ta, see you later, darlings."

Darlings. Pandora fumed, glaring at the back of the blond head until it disappeared behind a tall man.

"Pandora, I can explain—" Rogan began, his forehead beading with nervous moisture. Unconsciously he dabbed with the handkerchief.

"Oh, sure you can, *darling*," Pandora said sweetly. "Just like you can explain away the green-leafed shirt you wore while on the beach with your last

478

whore. Well, you can just take me home, Rogan Thorn. I am suddenly very much tired of all this inane chatter and phony glitter!"

Helpless to stop her in front of all these people without creating a scandal, Rogan found there was nothing left to do but follow her furious wake as his strides ate up the distance she had put between them.

Chapter Forty-five

Because of her seething anger, Pandora's apprehension had flown. She was a mass of conflicting emotions: angered one minute, fearful of the future the next, jealous, frustrated, happy only occasionally.

Happy hardly ever, really, Pandora was thinking as she paused at the top of the stairs hearing Rogan's voice and another male one floating up to her from the hall. It was the doctor and she caught the tail end of his sentence.

"... could cause amnesia, but only up to a certain point. I see no reason for it to linger, though."

Me? Are they talking about me? Pandora wondered, her long lashes fluttering quickly.

"*Will* she remember?" Her husband was asking Dr. Hoyle.

Pandora picked out the concern in his voice, and something else. He sounded almost impatient to have something over and done with.

"Oh, yes," the doctor said with a little laugh.

"I wish you could convince me of that."

"She'll do that herself. By the way, where is the expectant mother?" He chuckled. "So you think, you said. I'd like to have a look at her myself. You'll need a doctor for this occasion, you know. You should have called me sooner, Rogan."

Pandora swooned against the banister. *Expectant.* Rogan knows? She took a step backward. How can this be? She wasn't even sure herself. Or had she been kidding herself into thinking otherwise. A dew of sweat began to form on her upper lip.

Rogan's voice rumbled up the stairs. "Well, come along then, Hoyle. She should be up by now, and if not, you can come around later."

Flying to her room, Pandora took off her bodice and jumped into the yet unmade bed, thankful that Nan had not come in to straighten her room. She moaned, realizing she still wore her shoes. Her heart pounded in her throat as she prayed that the doctor wouldn't lift the covers to take a swift look at her to determine whether she was with child or not. Could he tell this just by looking her over?

She froze when the door opened. She squeezed her eyes shut tight, but could feel her eyelids quivering from nervousness. Oh God, don't let them come over to the bed! She felt as if she might relieve herself right on the spot, for she had forgotten to go to the bathroom upon arising. She wondered briefly if anyone had ever died from embarrassment. Well, if they came to her bedside, she would surely be the first to do so.

An eye narrowed on one side of Rogan's face, while on the other his eyebrow shot up. His eyes flew over the room then, snagging on the nightgown and peignoir folded neatly over the back of a chair. He studied the curvaceous bulge in the bed and concealed an amused smile from the doctor.

"She is still sleeping," the doctor said softly, frowning toward the foot of the bed.

"Yes, Hoyle," Rogan spoke up loudly. "Will you come back later, then?" He shot a parting glance at the covers yanked to her chin.

The door closed on the doctor's reply and Pandora felt her breathing return to normal and her heart beat steadily once again. A closer call she had never known. Flinging back the covers, she went to the wardrobe to find another dress to wear.

Rogan was seated at the breakfast table when she entered. She could not see his face, for it was completely hidden by the newspaper he was reading. Smoothing her aqua brocade skirt, she went slowly to seat herself at the end of the table, avoiding looking down the table's length to him again.

She felt mixed emotions as she picked up the teacup to take a sip, but then frowned, noticing that it was empty. The newspaper rustled and Rogan's face peeped out before going back inside.

"Do you always drink invisible tea?" he asked with a tinge of amusement. He heard the cup rattle in its saucer.

"No!" she snapped, reaching for the china teapot and beginning to pour when his second question struck her.

This time he stayed behind the paper. "And do you always sleep with your shoes on?"

Pandora froze her hand in midair. The tea she was pouring spilled over the rim of the cup and made steaming splotches on the tablecloth. The teapot thudded to the table as Pandora rose and fled the dining room in a fit of tearful sobbing.

Wizan, pausing in the doorway, heard her heart-rending cries rising up the stairs to the thumping accompaniment of fast-flying feet. Rogan had emerged from his newspaper to watch her hurried escape from the room. His brooding frown met with Wizan's for a moment as they both contemplated Pandora's injured female pride.

"Ah, very big sign," Wizan piped up, sounding wise.

"What's that?" Rogan snapped, not meaning to sound so harsh.

"Confucius say woman who cries easy has swallowed big watermelon seed."

Rogan's voice turned cold and distant. "I'm not so sure she hasn't swallowed a cowardly lioness instead. One minute she spits and claws and the next she mewls and cowers like a frightened kitten!"

"Ah, yes, Confucius say—"

"Shut up, Chinaman!" Rogan finished for Wizan.

Pandora overslept the next day and filled yet another miserable afternoon at the dressmaker's. She hated the gossipy place with a passion, but Rogan had pressed her to be fitted for a wedding dress; the quiet affair would take place the next Saturday, very privately with only close acquaintances and friends, he had mentioned just this morning before he swept out the door on his way to the office.

Pandora had her own drawing account at the bank now, and a small jet-beaded drawstring purse full of "spending money."

The bedroom had become a room set apart from the rest of the house, and after they had exchanged good nights with each other every evening, Rogan went to his uncomfortable couch and she to the huge brass bed.

Would the storm in their relationship never end? Even after their holy matrimony? Simple reasoning told her it was not very likely.

The hours slid by slowly, painfully. She missed Iola and Cara terribly. Who was there to keep her company? The only soul who made her smile, halfway, these days seemed to be Wizan.

The clock on the landing struck imperiously, to remind her that this was Thorn Mansion on Nob Hill, where life was ordered and systematic, and went on no matter what the circumstances.

Rogan had announced he'd be late in coming home from the office. What did it matter? she had told herself; when they were together in the dining room or the living room, she might as well be alone for all the attention he showed her.

Unable to stand the quiet bedroom any longer that evening, Pandora jumped to her feet and tossed aside the novel she had been reading. It was then that she again noticed the mysterious envelope the maid had brought to her earlier, saying Mrs. Thorn should open it immediately. It had been delivered by a man in sailor's clothing. What Nan had been saying hit her now as she came out of her fog of despondency.

Pandora had hidden from Rogan all of the invitations to parties from the elite of San Francisco. She had *had* it with those party-goers like Sheila Meade who had nothing better to do than gossip about one another. The envelope she held in her hand couldn't be another invitation—or could it?

Pandora sighed. She might as well see what it said. She ripped open the seal, flipping out the short letter. "Let me see: *'Soon you, Pandora, are going to die.'* What?"

Signed *The Wizard*. The paper rustled ominously in her hand, in the stillness.

Pandora gulped and her stomach gave a lurch. The Wizard? The one at Millers' party she had attended with Sarah Wolfington? The very same clown with the bag of tricks?

A chilling sensation overwhelmed her as it had the day before when she had gone up into the tower attic where the airless, too-hot room had seemed to close in on her. She had gone there to see if Rogan had transferred her trunk there with the others. She had caught a glimpse of something—an outfit, a bag of tricks. . . .

Pandora was suddenly trembling with a new and different kind of horror. Rogan had learned that she had gone there. How, she didn't know. Surely not Wizan, but perhaps one of the maids had seen her stealthily going up and had reported this to Rogan. He had glowered across the dinner table at her.

"Stay down from there, Pandora. I mean it. Anyone could fall"—he had said almost ruminatively—"with the steep turn of the stairs."

Others had gone there with the trunks, why not her? But she had not voiced her inductive reasoning.

Methodically Pandora now went to light a lamp to take with her; a glowing taper remained by her bedside table.

Upstairs. She must see for herself. Lightning suddenly darted outside the hall windows and she started. But undaunted she crept onward, upward.

Rogan stepped across the threshold and shed his raincoat and hat in the entry, handing them over to Freyda who had just now come downstairs. Lightning illuminated the shadowy places across the floor, seeming to reach gropingly toward the staircase and to flicker at the first step. Rogan stared there, mesmerized for a moment.

Raindrops glistened in places where his hat had failed to shield his face from the downpour. His green eyes leveled at Freyda and she drew back a little from the intense brooding look in them. There was a snap of irritation recognizable in his voice.

"Where is Pandora? Upstairs again," he seemed to answer himself.

For a moment Freyda was flustered by his manner. "I vas just up there to knock. Dinner is ready, I vas going to tell her, but no answer. Maybe she vas asleep again?" She shrugged, cowering a little as she clutched at the damp articles of his clothing.

"You can hang those up now, Freyda. Tell the cook to keep dinner warm." He shot a glance up the stairs. "We'll be down shortly."

Rogan turned the doorknob very quietly. The small night taper on the bedside table had been lighted beforehand, perhaps by Freyda, or Pandora herself. It tossed a pale flicker into the shadows. When lightning flashed momentarily illuminating the room, there was no sign of life.

* * *

The way up the steps loomed dark and forbidding; two coiling flights up into the uppermost attic tower, more frightening in this storm than the murky bowels of the mansion. Picking up her skirts, Pandora darted glances over her shoulder at the dark from which she had just risen. The lamp in her trembling hand was warm and shed wheeled spirals of light as she made her way lightly up the curving stairs. She halted at the tall, narrow door, her heart thudding against her breastbone. The knob turned under her hand with an eerie, grating sound, but she had come this far so she forced her legs to move inside the room, slowly, nervously. Her palms were wet and her hands felt swollen right to the tips of her fingers.

She gasped. The slanted eyes of a painted hobby-horse stared directly at her from the dark recesses of piled-high crates; she wondered for a crazy moment if Rogan had long ago mounted that black-lacquered saddle and ridden the white horse off into a child's fascinating dream world of warring knights, princesses, and hideous dragons with green scales and flaming red tongues. She would have laughed at her imagination were she not so scared in this foolish search on a dark night of storm and lightning.

Aged floorboards creaked as she roamed slowly about the round room, and occasionally lightning danced across the Medieval square windows, invariably causing her to start. She held the lamp high to peer into the scary corners. *There* was a curious trunk. She lifted the lid, but just some old, musty papers with a yellowed look to them greeted her. When she read a few by the light of the lamp, she learned that Rogan's grandfather and father were buried in the Thorn vault at Laurel Hill Cemetery. She shivered. No mention of a female parent, a mother.

She set down the lamp as she passed an old chipped table. There were more stored trunks, great heavy leather bulks with silk-lined lids and trays, and brass fastenings as big and shiny as harness buckles. THORN. The name was stamped inside of each and every one, alongside that of their Paris maker, and all smelled faintly of sachet.

There was the trunk in which she had seen the costume, when she had peeked into it for just a moment the day before!

She opened its heavy lid as though she expected a hellish thing to leap out and devour her entirely. The wizard costume and all the magical tricks of the trade. Her pulse raced and an awful ringing began in her head.

"The wizard—Rogan—the wizard," she repeated, staring at the costume in horrible fascination. It was Rogan who had charmed the Millers' party with . . . these.

"No! No!" The sea water of her nightmares, the worst, washed over every nerve end. "Oh, God, no . . ." Terrified thoughts collided with each other as she surmised that Rogan . . . wanted her . . . dead . . . the land. That was it, but why, oh why, hadn't he tried to do something before this? Why now? Why was he threatening her with the letter?

Dizzy, she hunkered back on her heels, tottering, then putting a knee to the floor to keep her balance. This could not be happening!

"Oh, Lord, let this not be so. Please, have mercy,

show me that Rogan is . . . not the one." Then, he had never once loved her . . . all those women. Sheila. Leilani. Candy. Even Cara. He had been playing her for a fool all this time, while he played his dangerous game of murder. She shook her head.

"No." She was petrified with both fear and bewilderment and her stomach turned over when she heard the click of the door, the grating sound . . . then the soft motion of someone entering. At the same time lightning flashed in a giant flicker.

Her heart pounded in her throat as she whirled about to find Rogan, just as she knew she would, standing there behind her. She couldn't faint now; no, she might never come to, alive, if that were to happen.

He moved quickly around her. "Find something interesting, love?" he asked softly, ominously, with the roll of thunder.

It could not be, no, no. Yet she could not swallow as she gazed at his strong long-fingered hands, beautiful man's hands reaching out to lift her quivering to her feet. To have those hands at her throat, to know she was alone in a shadowed attic with a man who could have been a murderer, was to desire to turn and flee. There was still time; his grip was not strong on her yet.

"Pandora?"

Her fear flew back in time. It could not have been Rogan out there on the beach—Akoni's murderer— her heart still cried it out passionately, defensively as his glittering eyes darted from her to the open trunk. Their green darkened to that of a dark forest. She was going to pieces inside. Remembering. A flash of heat passed from him to her. Was this the awful fate she had finally come to?

"Pandora, are you all right? You look as white as a ghost." Said softly, barely audibly in the thickness of the fog swirling about her. He stared and she felt him tremble with something she was afraid to fathom.

It was too late to fly now; she could not run, not down those stairs— "Anyone could fall," he had said, "with the steep turn of the stairs." The words stuck in her throat and she struggled to bring them out.

"Tell me, Rogan, tell me . . . the truth about Akoni," she begged, leaning on his strong arm for support.

"About Akoni? Whatever do you mean, sweetheart?" he asked, with only the merest hint of unguarded surprise crossing his face.

"It was not an accident." She gulped. "You know that," she went on passionately, stirred to reckless courage stronger than her terror of his callousness. "It was—murder."

Alert wariness flickered in his green eyes, now sardonic. Yet there was a hint of swift calculation, a certain kind of feeling-out in his voice next. "Hardly a word to use lightly. What do you mean, and who do you include, when you say—murder?" His grip tightened on her arm now.

The thud of her heart became louder, like thunder, in her ears. "You didn't do it? You were not there— were you?"

"No, Pandora, I was not there. Don't you know?"

He seemed to be feeling her out. But his words were spoken with infinite pity and with a little contempt, she decided foggily.

Pandora was staring, staring. Shuddering and dizzy with shock, she saw a bloodied dress . . . a knife. Her knife.

"What do you see, Pandora?"

Her hands flew to cover her face, hands that shook like lighting butterflies. The close attic was spinning, he was coming at her with . . . the knife. The lovely steel of death was lifting now.

The Wizard. *Soon you are going to die.*

She backed away from Rogan, back, back, until her thighs brushed the windowsill. Lightning flashed and thunder crashed with a deafening roar, and at the same time the window latch came free with a rattle and the window burst wide and banged against the house. Rain blew in. Rogan started forward just as Pandora whirled, the wind snatching at her hair, swirling about her, giving her the look of a lovely but demented witch. Her hands clawed the air futilely. Her eyes were wildly looking down . . . down to her death. Rogan was pushing her out. . . .

"Pandora!"

Chapter Forty-six

Rogan moved fast. He caught Pandora before she could plunge from the window to her death.

With the lamp to light the way, and her legs draped over one arm, he carried her carefully down the spiral staircase to the bedroom where he turned the knob and kicked the door open. Trembling himself, he bore her quickly to the bed, untangling her arms from his neck.

"So cold, my love," he muttered, "you are so cold." He piled quilts from the closet over her, tucking her into a cocoon.

A concerned look melted the lined harshness of his face as he left her to kneel at the hearth to stir the ashes, and to heap coal until a flame was born.

"Now, brandy," he muttered absently, rushing out with hurrying steps to find some next door. Wizan came, but Rogan waved him away.

He crooked an arm about her shoulders and held the shaking tumbler to her lips. "Drink it for me, sweetheart."

Pandora stirred and moaned, staring up into his worried face through her haze.

"You are back. You called me sweetheart. You

492

were supposed to . . . kill me. Why didn't you? Don't you hate me?"

She sipped, then coughed as the fiery liquid burned all the way down.

Rogan puzzled over her words, but only said, "More. Please try to drink more."

"Why?" She stared into the glass, imagining she saw poison.

"Don't talk, sweet. Just drink a little more." His voice cracked. "I'm going to send for Dr. Hoyle."

She grabbed his wrist. "No. Don't like doctors." She breathed the plea.

"Will you be all right?" He raked his fingers through his hair. "That was a dumb question."

"Yes. Dumb," she echoed. The liquid was beginning to bring her to her senses. Why wasn't she dying? "Talk to me, Rogan."

A sweetness washed over her that made her heart contract when she caught his worried look and noticed that the forelock she loved had fallen over his high forehead.

He smiled, the corners of his lips lifting in a quiver. "Tell me what you'd like to hear."

"Just talk, please?"

He merely picked up her hand to plant a warm kiss into its palm; so white, he was thinking.

"Rogan?" she tried again. "The fire at Summit House . . . who started it?"

"Haven't I told you?"

"I—I do not remember."

"Bo Gary was the culprit."

"Why?" she wanted to know.

"Because . . . he realized, even if a certain fool

493

didn't, that that someone had begun to fall in love with Dora." He put his larger hand over hers, squeezing with innate strength.

"In—in love?" she murmured in puzzlement.

"Hmmm—yes," was all he said.

Her eyes turned heavy-lidded. "I am so . . . very tired. Do you mind—?" Was she dying now? She certainly felt that way.

Rogan rose swiftly from the bed; she could see him moving to the bureau drawer where her many new lacy nightgowns were. *He knows everything*, she pondered dimly. There were so many questions yet unanswered, though; why couldn't he solve the riddles for her before she died? He was a magician, wasn't he?

With a nightgown meant for cooler nights in hand, he moved back to the bed to help her slip it on, his eyes never leaving her rounder curves, her full breasts. Then she fell immediately into slumber while he sat watchfully, like a concerned and loving parent at the bedside of a sick child.

Rogan stared thoughtfully at her lovely face in repose. His gaze slid to the flatness of her abdomen and belly; when she stood, though, a little rounded curve showed; that hadn't been there before on the island.

"A baby," he groaned softly, sick with jealousy. He had never known this emotion, before Pandora slipped so softly, so gently, and yet so disturbingly into his life.

His mind whirled from that disturbing thought to yet another. How did she truly feel about him? If she had needed him, she would have said so. She had not invited him to share the bed even once. . . .

He barely whispered to himself, "What will I do if she should love this baby when it comes more than me? There will not be enough of her heart to share with me; she will be drained of emotion, such is the care of a child. I need all of her, her very heart and soul."

Where was the fairness of it all? he groaned. He had never known the love of parents or the happy times a family could share together. He had been denied this through his youth right up to manhood. His father Elijah had ignored him for his many mistresses. His mother abandoned him to a houseful of servants and a grumbling grandfather. If not for Wizan, he would have died from loneliness. He had always been a lonely man, even with Wizan to care for his many needs.

Rogan bent down to Pandora. *Oh, my sweet,* he thought. He ached to hold her against his heart.

He straightened with a deep sigh of regret. The completeness of love was never to be his. Never. Never.

Pandora stirred in the bed, nestling her cheek against the pillow and murmuring softly as she came half-awake to see through slitted eyes the red glow cast by the crackling fireplace. Outside, the rain continued to hurl its wet fury against the windows, but inside, in her bed . . . this was no pillow beside her. There was a half-naked male form pressed to her side, her arm wrapped around his sinewy shoulder.

Her eyes flew over the close face. "Rogan," she breathed, feeling her heart thump against her ribs in excitement.

He ran a finger along her collarbone, murmuring, "You slept for several hours, sweetheart." There was a catch in his voice.

"I am alive," she groaned huskily.

He chuckled. "I can feel that for certain."

"Oh, Rogan, I don't care anymore if you want to . . . to be rid of me, for the grant to the land. You can have it—all yours."

"Be rid of you?" He laughed shortly. "Why should I want to be rid of you, and whatever gave you that idea?"

"You . . . do not?" She blinked into the green eyes devouring her lips, her hair in its dishevelment. Then he kissed each one of these.

"You've had a bad dream, that's all."

She clung to him with her heart full. "Hold me closer, Rogan, kiss me. Oh, kiss me!"

The rains swept over the mansion while Rogan did as she asked with much pleasure, beginning a slow-moving kiss that started at her lips and moved to her chin, leaving hot trails of moistness along her flesh. He proceeded to her throat, then lower and lower. When he felt her stiffen, he raised his head.

"What is it?" He rasped the few short words out with difficulty.

"Rogan, why didn't you tell me . . . you were the wizard at Millers' party?"

He shrugged against her. "Strange time to ask when I'm dying to make love to you. But yes, I was the wizard and until now I never thought to tell you. I mean you knew I behaved very poorly there in the garden, like a lecherous rogue who would have swallowed you whole had you fallen to my advances. I regretted that afterward, but you had gotten under my skin and I could do nothing else but try to rape you right there in daylight. I was angered about so many things."

"Please, tell me more about the things that pertain to your past," she begged with her dewy eyes on him.

"All right." He sighed, pulling her up gently as he placed the pillow against the headboard for them to rest their shoulders on.

"Those things in the attic, the costume, all of them belonged to my father, Elijah. He was a magician as you may already have guessed. Many had come to see him, from far and near, to marvel at his tricks and *Thorn Illusions*. People called the unusual things he performed supernatural . . . there was even a naughty ballad of the Thorn legend."

"Why didn't you follow more in his footsteps?" She purred against his shoulder; she was feeling so secure and happy.

"Oh, he taught me all the tricks of the trade, all right, but my interests didn't lean in that direction. Like my grandfather, ships were my first love as a young man."

She took a deep breath before posing the question to him. "What about your mother?" she asked.

His lips dragged down at the corners and a dim light entered the green of his eyes. "I never knew her. There was a woman years ago who had come begging"—he shrugged—"but, she was not my flesh and blood; I'm sure of that now."

She peered from beneath tawny lashes up at him. "Rogan?" she said, to shake him from his sudden depression.

He brushed a kiss over her forehead. "Yes? What else would you like to know?" he asked, sounding drained of emotion.

"I—" She bit off, unable to ask him what bothered her most. She had to give him the benefit of the doubt, even if only in her own mind. He could not have sent that note to her signed The Wizard. Someone else had . . . someone who wanted her dead. Someone who was indeed after her land, and perhaps more. Yes, somehow it was all connected with a very dangerous person—a man. . . . Something inside said her murderer—Akoni's murderer—was a man.

"Rogan, I—I want you to be very careful of whom you come across." She squeezed his arm, to impress what she must say next. "I've reason to believe someone would very much desire to destroy us both. There is someone who will do crazy things to tear us apart, threaten—" She halted here, determined to find this dangerous man herself.

He hugged her closer to his side. "Who would want to hurt you, sweet? You are precious to everyone you meet."

"To you, too?"

"Especially to me."

"Why then have you sought to avoid me so much these last several weeks?"

His gaze went to the hearth to keep her from seeing his reaction. "I thought you were . . . ill and didn' want to be bothered, so I took my rest in the study.'

This was not the whole truth, he realized.

His eyes were very big now, very green—a jealous kind of green that he concealed from her. She did study his profile curiously though, and decided she knew more.

"Are you happy about our baby that—that I am going to give birth to—in less than seven months?" She looked sideways at him. "I do not need a doctor anymore to tell me this." She turned to face him fully with her long fingers cupped around his chin. She lowered the bodice of her nightgown to show him the riper fullness of her breasts as she freed them. "See? My breasts prepare for the nursing of our baby." She dragged his glowing eyes lower as she kicked the covers down to her feet and lifted the hem of her nightgown to expose the golden triangle of hair, and miraculous roundness of her belly. "And here, your seed grows within."

She looked down at him then to where his manhood strained to be released from its material confines. Indeed he felt his turgid flesh against the lighter cloth of his trousers, the only article of his clothing that need be removed in order for him to be joined with her honey and flesh.

Pandora surprised him by unbuttoning his pants as fast as she could work them free. His manhood stood large and completely naked. Even more surprising, she helped him remove the trousers and then climbed unceremoniously on top of him, positioning herself for his entry. He gripped her slim arms to halt what ecstasy she had begun.

"You'll be hurt this way—the baby," he nearly croaked out from excitement.

"Don't be afraid, darling; you won't hurt me or the baby. I will do it all." She peered down into his eyes. "I will—"

And she did. She did.

Much later Rogan smoothed the tangled hair from her damp, sleeping face. He palmed her belly with the gentlest of caresses.

I have you, my cherished passion flower. We have this babe growing from out of our endless love. Complete. To share forever. I will take you both and hold you as a family, forever, sweetheart, to be kept close to my heart.

What could go wrong now with such dreams fulfilled? Rogan slept, peace and joy warming his once-lonely heart.

Chapter Forty-seven

Pandora sat at the dressing table to brush out her hair. It was terribly tangled. She smiled, her lips drawn upward sensually. The tangles were due to Rogan's having entwined his fingers in her tresses during the night when he had awakened hungry again for the full measure of their new and exciting kind of love.

She remembered just that morning, flushed from their love-making, when Nan had entered to put away some clothes she had washed and pressed. Pandora had stared at the green-leafed shirt, but she was determined not to let this depress her. She had been still staring at it when Rogan had come up behind her, a towel wrapped around his naked shoulders, and pressed a kiss on her neck.

"Does that shirt especially interest you in some way?" he asked. "If you like it that much, I'll have a hundred more made just like it and wear one every day of the week."

"No!" she blurted unthinkingly.

He turned her about to face him. "If you feel that way about the shirt, maybe I should go ahead and burn the thing." He smiled down into her quiet face.

"You don't have to burn it, Rogan. It is just that . . . the shirt reminds me of . . . Candice Randall for some reason."

"Candice Randall!" he snorted. "Well then, I really *will* burn it!" He continued to study her face measuringly. "Ahh, maybe I should have let Fred keep the shirt. But, as he didn't want it, he returned . . . the shirt . . . because . . . Pandora?" His face lit up suddenly. "Oh, yes . . . now I see. Fred—ah—had a midnight tumble with Candice on the beach— So, that's why you thought . . . Aha, you think *I* laid her. Don't you?"

"Oh, Rogan! I am sorry for being such a jealous fool!" She looked aside, embarrassed. "I even thought you and Sheila Meade had—"

"Oh. You heard about me taking her home, only from the wrong source of gossip. Probably the worst tongue-waggers in town!"

"Oh, yes. You should have heard them, Rogan. They called you and Elijah philanderers!" She remembered the dressing-room gossipers and their evil whispers.

Rogan cleared his throat. "A man's past sure catches up with him one day." He sighed. "I was like a candle, burning at both ends before you came into my life. I had become jaded, and of course, you know which end of me had burned out!" He chuckled.

Again she recalled the gossipers saying that very same thing. But Pandora said nothing about that now.

"Oh, my sweet," he murmured against her cheek, taking her in his arms, keeping her close while the reveled in each other's company for a long while.

*　　*　　*

The very next day, at Rogan's soft-spoken request Pandora allowed Dr. Hoyle to examine her fully; there was no doubt now. The pregnancy had been officially confirmed. She knew that Rogan had been jealous of the baby coming, knew what he had been through as a child and recognized the sheer loneliness of his existence without love. But now Rogan welcomed the fact of her pregnancy with something close to wondrous love.

Love. He had called her that repeatedly as they had *made* love. But did he truly mean it in the essence of the word? When would she know for certain? When he said it in the full light of day?

With Rogan gone off on some mysterious errand with Bo Gary and an even more mysterious man, Pandora began to think that the stranger had appeared somehow familiar to her. But from where? When?

Alone again, Pandora knew she must search her memory for answers, ruthlessly rake it. Not to find the one who was determined to end her life, but mostly to put a name to Akoni's murderer. She believed them to be the same man. She would not rest until the puzzle of her past had been solved.

She could not hide the note signed The Wizard from Rogan forever. But something told her that she must wait to see if she received any more; however, there was something that could not wait.

Any recollections of the horror-filled beach scene eluded her and thereby she was led deeper into a morass of fearful doubts and unspeakable suspicions. What would free her mind from torment?

Who could give her a key that would deliver her from darkness and lead her into light?

Hope. She was going to put it into action.

In spite of a heavily banked sea fog that had begun to move inland, the bay water that washed at the wharf pilings was a molten gilt color while the sky seemed to be torched afire. Red—like the color of blood.

At the Embarcadero, Pandora stepped from the rented carriage and made her way by foot onto the docks amid the last-minute jostling and confusion of express wagons and handcarts. She had paid the driver, telling him not to wait; she would walk home. In minutes dusk would creep along the wharves and the first wraiths of fog would come. How quiet and lonely the long pier ahead of her was now that she had come this far. She should have had the driver take her all the way, but it was too late now. She was almost there.

Her sense of all the life in the bay area diminished, though, as she began to feel that someone was close behind, stealthily tracking her. No time to think of *whom* that might be.

Pandora gathered up the trailing of her skirts and walked toward the *Promise*. There was an eerie deserted look about the ship, for neither the fo'c's'le nor cabin lamps had been lighted. Bo Gary must be off somewhere; maybe to Chinatown to see Susie whose father had had a change of heart regarding the possibility of their marriage, an ecstatic Bo had told Pandora this just yesterday.

Darting glances over her shoulder, Pandora has

tened across the deck and went aft. She could see the dim outline of the cabin door and was hoping it was open. She plied her hand to the knob, still glancing over her shoulder, still feeling as if someone were nipping at her heels. Inside the cabin she fumbled about and found a match where she remembered Rogan kept them. The sharp scratch of the match grated on her nerves and the smell of sulfur drifted up to burn her nostrils. She inhaled a whiff of kerosene as she lit the lamp. As a bright flare of yellow light was cast about, the shadows dissolved or were chased off into the corners. The sea chest took shape. She hurried to it, hunkered down, and tossed open the heavy lid. A breath of frangipani and crushed orchid blossoms lingered, stronger than the waft of champhorwood.

Not here! Who could have taken the knife and dress out of the chest? Rogan? It must have been him. Again she was clutching at the frayed strands of hope in her mind.

"Oh, I shall never remember now!" she moaned. Oh, Lord, just when she thought perhaps she could remember! What now!

She jerked her head upright. Slow footsteps were crossing the deck and were coming aft. She felt an icy fear creep into her heart, and it was all she could do to control the chattering of her teeth. Who had traced her here? She had never been as afraid as she was now. She glanced around seeking a means of escape. Dear God, which way should she go?

Pandora stared at the closed door when a quick, peremptory knock sounded. She clenched her hands into tense balls of fear. The telling moment had come. If it was Rogan, she decided here and now, if he still meant to kill her, she would gladly die for him! But dear God, it could not be. Don't let this be her love!

But before the door opened, Pandora breathed a sigh of relief and felt glad tears smart at her eyelids. She had realized that Rogan would never knock at the door to his own cabin!

"C-Come in," she called softly, steeling herself for the unveiling of the murderer.

He was only a blur at first, a tall shadow of gray against black shadows. Suddenly he stepped forward and his form was outlined for her. Standing there, distinct, unmistakable, against the bulkhead of the cabin, his eyes swept her in a single glance. Something glinted in the man's hand.

"Oh! My knife . . ." Pandora trailed off with a short gasp, then she met the blue eyes that were fathomless in the hazy light—or was it merely the fuzz in her brain that made the room seem so dim?

His narrow mouth was tight, so terribly familiar. She should have seen it long ago. Riddock! The murderer of her first husband!

"Of course; how stupid of me to have been so blind," she said slowly, almost in a whisper; she was mesmerized by the turning blade in his hand.

All that had been on her mind up to now was to clear Rogan of guilt. Riddock had never entered her mind. How ironic life was.

There was a second pair of footsteps on the deck now, heavy and clumsy, not quiet at all, thudding through the dark, and another knock, louder. Pandora received her second shock this night. This man was the one from her nightmare; he had always been chasing her. She knew who it was even before he stepped in. Those footsteps had followed her before —in reality.

"Hey, it's me—Riddock?"

Walter untensed his shoulders and called out. "Come in, Sly, you're just in time for the fun to begin." With courage renewed, he sneered across at Pandora.

The door was pushed open and there stood, framed on the threshold, a huge bear of a man, his torso incongruously out of proportion with his spindly legs; his face, with its huge bulging eyes, was reminiscent of a frog's—something out of one more monstrous nightmare of hers. Yes, he had followed her that day right before the accident with Rogan's carriage. In fact, he had been the cause of it!

The cabin reeked of Sly Binks's horrible breath, as like a blinking frog, he squinted once in the sudden glow of lamplight. His eyes regained their hugeness and raked over her figure with a lust that shone clearly in those popping orbs.

"Oh . . . God . . . no—" Pandora shrank against the bunk. Would she be ravished by him now? If he even tried, she would dash for the knife and plunge it into her own heart!

Walter lurched toward Pandora and his fingers grasped the clasp of her cape. With deliberate cruelty his knuckles pressed hard into her throat. She tossed a hasty look at the man, Sly, and saw that he was tilting an uncorked bottle to his mouth and looking over his shoulder as if he expected to find a demon suddenly standing there. Walter grasped the cape harder and shook her as one would a dog by the scruff of its neck. She had not realized that his leanness could possess such strength.

"What do you think you are doing . . . Walter?" Pandora found the voice to croak out.

The bear-frog came alive behind Walter. He stared stupidly at the other man's back, and then riveted his gaze on Pandora's eyes that blazed their hatred. There was not much fear there that Sly could see, though, and this made him begin to feel a bit uneasy. But tossing another gulp of the fiery liquid down his thick throat, he recalled all the promises of wealth Riddock had made to him.

"Poor Pandora, heh, Dora?" Walter drawled. "Does my big friend scare you? Well he should, because he's going to have you if you don't agree to our plans. Hear . . . bitch, do you hear?" He shook her again.

Pandora merely stared. Walter's blue eyes were aglitter with scornful, silent laughter. He was indeed clever, cruel, this Walter Riddock, still arrogantly certain he could manipulate any circumstance, control any situation, any human being. Like the stupid blob behind him, Walter's heart knew no kindness. Riddock smiled now, but it was only an ugly stretching of the lips.

To think that she had almost married this demon, Pandora thought now, the idea almost making her retch at his feet. To *think* that she might never have known Rogan's love. This in itself was more frightening to her now than what was happening.

"What do you gain by holding me here?" she blurted out. "Rogan is my husband now; he loves me"—she almost choked this out—"and he will come for me. He will kill you, Walter. You will never get away from him if you harm me. Please let me go before that happens . . . please! I beg you to release me and to forget this insane foolishness."

He snorted. "Shut up, bitch, and listen to what I have to say. We are going to make plans, you and I and Sly Binks here."

Stupidly Sly put in, "Ain't it clear he don't want to let you go?" He eyed the knife that Walter had left carelessly, or deliberately, on the cabin table.

"A short while ago you were saying how stupid you were," Walter kept talking to Pandora, ignoring Sly's remark. "Tell me more . . . pretty *Dora,*" Walter ordered with a curling of his lip.

Recollection, detailed recollection, flooded back as she stared at the knife—hers. It was all becoming horribly clear. She could see him stabbing Akoni with it, over and over. . . . She had passed out. . . . She had completely wiped his handsome face from her mind . . . until now . . . today he had come here before her and filched the knife from the sea chest. He had meant to do Rogan harm, kill him with her own knife, blame it on her, as with Akoni, she realized now with a painful wrenching of her heart. She almost staggered back from him at her next thought. But he caught her and snatched her upright by the cape again.

"What's the matter, *Dora?*" he ground out sarcastically. "Come, do tell, *Mrs.* Thorn from *Snob* Hill, what were you just thinking?"

"Wh-Where is Bo Gary?" she whispered brokenly, afraid Walter had hurt him—or worse.

"Who?" Walter whined the question on a high note. "Who the *hell* is Bo?"

"N-Never mind. He is just—a cabin boy," she said quietly with an inward sigh of relief.

Walter finally released her, with a little backward shove. Pandora lifted her hand to her throat and gingerly touched the spot where he had almost strangled her, willing away the imprint of his hand that had made her skin crawl and still did.

"Now," Walter began, pausing to light a black cheroot, "as to the reason for this visit—uh—I mean this gathering. I should say it was your note that first brought me here tonight. Don't look so surprised. . . . I know you planned to use your wicked blade on me. Hah! I turned the tables on you! Damn!" He puffed on the cheroot until the tip glowed fiercely, and his nervousness was plain. Then he coughed, choking. "Arghh, these things are killing me!" He stabbed out the offensive cheroot in a tumbler and went on as if he hadn't nearly choked to death. "I saw your carriage, anyway, and followed you back here. I knew it was you, Dora, when your lovely face peeped from the carriage as you passed mine at the corner. As fate would have it, my lucky moment had arrived! You knew it, too; you had a feeling, hmm?"

"Yes, I—had a feeling," she confessed, stalling for time.

Walter brushed ashes off his shirt before going on. "I was nearly ecstatic when I noticed where you were headed—and alone! But you didn't fool me with that urgent note of yours saying you had business with me. I surprised you instead of your surprising me. I knew what you had in mind, sly little Dora. Your business was . . . ?"

But Pandora, thoroughly confused, did not know what he meant.

He bent to peer at her closer, running his hand up her thigh over her skirts. She cringed and he snorted into her face. Unmoved by the feel of woman, he straightened to stare down in fascination at the knife.

"What do you mean to do?" Pandora asked softly, seeing where his eye was trained.

"Ah! The knife? You keep staring at it, too, lovely Dora. Want to know who I intend using it on next, hmmm? *Hmm?*" He hummed this last louder.

Pandora gasped in outrage. "You! It was you who sent me the threatening note signed The Wizard. You meant me to believe it was Rogan who would murder me."

"Yes. I recognized Rogan's signet ring at Millers' party, and from across the room at that. Pretty keen eyes, wouldn't you say? I knew Rogan was the wizard. Too bad you didn't see the ring yourself. He has several of them, I hear. But you were too busy gazing up into those wicked green eyes. How disgusting! I bet he even laid you out there in the garden!"

"You—oh, God! You killed Akoni Nahele!" she cried.

There! It was out, she had said it.

Chapter Forty-eight

Walter blew on his immaculate fingernails and turned his long, sculptured hands over.

"Naturally," he said. "It was too bad for Nahele that he sold that plantation out from under my nose. Damn it! I had first bid on it, but Thorn came along and snatched it out from under my nose. Just as he snatched up everything, even you. He even started that fire at Summit House. I'd wager my finest ship on it!"

"No!" she said too quickly. Then, "I mean . . . how could he have? Rogan was not even at the wedding."

"Oh, he was there all right. He had his covetous eyes on you, too; don't tell me you didn't see either."

"Well," she began to lie, "I did not see him." She wanted to confuse Walter so he would not know Bo Gary had started the fire. All because of love! Sweet, sweet Bo, so romantic. Because of love, yes. Rogan loved her, she was certain of that now.

Walter snorted. "That's not important. You'll soon find out what is. Let me go on. When the time had been ripe, after I had made you my wife, I had meant to—ah—see that you had a little accident—

512

like a fall down the stairs. But murder?" he chuckled evilly. "Oh, no, dear Dora, that never even entered my mind. Me? Never!"

Lying through his teeth, Pandora thought. Liar! Liar! Slow hot tears began to seep between her eyelids . . . tears of anger, of frustration. Her love for Rogan made her heart turn over.

Walter went on despite Pandora's dazed look. "That bastard Thorn always was one step ahead of me, always ruining it for me. But no more, not this time. I hold the *cards* now. Ha! I'm The Wizard now. You see, lovely Dora, you are going to go back to the house, steal the deeds to Nahele plantation, his and yours, and then, my dear, you and I and friend Binks here, we are going to tamper with them—change a few names."

"No, never," she said softly. "I would rather die than give Rogan's deed into your slimy hands."

Walter was about to lift his hand to slap her when there was a sound of hoofs along the wooden pier and a rumble of wheels. They could hear a carriage and pair pull up abruptly at the Thorn gangplank.

Pandora started forward one step, but halted. "Rogan. I knew he would come." Then she couldn't contain herself and cried out for joy.

Rapid footsteps came across the deck. Sly Binks swiped the knife from off the table and splayed himself against the bulkhead behind the door. Pandora saw the ready blade hoisted in the air, the blood lust shining in his frog's eyes.

"No! No!" Pandora shouted.

Walter swung Pandora against his chest and clamped his hand over her mouth to keep her from shouting another warning. Pandora tried kicking back at Walter's shins, but her heavy skirts weighed down her efforts. Above the hand that muffled her cries and sobs, her eyes were wild.

This time there was no knock; the door crashed open. Before Sly could swing the blade down, he was squashed to the bulkhead like a swatted fly. Using the little sense God gave him, Sly concealed the weapon in the bulk of his trousers when he saw the gray barrel of a long-nosed pistol peeping through the crack in the door.

Green eyes narrowed to take in the situation in a flash. Hearing a moan behind the door, Rogan waved the nose of his pistol for whoever was hiding to come out. Upon seeing the pistol, Walter had released Pandora, and stepped back gingerly.

"Pandora," Rogan said, nothing else.

She knew immediately that he wanted her to come and stand at his side, where she would be safe. He caught her arm and tucked her swiftly behind him, out of harm's way. He waved the two men together, so he could watch them in case there was trickery afoot. His eyes narrowed with menace, and the two bumped closer together for what protection they could find. Their thoughts careened from fear while Rogan held the wicked gun steady on them.

"Let's go," Rogan ordered, waving them out the door but keeping a cautious hold on both his precious possessions.

Pandora hugged Rogan close; meanwhile she rambled on in a quavery voice. She had never seen Rogan so angered, and the pistol he held so ominously and expertly made her wonder for an instant how many times before he had been in a dangerous situation such as this. The other two were greedy and demented; that was certain. And they were not all that safe yet, Rogan and Pandora, for still they must get through the dark pier. She continued to ramble as they made their careful way across the deck with the two shuffling before them like prisoners.

"Rogan . . . I did not know then, at the time, it was Walter Riddock . . . when I would have married him—"

"Did not know what, sweet?" he asked, keeping one eye on the pair in front.

"I could not remember . . . until . . . until tonight when he—Walter—came at me with the knife. My knife! Akoni had persuaded me to come out—outside and meet his friend. Akoni was very drunk. He wanted to—to *take me* in front of . . . of Walter . . . to show him how a Hawaiian consummated his marriage!"

Rogan squeezed her arm painfully. "Pandora. Not now, later love, tell me later!" he ground out, unmindful of the fact that he spoke harshly to her.

"It must be out now!" she yelled. Then her tone softened. "They argued. Riddock went away, he said the mating act would sicken him. . . . Akoni was offended . . . drunk as he was. I could not allow Akoni to take me . . . there on the sand. *Our* sand," she wailed, looking up at him soulfully. "Walter returned from out of the dark and flew at Akoni. . . . There was so much . . . so much blood, it looked black . . . black as the night!" Pandora caught her breath before she rambled on. "It was Walter! Walter . . ."

"I know, Pandora. I have just discovered this myself."

"Rogan!" she screamed, clutching wildly at his sleeve.

"Enough, Pandora!" Rogan shouted, tears burning his lids as he shook her fiercely.

Sly, seeing his opening, yelled like a wild Indian and, swinging about, lifted a kick to the pistol. Helpless, Rogan stared as the gray metal left his hand. He cursed then, biting his lip and drawing blood.

Now there was silence on the fog-hidden pier. Ripples of inky water washed against the pilings and seemed to swallow up the last hope for Pandora and Rogan to leave the wharf safely. For a moment they stared—all of them stared.

"Hah! What now, Thorn?" Walter howled in half-won victory; Sly still packed the knife, he knew, and this made his smile one of nasty bravado.

But Rogan saw red and whirled about to silence the man by smashing a fist into his face with such force that Walter crashed onto the dock. A long silence followed while Walter recovered from the stunning blow. Walter shook his head to clear it, and hunched his shoulders to finally unbend and stand again. Rogan went for him anew, with ready fist balled hard.

Sly merely stared stupidly, his reaction hovering in limbo somewhere.

"Defend yourself," Rogan drawled, but halted when he saw the other man holding the black-hilted knife.

Pandora nearly swooned. Her knife had killed

Akoni. But not Rogan; she would never let that come to pass. She backed around Rogan cautiously.

Rogan was cursing himself for not having packed the other pistol. Sly Binks, damn him, would back the coward Riddock to the end.

Walter sniffed in derision. "I think I've hated you forever, Thorn. Now you've given me the chance to even the score with you—for all time!" He laughed, and in his voice there rose an undercurrent of hysteria.

"I am not dead yet, Riddock," Rogan answered with deadly calm. He refused to yield to his enemy the satisfaction of thinking he was the victor already.

A blade went singing through the air. An evil laugh followed it. Instinctively Rogan ducked, and the blade which merely grazed his shoulder buried itself to the hilt in a rope coil. Before he could reach it, Binks lunged at him and they crashed to the dock together. The huge man pinned him down easily; Binks was heavier and stronger by far, and Rogan was rendered helpless. He struggled, fighting for breath with the hulk of Binks atop him.

Pandora screamed, for she, too, had been rendered helpless to come to Rogan's aid—Walter had flung her to the wood, where she still lay stunned and helpless.

Suddenly, Rogan felt the cold point of a blade at his throat.

Riddock had retrieved the knife.

"Sly," Walter snarled, "where is your own weapon—*your* knife?"

Sly was breathing heavily from exertion as he answered, "I forgot ta bring it."

The pain that Rogan felt when his flesh was nicked aroused him from his numbed state. He realized that Walter, bending over him with the knife, intended to kill him. The knowledge that he and Pandora might never love again enabled Rogan to call on his last reserve of strength. Freeing one arm from the massive frog's steely hold, he caught and held Walter's wrist, then, half-blinded by his own sweat trickling down, Rogan called up his will and wrath; now his anger grew cold and methodical.

"Rogan! Watch out!" Pandora shrilled at the top of her lungs.

The sound startled Binks, and Rogan saw his chance to be free from the devil and grasped it; with sheer physical strength, he rolled out and onto his right side, in the same motion dragging with all his might at the wrist that held the blade. The knife flipped free, and Pandora shook herself alive and grabbed it. She bent and tossed it far into the air; it clattered along the deck, slid, and then dove to a watery grave.

After she heard the knife, her knife, splash into the water, never to be seen again, Pandora's attention returned to the immediate scene. Rogan was warning her to stay back.

Rogan had hauled Sly Binks to his feet and smiling coldly, he was punching Binks furiously raining blows across his dim visage and body. Rogan was supple and muscular, and he was an expert fighter. Though his opponent had greater strength, Rogan was faster and more agile on his feet. He continued to pummel Binks until the muscles in his arms ached and screamed for mercy. Blood, muc blood appeared on the battered frog face and Binks's eyes swelled and became glazed, giving him the look of a hideous monster. Rogan halted the beating only when Binks crumpled to the wood and finally lay still.

Walter, his eyes darting for a means of escape, stopped to stare down at his man. Wild-eyed he peered up at Rogan and gasped upon seeing the unconcealed hatred in those eyes that were glowing like green beacons.

"Not much protection for you now, is he?" Rogan indicated Binks with a jerk of his head; he breathed easier now that the deed was done.

Dumbly Walter stared back at Rogan, only for an instant, and then he went crazy and lunged in a futile attempt to do battle. No match for Rogan Thorn, Walter was knocked down over and over, hauled to his feet, and punched like a bag again. When Rogan finally stood undecided whether to revive Walter and beat him some more, Pandora rushed to his side.

"Look, Rogan, look," she softly drew his attention from the bloodied man. "Bo Gary is coming!"

Rogan chuckled low. "Right in time to clean up the mess, huh?" He jerked his head back to fling the strands of hair from his eyes.

"He has the police with him"—she gaped—"and the other man, the stranger who was with you today, who looked so familiar to me."

Rogan was bussing his bruised knuckles. "Oh, him, don't you remember him from the luau? Jameson, from Hawaii, Honolulu police. Uhmm, the man with the smoke forever in his mouth?"

"Rogan, you knew Walter would try something

tonight, just as I did!"

"I found the little note, earlier today, but realized it was Walter's handwriting. Ah, but I was worried about you. I prayed it would be all over tonight, and that you would not be fearful of me any longer as the murderer. All things seemed to point to me, this I realized after I found you in the tower attic. Today I was afraid to put you through what Jameson had planned. Why did you come so early after you received the note Jameson planted?"

"I received no note . . . oh, the folded paper on the hall table?"

He nodded. "Yes, it said for you to come to the *Promise*. We sent Walter one, too. . . . I'm sorry. . . . Jameson signed your name to it. It was part of the plan. . . ."

"So that is what Walter meant by the note!" she exclaimed, enlightened.

"God; I almost didn't reach you in time!" He lifted her hand to kiss her palm tenderly.

Pandora sighed. "God answered my prayers, Rogan. He released us from our torment, I just know it. From now on I shall always believe there is hope when the path grows dark before me—*us*."

"Us."

Pandora nodded lamely, staring down at Walter. "It is all over for him now, darling; he will never steal our home in Hawaii from us now."

"My sweetheart, you don't know how happy I am to hear you say 'our home,' and it shall always be our second home. The mystery is behind us now. The police have the arrest warrant; Walter will be put in prison for the murder of Akoni Nahele and also attempted murder. Perhaps he will be taken to Hawaii. I don't know, but could not care less." He bent to her wearily and kissed her soft lips tenderly.

"Oh, love," Pandora murmured between their light kisses.

She gasped when she saw the smear of blood on his chin, but it was only a superficial wound; otherwise he would have lost more blood, and still be bleeding.

Bo Gary skidded to a halt at the Thorn pier and the police at once came to bend over the two men. Jameson shook his head when he took in the battered gore of the frog with the bear's body. Then he straightened, holding the torch high, as he swept his dark eyes over Rogan Thorn. Jameson lit his smoke with the torch. There would be many questions that needed answering, but Rogan and Pandora were prepared for anything now.

Bo winked as he helped the officers half-drag the prisoners off the pier, and Rogan nodded his appreciation of a job well done. Then the drama over, alone with his wife, Rogan looked up to the sky. Distant, pink clouds were showing in the east, being born above a peeping morning sun.

He dropped his face slowly, close to Pandora's.

"I love you, *kuu ipu*."

Pandora started at the suddenness of the endearment she had never heard emerge from his lips in the daylight. She wrapped her arm about his waist and they smiled, swimming in each other's eyes. They touched. They squeezed arms, and each tenderly brushed back the other's hair. The intense emotion they felt made them tremble.

Daylight. Only from love does strength grow, and

Pandora loved her man and told him so softly, tenderly, as the golden California sun burst into full glory over the horizon.

The very next Saturday, after they had rested, Pandora and Rogan married with God's blessing at Trinity Church. Her wedding dress this time was pale aqua and silk tiare, and lavender orchids adorned her crown.

During the ceremony when she felt a fluttering deep in her womb, as if the baby knew its first happy thought, Pandora felt joy beyond her wildest imaginings. She stared up at the sky as her heart swelled with love.

Yes, Linda beloved mother, you were right, when all else fails there is always hope.

Epilogue

Morning sunshine streamed through the window of the bedroom.

"I looked at you and I knew. . . ." He stood behind his wife, his legs planted wide while his hand reached down to lovingly smooth back her gold-threaded coppery tresses.

Pandora knelt by the open trunk of *koa* wood. Foaming out of it was a shimmer of brocades; there were satin robes and tunics embroidered with dragons that breathed out coiling flames of red fire, and Imperial silks from Suchow. Aqua, red and black, turquoise, ice-blue over cream, dove-gray—all hers.

"What a perfect honeymoon gift, Rogan! Iola will have such a time stitching up her creations when we settle at Briar Rose for the summer to honeymoon . . . finally. Belinda will have her own tiny muu-muus! Oh, darling, these are so beautiful! Thank you!"

"Naturally, beautiful, just like Mrs. Thorn," he murmured deeply to his loved one.

When she turned on her heels to rise, he lifted her into his arms to stand against him. He brushed her forehead with a kiss that sent delicious tingles of delight coursing through her blood. Almost a year had passed since they had been wed at the church and their love for each other had grown immeasurably, each new day being more delightful than the one before, each kiss and caress reaching the same height of bliss they had known from the start . . . and now they would soon honeymoon.

"You were saying . . . ?"

"I looked at you and I knew—that first day the *Baghdad* brought you to me—I had found something precious and everlasting. . . . You swept me off my feet!" Rogan exclaimed, petting and cuddling her.

She chuckled low. *"You* swept me off *my* feet!" she corrected playfully, recalling how he had swept her to his mansion on the hill while thinking she was totally unconscious.

Arms wrapped about each other's waist, they drifted over to the jonquil-yellow crib to peer down with adoration aglow in their eyes at the infant girl asleep there. For a fleeting moment Pandora envisioned a pair of ominous dark-blue eyes, a lad with intense dislike in his little heart. And then, just as quickly, the image of Adrian Dancer vanished and she was again gazing at her beautiful daughter with a heart full of love.

"She'll be three months old soon," Rogan murmured with pride. He had no regrets that Pandora would never give him another child. The birth had been very difficult and Pandora was indeed lucky to be alive as was the tiny girl. All that mattered to Rogan was this new-sensed love between them as a family.

"Why did we choose the name Belinda, darling?" he asked, having forgotten in his worry over her health the past few months.

"Because it's a Spanish name . . ." There was a hint of mystery in her tone when she said this.

"Oh . . . *that* answers my question?" he said close to her ear.

"Don't you remember when you slipped into the room and I said that you should not worry so, the baby would be *beautiful?*"

"And what if *she* had been a boy instead?" he wondered now.

"I knew it was a *her*. Belinda—Spanish—the beautiful. Also, named after my mother."

"Bella-linda," he said, enlightened, "and so she is just as beautiful as you, her mother, *and* your mother surely must have been."

Pandora turned in his arms in order to nuzzle her cheek at his throat. "Will we be dining in tonight, Mr. Thorn, or will we mingle with the socially elite crowd?" She hid the mischievous twinkle there in her eyes.

"Ah . . . no. I think from now on we'll stick close to home . . . let our hair down. Let those others posture and giggle behind their hands with their inane speech and remarks. Lord, they don't impress me anymore . . . only you do. What do you say to that, Missus Thorn?"

His eyes shone gossamer green as he swooped her up and carried her to the bed in the adjoining room. On the way, between kisses, she said into his mouth, "I shall show you, now. . . ."

She did, and his kisses soon became more. . . .

* * *

They lazed in their love all the morning long while their daughter slumbered peacefully in the next room. The dark ghosts of loneliness and fear that had flitted to and fro like eddying leaves had been swept away, leaving in their place the fullness of joy for evermore.

They were a family at last.

GOTHICS A LA MOOR—FROM ZEBRA

ISLAND OF LOST RUBIES
by Patricia Werner   (2603, $3.95)

Heartbroken by her father's death and the loss of her great love, Eileen returns to her island home to claim her inheritance. But eerie things begin happening the minute she steps off the boat, and it isn't long before Eileen realizes that there's no escape from *THE ISLAND OF LOST RUBIES*.

DARK CRIES OF GRAY OAKS
by Lee Karr   (2736, $3.95)

When orphaned Brianna Anderson was offered a job as companion to the mentally ill seventeen-year-old girl, Cassie, she was grateful for the non-troublesome employment. Soon she began to wonder why the girl's family insisted that Cassie be given hydro-electrical therapy and increased doses of laudanum. What was the shocking secret that Cassie held in her dark tormented mind? And was she herself in danger?

CRYSTAL SHADOWS
by Michele Y. Thomas   (2819, $3.95)

When Teresa Hawthorne accepted a post as tutor to the wealthy Curtis family, she didn't believe the scandal surrounding them would be any concern of hers. However, it soon began to seem as if someone was trying to ruin the Curtises and Theresa was becoming the unwitting target of a deadly conspiracy . . .

CASTLE OF CRUSHED SHAMROCKS
by Lee Karr   (2843, $3.95)

Penniless and alone, eighteen-year-old Aileen O'Conner traveled to the coast of Ireland to be recognized as daughter and heir to Lord Edwin Lynhurst. Upon her arrival, she was horrified to find her long lost father had been murdered. And slowly, the extent of the danger dawned upon her: her father's killer was still at large. And her name was next on the list.

BRIDE OF HATFIELD CASTLE
by Beverly G. Warren   (2517, $3.95)

Left a widow on her wedding night and the sole inheritor of Hatfield's fortune, Eden Lane was convinced that someone wanted her out of the castle, preferably dead. Her failing health, the whispering voices of death, and the phantoms who roamed the keep were driving her mad. And although she came to the castle as a bride, she needed to discover who was trying to kill her, or leave as a corpse!

Available wherever paperbacks are sold, or order direct from the publisher. Send cover price plus 50¢ per copy for mailing and handling to Zebra Books, Dept. 3060 475 Park Avenue South, New York, N.Y. 10016. Residents of New York, New Jersey and Pennsylvania must include sales tax. DO NOT SEND CASH.

THE BEST IN HISTORICAL ROMANCES

TIME-KEPT PROMISES　　　　　　　　　　　(2422, $3.95)
by Constance O'Day Flannery

Sean O'Mara froze when he saw his wife Christina standing before him. She had vanished and the news had been written about in all of the papers—he had even been charged with her murder! But now he had living proof of his innocence, and Sean was not about to let her get away. No matter that the woman was claiming to be someone named Kristine; she still caused his blood to boil.

PASSION'S PRISONER　　　　　　　　　　　(2573, $3.95)
by Casey Stewart

When Cassandra Lansing put on men's clothing and entered the Rawlings saloon she didn't expect to lose anything—in fact she was sure that she would win back her prized horse Rapscallion that her grandfather lost in a card game. She almost got a smug satisfaction at the thought of fooling the gamblers into believing that she was a man. But once she caught a glimpse of the virile Josh Rawlings, Cassandra wanted to be the woman in his embrace!

ANGEL HEART　　　　　　　　　　　　　　(2426, $3.95)
by Victoria Thompson

Ever since Angelica's father died, Harlan Snyder had been angling to get his hands on her ranch, the Diamond R. And now, just when she had an important government contract to fulfill, she couldn't find a single cowhand to hire—all because of Snyder's threats. It was only a matter of time before the legendary gunfighter Kid Collins turned up on her doorstep, badly wounded. Angelica assessed his firmly muscled physique and stared into his startling blue eyes. Beneath all that blood and dirt he was the handsomest man she had ever seen, and the one person who could help beat Snyder at his own game.